SEEDS OF HARMONY

A HARMONY NOVEL

ANDREW ELGIN

Cover by: Zoran Petrovic/on Fiverr as Visual Arts

Copyright © 2017 by Maggie & Nigel Percy

ISBN: 978-1-946014-14-6 (Ebook version)

ISBN: 978-1-946014-15-3 (Paperback version)

Sixth Sense Books

150 Buck Run E

Dahlonega, GA 30533

Email address: andrewelginauthor@gmail.com

ALSO BY ANDREW ELGIN

The Harmony Series

Finding Harmony, Novelette prequel

Songs Of Harmony, Book 1

Ambassadors Of Harmony, Book 3

CONTENTS

"If I'm going to sing like someone else, then I don't need to sing at all" - Billie
Holiday

To Maggie. Together we make lovely songs!

PROLOGUE

H aven and Harmony: two planets circling the same sun. Neither were anywhere near a center of human civilization, even using astronomical measurements. They were far from any trade route when they were first, accidentally, discovered. They were essentially unknown and unnoticed in an unexplored, minor part of the galaxy.

A vast ship, a colony class ship, immense in size and aspiration, carrying everything needed to jump-start life on a new planet, had malfunctioned. Traveling at immense speed, its target planet long since lost, its systems saving the colonists for as long as possible until certain life-threatening parameters were breached, it finally tumbled out of the blackness into this isolated system. With nothing familiar in the skies or the stars to greet them, the colonists awoke to a new destination, a different system. Their observations and measurements at first confused them before they finally accepted that fate had decided they should live here, not be dead and desiccated, traveling without end in the vastness beyond. They blessed the luck they had had which had brought them to this system when they could so easily have come awake in emptiness and lived briefly in despair, dying one by one, alone.

They chose the inner of the two available planets. It was rich with everything they would need from the very start. The outer planet, with no easy accessible metals, was further out, traveling on a slower path than Haven. The choice was obvious. As was the name.

Seen from the edge of the system, Haven seemed to hurtle, where its sister glided. Yet, to the grateful, lucky, new inhabitants, the seasons seemed normal. All that they missed was a moon to light their nights. But they could live, were living, without one.

It was only after they had forged the beginnings of a fresh, world-spanning civilization that some, still amazed at the fate which had carried them to this system, wondered whether they had made the right choice. They wondered if they should be taming the planet, digging into it, carving it and sculpting it to meet their dreams and desires. It seemed, they said, to be disrespectful to their savior. Perhaps the other planet would have been the right choice. No metals would have meant a closer relationship with the planet. After all, they had left a planet behind them gouged deep and drained of everything it had to offer. It was why they had left. Did they have to repeat that here? It seemed this was a chance to live differently.

And so some of the people, looking for a new way of living; a way which seemed to have been offered them, took a ship to the outer, slower planet with its beckoning moon and named it what they dreamed of: Harmony.

But their new home was not easy, nor welcoming. There were trials which tested the resolve of them all. Some were found wanting and, sadly acknowledging their weakness, said farewell to their dream and traveled back to Haven. They left their companions and set off on the ship they had arrived in, determined to at least hold high their heads at having attempted to follow their dream. But they did not live to proclaim their pride. Not one survived the return journey. The cause was never established. Apart from the bodies, there were some samples of plants and some recorded stories of strange things that had been witnessed or perhaps experienced, tales which made little sense and soon became myth. The name of Harmony became a fable of a place where people lost their rational abilities or sank into something only slightly above a stone age. It was no longer a place to dream of.

The relatively small band left behind on Harmony, now completely isolated, took up the struggle to survive, as well as to understand the planet they now called home. They strove to listen to it, to become close to it in a way they could never have considered on Haven. And, slowly, very slowly at first, they spread and they learned. They learned of the planet, but they also learned of themselves, and the knowledge they gained brought them new understanding and began to change them in subtle ways that, because they were gradual, became accepted as normal. To them, Haven became a memory of a distant place of belching smoke and blinkered ignorance where people confused progress with wisdom.

As they grew slowly in different, yet still human, ways on Harmony, so those on Haven grew in the same way humanity always had done. Industry and government, education and politics, exploration and invention became more intricate and less personal and always expanding. And all around them, in the moonless night sky, the unknown stars shone and teased them with the need to find their own kind. But to do that required immense efforts, driving leadership and constant investment of energy and inspiration to a common goal. Whenever those elements existed at the same time, they were never harnessed effectively or for any length of time. And most of the time they did not coexist.

The original colony ship had been gutted, re-shaped as the basis of factories and mines and machinery, as it had been designed to do. Some small ships were used to dismantle and transfer the colony ship to the planet's surface, piece by piece. Those tiny offspring themselves broke down eventually. But, before the last of them disappeared, a new one was built. Better design. Better engines. But there was nothing for it to do. It served only one purpose; to provide a tangible connection with the stars in the night sky. When that began to fail, another was built. And then another when the second was failing. But none of them could travel into the endless space beyond the system. They represented the deep desire to find the rest of humankind, even if it could not, yet, be accomplished. The ships were the communal response to a shared dream.

Despite having the ability, there was hardly any contact made between Haven and Harmony, because Haven felt there was no need. No metals meant no progress to those on Haven. Harmony had been a failed experiment early in Haven's history. It was a planet for the curious only.

3

Not for anyone who wished for the stars. Once in every several generations, a ship had been sent, but there was no real purpose to it beyond the technicality of the voyage itself. After such fleeting visits, tales were told of a strange affliction, a curse whereby nobody could leave Harmony alive if they stayed too long, or ate any of the food or drank the water. Those on Harmony came to resent such contacts, seeing them as unwanted invasions of their privacy and as intimidatory displays. Whatever commonality might have existed eroded over time until those on Harmony believed Haven an unspecified but potent threat to their way of life, and those on Haven believed Harmony to be both uncivilized and stagnant in ambition. Not that that stopped them from using Harmony to exile the very occasional high profile 'irritant', when a visible, but expensive, 'mercy' was politically valuable. Plus, it was technically useful for testing new ship designs. In living memory, an armada had been sent to Harmony; supposedly to establish a base for deep space exploration. But it had failed in strange and unexplainable circumstances.

So the two planets, carrying the same human seeds at different rates around the same sun, nurtured and grew them in different mediums to have different aspirations. Harmony passed slowly and gently through the same seasons that Haven, by comparison, slid through with a seemingly headlong rush.

And there were the beginnings of a new idea germinating in the system. Nobody could say what started it or where it originated, but it had the potential to become larger. Whether it would grow into something worthwhile, something viable, remained to be seen. And the sun remained in the center, pulling the planets along, like children.

1

LARRICK

L arrick was on his hands and knees in the long grass at the back of one of the pigsties trying to find the hole in the wall where the rats were coming in. He had volunteered to do it so that he could spend some time on his own generally out of sight and have the chance just to stop for a while and rest a bit: enjoy the day for a change instead of working, working, working. He must have dozed off, for the sun was much higher now. He had started up guiltily before hunkering down and scuttling crab-like back to the pigsties in case anyone saw him. He was now poking around, his head close to the ground, looking for any holes when he heard the sound. It wasn't one he recognized, being more like a short, loud pop than anything else. Puzzled, he peered around the corner and saw someone looking as if they had tripped and fallen. He shook his head at the clumsiness of someone -- was it Haller laying there? -- tripping on flat ground. He was about to go and help, because it was obvious Haller wasn't moving, when he heard the same sound again, only this time it was followed by a cry of pain. Then he saw a strange, helmeted figure sidle from the sty with his or her back to him He, or she, was wearing camouflage. It was so strange to see, so out of place. But whoever it was was also carrying something high up, tucked into the shoulder. Larrick put his hand to his mouth in shock and fear. A weapon!

There were more explosive sounds which he now recognized as shots. The one soldier he could see still facing away from Larrick, walked slowly away from the stye and past Haller as the gun swung back and forth. Pausing briefly by Haller, the soldier pointed the weapon down and shot Haller twice in the head, causing the large body to spasm in reaction, bouncing slightly with each shot. The number of shots further away increased and so did the shrieks of fear and pain. There was some shouting but it seemed mainly to be from the soldiers calling to each other. The pigs began to squeal, adding to the calls of cows and sheep: a swelling noise drumming at Larrick's ears.

From where he was crouched, Larrick could only see Haller's body, now missing part of his head. Too numb with fear to move, he was unaware of the tears streaming down his face or the way his whole body was shaking. His breathing was ragged and he slumped against the wall, turning away from Haller, his neighbor. With each shot, each cry of anguish, each half-heard pleading voice, he shook and closed his eyes only to open them and stare sightlessly ahead before the next one.

Gradually, the shots came further and further apart and the soldiers' calls took on a less urgent tone. He had no idea how long he had been there. By now he was hugging his knees to him, too frightened to do anything. Finally, he heard some soldiers closer than the rest entering the stables closest to the pigsty.

"How many do you think there were here?" asked one young-sounding voice.

"I don't know. Fifty maybe? More than the last place anyway." This second voice sounded older, rougher. "Beats me why anyone would even want to live like this. Look at it. Dirt and rags and nothing else. No luxuries. And if you want something, you have to make it yourself. Absolutely crazy people. They're insane."

"But why do they do it? Live like this, I mean?"

"Because they're not right in the head, are they? Take a look at their homes for starters. Why would anyone choose to live inside earth walls and under grass roofs when you've got a perfectly decent town nearby? They have to be crazy. We did them a favor. They had to be dead inside to live like this. Dead inside but didn't know it."

There was a pause and the sounds of shuffling and cows protesting.

"Are you any good at making these things move in the direction you want?" asked the young voice.

"Just give 'em a good slap on the rump to get 'em going, then prod 'em to keep 'em going. It's not hard." There was the sound of a slap and another cow protesting. "Ain't you ever seen a cow before?" There was incredulity in the voice.

"Not up close. Not like this."

"Well, let's get them loaded and then we'll come back and round up the pigs. They're the ones you have to watch out for."

"Why's that?"

"You'll find out soon enough. Now let's get going so's we can torch this place and finish with it."

The cattle made their feelings plain amidst the shouts and calls. Larrick listened to them until those sounds were lost amongst the general noise and confusion going on. He wanted to move, to do something, anything to prove to himself he was still alive, but he was locked in shock. He tried to say her name, to say 'Shelleer', but something in his throat caught and he could only gulp in spasms. All he could think of was the older voice talking about the pigs. They were coming back for the pigs and they would find him. And then they would kill him like they had killed all the others. But she wasn't here with him. She was dead. They had shot her and he hadn't even been able to recognize her voice.

Something inside of him at last let loose of his limbs and he found himself scrambling on hands and knees through the grass, heading for the bushes and, further, for the trees. There was no plan, only the urge to leave this behind and not be killed. Nothing else counted. He scrabbled on and on, his lungs screaming at him, every part of his body aching, bruised or cut. Only when he could no longer move, only then did he allow himself to think of her, of Shelleer, his wife, his beautiful, young wife. And the tears flowed as he thought of leaving her behind. The guilt of being alive crushed down on him and he hugged himself as he saw the smoke rising in the distance, knowing that his life was over. Nobody needed to shoot him. He was, as that soldier had said, dead inside. Dead. He knew it for certain.

He waited in misery until the soldiers had left and fire had died out and the smoke was only a few wisps before going back. He wanted to do... something. Say farewell? Apologize? Let them all know he would remember them?

The homes they had built had all been burned or pulled down. Fences had been torn out and the crops had been set on fire. But worst of all were the bodies. They lay where they had fallen. A few he recognized from their clothing, but the rats had also found them. They were still feasting when he arrived and he screamed and kicked at them. He wanted to find Shelleer, but also wanted not to. Then he recognized her hair: that long braid where ribbons twined in and out. She was facing away from him as he knelt, her limbs spread as if she was about to run, the ground around her dark from her blood. He stroked her hair and found he lacked the courage to see her face again. He tried to say something to her, to apologize for being alive without her, but his voice failed him. Looking around he felt useless and irrelevant; a helpless fool. He realized that there was nothing he could do or say here that would have any meaning at all, least of all to him. So he turned his back and left, empty of tears and of hope. If he was to die, it would be somewhere else; on his own and wrapped in his own guilt and shame.

He walked. The direction didn't matter. He kept walking away.

2

THE SLEEPER

Javin fought to become fully awake. He was drenched in sweat, his heart pounding, as he struggled to overcome the fear, fighting to get away from it. He gulped air noisily as he tried to sit up and leave the dream behind. As he struggled, he felt the fear lessen a little. But as he began to regain some sense of who and where he was, Meldren began to cry out in her sleep. Her arms and legs began thrashing and she started to make a disturbing sound of one continuous note somewhere between a wail and a moan, rising higher and higher to where it would have ended as a scream. Instead, he shook her shoulder. "It's all right. It's over. You're safe. You're safe."

She gulped and swallowed as if her throat was dry and breathing was difficult. She blinked and looked around in the pale moonlight, disoriented by whatever she had experienced.

"What happened?" asked Javin, grateful to focus on her and thus push his experience further away.

"I had a bad dream. A really bad one." Her voice was shaky.

"It looked like it. I had one as well."

"You? What? When?"

Javin's heart rate was almost back to normal. He wiped his forehead, the sweat cooling on it. "Just now. I'd just woken up because of it, and then you started moaning and thrashing around."

Meldren sat up and rested her head on Javin's shoulder, still breathing deeply, and brushing her long, red hair from her face where it had become stuck with sweat. She pushed the rumpled bedding from her to try and cool down. "What was your dream about?"

"Not a dream. It was a nightmare. One of those you can't seem to stop." He put his arm round her shoulder, peering sightlessly into the night as he tried to recall the details of what had happened. "I was in a boat, a small boat. Fishing I think. The sea was calm. It looked flat. We were well away from the shore. I could see it in the distance. And then... then there was a huge fish. No, two. There were two of them. Very big, and they were suddenly fighting near us. Coming up out of the water. And there was someone else there in the boat. I didn't see him -- it was definitely a him -- I didn't see him but I knew he was there, whoever he was. Anyway, then suddenly there was this huge black tail smashing down on me. Big and fast. I managed to jump away from it, I think, and then everything went dark, like I was under water. It felt completely real. The other person was dead. I knew that somehow. But the worst of it was that I knew it was my fault. I knew it." He shivered at the memory. "That's all I can remember. I was right there. All the details were so... perfect. So real." He gave another small shudder as if to shake off the remains of the dream and then gave Meldren a gentle hug. "What was yours? The same?"

Meldren shook her head in dismissal. "I don't want to think about it."

"I understand, but it might mean something. Two of us having nightmares? It could be Harmony doing something. Although if it is, I really don't like it."

Meldren was silent for a space. "It's not Harmony. I'm sure of that. Not Her directly, anyway. And, if She is trying to tell us something, I can't begin to think what it might be." She took a steadying breath. "All right, I'll tell you. I was being attacked. Actually, I was being raped." Javin stiffened at the words but forced himself to say nothing. "I don't know who it was. I never saw the face, but it was someone the 'me' in the dream knew. He was big. Much bigger than me, and he was sweating and it was smoky, wherever it was. I think we were inside some sort of building. Nothing like this one. No straight walls, more curving. But it felt like it was my home. I don't know where it was. There was a dog there as well. Big and white. It was my dog. I knew that in the dream. It was trying to stop him, snapping and snarling. He looked away at the dog and I... I hit him. I hit him on the head. With a stone, I think. It was in my hand. Really hard, I hit him. He fell down on his side." Her voice tailed off into silence. Javin hugged her to him, stroking her hair, reassuring her.

"I'm sorry. That must have been awful. I can't see any message in that. Nor in mine. Two nightmares. But two different nightmares which happened at the same time? That's not a coincidence."

He had no idea what it might mean but he knew he wanted to shake off the residue of the nightmare. He came to a decision.

"Well, I think we've slept all we are going to, tonight," he said, swinging his legs out and heading for the pitcher of water, using the moonlight to avoid stubbing his toes. "Let's watch the sun come up and have a drink of water. I'm cold now I've stopped sweating, so bring blankets while I pour."

Sitting at the table with the blankets thrown over their shoulders against the night chill, he held her hand. "How do you feel now?"

"Oh, I'll be fine. I know it was just a dream. But it was so real."

"Mine, too."

She sipped at the water. "You were right, though."

"About what?"

"About it being a message, I think. The two of us having nightmares. That's not normal. There has to be something more to it. But why did we have them? That's what I can't understand. It's not like it was with Harmony. When She showed us things, those were vivid. But not like the nightmares." They both thought back to the first time they had Harmony come to them. They had both experienced very vivid dreams or visions, but they had each had the same one at the same time. This was different.

"I'm with you," said Javin. "Yes, Harmony can be a little frightening, but Her frightening was more for a definite purpose, a way of telling us something. What can these dreams tell us? That bad things happen to people?" He shook his head. "I can hear your song and it's still in tune, still sounding as it should," he said, referring to his ability to hear the

11

songs which, they had learned, created the world and everything in it. "Nothing else sounds wrong. And neither of our sprites made a sound like they would have done if it was Harmony." The snake-like creatures that were normally wrapped around their necks during the day were coiled together as usual at the end of the bed.

"We were meant to have those dreams then?" She sounded skeptical. "But what was the point of having them?"

"I don't know." Javin pulled his blanket a little closer. "My dream was me, the dream me, almost dying, and in yours, you were being attacked and could have been killed, I suppose. Both violent dreams." He ran his fingers through his hair, tugging on it in his frustration to understand. "Violence. And it felt so real." He blew out a sigh of annoyance. "I don't like not knowing."

"Can you feel anything coming that might help understand this?"

He paused as he let his mind wander ahead to see if he could sense anything unusual. It felt smooth and flowing as it normally did. "No. Only Amleek arriving with the boat tomorrow. Well, today now."

"Same for me. And there's nothing violent, nothing wrong in the feel of that." Meldren finished the water. "I don't like this dream and I don't want another one or the same one. There has to be some sort of reason."

"If it is Harmony in some fashion, then I guess we're going to find out soon enough. She'll find a way to tell us. She always has." He had a thought and paused a moment to close his eyes again. "Mel? There *is* something, some little thing. A prickling in my head. It's not a song. But it's something. I think I *am* picking up something. I don't think I was feeling far enough ahead. It's there. Out there." He opened his eyes and gestured with his hand in front of him. "Can you feel it at all? It's faint and maybe I'm making it up. What about you?"

She, in turn, shut her eyes and took a relaxing breath, the better to feel her way into the future. "Maybe. Maybe there is something." She looked at Javin in the dim light, half-dressed. "It's not clear. I can't get a good feel for it. But it's there. Are you sure it's to do with our dreams?"

He tapped his head. "There's a definite link in my mind somehow. It feels like there's a connection between it and what happened tonight. But whatever it is, it's not happening today. At least I don't feel that. Sometime later. Maybe a lot later." He suddenly shivered, not from the cold. "Whatever it is, it's got the feel of something big. But I suppose I would think that, if I can feel it from this distance. I wonder if we're going to like what it is?"

Meldren gave a throaty chuckle. "Now that would be worth knowing. But, assuming that is in the future, let's go back to bed."

"I am a bit cold now," he admitted.

"Do you have to be so practical?"

"Ah. I see. No. Not at all."

BY THE TIME AMLEEK'S LITTLE BOAT TURNED UP, BOTH OF THEM HAD SHAKEN off any lasting feelings about the nightmares. They were dressed and had slung cloaks around themselves against the cool wind they knew they would feel on the open ocean between the island and Littlehaven. Amleek, the stocky little sailor, bronzed from the sun and the wind, was sitting on the bottommost of the rough steps which had been carved out of the gentle slope leading up from where he had tied his boat. It would have been grand to have called it a harbor or even a dock. Grand, but wrong. It was more truthful and accurate to say that the avenue of smooth, salt-stained boulders shouldering up from the seafloor was sufficiently wide for him to nose in between them and tall enough for the boat to be sheltered by their size. The slight angle in the avenue about half way in also served as protection from any but the strongest waves. It was an entirely natural phenomenon, neither Javin nor Meldren having had anything to do with it. But the fact of its existence seemed to indicate that it was ready and waiting for someone to use it. Perhaps it had only appeared when it was needed. Whatever the true cause of the small harbor, Amleek's boat was riding the gentle swells inside it and he was chewing on some dried fish, staring out to sea by the time his two passengers arrived at the top of the steps.

"Tell me again, why I have to go in that really tiny and scary boat of his? I can sing us to Littlehaven and back." Javin spoke quietly, reluctant to start down.

"Because we're trying to live normally, remember? We can't do everything with songs." Meldren answered just as quietly. "And, besides, it's a good thing to face your fears and not run away from them just because it would be easier." She ignored the face Javin pulled and continued. "We've had this conversation before. It's a good way of getting used to being with people again. Having just him at first and then, as we get closer, getting to be comfortable with all the people in Littlehaven." She smiled and planted a quick but thorough kiss on his cheek. "Plus, I really like it." And before Javin could argue, she stepped ahead of him, calling and waving. "Amleek! Good to see you and your boat again. Thank you so much for coming."

Amleek stood and, spitting out some un-chewable portion, wiped his mouth with the back of his hand before waving back. "I was going to wait until the wind eased later today before going back to give you time to get ready." He wiped his hands on the ground to clean them. "I've never needed to come find you. I guessed you'd know I was here." He turned his face to the ocean, using his chin to point. "The weather feels good for a day or so. It seemed right enough to come now." His tanned face eased naturally into a mass of wrinkles under the wide cloth headband when he smiled. He pointed to his throat and then to Meldren. "I see you've still got those creatures on you," he said, referring to the sprites which were now around their necks. "Are you willing to trade yet?" It was a ritual, repeated every time he arrived. And every time it was answered the same.

"You know very well that they found us and we like them enough to keep them." She rested her hand against the sprite coiled comfortably around her neck. "And we don't really know what exactly they do, if anything. And, no, you can't have one, unless you find one of your own." The part about not knowing what they did was half true. Harmony had told them that they were a way to allow Her to communicate more easily with both her and Javin. But neither really knew what they were or how they did what they did. Amleek would probably have given them free trips forever in return for having one of their sprites for himself.

She turned to Javin and held out her hand, smiling in a sweetly fierce way. "Come on, let's not keep Amleek waiting."

Javin gave a thin smile as he finally stepped aboard. He could find no good reason for trusting this unsettling craft, despite the fact that it had conveyed them back and forth more times than he wanted to count.

Amleek had been happy to ferry them to and from Littlehaven, the nearest port, on an occasional basis. Every so often, he would turn up and they would know it -- having sensed or foreseen him -- and then take the day to travel and trade. He turned up when he felt the wind was going to be favorable and the weather fair, and when he thought sufficient time had elapsed since his last visit. There was nothing rushed or permanent in the arrangement, but it suited both parties. As payment, they traded herbs with him, fruits or whatever else was in season in their small garden. Plus, Meldren had taken up making baskets of various sizes and Amleek had thought them good enough for payment, which had pleased her greatly. Once in Littlehaven, they could acquire supplies, trade herbs with Abalan the healer, or just become used to being amongst people again: a tiring experience which made the isolation of the island a necessity for them.

Javin had reluctantly agreed that the two of them should try to live as normally as possible, even though they had the ability to create anything they might want from song; for songs, they had learned from Harmony, created everything, if only you knew how to sing them. Living normally had come to include growing their own food, as far as possible. Their garden provided them with some food: fruits like the small and tasty pok berries and the well-named slipsweet, some root vegetables and leafy greens and the inevitable simesh bush: the leaves used for making the popular hot drink. The garden provided enough produce to add variety and also gave them something to focus their energies on. Anything else they required they obtained from visits to Littlehaven.

Meldren had been very firm in her views. "You can't just hide away, Javin," she had said. "If we can hear Harmony, feel Her as we grow our crops, we should also see Her as well. And we can't do that by staying here on our own. Being with others, even for a little while, won't hurt us, and it will allow us to hear other songs from other places, get a feel for other things. If Harmony does speak to us again like when we were first together, we had better be ready for her. And we won't be if we hide ourselves away from everyone on this island. And, before you say we could hide and nobody would know, you're still missing the point of it all."

And that had been the end of that.

It still didn't make him feel any better about setting foot on the boat. "It's a bundle of twigs held together with spit, probably, and bits of old fish that Amleek can't eat. It's small and it moves all wrong and I have trouble hearing the ocean and any danger. It's a bad way of going anywhere," he muttered.

"And yet still we're going to do it," said Meldren brightly. "You can listen all you want for any problems coming up. But, unless I hear them as well, we're going to Littlehaven on that bundle of twigs."

To be fair to Amleek, his boat was indeed made mainly of bundles of reeds tied together to create a platform for the solid decking, where the small cabin gave shelter from bad weather and helped the short mast keep upright. But those bundles were large enough and long enough to ensure there was enough room for at least six people. Indeed, it was large enough to sit and rest comfortably against the bulwark formed from the topmost reed bundles and still have some protection from the wind. And the reeds were made more secure by the wide, strong strands of a type of weed called ship-weed, which could be dried and hardened into a durable and waterproof cladding for the hull. Not that that knowledge was of any consolation to Javin. He simply hated the motion the boat made.

The island slowly dwindled behind them and the shore ahead changed from a vague haze with no shape to it to a more distinct coastline. No matter how good Javin might be with songs, he seemed incapable of feeling lively on any of these voyages, choosing to curl up, head on his knees and cloak wrapped tight around him. Meldren, on the other hand, was happy to chat with Amleek about his family, the weather and the state of fishing now as compared to the past, indeed any subject at all.

They finally made the cove which gave the town the reason for its name and stepped ashore after arranging to meet Amleek in the same place tomorrow for the return journey; it being too far to travel there and back in daylight.

"Was that boat like the one in your dream?" asked Meldren when they were out of earshot of Amleek.

"No. In the dream, it seemed bigger, more substantial. But, it was over quickly and I might not be remembering it well. Maybe I just like the idea of bigger boats." He smiled weakly.

But Meldren would not leave it alone. "Are you saying it wasn't made of reeds?"

Javin thought back. "No. I'm sure I'd recall those. It seemed... smoother? Not having those bundles anyway. Why are you asking?"

"I think we should look out for any boats that were made in the same way as you saw in your dream. It might help us understand more about it all."

"Maybe so. But your dream had you inside a strange type of house. What if your house and my boat are from the same place, days and days and days away? A whole season, perhaps? Or maybe we just made them up? How do we know they were real?"

"Two reasons. First, anything that vivid had to come from Harmony in some fashion. And, second, She has never shown us something that wasn't real. I don't think She can. That's why I want you to keep an eye open for a boat like the one in your dream."

"But I thought we'd agreed Harmony wasn't involved."

"Not directly, that's for sure. But it makes sense the more you think about it. We're living on Her and everything that happens is due to Her songs in one way or another, She has to be involved in some fashion. Even if She's just allowing it to happen. She knows. Somehow, I'm sure, She knows."

"If only we knew anything."

"That's why you have to keep an eye out for one of those boats you saw."

"Fine. I will."

"Good. Now, can we go eat?"

"First, let me sing my stomach back to how it should be, not how it is."

Meldren smiled and wagged a finger at him. "Don't take long. I'm hungry and I don't want to wait."

As the evening began to spread softer shadows and the activities of the harbor began to take on a slower, quieter rhythm, Javin and Meldren sought Orland's place. They had spent the afternoon profitably trading several bundles of herbs, some leather, some stories from Javin's past, a simple healing of a headache and one of Meldren's small baskets -- 'ideal for holding all sorts of small things', she had said. As usual, they were going to stay the night at Orland's. He was the gentle, lean man with large hands, a wide smile and a balding head who had taught Meldren to cook when they had first arrived in Littlehaven, before moving to the island.

That night, as usual, Orland shared a meal and talked, swapping news and recipes with Meldren. Eventually, he left them alone, promising them another fine meal in the morning before they left. They were soon asleep, tired with heads rubbed thin from interacting with the people in Littlehaven, a line of pain beginning to growl above their eyes.

Deep in the night after the moon had set and the stars alone glittered, Javin awoke in tears consumed by an overwhelming awareness of loss. He sobbed quietly, feeling utterly alone. It was unbearable and yet, there beside him, Meldren was sprawled in casual sleep. At first he was not able to accept her presence as being real. There was a sense of separation so complete that he could not even begin to comprehend it. He felt so desolate, so empty of everything that even reaching to touch Meldren's hair meant nothing to him.

A part of him did not believe the emptiness to be true. He was with Meldren, he told himself. He was in a room of Orland's, he said silently. He was not alone. A tiny part of his mind called to him, that this separation and loss he was feeling was not the truth of who he was. And so he gradually pushed the feeling away to a point where he could still see it for what it was, but could recognize that it was not him even though tendrils of it still clawed at him. Taking a deep breath, he felt battered by the emotions he had experienced and confused as to why it had happened. He could recall no dream, no hint even of a remnant of a dream which might have triggered it. Yet there he was, still reeling from it, still aching from the loneliness he had felt.

As he began to recover his poise, so Meldren began to murmur in her sleep. Her arms began to move, her hands making clutching motions. He could not see her face clearly, but he thought he saw a deep frown -- or was it fear? -- on her face. For a moment he was undecided. Should he wake her or let it pass? For a moment, the movements ceased and she appeared more peaceful. But then, suddenly, her mouth gaped wide as she drew a deep breath and she began to scream. It was a scream of loss not fear, of a witness, not a participant. It would have continued into a sobbing remorse had he not swiftly shaken her awake, calling to her, reassuring her. He could tell her eyes were open as he caught the glint of moisture in them reflecting the dim light.

She grabbed his arm, her fingers digging into him painfully, drawing him down to her, her gasping breaths brushing his face. For a moment, she was unable to speak. He could feel the fear still radiating from her. "You are with me. Everything is safe here. You are safe here with me." He spoke softly, reassuringly, trying to drag her back from whatever had claimed her in her sleep. "Everything is safe here. We are at Orland's. In Littlehaven. It is night. I love you. You are safe."

He kept repeating these and similar phrases until he felt her breathing begin to slow and she relaxed her grip on his arm and the tears she shed were those of release rather than of tension and fear.

When he felt it to be right, he helped her to sit up, pulling the pillows behind her and dragging the blanket up to her chest. Then he knelt beside her, stroking her hair from her face and wiping her tears gently with his thumbs.

"Can you speak about it? Was it the same as last night, back on the island?"

He felt the movement of her shaken head in the darkness, her breathing still labored. "No. Not the same. This was a different one." She blew out a breath. "Just as bad, though. Or maybe worse. I don't know." She paused a moment. "I hope we didn't wake Orland." She listened. "I can't hear anyone moving about." She lapsed into silence again. He let her take her time, just resting his hand on her leg to tell her he was there, and she was safe.

Finally she spoke. "Last night, that was bad. It was happening to me. I was being attacked. But this dream tonight, that was different. It was not me being attacked. The dream 'me', this time, was looking on. I was watching a house burning down. In the dream I knew the house. But the worst thing was I knew there were people in there, people I loved. And they couldn't get out and I couldn't get in. It was awful. I was watching the fire kill them and there was nothing I could do about it. I could hear them screaming. The screams were the worst part of it. And all I could do was watch and listen to them die, and do nothing. They were people I loved." Her voice sank to a murmur. "It was awful to watch. Awful."

All he could do was hold her and give her time to recover. When he thought she was calm, he told her about how he had woken feeling desolately alone.

"It wasn't anywhere near the same as your dream. I couldn't recognize anything or anyone. All I had was that awful, terrible feeling of being alone. Even though you were there, right next to me, I still had it. It made no sense. And yet, with your dream, I think perhaps it does make some sort of crazy sense."

"I can't think how it makes any sense," murmured Meldren.

Javin moved to sit closer to her. "Last night, we both had strong, frightening dreams. Nightmares. And tonight we had our sleep invaded again. But first, I wanted to ask you if you had ever heard of anyone's talent being that of sending emotions, visions, dreams, things like that which would completely take you over? Is that possible, do you think?"

Meldren thought about this. "I don't think so," she said at last. "At least, I've never heard of anything like that. And the fact that it's in two different places, here and the island, that makes me think it can't be. I would have thought you'd need to be near someone to be able to do that. I'm just guessing though. I mean, speakers have to be near the people, touching them, to hear what they need to hear."

"Hmmm. That's what I thought. Hanlar and Paysa could speak to each other over any distance, it seemed, but that wasn't strong, it was just something they heard, like a normal voice." Javin had lived with the couple and their daughter after arriving on Harmony. It was from them that he had learned not only about the physical demands of farming but also about the variety of talents that people of Harmony all had to one degree or another.

"So, if it's not a talent, and it's definitely Harmony, what does that mean?" asked Meldren.

"Between us we've had four different dreams about four different people, or so it seems. And it's all been very real. I don't know who had that awful feeling of being alone, but I do know it wasn't me." Javin half-turned to Meldren. "What if Harmony is warning us about the people? What if She is telling us that we should be on the lookout for them because they are dangerous?"

"But why not show us their faces? After all, She showed you my face in your dreams, didn't She? So why not theirs?"

"I wish I knew for sure. But why couldn't it be that they are dangerous in some way? Perhaps we're being shown what's going through their minds. You were attacked and you watched people burning to death. Couldn't that be us burning?"

"I don't think so. It doesn't feel like that. But why was I, the dream 'me' that is, why was I so upset by it? It doesn't make any sense, if I was also the one being burned alive?"

Javin was quiet for a while. "It seemed like it made sense at first. But when I say it out loud, it really doesn't, does it?" He gave a quiet snort. "I sound paranoid, don't I?"

"Paranoid?"

"Ah! The foreign language thing again." Coming from Haven, the other planet in the system, Javin sometimes used words or phrases which meant nothing to Meldren. Sometimes, though less frequently, it worked the other way. Obviously this was another of those words that made no sense to Meldren.

"It means you spend all your time thinking that somebody is going to attack you in some fashion, even if nobody is."

"But what if somebody does attack you?"

"That doesn't mean you're paranoid. It means you are attacked."

"So you have to think about being attacked before you are attacked to be paranoid?"

"You don't have to be attacked to be paranoid about being attacked. Look, why are we talking about this anyway? It's got nothing to do with the dreams."

"Are you sure? After all, you're saying that we could be attacked somehow."

"That's what I started out thinking, but it doesn't make much sense when I say it out loud, does it?"

"Not really. So you *are* paranoid then?"

"No. You can *sound* paranoid, but not *be* paranoid. Can we please change the subject now? This is getting even more confusing."

Another silence before Meldren spoke. "Your colors? They were not as strong when you were speaking about being attacked. It's not the right way of thinking about it from what I saw. All the colors were there, but pale compared to how you are normally." The colors she spoke of were what she saw with her talent. To her they were visible around people all the time. Indeed, they were around any living thing and it helped her to understand, to 'see' if people were telling the truth or how they were feeling. It was also another reason for the difficulty of being amongst too many people for too long, because then the colors became overwhelming. She knew Javin trusted her interpretations of what she saw. Then she added what they were both thinking. "But we did both feel that distant something. That distant big something. If the dreams are linked to that..." she let the sentence drift off into the dark where it prowled around them both, preventing them from going back to sleep.

AFTER THEIR RETURN TO THE ISLAND (KNOWN AS THE SLEEPER BECAUSE, from a distance, it looked like a person lying on their side), they felt a little better and were able to shake off the effects of the dreams. They could come to no useful conclusions about them, however. Just when they thought that it was all in the past and done with, they experienced two new nightmares.

As before, Javin was the first to wake, terrified, as he had dreamed he was falling. Whenever he had any 'falling' dreams like that, he had woken with a jerk and a catch of his breath before he landed. It had always been only a sense of falling with nothing beyond the sensation. Not this time.

"Aaaaaagh! My legs, my legs!" He moaned with the intense pain, certain that both of his legs were not just broken, but had bones shattered, pieces piercing his skin. He had fallen from a high place, a rock, a cliff or something like it. And he had seen, and felt, the ground rushing to him. He had been trying to land and roll to avoid the shuddering contact, but he had landed on another large boulder. The face of it slanted the wrong way and all of his energy had streaked down his legs into his feet, shattering bones as it did so. It had been so real, so true. For a moment, he could not move for fear of further agony. He lay there, clutching at the bedding, trying to not scream, trying not to move. Slowly, he took in the fact that he was in his home, in his bed, and his brain told him his mind was lying.

His breathing came once more under his control, and the sweat began to dry. The reality of the pain began to move away from his mind. He could still feel the vivid sensation of the fall and the sickening crunch of the landing, but it was something now he could begin to feel a distance from. As he did this he realized that if this was the same as before, Meldren would very soon be in the grip of another nightmare. He half-turned to her, intending to reach out and rest his had on her shoulder when she suddenly convulsed, sitting upright, arms stretched ahead of her, hands trying to grasp something. As she did so, she screamed the word 'No!' so violently, with such passion that Javin was almost thrown back by the power of it.

That one word carried in it denial and terror and pain in equal measures. Again, she called out, and the word became thinner, longer and sliding into an aching scream. Javin lunged for Meldren, trying to bundle her into his arms, break whatever had hold of her mind, draw her to him and protect her. He battled against her thin, endless scream with his own words. "No. No. Wake up! You're safe. It's over." Clasping her to him, he felt her convulsive gasp for breath as her lungs finally emptied. "Meldren. Wake up! Wake up! I'm here." And then she gasped once more, then again, and relaxed her arms and her neck so that her head nodded forward as she gulped in air. He kept murmuring and reassuring her until he felt her relax even more.

He drew her back against him to rest, his arms a cradle for her. She wiped away her tears and sniffled a few times. Javin gave her time to gather herself. She hooked her hair behind her ear with her fingers as she took another deep breath or two before finally feeling composed enough to begin to speak.

"It was the worst one so far." As before, her voice as she began was empty of emotion, having had it all drained from her. "This time, it was a child, my child. No more than a toddler. I couldn't stop her. Couldn't help her." Another deep, slow breath, blown out in a steadying sigh. "I know it was a dream, but it's hard to speak about it. It was my child and she... she died. She fell and she died. In a well. She hit her head as she fell and the neck snapped and... that was it. She was beside me and then she... she fell. I was too late. Just too late by a second. And she was dead and there was nothing I could do." Another cleansing breath. "It was the worst one so far. The absolute worst one." She stroked Javin's arm as they sat together in silence. "If I had one," she said finally, "then you did, too."

"Yes. I did. This one was bad as well. This time, I was falling. I don't know where I was, just that I was high enough to make the fall a bad one. I don't know why I was there or what I was trying to do, but I fell. I tried to hit the ground and roll, but my legs got smashed to pieces. Shattered. I could even see pieces of bone sticking out."

Her grip tightened on his arm as she reacted to his words. "Why didn't you scream? You might have woken me up if you had."

"I think I passed out. In the dream, that is, I passed out. I woke up here, not in the dream, sure that I was crippled. The two me's, the dream me and this me, they got confused."

She took one of his hands and held it out before her. "Your colors are getting stronger again."

"I'm fine now. Just feeling a little bruised in my head, I think. It's something I know I experienced somehow, but it's not that real anymore. And you? How are you now?"

"Like you, bruised. Feeling raggedy. I can still see it, but the pain isn't there now. Just a sort of emptiness, a feeling of, I don't know, sorrow?" He could feel the little shift of her shoulders as she shrugged. "Not surprising, really, I suppose."

"Are we going to be shown every single painful thing that has happened to anyone on Harmony?"

"I've been thinking about that as well." Meldren's voice was low. "Whenever Harmony showed us something before, there was always a reason. She wanted us to know something. And, when we had seen it, there was something She wanted from us, something She wanted us to do. These dreams, these have to be the same thing, don't they?" She sounded hopeful. "It's not like we can ask Her what She means, can we? Or maybe we can. I don't know. I don't see how, that's all."

"But how many more times? That's what worries me." Javin shook his head. "You're right, I don't know how we could ask Her. But, maybe, with the sprites, we could do... something?" Usually, when they slept, the sprites left their necks to curl together nearby, sometimes on the floor, or at the foot of the bed, moving back to their positions on Javin and Meldren each morning. They seemed to know when to leave and when to return. Neither Javin nor Meldren called to them or did anything more than feed them whenever they fed themselves. Some few scraps of food was all they needed, apparently. Neither had been seen to drink. They were still very much unknown. But, because Harmony had spoken to them directly using the sprites in some fashion to allow Her words to be heard, Javin and Meldren were more than happy to have them as companions. To the uneducated eye they looked like long twigs with small leaves or buds at irregular intervals along the slim bodies. They looked identical. Neither Javin nor Meldren could point at one and claim it as their own. They had become used to them around their necks, the small heads with the sparkling, black eyes always rested in the hollow of their jawbones, peering forward.

They were silent as they each tried out various ideas. Then Meldren spoke. "Javin? Have you felt ahead again, like we did with the first dreams."

"No. But I will." And then, he let himself drift inside and followed, not the dreams, but the source of the dreams, the music of their creation. Once he had found that, he slid his attention forward to where the dreams' songs faded and left him in a new place. "That's strange."

"You felt it, too?"

"It's changed. It's different somehow. Or maybe the same, but bigger. Is that how you felt it?"

"Yes. It could be that the whatever-it-is is nearer. Or, perhaps it's just getting clearer, like a storm that starts off as a small cloud, but ends up with lightning and thunder and lots of rain."

Javin wrinkled his face. "Not a nice picture. A storm? Coming here? From where? And in what form? If it's anything like these dreams we've had, then I can't say I'm looking forward to it."

25

Meldren nodded in agreement. "Do you think there is a way we could ask Harmony for more details? Find out what it is we're heading into? When we were in Littlehaven, we made it clear that we needed somewhere else to live. That was easy, because She dragged us out of bed one night and showed us this island. But, asking for explanations about something? I don't see how we can do that. Unless... ."

Javin completed her thought. "Unless we ask Her to come and speak to us again. It wasn't that painful, but could we even understand what it would be about? After all, what bothers a planet might mean nothing to us. And if it wasn't bothering Her, we wouldn't be having these dreams, would we? And would She come anyway? I got the distinct impression that when She spoke with us last, it really was the last time She would do that."

The rest of the day was spent in fitful activities and silences. Both felt an irritation, rubbing at them, chivvying them from place to place, never allowing them to relax. By the time night came and they were getting ready for bed, they both felt tired and alert at the same time, hoping for a clear and easy sleep, but fearing it would not happen. Nevertheless, they both fell asleep more quickly than they had imagined.

In the depth of the night, Javin woke up. There was no fear, no horror he was escaping from. He was simply and suddenly awake and alert. Meldren's hand reached for him and he gave a gentle squeeze.

"Did you have a bad dream?" she asked, her voice a soft murmur in his ear.

"No. Not this time." He answered her just as softly. "I'm just awake."

"Same here, just now. Did you have any dream you can recall before that?"

He eased himself up a little to rest his shoulders on the wall and could feel Meldren doing the same. "No. You?"

"Well then, perhaps we're just awake together."

Javin was about to answer when he felt the familiar touch of his sprite as it glided in its strange, silken, swift fashion up his arm to his neck. Instead of taking up its normal position, it continued to his head where it stopped after having wound itself in a band above his eyes. "Meldren? Is your...?"

"Yes. My sprite's round my head." A gasp. "She's coming!"

And then, the music, the wonderfully beautiful, enthralling music came to them. If an orchestra could breathe and speak in such a way as to make clear words out of the combined individual notes, that would have been something like the sounds pouring into them now as they were held in fascinated wonder once more.

"Discord came to you." The symphony of sound formed the words and enfolded them in something like sorrow; minor chords filtering through. "This discord... hurts... you must give them my song again." The phrasing and intonation of the words made it clear that this was a difficult language for the speaker; one with which She struggled to find clarity of expression. Simple words, basic terms and unsophisticated ideas were all that were available.

As before, both Javin and Meldren fought to think clearly. They were able to form questions in their minds, though they could not speak but there was no fear in either of them. There was so much love, so much tenderness surrounding them both. They formed questions for themselves, for Harmony, for help, for understanding. It was becoming clear that this was a subject almost beyond the bare abilities of the restricted language.

"Father is... singing?... making?... a song... New. A new song." The spaces between words and sentences were liquid with possibilities, hinting at harmonies and lyricism beyond comprehension. "It is small... not strong... . But... it can grow... more." Another enchanting space where music and thoughts and words swam through each other. "Discord is pain... much pain... discord is not hearing... realness... not hearing... songs? My song?" There was uncertainty over the right phrases to use as the sounds swelled and shrank, seeking the perfect tone, the perfect harmony of expression. "Father's song needs... hearing... beyond this family. Small pain here... can still hear realness... if discord is not too... grown?... big?... long?" Harmony seemed to know what they were thinking.

There was a surge, a pulse, in the intricate chorus speaking to them, much as the sea moving to the shore. "Pain songs... discords... are coming. You hear them in your songs... they do not hear... my songs... full?... real?... true? They must hear realness... must hear all of it... must... hear again." A pause, and it almost seemed as if there was a searching, a thinking going on beyond the reach of their senses as they lay there. "These are the first... singers?... seeds?... of Father's song... They must hear again for Father's song to sing loud... to sing to other brothers and sisters... They must... hear?... make?...their own songs... bright?... strong?" Again a withdrawal before the polyphonic surge, the mellifluous sound, returned. "Others must hear and learn... Songs must be... here in me... and in others... All pain is discord, is not hearing truth?... Not hearing the real is pain... . You will... help?... sing?... to stop the pain, to hear realness... to sing Father's song. The pain here is... a beginning... a seed. More seeds will come... ."

There was a withdrawal of all sound as they both held their breath, waiting for the return which never came, and then there was the normal silence. The voice of a thousand complex, multi-voiced instruments, capable of infinite variety and subtlety had left them as suddenly as it had arrived. As ever, it left them empty, yet with a feeling that they had been touched by grace. They felt blessed and also, as usual, puzzled by what the words had really meant that they had heard so clearly.

The sprites slid back down in that fluid fashion of theirs and left them to curl up together at the foot of the bed again. "No. I have no idea, so don't ask," said Javin quietly, almost as if to himself. "Not yet, anyway. Not yet."

Both sat in silence, sinking back into the memory of the encounter.

Meldren sighed quietly. "It was an answer, I suppose. Of a sort, anyway. I know it was about new songs, about pain, about hearing new things and we're meant to do something. But what are we meant to do? There was something to do with hearing songs. But whose? Hers?"

"'Pain songs,' She said. Discord. Doesn't sound like something I want to hear." Javin said, trying to sort out the message in the beautiful but crippled language they had heard. "'Father' is the sun, yes? But I thought He was responsible for the big stuff, not on this planet. Not on any planet, come to that. So why is His song somehow important to us and what we're meant to do? And what are those pain songs anyway?"

Meldren had slid back down under the covers against the chill of the night. Unlike the last time when Harmony had contacted them, they had not lost hours and hours in hearing Her. It was certainly lighter, now, but it was still recognizably nighttime. "She said that pain was not hearing the true songs. Her songs, I suppose She meant. And we are meant to change the songs with pain into songs that are of Harmony. At least, that's what I think She meant." She tugged gently at Javin's arm to have him slide down beside her and close off a draft.

He did so and they turned to where they were absent-mindedly spooning, gaining warmth from each other, but both furiously thinking about what had just happened to them. He brushed Meldren's hair from his mouth. "Sometimes, I really don't know that having an explanation like that is such a great thing. It hasn't helped us. Then again, She didn't say anything about the dreams. Maybe we've had all the bad dreams. Maybe they were the pain songs She meant. Maybe they weren't." He puffed a breath that tickled on Meldren's neck.

"The dreams have definitely been painful, for us if nobody else. And they seemed to be of other people. Perhaps that's what She meant about pain songs. It may be their pain we've felt." She sighed. "It's all guesswork, isn't it? We know so little. But, at least we have had some sort of warning about something which is going to happen sometime. And that's probably the thing we've both felt." She gave a low chuckle. "Doesn't sound very helpful when it's said like that, does it? I mean, it's beautiful when She comes to speak to us. Absolutely beautifully, unbelievably wonderful. But, when you think about it, not very helpful."

Javin answered with a hug. "At least, we're not feeling sick because of Her visit. That's got to be an improvement." He ran the visit through his mind again. "Like you say though, not that helpful."

AMLEEK, LEANING BACK AND HOLDING THE BOAT STEADY AGAINST THE LAND with the rope, squinted thoughtfully at Meldren as she and Javin helped the woman safely to land. Meldren caught the look and raised her eyebrows in question.

"I know about weather," he said.

"But...?" prompted Meldren.

Now it came to it, Amleek looked a little uncertain. "The weather is one thing, but people... I suppose you do know what you are doing?" He tilted his head at the woman and Javin negotiating the steps a little unsteadily. "Doesn't look, well..., doesn't look as if it's going to be easy, is all I'm thinking. Not with the others as well. And all these trips, they certainly make for good trading. I'm not complaining. How many more are you going to be taking on? Not that it's my business. It's just that, I've got to liking the two of you, is all."

Meldren gave him a warm smile. "Amleek, I like you, too. So does Javin, whenever he's on dry land, that is." Amleek grinned. "And I truly appreciate you looking out for us. But I can tell you here and now, this is the last one we're going to be looking after. For as far as I can see, that is."

Amleek thought about that for a moment, sucking at a tooth, and appeared to be happy as he gave a small nod. "If you're happy, that's good enough for me. I'll keep coming as and when, if that's good with you?"

"Always, Amleek, always. And are you happy with the trade for this trip or is there something else we can do to make it even?"

The lithe, tanned man shook his head. "No, this is good. I'm thinking I've got the better part of this deal lately. The herbs for my sore muscles are good, as are the baskets. Always a need for good baskets in what I do. We're definitely good. We're going back to the old way then? No big rush anymore?"

"That's definitely the last, Amleek. You can take your time from now on as it used to be."

He considered that a moment before nodding. And with that, he touched two fingers to his forehead, flicking them at Meldren in quick salute before he hopped aboard, pushing the boat from the shore with his foot, then using a pole to nudge it between the boulders back out into the ocean. Meldren waited until he was clear and he had turned back once to wave farewell before she too started up the steps to the flatter ground where Javin and their new arrival would be waiting. By the time she reached them and looked back, Amleek's boat was heading away in the breeze and she could just make him out leaning against the small cabin totally relaxed and at ease on the water.

Javin smiled at Meldren, feeling better for being on firm ground. The young woman beside him was gazing around her. One hand was continually stroking her long, neatly braided black hair as it fell over her shoulder. Her face had a vague smile on it, as if someone had attached it for her, thinking that was how a smile should look. Her eyes, however, were looking at something no-one else could see. "Shall we keep her with us for a short while as we build her a new home, do you think?" He said it in a voice meant more for the woman to hear a voice than as a question. He already knew the answer.

Meldren nodded. "Of course. And some food, I think." She began to walk. Javin held the woman's elbow as if to guide her. She hesitated a little but then began to move after Meldren, still stroking the braid and still carrying the empty smile.

It was later that night, after the woman had been helped into her new bed in a side room previously sung into existence by Javin and Meldren as temporary shelter for the newcomers, that the two of them were able to talk freely.

Javin looked tired, Meldren noted. "She is the last of the pain songs, isn't she, Javin?"

Javin looked up and nodded. "Her name is Perray. And, yes, she is the last one. And I know that because... ," he shrugged, "because I just know it the way we know these things. You felt it. I felt it. It's the truth of it. But I still don't understand the how and the why of it all."

Meldren began to allow the tiredness which Javin was showing to creep into her now. She stifled a yawn. "The 'how', I think, is easy. If Harmony wants someone to be somewhere, then I suppose She will arrange it so that that's where they are. But, even so, how She got them to Littlehaven with only days between them... that's amazing. Just seeing them was like having spikes in my head. I won't miss that!" Eyes wide, she remembered how it felt, how it had changed, as soon as they had just thought of taking the person with them. The urgent feeling, the push to hurry; it was a cramping in the head that only let up once they were aboard the boat. It didn't seem to affect the ones they approached, only the two of them. The pressure to leave had started two days before they met the person in Littlehaven and it coincided with Amleek arriving. A restless night and then the sharp stab of pain in the head the next day as they saw the next person Harmony had singled out for them. After the first of the passengers, Meldren had asked Amleek to come back as soon as he could. She couldn't say why, only that she knew it. He had shrugged and nodded and was back within a day or two; the routine kept up until this last one, Perray, had arrived.

"The number of dreams and the number of people here match up." said Javin. "So they are here now. That's the 'how' part, I suppose. But the 'why' of it? That escapes me. Why us? Why them? Why now? Why here? Just, why? About everything."

"They're all in some kind of pain, aren't they?" said Meldren. "That *has* to be the pain songs Harmony meant. I mean, it feels right. It's painful to us, listening to them. And, if I remember correctly, She said that pain was about not hearing Her properly. So we must have to do something for them. There's a next step. For you it's the 'why', for me, it's the 'what'."

Javin yawned and rubbed his temples. "Has anything changed? Can you feel anything about this? For me, I really don't feel comfortable with these people here. They need help that I don't feel capable of giving. They're damaged and hurt. Badly hurt. Just being near them, it hurts to listen to them. Pain songs is a good way of describing what they sound like. I'm worried that we're going to make things worse. It was easy to bring them here. But, now what? That's what I mean about asking if anything's changed; if we can feel what's meant to be happening."

In answer, Meldren leaned back and stretched her neck muscles as she took a slow, deep breath and let it out in one long sigh. She shut her eyes and felt for anything which might help or guide them in what to do with the people now living on the island. She tried to slip far enough away to where she could hear their songs but not be disturbed by them. Once she had that distance, she began to follow the song of Javin in the hope that it would lead her forward. Nothing. Her tiredness was making it more difficult. She tried again, this time listening to the song of this, their home. Again, nothing that helped. Finally, she simply allowed herself to relax into the songs around her, not only in her home, but broader, on the whole of the island, letting them blend together; the rocks and the wind, the bushes and the earth. The familiarity of it all in its wonderful complexity relaxed her still further and she let her mind move with it. As she did so, she sensed that, somewhere in the music yet to be heard, a new sound was striving to be heard. It didn't feel in any way familiar. But, at the same time, there was something about it -- the cadence? the rhythms? -- something which she could perhaps begin to recognize, given enough time. It was both elusive and yet inevitable.

She opened her eyes to find Javin watching her, eyes narrowed as he was, undoubtedly, listening to a part of what she had heard. She linked her fingers behind her neck and stretched, pushing her arms back. Relaxing and letting her arms slide down again with a sigh she said, "Something is ahead. It's nothing I've heard of before. I don't know how it relates to these people, except I know that it does. Something we've never heard before, either of us. And that doesn't help at all with what we're meant to do with these people. Except we have to do something."

"Let's get some sleep and deal with this tomorrow," Javin said, stifling another yawn.

"Not yet we can't. We have to check on the others first. We've been away for a night and two whole days. Can't sleep without making sure everyone else is fine." With that, both she and Javin went to that place inside themselves that had been opened up by hearing Harmony. They sought out the songs of the other seven people they had brought back to the island. Both listened to each one in turn, finding it, hearing it, hearing the pain in the unbalanced song, the lack of harmony, accepting it for what it was and judging it for any sort of imminent danger and then moving on to the next.

Javin was first to complete the check and was waiting when Meldren opened her eyes. "I didn't hear anything new in their songs. They're still not the songs I want to listen to but, at least, they haven't changed in any important way I could hear. Was that the same for you?"

Meldren nodded. "Yes. The same for me."

"Good. Now can we go to bed? Looking after people is really not one of the things I enjoy doing. There had better be something good at the end of it all." He reached a hand to Meldren and helped her up.

"We've got to get through it first," she said. "And I still have no idea what it was that I sensed about this."

———

THE NEXT MORNING, AS WITH EACH OF THE OTHER NEW ARRIVALS, JAVIN AND Meldren were up and about well before dawn, despite being so tired the night before. They wanted to have everything as ready as possible for Perray and set off at a brisk pace, eating fruit and some bread they had brought back from Littlehaven as they went, to a place they had earmarked earlier. The island had both more rolling hills and was wider than was apparent from the sea. The 'head' was relatively flat and the 'shoulders' of the cliffs hid the fact that the land sloped down from them, away from the rocky shore. Following the body down from the head end, there were various pockets of hollows and hillocks on a generally flat plain until the land near the 'hips' began to rise with the cliffs and form a long range of hills in the center from which the land fell more or less steeply on the side away from Littlehaven. From there, the cliffs forming the 'legs' fed into a long stretch of land filled with scrubby bushes and shrubs before easing down gently and slowly to the sea at the 'feet'. What this meant for Javin and Meldren was that there were many places they could sing simple homes which could have sea views or not, according to desire. More importantly, the breadth of the island meant that they could house these newcomers and still be within easy distance of all them. Their own home was at the 'head' of the island, nestled in a dip for protection from too much wind but with an easy walk to the very tip of the island and the wonderful ocean view it offered.

The place they were heading to was where they would sing a home for Perray. It would be private enough, not far from the cliff edge, but with a screen of vegetation to block the weather. The cliff at this point was not that high, but there was no place on the island, other than the harbor and the far 'foot' end, where there was an easy slope to a beach. To access the shoreline anywhere else either involved scrambling down a slope which usually had a steep incline at one point or another, or climbing down a cliff face. Javin and Meldren had no way of knowing if any of their visitors would attempt suicide by jumping off a cliff. They hoped that, if Harmony was involved in bringing them together, She would stop them from doing that. Nevertheless, they had made sure that each location had bushes and shrubs between the home and the cliff edge to lessen any temptation.

The two of them worked efficiently, as with the other homes they had created for the previous arrivals. First they agreed on the orientation and precise location, and then they set about creating it. To an onlooker, what happened next would have seemed very strange. They stood, side by side, holding hands, eyes shut and began to make small, low sounds, as if seeking a tune to follow. These sounds gradually became louder and took on a more rhythmic aspect, almost a recognizable tune. The sprites unwound a little from around their necks and stretched out and up, their slim bodies pulsing with more sound; sounds which were less obvious to the human ear but which acted as a backdrop or counterpoint to those made by the two humans. It was as if the sounds the sprites made wove in and out of the human voices creating something more potent and more dense somehow.

As these sounds, which were almost songs, grew, so they became more complex, and the onlooker would have not been able to hear some of them. But, nevertheless, they were there. The effect was as if the air was being woven into something else, as if clouds and wind were becoming something new and different. Accompanying these notes and harmonies, rhythms and chords was a feeling that what could be seen and touched and felt and experienced by the observer was, somehow, not as real as was first imagined. There was a challenge to the senses which began in the ears with those strangely familiar and haunting sounds, but which continued with the eyes. For there, in front of the singing humans and their accompanying sprites, a building began to take shape, seemingly out of nothing. If challenged later to describe what happened, the response would have had to include phrases like 'fading into being', or 'shimmering', or 'appearing out of a mist'. And each phrase would have been inadequate.

As the singing continued, walls, roof, table, chair, the simple necessities of a home took shape and solidified. Even a fire and some cooking stones as well as plates to eat off and mugs to drink from and some dried meats to provide the first meal. The chosen location was on the side of the island where the beach below was sand, not pebble, and the land sloped gently down for most of the way before the inevitable drop-off. The home being sung into existence was just below the top of a gentle hill, sheltered in a slight dip by fruit trees and shrubs from the heaviest winds. Before finishing, they also made sure to sing up a spring close by for water. All of the homes for the other people they had brought back had been created in the same way. None of them was further than an easy morning's walk from where Javin and Meldren lived. This one was one of the closest. Some were close to the sea, others in more secluded inland locations.

The construction, if such a method can be called that, concluded with the humans letting their voices fade and the sprites returning back to their usual positions around their necks. Javin and Meldren took a few deep breaths to relax after focusing so closely and visually checked what they had caused to come into being. They walked in and tested the chair and table and made sure the door closed and that the roof looked weatherproof.

Satisfied, they mentally checked on each of the other inhabitants again to reassure themselves they were all there, and as well as could be expected.

Only then did they return to their home and to Perray after checking that she was still asleep. They had sung her relaxed and sleepy the night before, on the off chance that she would be unsettled in a new place. They had woven sleep into her song before they left to ensure she would not wake up alone.

"What do we do when she's awake?" asked Javin.

"What do you mean?"

"I mean, if she is the last one -- and she is -- what do we do next? We've got seven others living here. We feed them and we have made homes for them. But what do we do now? Are they going to stay here forever? Harmony must want something more than that, surely?"

"That strangeness I sensed yesterday? That feeling that there's something going to happen, and it's to do with the island? It's still there. Perray's arrival hasn't changed that. Perhaps just having them here, together, is important in some way." She shook her head in rebuttal of her own words. "But that's not right." She played with some loose strands of hair, her gaze unfocused, as she tried to find the words she needed. "If I think about them now, all eight of them, it's as though something has been loosened, let go, in some way. There was always a tension before. And now? It's gone. Something's changed with her arrival. Before, it was as though we were waiting. And we were. We were waiting for them all. But now, that's over with." She brought her focus to

Javin. "It's time to do something now. No more waiting. But, what that something is, I don't know yet."

Javin shut his eyes to listen to the songs and to himself a while. Meldren was used to this by now and re-tied her hair back into a neater arrangement as she waited and watched the colors around him shift and flow with his concentration. When he opened his eyes again, he nodded in agreement. "Yes. It's like something's pushing to come through. Something we have to do. But what that is, I can't hear at all."

Meldren gave a quiet snort of amusement. "You know what I think all this is about? It's about Harmony testing us. That's what I think. We have to work out what it is that we have to do. I don't think She's going to come and tell us. Not in any way that would make sense, that is. I mean, when She did speak to us last, it wasn't exactly the clearest thing ever, was it? No. I think it's a test."

"So, it's a test. But why? And a test of what? And what happens if we fail and also what happens if we pass? And would we know the difference?" Javin's face showed his confusion.

"Oh, we'd know. I'm sure of that. Somehow, we'd know."

"Eight people and none of them... ," he tried to find the right way of describing them and failed. All they knew, so far, was that none of them wanted to speak of the past, or why they had made such a piercing sound in Javin and Meldren's heads.

"They're all wounded and in pain." said Meldren. "That much we know. They are carrying pain songs, according to Harmony's definition. We can hear those songs."

Any further discussion was cut short by Perray appearing in the doorway with that same vacant smile she had worn the previous day and she was still gently stroking the braid.

"Are you hungry, Perray?"

"Pep. Call me Pep. I like being called Pep." The voice was, to Meldren, colorless. It contained nothing; no emotion at all. It was flat and dull, just like the colors around her.

"Pep it is. Would you like something to eat and drink, Pep?"

A vague nod and she walked to the table where Javin got up to offer her his seat while Meldren poured some juice, laid out the rest of the bread, some dried meat and some fruit.

Pep ate slowly, one hand touching her braid and her eyes gazing sightlessly as she chewed. Meldren sat to one side and watched her, her eyes narrowed as she watched the dull, slow-shifting colors around the woman, trying to assess what was happening to her. Javin appeared to be doing something similar in his own way. Pep seemed to be oblivious to the scrutiny and munched her way slowly and steadily through a good portion of the food as if to a funereal tempo in her head. Finally, she took a large swallow of juice and sat back. Not once had she stopped touching her braid.

Javin shot a questioning look at Meldren who responded by leaning toward Pep and lightly resting her hand on the woman's arm. "Shall we go and see where you can stay now?"

Pep nodded, without looking, but it wasn't until Meldren stood up and tugged lightly at her shoulder that she also stood, her expression still the same.

The walk to Pep's home took much longer this time, because Pep walked as slowly as she had eaten. Every step was deliberate, just as it had been when they had first seen her in Littlehaven; stalking her way through the people to some unknown destination before they had interrupted her progress and brought her here. When they finally arrived at the new home, the sun was bright and hot, throwing sparkling points from the ocean below. The cool spring water bubbling over the edge of the pond looked refreshing. Pep was shown around, and she handled every object as if it was fragile and precious. Then, she was shown the dried meat and the fruit trees outside and was told that it was all for her to eat. She gave a smile which touched only her lips and Javin and Meldren took their leave, all the while sensing as best they could, how Pep would fare on her own.

The next day, Meldren and Javin were sitting on their favorite spot on the island; on the headland not far from their home. It was the highest point of the island from where the only things they could see and hear were the sky and the sea. The two of them were sitting on soft mounds of earth which looked like boulders trying to force their way up under the soil.

Meldren asked, "How do you feel now when you go to Littlehaven?"

"Still painful after a while. But, now you make me think about it, I'd say that it's not as painful, or not as quick to be painful as it used to be."

"That's what I was thinking. Perhaps we're getting better at being able to control it, control how much we let in. Maybe, one day, we'll be able to live surrounded by people."

Javin pulled a face. "Maybe we'll be able to, but that doesn't mean I'll want to. I like it here, just you and me."

"Except we're not alone, are we?" Meldren sighed. "I suppose we'd better check in on them all. I want to see if Perray is... ."

"Alive?"

Meldren smiled ruefully. "True, but not how I'd want to put it. Shall we?"

They closed their eyes and let their attention find the people that were now sharing their island. Together they checked in on each of them, listening to their songs, judging how they were by any changes they heard from day to day.

After a period of listening, Javin said, "She sounds strong enough to me. So that's one thing less to worry about."

Meldren fidgeted with her hair. "What is going to happen to them and what do we do? I am still no clearer about that."

Javin thought about how we wanted to say what he felt. "The point is, do we have the right to do more than just listen to them? What was the purpose of bringing them here?"

Meldren said, "You used to listen to me when I was working in Littlehaven, and sing me better. That was to help me. Aren't we doing the same thing for these?"

"It's not the same, I think," he answered. "But, it might be that you have given me an idea." Meldren cocked an eyebrow. "I did listen to you. Because I could and because I wanted to. We can hear these people, but I don't think they can hear anything at all."

"You mean, they're deaf?" asked Meldren, looking surprised. It was a term meant for people who could no longer hear Harmony because She had withdrawn from them. It was fatal. It was that isolation which killed them somehow, because there could be no life on Harmony which was separate from Her. Javin had once stumbled across an entire village where all the inhabitants had become deaf and died all at the same time and in the same place for the same reason: Harmony withdrawing from them.

"No. Not deaf. She is still there for these people, otherwise they would be dead. I think the pain they have, the pains in their minds, are stopping them from hearing Her."

Meldren pondered this a moment. "They might not want to hear Her anymore. If they suffered badly in some way, surely they'd believe that Harmony should have saved them, helped them. Why would they want to hear Her in that case?"

"Which brings us back to the beginning again, doesn't it?" Javin shifted to sit on the ground with his back to the mound, gazing at the sky. "Or, maybe it doesn't." He sat up straighter, his head to one side, as an idea occurred to him. "What if we are here to help them hear Harmony again? That isn't the same as healing them, is it? From what I remember, Harmony said the pain songs stopped Her being heard, didn't She? So... ," Javin spoke slowly as he followed his thoughts, "if we can help them hear Harmony again, hear Her songs, then it's up to them how they want to be, isn't it? If they want to still be suffering, that's their choice, yes?"

"Wouldn't hearing Harmony heal them anyway?" asked Meldren.

"Not necessarily. If they want to hurt, they'll hurt. If they don't, they won't. Just because we can hear Her doesn't mean that we don't get sad. It's a choice for us and for them."

"So what you're saying is that our job here is to help them hear Harmony, not heal them? But, it might heal them if we do?"

Javin nodded. "And it certainly won't heal them if we don't do anything at all."

Meldren thought about it a moment before asking the question which was still bothering Javin. "Why us?"

He spread his hands, palms up, to show his ignorance. "Because we can? Because Harmony trusts us? Because somewhere out there are other people like us and She's seeing who can do what? Because it's a test of something that we'll never understand? I really don't know."

Meldren murmured an agreement. "They're here. We're here. It's obviously not an accident. We've got to do something, so why not get them to hear Harmony again?"

"If I'm wrong about them not hearing Harmony, so be it. But it does make sense, bearing in mind what She told us about the pain songs."

Meldren, seated by now next to Javin, leaned into him to give him a kiss on his cheek. "Well then, my little genius, what exactly do we do next?"

Javin smiled at her as he wrapped an arm around her shoulders and hugged her to him. "Ah! I like the simple questions."

"And the answer would be... ?"

"Absolutely no idea at all. So I think we'd best start out by going to visit them and see what happens. Who shall we see first?"

"My choice?" she asked. Javin nodded. "In that case, I think we should go and see Isselta first. She's the youngest by far and bad things shouldn't happen to children. She's my choice."

As they were walking slowly back along the clifftop path, Javin asked, "Why haven't we done this before? Why haven't we asked them what happened? Should we have done? We've just let them be since they arrived. Was that right?"

"Ah, but we did, my love. They didn't want to say anything. Isselta wouldn't speak at all. A bit like Perray. The others didn't want to speak about what happened, but Timoss, for example, will talk about anything at all, whereas Dennet will only talk about the types of fish he can identify by their color. Farran? Well, he's wrapped in his sadness about whatever it was the happened, and Enrick's pretty much the same, They'll talk about anything, except what happened. Neither of us felt like pushing them. The two women, Allegara and Carmeena, they're carrying sad tales as well. Everyone's sad and empty and probably filled with anger deep down. But nobody's as young as Isselta." She halted and Javin swung round to look at her. "Think of it this way. We have given them time on their own to do whatever they needed to do. And now we both know, we both *feel*, that we have to help them more. And that's what we're doing."

"Harmony at work again, isn't it?" He gave a wry smile. "But, you're right, of course," Javin said. "As usual, you are right. But it still doesn't change the fact that I have no idea what we're going to do."

Meldren reached for his hand and started walking again. "I so love it when we think the same way. And anyway, we're not in this by ourselves, are we?"

"Were we ever?" he replied.

3

SHARMEENA

Sharmeena passed her fingers through her hair and made a wry face as it caught on the callouses. She inspected her hands and wished, once more, for the perfect nails and smooth skin she used to have. She had never told anyone, not even her beloved Perrott, that if she could have just one thing back from her old life, just one treat, it would be a manicure. She let out a soft breath of amusement at what his reaction would be if she ever did tell him. Shaking her head at the image it conjured up, she turned her attention instead to her surroundings. Poor, stubby, dirty nails and hard skin aside, this was a wonderful place. Here she was beside a beautiful, tree-ringed lake which supplied all the fish their community would need. Beyond, in the open, small herds of sheep and cows were watched over. Her home, like everyone's, was a simple construction of hides and poles, easy to setup and take down when they needed to move on. Life here was peaceful and there was enough for everyone.

Sure, it was hard work at times, but to be in this place, away from the towns and the cities and the noise and the pollution, to be amongst other like-minded people was wonderful. She had never been this happy before. When she had first met Perrott, she had been working in a factory that made upscale consumer electronics she couldn't afford. But Perrott had met her at a party and they had got along well. Really well. And then, after a time, he had let on that he was interested in this Revivalist idea.

"We never get to see the seasons properly anymore," he had said once as they had sat on the small balcony overlooking the industrial estate where she worked. "Nobody's interested in letting us live how we want to live. The government only wants us to produce and to pay taxes. And for what? What do we get out of it?"

Later, he had shared with her some of pamphlets he had which spoke about the movement and how it was growing. He didn't say how he got them or who from, but it was evident he didn't want anyone else to know he had them. She loved him for trusting her. What he said seemed to make sense to her. Sharmeena had heard vague tales of people leaving the towns and going to the countryside, but it didn't make much sense until Perrott began to explain it to her. He even invited her to come along to one of the meetings and listen for herself.

It had been held in an old warehouse outside of town and Perrott had vouched for her to two impressively muscled guys. Inside, there had been speakers who talked about what they all needed to do, how they should organize themselves, in order to live the life they wanted. It had opened her eyes. Before, she wanted to listen to Perrott because she loved him. But after the meeting she wanted to be part of it, this Revivalist thing. She realized that she hadn't bothered to listen to herself and what she wanted before or what would make her life better. That all changed.

She brought her attention back to the present and to spinning yarn, giving the spindle a flick to get it moving and slowly drawing the yarn out before wrapping it around the shaft. She was proud of her ability to make fine, strong yarn. It was something she made herself and which she and everyone was going to use. She had a place here. She had an importance here, unlike her factory job.

As she worked her way through the coiled wool roving she had made earlier, she realized that everything was quiet. It was a different sort of quiet. The planes she had seen flying overhead the previous days had stopped. They had circled for a while before moving off. Everyone assumed that people just wanted to see what a Revivalist community looked like. Tourists from the air. But this was much quieter than the absence of planes.

She dismissed it and went back to spinning yarn, enjoying seeing the bundle grow as she sat beside the lake. Dimly she became aware of another sound, soft at first but growing in intensity. She frowned as she listened, trying to place it. Then she realized it was the sound of vehicle engines, not like the planes. It was something she hadn't heard ever since coming here with Perrott. She had given up her small apartment and virtually everything in it to follow him here. She loved him more than ever and she was sure he loved her back equally. At first, it had been hard and she had doubted her decision, but he had looked after her and helped her to learn how to become a part of the community and be more free than she could possibly have imagined. It was, she now knew, the best life she could possibly have. But the sound of engines was not part of that life. She was vaguely interested in why people might be coming to see them when everyone knew that Revivalists didn't use engines.

Thinking it was just another tourist intrusion, she settled back to concentrating on finishing the roving and winding the yarn into a neat ball. Just as she laid it by her side and rubbed the muscles at the base of her neck with her free hand, she became aware that there was someone pointing something at her. Someone she didn't recognize. Stirred by a sudden unease, she turned to get a better look. And then there was a sharp pain and heavy feeling in her chest and she toppled backward, the spindle falling from her hand as she fell into blackness.

4

THE SLEEPER

Isselta was sitting in the sun. She had the lanky, angular frame of a tall but young girl, but her green eyes belonged to a much older person. There was a bruised look to them, the brows pulled down against some hidden pain which was echoed in the taut lines of her mouth. Her dirty blonde shoulder-length hair was tapping and curling in the breeze against her face which had the delicate chin and soft not-yet-finished features of a child. She was a strange mixture of youth on the outside and age inside. Her eyes were closed as she rested against the wall of her small home. She looked at peace from a distance, but closer, her shoulders were tight and the muscles of her jaw were bunched. Both Javin and Meldren could hear the turmoil in her. It had not changed since their last visit.

They sat on their haunches nearby, letting the cooling breeze refresh them, waiting for the girl to recognize and greet them. Eventually she opened her eyes and gave a smile which meant nothing, her eyes avoiding contact. "Hello."

"Hello, Isselta," said Meldren, aware that she was feeling her way into this meeting, having no clear idea where it was going or what, if anything, would be revealed. "How are you today?"

A grudging nod as the girl looked down at the ground. That was her usual response. Rarely was there a conversation.

But, now, Meldren was intent on doing something more. On the way there, both she and Javin had felt that same push in the back of their heads they had experienced back in Littlehaven. That's what had made them certain then that they were doing the right thing, if only they knew the exact details of what that right thing was.

They had talked it over as they walked.

"Could her song give us some clues as to what happened? Or her colors, maybe?" asked Meldren. "I know we have to do something, but I don't know what."

"What if... ," began Javin, thinking aloud. "What if we listen to her song and try to find out *how* it got to be that way?"

"I don't understand."

"Well, if there's a song of a flower, then it has to be related to the song of the seed it grew from, right?"

"I suppose so."

"Think of Isselta as the flower. She's like she is because she grew from another, smaller song. At some point, that song was interrupted or altered somehow to make her how she is now. Agreed?"

"I suppose so. Yes."

"What if that smaller song is still there inside her? I've never tried it with anything, but it makes sense. If we can find that small song, the early song, and then follow it--,"

"Follow the song? How?" asked Meldren.

"It has to be inside her still in some form just as your childhood is still inside you. If we can hear how it *was* and then hear how it *is*, perhaps, and it's a big perhaps, that might tell us what happened."

Meldren walked on in silence, thinking it over. Finally she said, "Why not? I can't think of anything better to try because her colors only help me to see how she is, not how she was. But only one of us should do it."

"Absolutely. And I think it should be you."

"Me?" She looked aghast at the thought. "You're the one who can hear songs better than me."

"Yes. But I never had a dream which made me think I was female. I only dreamt the male ones. At least, I think that's what I did. I think it *has*

47

to be you. You already have had a connection with her that I can't match. You should do this for her."

Which was why Meldren was now making herself more comfortable on the ground, letting the jangling song that was Isselta become more prominent in her awareness. She heard the discordant nature of it and knew that the dissonance and fractured tunes hid deeper, darker, more somber notes.

Knowing that Javin would be listening in and both sprites would also be on the alert, Meldren closed her eyes, the better to hear. At first, she could do nothing but hear the present cacophony of Isselta. She fought to hear what could be the echoes of earlier sounds mixed in with the present turbulence of noise. Here and there she thought she could -- not hear it as such -- sense it as a lightness. That lightness, hidden deep, was, Meldren guessed, Isselta's early childhood. It was the memory of her childhood, still there as a separate and identifiable tune; a lightness which had its own clarity once the present chaos was isolated.

Meldren strained to hear that song, the ripples, the harmonics and the happiness within it. She sought to follow it despite the fact that it was a song which Isselta herself wanted hidden inside her. Listening to it, Meldren began to automatically sing fragments of it, humming it, bringing it into relief. Slowly, carefully, painstakingly patching it together, Meldren hummed the song of Isselta's youth and carefree days, enjoying the feelings it brought with it. Gently, as gently as sunlight fades into the night, Meldren found the memories begin to darken and take on heavier tones, minor chords, slower rhythms, discordancies. The emotions gradually changed to be more fearful and wary. She strained to hear what the song was holding, what reality it kept to itself. She followed it where it took her, the emotions becoming stronger and darker. And then, without warning, Meldren was overwhelmed with pain, fear, terror, helplessness and she was back in the first of the nightmares she had experienced.

She was unaware of her screams, only that Javin was shaking her, and her arms and legs were thrashing against an assailant no longer there. And then, when she opened her eyes, she could see the clouds above her. She could also hear someone else crying; sobs being wrenched from somewhere deep inside. And then she knew, without asking, that Isselta had experienced the same thing. The assault, the fear, they were Isselta's. The nightmare was not Meldren's, it was the girl's. It was the song Meldren had followed and sung. She gasped for breath, pushing at Javin as she struggled to sit up. Javin's face showed the concern of having two people, both crying, both scared about something he could not see, not knowing who to tend to first.

"I'm all right," she said, struggling to shake off the terror and the memories it held. "Let me get to her." Blindly, she pushed past Javin, knowing she would have to explain it all later, and scrabbled on her hands and knees to where Isselta was sobbing so hard that it sounded as if she were being sick. The girl's hands clenched and struck at the ground and a toneless moan escaped between the sobs. Meldren knelt and wrapped her arms tight around the girl, clasping her to herself to act as the rock to which Isselta could be drawn for safety and to anchor her here in the present, feeling as she did so the heat radiating from the girl, feeling the bones in the slender body moving, shuddering as Isselta gulped for air. She shook her head at Javin as he moved into her line of sight, questions large in his face, to say *not yet, not now, but soon.*

"I know what it is. I know what happened. You are not alone. Come here with me. Don't be alone anymore. It is safe. I am here." The words Meldren spoke were said without thought. They were simple, honest reactions to what she had seen and felt and heard. They were the words that a mother would sing to her child to reassure her. The songs they made wrapped themselves around Isselta.

Gradually, the heaving sobs began to subside, to slide down the scale and sink into irregular gasps of breath, becoming just shudders of breathing and the moan trailed away into nothingness. At the same time, Meldren could feel the slim body beginning to relax, the furnace of her body damping down. She gestured at Javin to take off the cloth bandana he wore to keep his hair in check and she used it to gently clean up Isselta's face, while still holding on to her tightly. And, as she did so, she heard the chaos of Isselta's song begin to break and soften into something which had harmonic chords in it pushing back at the earlier dissonance.

A few minutes passed until Meldren was sure that Isselta was going to be fine without being held. She eased the girl back against the wall and shifted around until she was able to sit beside her. Javin had been watching, and listening, and was seated just off to one side. They were all silent as they each sought to process what had happened.

Isselta's eyes were red, as was the tip of her nose, and she used Javin's cloth to wipe at the remaining tears. She offered it to him, but he motioned that she should keep it. Meldren had no idea what to do next. It was one thing to know of something but another matter entirely to deal with it. The best she could think of was to ask, "How are you feeling now?" And she felt how useless a thing that was.

Isselta took a deep, shuddering breath, her small chin still quivering, before answering. "What did you do?" There was an accusation in her voice. "And why did *you* scream?"

"I wish I knew," said Meldren. "I wanted to help you, to stop you feeling so hurt. But I felt, or experienced somehow, what happened to you." Isselta paled as she spoke and Meldren hurried on to reassure her. "What happened was not your fault. It was awful. Terrible! But it was not your fault." Isselta watched her cautiously, not yet willing to believe or trust Meldren. "I had a dream," continued Meldren. "This is going to sound ridiculous, but it's true. Long before I met you, I had the exact dream that showed me what happened. I woke up screaming. It didn't feel like me in the dream, only that, in a way, it was. It was a long time ago." Isselta looked to Javin who nodded solemnly in confirmation. "And just now, here, I had that same thing happen to me again. Only now I know I had dreamed of what had happened to you."

Here, Isselta shook her head with a look which said plainly that she wanted to hear no more. But Meldren pushed on as gently but as firmly as she could. "What I did, I think, was stop you from hurting yourself anymore." Again, that cautious, questioning look. "You were hurting because of what had happened. You didn't want to think about it, about the attack, but it was there, like a pressure inside you, pushing and pushing to be seen and heard and remembered."

"But I never wanted to think of it again!" Isselta wailed. "Why did you make me?" Her fists balled again as she fought against fresh tears.

"I didn't know that's what would happen. I only wanted to help you."

"Why didn't you leave me alone? You had no right!"

The words were flung like stones and Meldren flinched as each one struck, knowing that to answer them honestly she would have to admit that she had invaded the girl in an incredibly personal way; that she had listened to the most private songs inside her and, more than that, had altered them because she, Meldren, had felt it was the right thing to do. Not knowing how to admit to any of that, she answered instead by saying, "Harmony asked us, Javin and me, to help you and the others on this island with us. But She didn't tell us how. That part, just now, that was my doing."

Isselta's face twisted in anger. "Harmony? This planet? The one we're all told will look after us? The one that's meant to be so special?" She waved her hand in disgust, dismissing the idea. "Where was She when my father was raping me?" She saw Meldren's face. "Yes, my father! Didn't you know that when you had your little dream? That makes you think again, doesn't it?" The girl's voice was low. Sibilant. "Did you enjoy watching it happen? Was that fun for you afterwards? What did Harmony do when She saw him hitting me? Did She find me enough clothes to keep warm when I ran out into the blizzard? Did She do anything at all to stop it? To stop him?" Back to loud anger. "No! She watched it happen. She *let* it happen. She probably enjoyed it the same as you. So don't try to tell me that Harmony has any interest in me. I have no interest in Her. And, please, *please*, don't tell me that Harmony spoke to you about me! You felt sorry for me. You thought you could feel good about yourselves by taking me to this island. Don't try to make it sound better than it is by pretending that Harmony speaks to you and only you. Like you're some sort of special people. Just because you have those weird little things round your neck. That doesn't make you special. If you are that special, if that's true, tell Her to speak to me right now and tell Her to explain why She did nothing, *nothing*! to help me. If you want to go around playing at helping people, you go right ahead. But you can leave me out of it." She jumped up suddenly, challenging both of them to stop her. "You can pretend to help all the people you want, but you've finished with me."

She made to walk off, but Javin reached for her arm and, before she could pull away, said, "But you're alive and you're safe." Isselta was rigid with anger, but he continued. "And, unless you can swim a long way, you will have to wait for Amleek and his boat." He let go of her. "You can go anywhere you want on the island. Do anything you want. That's your choice. We won't stop you."

Isselta stood glaring into the distance, every part of her straining with anger, yet she was also trapped by it, unable to find a focus for it. Meldren felt guilty but knew things could not stay like this.

"You don't hear Harmony, do you?" Javin's reaction showed that he was not sure this was the best approach, but Meldren continued. "You don't, do you?"

"No. And I don't want to. I just told you that. Oh, but I forgot! You're special! You know everything about Harmony! What She wants or doesn't want." Sarcasm smeared her words. "Please, do let me know what Harmony wants of little, little me." She held up her hand to Meldren. "But before you do, you might want to ask dear, sweet Harmony what a murderess really needs." Her eyebrows rose in mock shock. "Oh, goodness. You didn't know that, either, did you? Yes, you special people, I killed my father. Is that quite enough of a confession for you now? Shall I tell you how I did it? Or would you prefer to have your little dreams about that instead?"

As she was speaking, Meldren was running through the dream again in her head, and recalled that she had 'seen' her dream self striking at her attacker. "And so you ran and ran and decided never to think about it again." She looked at Isselta, still standing, still heaving with anger. "You want to have Harmony speak to you, is that it? You want Her to tell you that She was wrong? I'll tell you what I think. You don't ever want to hear your father's voice. You don't ever want to hear Harmony. But, the worst thing of all is you don't ever want to hear yourself, your earlier, younger, happier self again. That's the true tragedy here." Isselta looked as if she could not choose between shock and anger. *At least, that's a change,* thought Meldren.

"People get hurt," she continued. "People die. Things go wrong. Things happen that you don't want to happen." She reached out and snapped a flower from its stem. "Here," she said, holding it out to the girl. "Here, take it. That flower? A bad thing just happened to it. I stopped it growing anymore. Does it sound sad and angry? Does it complain? Is it going to blame Harmony or me or both for as long as it can live? What about a fish that gets caught and eaten? Does a child who has just fallen over and got a bruise on it's knee from hitting a stone hold a grudge against that stone forever? Does it feel it's life is over?"

"But they're not the same thing."

"Why aren't they? Bad things happened to them and a bad thing happened to you. What's the difference?"

"They're not the same! I was raped! I'm not a fish and I'm not a flower. And how can a flower sound sad? It can't feel anything!" She hit it out of Meldren's hand.

"How do you know it can't?" Meldren pushed on, suddenly seeing that what she had started without thinking now seemed to have a purpose. She noted, peripherally, that Javin had his eyes closed, listening to what was going on in a different way. Also, she noted that both of their sprites were beginning to strain outward, as if becoming involved as well. "If you can't hear Harmony, then how would you possibly know what anything was feeling, what anything was like? You're too wrapped up in your own pain to ever want to hear anything else. You don't even want to know that you had a happier life earlier on. That means you're not even listening to yourself anymore, just some pain you want to keep with you."

Despite her need to strike out, Isselta said, "A flower can't feel sad, and I do know that once I was happy. You're wrong about that. You're wrong about everything!"

"Do you want to hear that flower? Hear what it really is, *how* it really is?" The challenge was quiet but undeniable.

"What do you mean, 'hear the flower'?"

Meldren repeated it. "Do you want to hear the flower as it truly is? If you think we're nothing special, then maybe you're right. Do you want to hear the true flower? Yes or no."

Drawn in despite herself, Isselta accepted the challenge. "Do it. If you can, then do it. Show me what a 'true' flower is like."

Meldren nodded and Javin opened his eyes and came a little closer to the other two. He and Meldren were now sitting facing Isselta who stood for a moment longer but sat heavily, avoiding their eyes as she did so. "If you want to hear this, then you have to stop thinking about what happened with your father. You can go back to thinking about it afterwards. But now, you need to stop that and let yourself think of the flower." As she spoke, Meldren offered up the small yellow flower again. Isselta eyed it but did not take it, so Meldren placed it on the ground before her.

"Now," she said, "look at it. Look at it and see it as clearly as you can; the colors, the shape, the size. Everything about it. Then, when you're ready, shut your eyes. It makes it easier to hear. If it makes you more comfortable, Javin and I will move back. We're not going to attack you."

Isselta shook her head, defiant. "Do what you like." But she did look at the flower and then, after one last challenging glare, she sat up straight and closed her eyes.

Meldren reached for Javin's hand and together they closed their eyes and felt for the flower on the ground. They heard its song and how that song fitted into everything else, including the three of them. Once they had the song clear, they held it and then began to move it gently into the slow roil of sound that was Isselta. They waited for a space, a pause to appear and then, as gently as they could, they put it inside her song to let her hear the sound. They held it there for a space and then, as they opened their eyes, let the song fall away. Just before it faded, however, there was a momentary and subtle change of key, a modulation which sank into the song as it entered Isselta. As they opened their eyes they saw the look of surprise on Isselta's face as she snapped her eyes open.

"What happened?"

"You heard the flower as it truly is; as a song. That's all. You heard the song of it."

"Music?" Isselta pointed at the flower. "Are you saying that's made of music?"

"Not music," said Javin. "A song. Music is something that can make you feel good or bad, change your mood in some way. But a song is more than the music. A song is a story, a tale, a making of something else that the music is just a part of. A song is creating something more lasting than any music is capable of. Music can make you have an emotion about the flower, but it's the song which makes the flower itself."

Meldren, though, had been quietly impressed at the leap of intuition in the question. She asked, "What exactly did you hear or see?"

Isselta was still not in a trusting frame of mind. "I heard something. A sound. But it was a sound which had a shape. It had the shape and color of the flower there." She looked almost embarrassed. "But saying it out loud makes no sense at all. You can't hear colors and shapes."

Meldren let the silence spread a while longer, allowing a little more uncertainty to take root in Isselta. "Isselta? You heard a song. That's true. But that song is just one tiny sound, because everything you can see around you is also a song. You were hearing a very small part of Harmony." Isselta became a little more rigid at that. "Harmony's songs: they are what everything here is made up of. Including us, I suppose."

Isselta pointed at the sprite now relaxed and back in its usual place around Meldren's throat, as was Javin's. "And that thing? What does that do? Why do you have those, each of you?"

Javin stroked his sprite with one finger and smiled. "We're not really sure. We think they help us hear Harmony better. Or maybe they help us sing better."

"You can make songs like the flower? Like Harmony?" Now there was growing curiosity replacing the outright disbelief and earlier antagonism.

"Not like Harmony," Meldren also smiled. "Just small simple things, like the flower. Like your home here, for example. We sung that for you."

Isselta, eyes narrowed, stroked the wall behind her with the fingertips of one hand, as if feeling for sounds inside it. There was still some skepticism evident when she spoke. "Songs? This is a song as well? And Harmony sings everything?" She thought for a moment, trying to come to terms with this new concept. "So Harmony made a song about me killing my father, about my father raping me? Is that what you're saying? That's sick!"

Meldren jumped in to interrupt that chain of thought. "No! Harmony doesn't make us do things like that. A flower grows in the way a flower grows. Harmony isn't going to make a flower suddenly fly away or become a fish. A flower, you and me, we are made of songs. But how we choose to sing those songs, that's up to us. But we can't be something we aren't. I can't suddenly turn into a boat or a mountain. That's why people are just people but in different ways. Your father was one type of person. But Harmony didn't make him rape you. He chose that himself. It's the way he chose to sing his song.

"It's like you can be a song, sing that song, but sing it higher or lower,

55

or sing in harmony with it or sing it out of tune, sing it loudly or quietly. But the main song, who you are, the central thing if you like, doesn't change. Your father chose the way he would sing. You reacted to it in a way which made sense of your song. And you had to if you wanted to live, to keep singing your song. And neither you nor Harmony is to blame for what happened. You did what you had to, but then you forgot to keep listening, keep hearing Harmony. You were so wrapped up in your pain that you blocked everything else out. And, if you can't hear Harmony, you can't be well because you're out of rhythm, out of harmony, you've lost the main song. There's no way you can know what your song should sound like if you cannot hear the other songs around you. Your sounds will be wrong, out of tune, making you ill."

Isselta had been listening carefully. Now she looked from one to the other as she sought to understand it. "*Every*thing is songs? So, if I knew the right sounds, I could bring my father back? Is that what you're saying?"

Javin puffed out a breath of surprise and admiration. "That's a question neither of us thought about asking for a long time. We're still not sure of the answer, but, as far as we can tell, it wouldn't work. Harmony sings everything. We have learned to make some small songs, but they have to fit in with what Harmony is singing. If you sang your father back to life, and I'm not sure that's even possible, then how would he fit back into Harmony's song? His song ended. You can't just push it back into what Harmony is singing and expect it all to be fine. I'm not sure what would happen, but I suspect it wouldn't be your father who came back. It would be someone else. The only way we think it could happen would be if you could persuade Harmony to have his song reappear." He shrugged. "It would have to be a really good reason that She could understand. And I'm not sure She does fully understand about how we humans think or feel. She gives us songs and lets us get on with singing them. At least, for almost everyone else, that's true." He gestured at himself and Meldren. "We seem to have been picked out by Her and don't have as much choice as other people." Another shrug, this time of resignation. "Not that we mind too much. It does have its advantages after all."

"Speaking of having choices," added Meldren, "that's what happened with you and the others. Harmony clearly told us that we had to do something about all of you. We had to help you in some fashion. But we're not really clear the best way to do that, as was obvious just now -- and apologies for doing what we did. Plus we're not clear at all on even why we have to do it." She winced in embarrassment as she spoke those words.

"So why do it at all?"

"Fair question, I suppose," agreed Meldren. "I think the best way of answering that is, at first, it was plain uncomfortable and nasty having Harmony speak with us. And, yes, She does really speak. Then it became easier, with these sprites, and we found out that, as a result, we had bigger, different talents than anyone we've heard of. But, the gifts we've been given make us think that we have a responsibility, a way of paying back Harmony for choosing us, even if, at times, it might be more pleasant and relaxing having been left alone."

Isselta considered this, the earlier anger pushed aside by her new focus. "What it comes down to is that you have no idea why you did whatever it was you did to me except that it seemed like a good idea, at least to Harmony's way of thinking. Would that be right?" Her voice was less accusatory, but colder now, more analytical.

Javin tilted his head in acknowledgment. "Put that way, I'd have to agree with you. But, if you were us, you'd probably have a different view." He leaned forward in emphasis as he spoke. "I can't persuade you that we're right and you're wrong. I don't want to do that. I can't even promise that we could sing you back to how you were, assuming that's what you want. But I think it's worth pointing out how quickly you lost your anger after you heard Harmony again. You are now singing your song yourself. As for what happens now? All I can say is that what you do next is up to you. We'll stay out of it, not bother you while you decide. If you want to leave, you can. We'll try to have Amleek here as quickly as possible. If you want to stay, but have nothing to do with us, that's your choice as well. To speak truthfully, neither of us knows what happens next or what Harmony's plans are. That means, I suppose, that whatever you choose to do is the right thing. It means you're singing your song your way. In the end, that's all that counts."

Isselta finally picked the flower up and studied it, spinning it gently between her fingers. After taking a sniff of it she looked up again with a slight frown. "I think I feel sorry for you both. You have all these talents, can do virtually anything you want and you say you have no choice about anything you do. That's not really, as you put it, singing your own songs, is it? And if you say that's what counts, then what you're doing here doesn't count for very much."

"But," said Javin, "we've chosen to accept not having so many choices. Isn't that singing our own songs?"

JAVIN WAS IN THE GARDEN BUT NOT REALLY DOING VERY MUCH. KNEELING and weeding had turned into sitting and looking aimlessly around him whilst half-heartedly jabbing the wooden trowel into the ground. Meldren had opted to scramble down to the beach and walk along it. They were both still preoccupied with the events of the previous day. They had tried to feel what they should be doing, but there was nothing they could sense which helped in any way. They were frustrated and didn't know what to do or not to do. As Javin had said, "There's no rhythm right now."

He knew that getting Isselta to hear Harmony had been a turning point. But he wasn't sure that it had been the right way to do it, even though he could not think of another way of achieving what Harmony had requested of them. And then there was Isselta's assessment of his and Meldren's life which, he had to admit, had stung.

He was about at the point of admitting he was wasting his time and of getting up and going to find Meldren, when he was startled by Isselta's voice. He had been too absorbed in his thoughts to have noticed her, so when she called out, he flinched with surprise.

"I've been thinking," is what she said.

Turning round he could see that she rather liked having startled him. "Yes?"

"Maybe you were right. About what you did to me." She scissored down to the ground in front of him, her slight, angular frame moving easily. He waited, noticing how thin she looked. Her gaze was direct and somewhat unnerving. Maybe it was the adult-inside-a-child dissonance, or maybe he was not used to her sharpness of mind.

"Perhaps you were right to do what you did. I've been thinking about it a lot since. And, yes, I do feel better about things, but I think you did it the wrong way."

"Well, I think that's a fair way of putting it," he offered.

"But I also think I know a better way," she said, ignoring him. "A way that doesn't have to be so rude, so forceful. So ugly. Because, the thing you did with the flower? That was what did it. There's something I can do now." She batted away his attempt to speak and continued without pause. "The important thing, the thing you said that was true, was that I couldn't hear Harmony any more. And that's what's wrong with the other people here, isn't it? They can't hear Her either, can they? So what I'm thinking is you need me with you when you try to help the others. I can talk to them, tell them what it's like, what happened to them."

She gave him a half-scornful look. "You can't do that. Having a dream is not the same as living through something. I have no idea what's wrong with them, but I know they have suffered. I've seen them. We don't talk much, but it's easy to see they've had bad things happen to them as well. It's like you and her collected them here. Like we're all cripples or something."

Again, she plowed through Javin's attempt to speak. "Anyway, the way I see it is that I have to help you help them heal. If nothing else, it will stop you two from bursting in on them like you did with me. And that's got to be better for them. I don't really know them, but what you did to me, that's not the right way of doing it. So I'll help. But after that? I don't know. Maybe I'll leave. Maybe not. But I thought I should tell you before you both go off and hurt someone else." She stood up as easily as she had sat, hooking her hair behind her ear as she looked down at him. "Come and get me before you do anything else." And away she went, leaving Javin open-mouthed behind her.

When he eventually located Meldren she was sitting on a large, smooth boulder staring sightlessly out to sea. She smiled absentmindedly at him and patted the boulder, inviting him to sit with her. When he finished sharing what Isselta had said, she was in a lighter mood.

"That makes sense. If she can get to them somehow, make them realize that she understands what they're feeling, maybe we can then help them reconnect with Harmony more easily. At least, make it less of a shock." She smoothed out her skirt as she turned the idea over in her mind. "And she is also right that having a dream about something is not going to be the same as actually having something like that happen to you."

She picked up a pebble and tossed it gently in her hand a few times before letting it fall with a little sigh of frustration. "I've been trying to listen to the others to get a feel for their songs. And there does seem to be the same sort of small song going on in all of them. It's very close to what was in Isselta's songs. Maybe it's the sound of shock or terror or something horrible that happened. I'd never bothered to look for it before. But now I have, I think that's what it is." She looked at Javin. "Do you think that was a good thing to do, listen to them like that?"

He nodded firmly. "Absolutely. We are trying to help them. And, maybe now with Isselta with us, we can do that more easily. Mind you, I have no idea what exactly she will do. But, what she said is definitely better than anything I've been able to think of."

"So who shall we visit first?" asked Meldren.

"I was thinking either Timoss or Dennet. Dennet probably."

"Why him first?"

"Timoss is crippled. There's a physical thing there. If we help him hear Harmony again, he's still going to be crippled and in pain. I'd rather deal with Dennet first because it would be more like with Isselta. Get him hearing Harmony again and that's all we have to deal with... hopefully. I think, or hope, it would be easier with him first. Plus, he's the nearest to Isselta's age, so there might be something in common which could be useful."

Isselta was waiting for them outside when they were preparing to leave the following morning. She gave them a quick smile which almost reached her still bruised-looking eyes but volunteered nothing as they made their way to where Dennet was living. The only thing she said, in response to Meldren asking her what she proposed to do to help Dennet was to say, "I'll let him see what it's like to be alive."

Dennet had been one of the first to have been recognized as being involved in Javin and Meldren's dreams. He seemed fairly young, with black hair and dark eyes in a thin face. Unlike Isselta, he was always happy to talk but it was always of the same thing: about the best way to track fish underwater. It was obvious that his talent was much like Meldren's in that he could see colors around things, but he only seemed to use it for spotting shoals of fish, or perhaps they were the only colors he could see. He would often be found sitting overlooking the ocean, from where he would point out the movements of various types of fish. Meldren could also see the colors, but she had no idea what the colors meant. Dennet was happy, always, to instruct her. But any attempt to change the subject was ignored.

As the three of them came to his home, they found him seated some distance away, beyond the sheltering vegetation, staring at the sea as usual, the wind tugging at his clothing. He waved in response to their calls but didn't move. They decided to go to him.

Before Dennet launched into his usual description of what he was looking at, Javin pointed at Isselta and said, "You and she have something in common. Something she needs to tell you." He then beckoned Isselta to speak. Dennet watched her suspiciously, aware that his routine was being broken. Isselta seemed not to hesitate at all, but hunkered down in front of Dennet and reached out a hand to him. He began to shrink back from it, but she grasped his arm. She held his gaze with a fierce concentration. Dennet began to struggle against her grip, but she held him tight despite her size. Javin and Meldren looked on with concern, worried that they had been talked into doing something everyone would quickly regret.

"You've been hiding away, haven't you?" Isselta spoke quietly. "But I can see where you are. You're in there, looking at something else." Dennet's eyes opened wide. Isselta continued. "Shall I show you what I was looking at inside me? I was hiding, like you. You can't stop looking, can you?" Here, she leaned in even closer, ignoring the fact that Dennet was trying to pry her hand from his arm. Her voice lowered and softened until it became no more than a breath. "Here. This is what I was looking at." And she shut her eyes. Dennet stiffened suddenly and became still, his gaze turned inward for a moment. Then Isselta opened her eyes again, let go of his arm and said, "I can see you on the inside. You can't hide anymore now. You've seen me. I've seen you. I know all about it."

Dennet shook his head in denial, his voice pleading. "No! You can't know. I didn't mean to! It wasn't my fault."

Isselta put a finger to his lips to quiet him, a gesture of surprising tenderness and understanding, given her youth. "There's no point in hiding anymore. I hid, like you. But I'm not hiding anymore. So I'm going to let Javin and Meldren here make things better for you. They don't know what happened. They're just going to help you stop looking at it. And, if you want to go back and look again, you can. But you won't want to. I know. Now, be quiet and let them give you a choice of looking at something else."

She stood up, lifting a warning finger at Dennet, who appeared confused but no longer angry. It was her turn to beckon Javin and Meldren to do their work. As they did so, she sat to one side, looking out to sea with an expression on her young face that was difficult to read, but which had a hint of sadness to it.

After the singing of Dennet back to awareness was completed, Meldren stayed with him and began the slow process of helping him understand what had just happened. Javin left and sat beside Isselta, who had remained staring out to sea. He, too, gazed out for a while. Without turning to her, he said, "I know something's changed. Your song? It's not exactly the same as before. Something new has been added. Is that what you used when you were talking to Dennet?"

Isselta nodded.

Javin prodded gently. "What is it? What happened?"

For a moment, Isselta remained hugging her knees and resting her chin on them, staring away into the distance. Finally, when Javin still kept quiet, she half-turned to him. "When you sang me the flower yesterday? That was when it happened. Oh, sure, I heard Harmony. But something happened. It wasn't just me being able to hear Harmony. I also could see things. See what was going on in you, for instance. I saw what happened to you." She shrugged. "You did it to me without asking. So, when I could see you, I didn't care."

He waved her words away. "I'm used to having Meldren hearing me, hearing my song. I don't even think about it anymore."

"I saw what had happened to you. I'm not sure what it is I can do. But... ," she trailed off, trying to find the right words. "It's as though, when I looked inside you, and then inside him," gesturing back at Dennet, "I get to see the big stuff. The horrible things. Like you being drugged and kidnapped. With him... well, I'm not going to say. That's up to him to tell you. I looked inside him and inside you. And as soon as I did, I saw what had happened. None of the good stuff, none of the happy times. Just the thing he was hiding from. Looking inside. That's the only words I have for it. It doesn't sound like songs, does it?"

It was Javin's turn to shrug. "I don't see why not. After all, we can see things with our eyes, and we're songs. Seeing is part of the way the songs are. It sounds like you can see things that others can't, that's all. A bit like an 'eye' I suppose." It was the term given to those whose talent was being able to see things happening in the future or far away. "Did you have this sort of talent before?"

She shook her head. "No. Nobody in my family did. At least, I don't think so. We survived in the ice and snow and hunted. Too much hard work and cold to notice anything like that. It was yesterday after singing the flower. That's when it happened."

"Ah! That's what that was!" In answer to her unspoken query, Javin added. "Right at the very end of singing it, I noticed something changed in the music. Really small and subtle. And then it vanished. I forgot about it. But I'm sure that's when it happened."

"You didn't do it or have anything to do with it?"

Javin raised his hands to show his innocence. "Nothing at all."

"So why did it happen anyway?"

He couldn't resist grinning at her. "Well, if neither Meldren nor I did it, then don't you think that Harmony might be the one to ask? And, before you say anything, maybe it's not an answer either of us could guess at. And, just another maybe to add on, maybe you've already started doing what you were meant to be doing by helping Dennet." He touched her arm gently as he spoke, but withdrew quickly as she shrank back. "You do realize that what you can do now is going to be amazingly helpful to the others here? It will be much easier for us to help them listen to Harmony again. Meldren and I did a really bad job with you, but you're able to speak and act and live and be well again -- better than you were, at least. Maybe, just maybe, this is just another talent. Something that not many others have."

Isselta narrowed her eyes as she thought about it. "Have you ever heard anyone being able to do this before?"

"No. I've never heard of such a talent. Doesn't mean that someone somewhere else can't do it as well though."

Isselta had turned back to staring out at the ocean again and was again hugging her bony knees to her slim frame and wrinkling her snub nose. "I'm like you, aren't I? I don't get to have a choice in this. What Harmony wants is what Harmony gets, I suppose. And there's me feeling sorry for you two. But what's really worrying me is why would Harmony want anyone to have a talent like this?" She sat silent, the wind blowing her hair from her face, teasing tears from the corners of her eyes. She closed her eyes and bowed her head to her knees. Her voice was low and muffled when she spoke, the breeze taking it. "It means that there's going to be a need for it, doesn't it? There's going to be more broken people, aren't there?" Javin felt a tremor of something -- an unwelcome truth perhaps? -- at hearing the words.

OVER THE NEXT FEW DAYS ISSELTA, MELDREN, AND JAVIN VISITED THE OTHER people on the island and between them they reunited them all with Harmony. Most of them were, if not immediately happy, then at least accepting of the outcome. Of all of them Timoss was the most angry at being reunited with Harmony.

"I never wanted to hear Harmony again! Ever!" shouted Timoss after Javin and Meldren had finished. "It was because of Her that I ended up with these legs."

"What do you mean?" asked Meldren. She noticed that Isselta, who probably knew all the details, had removed herself and was sitting with her back to them.

"Talent! That's the problem. I had a talent. And Harmony loves giving talents, doesn't She? Well, you just gave me back mine; the one I never wanted."

Javin asked, "What's so bad about it?"

"You two and her over there and the others? I can hear you all. All the time now. Up until you broke into my head, I was alone. I was silent. Everything was quiet. I could sleep properly. It was beautiful. Peaceful." He squeezed his head and his eyes filled with tears of either rage or pain. It was hard to say which. Maybe both.

"Ever since I can remember, I've heard the constant noise of other people in my head. It's never-ending, going on and on. The more people, the more noise." Meldren and Javin exchanged knowing glances at this.

Timoss managed to gather himself enough to explain what had happened. "I couldn't control it. Even living with my parents was hard. It never stopped, even when they slept. I tried to control it, but when it didn't change, I thought I would find a place of my own, far away from everyone else. Or, at least, where people would only pass by and never stay. I was young and hopeful." He took a slow, deep breath and let it out in one long sigh, his eyes tight shut. "I was in a canyon. Only one way in and one way out. And I heard people approaching." He tapped his head. "Heard them inside my head. I was trapped. I suppose I could have stayed or pushed past them, but I tried to climb up and avoid them. I wanted to leave them behind and find some peace again. I was near the top and looking down when I slipped." He squeezed his eyes shut again.

"And that's when you broke your legs," said Javin. "When you fell." It wasn't a question.

Timoss nodded, tears leaking from beneath his eyelids. "I must have passed out with the pain. I remember seeing some bone poking through. The people helped me as best they could, but none of them was a healer. They were hunters. Only meant to be out a few days. They did the best they could. They set the bones as well as they could and gave me herbs which numbed everything." He gave a soft grunt of amusement. "The thing was, those herbs numbed my head as well. After a day or so, I couldn't hear them. Or, maybe, it was the pain which stopped me hearing. Whatever it was, it was because of the fall. And I wouldn't have fallen if I hadn't had the talent. And now, it's back again and you are noises in my head, in my life, and I want to hit you, but I'd never catch you with these legs. I hate you both, and I hate her as well," pointing at Isselta, who still had her back to them.

Meldren called Isselta over. The girl came with some reluctance and sat between Meldren and Javin facing Timoss.

"Timoss," began Meldren, "You know all three of us to some extent. We're all sorry that we've given you some pain back."

"Huh!"

"But," she continued, a touch of granite in her voice, "hating us -- any of us -- won't change a thing. If you want to go on being in pain, you go right ahead. Go on and feel really sorry for yourself, if that makes you feel better, but don't take out your pain on us." That made him look up.

"You are stupid if you think this is how it has to be. Because what you haven't yet realized is that you can stop the noise in your head. Javin and I have the same problem. Staying around too many people for too long is painful. It's not quite the same thing you have, but it's close enough. We chose to live on this island because it was away from people. But we've begun to control it. It's taken us a long time to realize that. We were really slow about it. Our excuse was that we had plenty of other things happening in our lives. But we're learning. But you? You were shown straight away. You said that the herbs numbed everything. And you've stayed numb ever since. The herbs didn't change you permanently. You did that to yourself. You were so frightened that you taught yourself to stay numb to Harmony. Until we came along just now, that is. The herbs helped, but you chose to remain deaf to Harmony. And, if you chose to switch off your talent once, you can do it again. Any time you like. But, no! It's easier to shout at people." Meldren felt anger and sympathy in equal measure, wanting to shout and to hug him at the same time. She took a steadying breath.

"Isselta has a talent. She used it to make it gentler for when we worked on you than it was when we worked on her. We hurt her badly, but she forgave us enough to offer to help the rest of you. I'm sure, if you ask her, Isselta will be able to help you find the right way to hold back the noise by finding it in you. But whether she is willing to help you, after what you've said, that's up to her entirely."

Isselta bobbed her head, her eyes wary. "I can do it if you want."

Timoss wiped at his tears and looked a little embarrassed, choosing to stare at the ground. "I'd like that," he mumbled. "I'm sorry."

"Well, that's settled," said Meldren briskly. And she stood and patted Timoss on his shoulder and gave an encouraging grin to Isselta. "We'll leave you two to it. Come on Javin."

Isselta and Timoss spent much time together in the days following, between them, they began to listen to and understand more deeply the songs of the world around them. Gradually Timoss learned that the noise he had always heard was nothing more than a part of a larger song and that, by allowing himself to hear Harmony more fully, the chaotic noise which had always been a part of his life could begin to fit into this larger sound and become, if not less obvious, then at least less disturbing, because it now had a purpose, a pattern to it.

As Isselta once said to him, sounding much older than she was, "My problem was that I didn't want anything else in my life. I lived inside my shell. Your problem is that you want everything you don't have; peace, health, sanity. You want out of your shell. I didn't like letting Harmony in. Why should you like blocking things out? It's just the same for both of us, only from different sides. If you hear Harmony fully, then you will be able to mend your leg again. Why would Harmony let us hear Her again if all we did was complain about what was wrong? Hearing Her will allow all of us to do things we didn't think we could."

The others were less conflicted about being reunited with Harmony's songs again. Their stories unwound from their hiding places deep inside them as Javin and Meldren worked with them, helping and teaching them. Allegara, for example, had been deeply scarred by finding her husband, or what was left of him after some big hunting cats had finished with him. She was an older woman with pale green eyes, thin lips and thin body. They had never seen her smile before, but she did allow herself a small grin as time passed and she let herself hear Harmony again. Her talent had been the ability to find things, locate people or places to fish or hunt, or where to dig for clean clay. She had minor talents but had never spoken directly of them. So when her husband was late back from what should have been a short hunt, she used her talent to find him. She never wanted to do any such thing again.

Then there was Carmeena. She had been the first to have been brought to the island. One day after hearing Harmony again, she began to speak to Meldren as if taking up an old conversation.

"I had a child once. Beautiful, she was. I can't even begin to tell you how beautiful. And alive! So lively and active and always, always happy. So happy." She paused and gathered her long brown hair and draped it over her shoulder. She was half-smiling, her dark eyes, brown like her hair, had a dreamy look. "She was... everything. Everything of my world was there in her. And then, she was gone." She held her hands apart, staring into the space between them as if to find her child there somehow.

"What was her name?" Meldren asked gently.

Still staring between her hands, Carmeena said, "Anna. She was Anna."

"That's a lovely name," said Meldren.

Carmeena nodded. "But she went. So suddenly." She brought her hands together and let them rest on her legs. "I was sewing something for her. A small cap to her keep her head warm when winter came. I was sewing it carefully. Small stitches." Her hands moved to illustrate her words. "I was proud of it. And she was there beside me and then she was away and gone. And I took so much care that I didn't notice. Sewing, sewing, sewing." Her hands moved quicker. Then she stopped suddenly and looked straight at Meldren. "You know how it is when you know something but nobody told you? It's just there in your head? As I was sewing, I felt Anna slip away from me. She vanished. Pop! There and then not there." She looked away and inward, seeing again what had happened. "And I went to where she disappeared and I knew she was gone." She pointed down. "There. Down there. Right at the very bottom. She was there and she was gone and the well was too deep for me to reach her and she was floating face down, her head at a wrong angle and never moving and I couldn't reach her and I saw her and she left me and I felt it and I was sewing and not watching her." All one breath ending in a gasp of agony of recollection and guilt.

But the telling of it had broken the dam inside her and Carmeena could begin to think about doing something more than reliving the agony every day. Meldren's eyes filled with tears and Javin gently and quietly sang a song to ease Carmeena a little.

Each person they had brought had similar tales of agony, sorrow and regret. Enrick and Farran eventually shared similar tales of loss of their loved ones. In Enrick's case it had been the rejection by the woman he had loved from a distance for many years. He was a bulky man, softly spoken with sad eyes, too easily hurt by rejection. In Farran's case the loss was of his partner, the only woman he had ever loved, could ever love, who had decided to break the relationship and leave him. In each case, their dreams had been cracked apart and neither could cope. Enrick had wanted only to be alone. Farran, his lined face and fringe of white hair making him look as weary and worn as he felt, had lost interest in living and had been a bony stick of a man before meeting with Javin and Meldren. Both, in their own ways, had been devastated and had turned inwards until Harmony was sung into their lives again.

Perray, or Pep as she insisted they call her, had been the last to reveal her torment. Again, it had happened without warning.

One bright day, Javin and Meldren had been helping her gather some fruits; berries from the bushes near her home. They had only intended to be there, not to pry or force any conversation, just be there with her. They were thinking of bringing Isselta along the next day. But it wasn't needed.

Pep was plucking some berries and placing them in a container Meldren had brought with her when she looked at Meldren and said, "Do you know how loud people can scream?" It was said in such a conversational tone that it took Meldren completely off guard. She could only stumble and stutter. Pep appeared not to notice, continuing to collect berries as she spoke. "It's very, very loud indeed. It's so loud that I can still hear it. Can you hear them? I think I can hear her better because one of them was Emalia. Em. She and I were twins. We could always hear what the other one was doing or thinking. I suppose that's why I can still hear her, don't you?" She continued before Meldren could answer. "I was Pep and she was Em. And she died. Did I tell you that? She died." She continued searching for berries, giving more to Meldren to hold. It was all so matter of fact that Meldren was having trouble realizing that this was the reason for Pep being here with them. "I was with the mandria. I like mandria. They are big and friendly and they don't mind me when I get upset. I was with them, you see? I had forgotten to check on them before. I should have done it but I forgot. So I left them all in the house and went to the mandria and I told them what was happening. And that's when I heard the screams beginning."

She finally stopped searching and turned to Meldren, a serious look on her face as if trying to teach Meldren something important. "They were all in there. And they are all still screaming. Big, big flames. Oooh! They were big and too hot for me. I burned my hands and my hair." She stroked her hair in that familiar way, a faint smile on her face. "But I had to say goodbye to them. I don't know if they heard me because of the screaming. Anyway, that was the last time I saw Em and my mother and my father and the father of Em's baby. They were all screaming." She paused with a quizzical look on her face. "I don't think I heard the baby screaming. But it was inside Em, so that would have made it hard to hear, wouldn't it?" She reached out to grasp Meldren's hands, spilling all the berries on the ground but not seeming to notice. "I don't want to hear them anymore. I've heard them for a long time. Do you think that will be a good thing or will they hate me for not hearing them anymore?" She dropped Meldren's hands and turned back to berrying, as if nothing had happened. It was, said Meldren later, the scariest thing that had happened to her in a very long time.

It was how they learned that Dennet had blamed himself for his father's death at sea, gazing at the colors on the land which attracted him more than watching out for dangers ahead of them on the ocean.

So it was that the dreams which had started this all off made sense as they were able to link them to each individual's story. Heartbreaking loss, sheer terror, agonies of guilt; all now made sense to the two rescuers. And that understanding made them at first feel sorry for the people. But it also made them realize how lucky they both were in comparison. And they had to deal with guilt they felt over that.

At the same time as listening and allowing them to speak, the two of them also gently taught their neighbors how to sing for themselves. Small songs, tiny songs, songs of a flower or a fruit. Singing to keep food fresh or to mend a hole in their clothes. The simple things they taught gave these broken people some feeling of control again, some measure of reassurance that things really could be fine and that their lives could take on a new meaning.

Over time, all of them were able to sing the simple songs without instruction. Isselta, although her eyes still had a remoteness to them, slowly lost her sarcasm and her anger as she helped the others to talk more about themselves. Apart from Isselta and her new talent, the others began to re-kindle their original talents, but this time within the songs around them.

As Meldren put it one day as she and Javin were tying some slipsweet seedlings to their supports, "It's like they are beginning to be able to see that they really have a place here and that any talent is just another way of harmonizing with what is already being sung."

It was Isselta who brought up the question which had slowly been forming around them all. In her usual, direct fashion, she had walked in on Javin and Meldren at breakfast without apology or preamble and asked, "Why are we all here and why is Harmony so interested in all of us? What's the point of this, of hearing Harmony and singing the small songs? There has to be a purpose to it all. That's what you always keep reminding us about, isn't it? That Harmony has a purpose? Well, don't you think it's about time we found out what it was?" Her face had her familiar determined look which, on anyone else as young would have been considered charming or even cute. But, in Isselta's face an older person still looked out from her eyes. She would never look as young as a child again.

Meldren beckoned her over to sit with them. Isselta did so, her feet just reaching the floor, but she had a tight grip on the edge of the seat and her shoulders held tension there as if there was an inability to relax fully with the two of them.

"We were thinking much the same thing," said Meldren. "You know now that it's not a simple thing, understanding what it is that Harmony wants. We've been trying to feel our way about this and we can't get a good answer, a clear answer, that is."

"Why not just ask?"

"We can do that, but how do we know what the answer is? Harmony can't speak to us easily, and when she does tell us things, it's often difficult to know what She means. Take you and all the others, for example. Both Javin and I knew you were all important and that we had to find you. But beyond that?" She shrugged. "We had to wait for the next thing to be shown to us. If it's something as simple as showing us where to live, that's easy for Her. But this is way more complicated than that." Meldren gestured at Javin. "Both of us have been trying to feel what is wanted but -- ."

"What do you mean 'feel'?"

Javin answered this one. "Everyone can get a feeling about something that's about to happen, right? But not everyone is able to let that feeling come through. It can be something as vague as waking up and knowing that the day is going to be a good one, a happy one. Well, Meldren and I, we try to feel the future and use that to guide us."

"You mean like an 'eye' does? Seeing ahead?" Isselta asked.

"Sort of. But 'eyes' don't see that far. A day or two at most is all I've heard of, and they have to know where to look. We're trying to feel things many more days ahead, and we don't always know where to look or what to look out for."

"Why?"

"Because Harmony is a planet. And a planet is a slow thing. Think of seasons and how long they are. I don't think Harmony is any good at planning what happens the next day or the next hour. She sings the long songs and lets us, the small, short ones, work out how to fit in. So we, the shorter songs if you like, are trying to feel what might be coming from Her, good or bad, fearful or happy, something with a flavor to it, a sound, anything which might help us understand more." He shook his head. "But it's difficult and we can only get the vaguest of feelings which are no help at all."

Isselta considered this, head bent, hair falling over her face and one foot swinging back and forth, lightly scuffing the earthen floor. "I think," she said, tossing her head up to get her hair out of her face, "that you don't have anything to do with the next step. I think you've done what Harmony wanted. You've been teaching us songs and singing and things. I think it's up to us next, the ones you brought here." She stared off into the distance seemingly unaware of the two others there as she thought. "I think it's like you've not been helping us so much as training us for something. I think we are the ones Harmony is working with now.

You two can take a rest now if you want. I'm sure you'll be needed again soon." Then she seemed to become aware of where she was again and looked at Meldren. "That's why it is so difficult for you to sense what Harmony wants. She doesn't want you to do anything. She wants us next." The girl nodded thoughtfully to herself as if confirming her own words. "Yes," she said. "That makes sense. I'd better tell the others." And with that, she jumped off and left Javin and Meldren wide-eyed and momentarily speechless.

"And she asked us about feeling the future? Do you think she has any idea how capable she is?" asked Javin.

"No. But it's kind of scary in a good way listening to her, isn't it?"

"She always makes me feel so... so...,"

"Slow?" finished Meldren, eyes twinkling.

Javin made a mock-angry face at her. "You're weeding alone for the next two days for that."

Meldren inclined her head, grinning. "It was absolutely worth it."

DESPITE THE JOKING ABOUT ISSELTA, IT WAS A STRANGE FEELING FOR BOTH Javin and Meldren over the following days to not only feel idle, but to be idle; to have no quietly persistent internal drive, no slow, deep awareness of a goal urging them on to achieve it. They had both sought out the truth of what Isselta had said. Each in their own way tried to listen, to sense in some fashion, what it was they had to do next. And each of them had the same feeling and came to the same conclusion that Isselta had been right.

"Do you think we should go and see how she is doing?" asked Javin, sounding a little peevish. They were both seated at the table, the remains of a meal waiting to be cleared.

Meldren was firm on that. "No. Absolutely not. That is something she is doing, whatever it is. It's not up to us. Not right now, anyway. Maybe later...? But not now."

Javin huffed. "You're right, of course. It's just that I'm not used to this happening. Sitting around, knowing that something important is happening, something that we were part of. And now we're not."

"How do you know we're not part of it? Could be we're just waiting for the next thing to happen. And then off we go again." Meldren emphasized her words with a sweep of her arm.

He frowned. "That reminds me of something else. Do you recall way back when we first started having the dreams? We both got a sense of something dark or heavy or unpleasant in the distance. This isn't it. This isn't the thing we felt, is it? That darkness isn't now, is what I'm saying."

"What are you saying, then?"

"I'm saying that I think you're right about us waiting for the next stage. And maybe the heavy whatever-it-is is the next stage waiting for us? What if we try to get a feel for it again? For all I know, it's changed and is never going to happen. But it would be good to know, if that is the case."

Meldren nodded agreement and they let themselves sink into the songs around them again, searching ahead, following tunes and harmonies, sensing the way the music flowed around them and in them. Sensing, if they could, the folds of the future and whether what they concealed could be heard or felt in some fashion.

When they had finished and had their eyes open again, they looked at each other with surprise.

"That," said Meldren with some feeling, "feels a lot stronger than before. How about you?"

"Me, too. Definitely closer, and definitely something big. Big? Yes! Important because of that? Certainly. But scary? Not so much." He shook his head. "Could you make anything else out of it?"

Meldren thought for a moment, trying to recollect all the nuances of what she had felt. "It's big, like you said. Important for that reason. Like you said." She wrinkled her nose as she struggled to find the words. "It feels like some big change. Everything changes. Not just us. It's like something that affects more than just us here. Wider, perhaps? I don't know the words for it. But I get the feeling that the change which will affect much more than just us, is also centered right here. We're at the middle, the center of it all in some way." She dragged her fingers through her hair, annoyed at not being able to be more precise. "I don't much like that thought; that we're going to be responsible for something that big in some fashion."

"Maybe not responsible, but certainly part of it."

Meldren disagreed. "If we're doing something, we're going to be the ones responsible for it. And it might not be something we want to do."

Upon hearing the truth of her words, the way the sounds of them fitted the song of what they had both just listened to, Javin experienced the same sense of uneasiness he had felt when Isselta had spoken on the clifftop after she had helped Dennet.

To shake it off, he pushed his chair back and offered his hand to Meldren. "Let's go digging around and making things grow. And after that, we can stare at the sea and the sky again. What do you say?"

Meldren planted a gentle kiss on the tip of nose. "Sounds irresistible!" They had gone just a few paces when Meldren half-turned to Javin. "And I feel the same as your colors look, and I don't know why either." Her face had a smile on it which hovered between hope and tears and she gave his hand a fierce squeeze.

Knowing that the feeling was not his alone eased the tension he felt.

As they started again, there was a fast-moving ripple which seemed to flick through the clouds. It looked as though they were lifted up higher before falling back into place again. At the same time, the ground they were sitting on rose and fell very slightly, as if the earth was liquid and a wave was passing through it. Javin and Meldren looked confused for a moment before realization dawned.

5

NEWGRANGE

K ris was trying to keep his irritation hidden as he listened to
Markin explaining at great length why they all needed to prepare
for a raid by government forces.

"Surely, you can understand that because of what I've heard, what
I've seen, we have to store our crops safely to stop them being taken
away. If we lose them --,"

"--Yes, I know," Kris interrupted, annoyed with himself even as he did
so. "It will mean we will be in danger of starving this coming winter. I
know that, Markin, but why now? What has made you so nervous?"
Inwardly, he winced as that word came out. Not what he wanted to say,
and Markin was not going to let it slide by.

"Nervous?" Markin plowed on, ignoring the placatory gestures that
Kris was making. He snorted rejection of the term. "I'm not nervous, I'm
doing what I'm meant to be doing, what I'm good at, which is looking
after all of you. And I say we need to be storing more food away in the
mountains beyond the waterfall where nobody can find it and take it."
He wagged a finger accusingly. "If we don't do this, and start making a
habit of it, we're going to seriously regret it. They'll either kill us or take
our food to feed themselves, probably both. I should have been saying

this a long time ago, but I never seemed to find the right time. Either that, or... ."

Kris winced inwardly at that, knowing that Markin was hinting that he would not have supported him. It was a splinter in their relationship and he felt the guilt of its presence. He waited to be sure Markin was finished before speaking. Kris felt older than his years. The strain of keeping this Revivalist community together never seemed to let up. Kris tried to sound conciliatory without being patronizing. "I know you are advising what you think is best, Markin. And I appreciate it. Really, I do. But you must know that any decision affecting the community as a whole must be agreed to by the majority. It's not something I can decide by myself. You will have to explain it to us all at the next council meeting."

The way Markin shook his head made it clear what he thought of that. "Oh, yes, they'll all be polite and listen and not hear a word I say." He thumped his good hand against his thigh. "They don't know what I know. They haven't seen what I've seen or spoken with the same people I have. It's my fault. I've let it go on too long. They're getting too soft."

Kris thought that the lives they were living now were anything but soft compared to what they had turned their backs on, but let it slide. "Sadly, everything you say might be true, my old friend. But it was you that helped organize the council and what it could and should do and what it couldn't and shouldn't do." Kris looked at the man before him, trying to see the younger face, the idealistic one, rather than this angry, old one. "I'm not going to dictate to anyone what they should do."

"Except to me, it seems," Markin grunted.

"I'm not going down that route with you. At the next council meeting, I'll let you have your say. I promise."

With the barest shake of his head, Markin turned and left the hut, walking in that distinctive rolling style of his, probably, thought Kris, to sulk somewhere. But then he dismissed that thought as being unworthy. He turned to make himself a warm drink. It was not weather to be standing around in. The cool, damp, autumnal weather dragged him down just as it dragged the smoke from the cooking fires close to the ground. However, his hopes of having time for a warming drink and of having some time to himself were shattered by Sten.

"Ah, Kris! A word, if I might?"

Stifling the automatic sigh, Kris summoned a smile for the tall man, blond hair in a ponytail flowing behind him, striding rapidly as he skirted the communal compost pile."Of course, Sten. Of course. What is it?"

"I really do think I am making progress with the trees." Sten brought himself to a halt at the doorway of Kris's wood-walled single room home. He paused, waiting for Kris to react, but all he saw was a certain vagueness on the older man's face. "You do recall I am trying to listen to the trees? They are the guardians of this place, after all. The elders, if you will?"

Kris did remember something of the sort and nodded, putting in place his warmly vague smile that hid his true thoughts. He hoped this would be short, but feared the enthusiasm of the younger man would make that unlikely. "Progress, you say?"

Sten's wide, easy smile flashed across his face. Kris wished Sten would look ordinary, tired and dirty like everyone else. "Indeed! I think I've found which of the trees are the true leaders here. They are the ones I have to make contact with." He pointed vaguely off to one side. "In a glade, not too far from here, there is a massive tree, a type of oak I think, which has the most amazing feel to it. I have established a real connection with it and I can feel it reach out to me in greeting whenever I get close." Sten had taken Kris's arm as he was talking and had led him to the table where they could both sit. Now he rested his forearms on the table and was leaning toward Kris in his enthusiasm. "At the moment, I'm in the process of swapping images with it, sharing concepts, if you will. Establishing a sort of common ground, a basic language. It takes a lot of time and patience and the right mental approach, but I'm utterly convinced that within a reasonable space of time from now I should be able to really understand it, understand what it wants from us here and how we can work together, synergistically, to create a true partnership. One which will be of benefit to both of us; the trees and Newgrange." His eyes were shining in his excitement.

Kris wished Sten would speak with a little less of his ex-university lecturer past. Enthusiasm was wonderful, but right now Kris wanted some peace and quiet to think about Markin and whether he was right or not. He pushed those thoughts away and tried to respond appropriately. "That sounds wonderful, Sten. That would be a great accomplishment, certainly."

"I think so too. And when we are able to dialog, so to speak -- pardon the pun -- I truly believe that Newgrange will be able to expand well beyond its present borders and become the premier example of how a Revival commune could and should be."

Kris smiled encouragingly and patted Sten on his arm as a part of his mind told him he was being overly patronizing. "I think you should keep on doing this, as long as your work in the commune doesn't suffer because of it."

"Of course, of course. I would never let that happen. Never. You can be assured of that." He made slashing motions with his hands in emphasis. Then he beamed another huge, perfect smile at Kris. "Anyway, I just wanted to keep you in the loop, up to date with what is happening. I'll be sure to let you know of further progress. Shan't keep you any longer." And away he went, much to Kris's surprise. Normally, he would have insisted on having a long, detailed political argument about the Revival movement in general and Newgrange's place in it in particular. Maybe, thought Kris, as he watched Sten stride away, he is actually making the progress he said. If nothing else, he was making progress in not staying too long.

He sighed at his weakness; that of thinking peevish thoughts of people who seemed to be intent on doing their best, and made himself a cup of coffee. The kettle was still hot on the stove. He damped down the fire a little to conserve fuel and then opened the tin and reveled in the smell. He allowed himself a bare half teaspoon, trying not to estimate how much was left, how many more cups he could look forward to. A luxury, to be sure, but he felt he had earned it. Sitting at the table, sipping the mug, letting the warmth spread through him, he looked out across the community. Here was a place he had helped to create, where people could live freely, become closer to the land. Farming and tending the land in ways which showed respect; collaboration, not destruction; sensitivity, not arrogance. Above all, it was about self-reliance; not looking to some distant government for approval and control. Those were the ideals which had started Newgrange. He took another sip of the coffee, determined to savor it. And that brought his attention back to the here and now. He wasn't sure how he felt about Sten and what he was attempting beyond the fact that there was an intensity there which he could admire. But the value of what Sten was doing? He wasn't sure about that at all.

Newgrange had changed. It had grown over the years to where he could no longer take it all in from the doorway. He mused at the passage of time and all the changes it had brought and the memories it had created. He was so deep in looking at the past that he barely saw the trees in the mist or the felt the cold air snagging at him, trying to leach his warmth away.

He had started this community. That was still so clear in his mind. Markin had been with him. But, more importantly, Ellenara had been with him, urging him on to chase his dream of self-sufficiency, far away from the cities and the towns. She had been as fierce in her beliefs about the government and corruption and militarization as he was. But she had died too soon. Killed by some faceless uniform in a skirmish in one of the local towns where they had gone to take what they had needed for Newgrange. The name, Newgrange, had been her idea. And he still missed her; the warmth, the intellect, the sheer drive to live as she wanted and the exuberance she had in everything she did. How could he not miss her? How could the pain not subside?

Back then, with her, that was the time when he could have out-shouted, out-argued Markin easily. He would have done so automatically and Markin would have shouted back and they would have both sulked for a day before forgetting about it. It had been the three of them, their shared passion, that had formed Newgrange. They had been determined to live as simply as they could. Some communities used more machinery, others less, but the basic ideals were the same. Newgrange was, from the very start, a place where the simplest means of living were embraced, and only the very extremes of deprivation were reason to deviate from that, and only for as long as absolutely necessary.

Newgrange had been nothing more than unused, unclaimed land many days away from any population center until the three of them had stumbled into it all those years ago. They had nearly given up hope of finding anywhere that felt right, looked right, had what they were looking for. Several days of toiling up through wild, untended forest, forcing a path where none had existed. Days of doubt even after examining the maps. They had determined that, if they went one more day without finding anything suitable, they would turn back. And then they had entered a clearing, this clearing he was sitting in now. And in the middle of it, the boulder big enough for all three to sit on and rest, as if it had been put there for them. This was the place for them. Clear, fresh mountain water within easy reach, soil of a good depth and vital enough for crops. Trees all around them to be cleared for lumber and fuel and tools. And, most importantly, it was remote.

It had grown here amongst the trees as cities dwindled, towns contracted and villages emptied. He sometimes found it hard to realize just how much change must be taking place across the whole planet and across time as well. Would Haven become some agricultural utopia, or would the technocrats reclaim the land and recreate the intrusive, industrialized, impersonal society he had left behind? He doubted it would ever be that clear cut again. Their vision of living away from cities and all that entailed had drawn others to them. The adherence to its central principle of simplicity had meant that it had grown more slowly than other Revivalist groups. Some stayed for a year before leaving to find an easier life. But those who remained became tougher and more determined to live this way. Disaffected, hurt, lonely; the variety of reasons didn't count, only that they were willing to work. Newgrange had slowly become self-sustaining, growing and making what was needed. The people learned the necessary skills as they went along. Sure, they had had hard times. But the point was, they had made it this far. They were able to feed themselves and have just enough put by for hard times.

And here was Markin, one of the originals, one who had shared their dreams, fought beside them, watched beside him as Ellenara died, had walked back with him, holding him upright as he had left her body there; here he was, warning him of doom and disaster. Markin was once in the civil police. His disaffection with how the force had become more militarized, more intrusive, had grown to be more vocal and persistent until he walked away from it. He had met Kris and Ellenara at a Revivalist rally about how to not just oppose the government but to turn away from it. The three of them had become allies and then friends. He had chosen to be their security in the early years, going out into the world to listen to what was happening, seeing the world fall apart, reporting back, fighting the troops, identifying the wanderers who wanted only to steal, not stay. He had developed a network of contacts, just as he had when he had been in the police. The fears of those early days had been real. Markin had had one hand crippled in the fight in which Ellenara had died. It was a constant reminder to Kris of his loss. His injured hand had meant that he had developed few, if any, skills to help in the community. Instead the security of Newgrange was a responsibility Markin he had taken on and would not turn away from. He had kept them safe, that was true. They had needed him at first. But now?

Kris took another sip of the coffee, letting the sharp tang of it take away the worries and the memories. He gazed out and saw the present and the past mingle together. No matter what else happened in his life, he would always be proud of this place and these people living his vision. His and Ellenara's. And, as ever, the thought of her took him away again in silence. It took him a moment to realize that there was someone tugging on his leg.

He looked down to find Pol looking up at him with the earnest expression which always melted his heart.

"Pol? What is it you want, my little one?"

In answer, the girl raised both her arms in the universal signal which demanded that she be lifted up. Putting his coffee on the table, with just the smallest of regrets that it was now cold, Kris obliged and placed her on his lap.

"What have you to tell me today, Pol? What have you been up to?"

The girl delighted him. Maybe she was how he had imagined his own daughter might have been. Or maybe he was just the right person to find fascination in one so young. Whatever the reason, he never minded her appearing before him, as he was always reassuring Jenni and Berd, her parents.

"I have been listening to the mushrooms," she said with the complete seriousness of a six-year old girl who followed her imagination.

"And?" prompted Kris, knowing that he had his part to play in this exchange.

She frowned. "They make tiny, tiny sounds that I can't hear properly." She paused, a slight pout showing. "And I want to hear them!"

"Of course you do," he agreed, reflecting her seriousness on the subject. "How big are these mushrooms you've been trying to hear?" In answer, Pol made a space between the two index fingers of her pudgy hands.

"That is very small indeed. It's no wonder they make tiny sounds." Pol nodded at the wisdom of his words. "What would you like me to do about them?"

"I wish you could make them bigger so I could hear them better. They make such pretty sounds."

It was Kris's turn to nod in agreement. "I'm sure they do. I would love to hear them myself, but I think my ears are the wrong shape to do that. Yours, though, are the perfect shape for hearing them."

Pol looked up at him with an expression he couldn't quite name. "Silly. It's not the shape of your ears. Ears don't hear them. *I* hear them."

It was an explanation which, Kris felt left much to be desired. So he changed tack a little. "Why do you think I can make the mushrooms bigger, Pol?"

She gave a huge sigh at the inanity of the question as if the answer was so obvious as to not be worth saying. "Because you are in charge of everything here."

Kris allowed her to see him smile, making sure this one was genuine. "Thank you, Pol. Sometimes, it feels like I'm in charge, and sometimes it doesn't. I don't think I'm in charge of mushrooms, though. They're going to grow the way they want to, Pol." She leaned against him, though whether in resignation or for warmth he could not tell, and he hugged her. "But thanks for thinking of me like that," he whispered.

She was silent for a while, snuggled up against him. Then she added, in a quiet voice, "Everything grows the way they're told, not always how they want."

In the fields beyond the homes on the other side of the village to where Kris lived, two figures, one large, one small, were completing their morning's work. "That's excellent, Endel. You've done beautifully. Well done." Semmik was lavish in his praise of the boy in an effort to get a smile from him. Indeed, the praise was justified. The boy had cleared the rest of the field, leaving tidy mounds of weeds at regular intervals along the side. "I think we should go inside now and get warm, clean up and have some food. Yes?"

Endel, as always, gave him a steady gaze and a slow nod, beginning to scrape his hands free of mud, finding tussocks of grass to wipe them on. As he did so, Semmik could not but help think that he and Marianna were making no headway at all. Endel looked as though he was maybe twelve years old, but acted as if he was much, much older. He had arrived one day out of nowhere. He had walked into Newgrange in the middle of a day looking awful. He had obviously not eaten for a long time and his legs and feet had shown the bloody marks of an arduous journey. There were scratches on his arms and hands, his clothes were ragged, his face dirty and his eyes had seen too much.

"Come along, then. Let's see what Marianna has made for us today, eh?" Semmik was all warmth and cajoling as he kept pace with the boy. "Perhaps she has finished making that jacket for you? Winter's nearly here and it will be good to keep warm, won't it?"

Together, the slim, silent boy and the talkative, broad-shouldered man came to the entrance of their home. It was made of logs, as were all the homes here, cut and laid with rammed earth closing the gaps. Simple but effective. A small ditch around the outside was to channel water away. Although it was but an easy hop across, Semmik had found two large stones, almost flat, and had laid them as a bridge.

At first, there had been just the one large room. But, over time and with help, a bedroom had been added and later a spare room for equipment and storage which was now a place for Endel. This arrangement left the original room for cooking, eating and, more importantly, Marianna's loom. The loom had been found in a museum, of all places. Marianna had casually admitted that once she had seen someone weaving on a show she had watched in the days before Newgrange. She had then been 'volunteered' to learn the craft. The loom had been brought back piece by piece and reassembled. Now, she was responsible for making as much material as possible for the entire community: a non-stop activity.

They had been there for over fifteen years, being amongst the earliest to arrive. They had been scared by the army raids on anyone who had spoken against the government, which had apparently included those who visited their small restaurant. They had watched in horror as their friends and customers had been taken away or beaten and killed for resisting. Fearing their own arrest, the two of them had run away one night, taking only a scant few possessions. They had heard rumors of the Revivalist movement and what it stood for, but didn't know much more. It had been luck that had led them here, stumbling along, cold, frightened and running out of food. They had been heading for the mountains behind Newgrange, not knowing that the community existed until they smelt woodsmoke. They had been met with wary, silent stares by people who held axes and lengths of old pipe and rough-hewn wooden clubs. And then Kris saw them and saw their pain, spoke to them and offered them a place.

"Well," said Marianna brightly. "How did it go this morning? Everything finished? I'm close to having your jacket ready, Endel."

Endel did not react.

Marianna bent down to be closer to Endel. "Would stew be good?" She smile briefly when she too received the slow, deliberate nod. She turned to the stove against the far corner where a pot was bubbling gently. She picked up three slightly misshapen pottery bowls and ladled some into each. She placed them on the table where a loaf of coarse bread and a knife, worn into a thin sliver of metal through use, were ready.

Endel blew cautiously on his stew before slowly beginning to spoon it up. When Marianna handed him a hunk of bread, he stopped long enough to look at her before returning to his food.

"What do you think of this bread, Semmik? Sarrah's trying something different, I think."

Semmik chewed thoughtfully and nodded. "It's tastier than before. It would be wonderful to have proper fine ground flour though. But, considering everything, this is good."

Sarrah Hander, several homes down, had taken on the job of

providing bread for those in the community who, for whatever reasons, didn't make their own but wanted some anyway. Marianna, for example, was too busy at her loom and there were several other homes similarly busy who welcomed Sarrah's baking for them. There was not always sufficient grains for flour, sometimes nuts were added. The flour was hand ground by Sarrah's sons, Bodren and Fillip; a laborious task which used hand-fashioned querns and took a good portion of every day to produce enough flour. She had the biggest oven and the most claim for fuel, which her husband, Flinder provided as he worked in the forest. Hard though it was, she had been baking bread for a very long time it seemed, with very few failures.

Other than that, the meal was eaten in silence. It was completed with some mugs of hot, weak tea made from herbs harvested and dried earlier.

"Thank you, my love. It was, as ever, delightful."

Marianna smiled her thanks. "Give me some old roots, some fresh herbs and some smoked meat and I can make anything. Anything, that is, as long as it is stew."

"You are a good cook. You know it. But, more importantly, I know it." Semmik sipped his tea. "I know you would have been a great cook, a chef, if only..."

Marianna placed a finger on his lips. "Shh. We promised not to speak of the what-ifs in life. This is where we are now. This is who we are. So," she added with a forced brightness, "what is it you have to do this afternoon?"

"Check all the animals. Make sure they are all healthy, have enough feed and so on. You know, the normal things. Endel likes the animals, don't you, Endel?"

The boy had been sitting still since finishing. He nodded in his serious fashion. He had done nothing else since his appearance almost a year ago. He had said one word, 'Endel', when asked who he was, and had said nothing more. Nobody was really sure if that was even his name. When asked where he had come from, he had pointed at the woods. A group of people had gone to search for any others who might have been with him, as well as being alert for any government forces who might have tracked him. They had found nothing and nobody. It was inevitable that he became part of the community. Semmik and Marianna, having a slightly larger place than most, had been the ones to take him in and feed and clothe him. He was never a problem, and that, in itself, was the problem.

As Semmik had said, it did seem as if Endel liked being with the animals. Semmik certainly enjoyed their company. They demanded little, were gentle, by and large, and he felt he could trust them. They, in turn, seemed to trust him so that he was always the one called on to help out when an animal was stubborn or was in the wrong place, endangering crops for example, or was caught in a thicket. They listened to him, is how he described it to Marianna.

Endel, on the other hand, appeared to be the one listening when he was with the animals. Sometimes, when Semmik looked up from the task in hand, he would see the boy standing to one side with an expression which was the closest to appearing happy as he ever showed. Eyes half-shut, he rocked gently back and forth and seemed to be humming a complicated tune whenever Semmik got near enough to hear it. But, as soon as he was near enough, Endel stopped the humming and turned that blank look to him again. Once, Semmik had asked Endel what he was humming. In answer, the boy had walked toward the cow before him and stroked it from head to tail, gently, in one, long sweeping motion and had then walked away, leaving Semmik confused as to whether that had been an answer or not.

SEVERAL DAYS LATER, THE MONTHLY MEETING TOOK PLACE AS USUAL IN THE storage barn; the largest available space. There were no seats, so people brought their own or took up whatever comfortable positions they could. It was crowded; so unlike the early days. Here there were perhaps eighty people all told, and the area under cultivation had grown to the point where the surrounding forest had been thinned dramatically and two new fields had been plowed and planted in recent years. Overall, the land sloped gently down from the range of mountains which began to rise in earnest some few kilometers to the west. The barn was at the top end of Newgrange, furthest away from where the only path entered. If followed, that path would lead, via several twists and turns and more kilometers than were easy to travel in a day, to a narrow metaled road, made narrower by the encroaching vegetation. It had never had much traffic, being little more than a way between two villages, both long since abandoned. Nevertheless, the place where the path to Newgrange started had been carefully concealed from any casual traveler with well-placed shrubs. It was deliberately not easy to find.

The meeting began with the usual reports concerning the state of the crops, the harvest, the animals as well as the tools and equipment they all used. Metal tools scavenged from the nearest towns and villages were wearing out and there were no more to be had there. The scarcity was forcing them to learn to fashion what they needed out of wood, clay, stone or whatever would serve.

Finally, Kris called on Markin to report. The bulky man heaved himself up with a sour glance at Kris. He scanned the familiar faces, scratching at his stubble with the remaining fingers of his left hand.

"Security. That's what I am responsible for. The security of this place and everyone in it. In the early days, I used what skills I had to organize us to fight those who needed fighting or to hide from those who wanted to find us. That's not been the case for a good few years now." He paused.

"I'm fairly certain that some of you think I go off and sit in the woods out of sight for a while and eat the food you produce, because, you know, I'm an old cripple." He held up his left hand to them. There were enough uncertain coughs and quickly stifled voices to show the truth of his words. "What you believe is what you believe. But, you should know something before I go on so you can, perhaps, understand why I say it. You know that before this place, I was in the police, yes? One of the things police do is have informers, people who know what is going on. And some informers are better than others. More reliable. I still have informers who travel around, seeing things, noting things. It's what I've been doing since the last meeting. Looking around, asking, watching, listening. Not like the hard work you all do here every day, is it?" He was challenging them to face what they thought of him in the hope that it would make them feel less antagonistic to what he he had decided to say. "Anyway, I hear things about the government and the Revival movement that you don't. Some of you don't want to know what I've heard and seen."

"Come on, Markin. Get to the point!"

Kris peered to see who it was, but it wasn't obvious. "That is not how this happens, and you know it. Markin's speaking and all you listen. *That's* how it happens. So, quiet!"

Markin turned and gave a grudging nod, surprised at the unexpected support. "As I was saying, I hear things. For example, the government does not have enough people to farm the land it controls. At least, not farm it well. It is also building a larger security force." He spread his hands to show the inevitability of what would happen. "The force will be used against us and people like us. It's inevitable. They're trying to maintain the old levels of society but with fewer people. They've got less coming in taxes, but they're paying the same to people, utilities, services and so on. They're losing production in heavy industry and crops, but people still need to be fed and stuff needs replacing." His gaze swept the audience again, noting the restlessness. "This isn't a lesson in politics. This is a warning. They are going to come after us. It's already begun elsewhere. And it's going to happen to us sooner rather than later. And that means that we need, now, to move as much of the harvest as we can out of here and into somewhere they don't know and can't find. And we have to be ready for that so that we can survive." The people stirred and muttered and Markin held his hands up again, as if against the tide of noise, to hold it back from growing louder.

"I know this is not what you want to hear. But it is the truth of it."

"And when will this happen? This year? Next year? Or will it happen to some other communities and not us?" Voices called out and Kris was not quick enough to stop them.

"You want dates and days and times that I can't give you. But I can tell you it *will* happen. And we need to be ready for it. Because I can guarantee that when it does happen, when people with weapons march up that path out there and start pointing them at us, they won't be asking us politely for food. They will take whatever they find and then they will kill us for having it. And then they will destroy our homes and everything we have built up, and we don't have anything to stop them. That's the truth of it. We think of them as the problem, and they think of us in the same way we think of vermin: taking what is rightfully theirs. You should know this: they will find us and they will kill us."

Kris moved forward to stop everyone calling out at once. "One at a time! Hands up for a question. Hands up or don't speak. You know the rules here." He pointed and called out, "Flinder. Your question, please. Everyone else, quiet down."

Flinder Hander was not a newcomer, nor one of the first to settle. He cared for the crops along with the others, but was also mainly responsible for gathering firewood and pollarding trees, occasionally making living fences in the old way by cutting and bending and laying branches so that they grew into an impenetrable barrier. A forester' s work was slow and hard, but he seemed to have some sort of affinity for working with trees and shrubs. Like most others, he had learned by trial and error and from scavenged books, the odd encyclopedia and dictionary and, in rare cases, faded computer printouts. He was known and respected as a hard worker. "You know I like living here," he began. "If it weren't for the work involved, Sarrah and I would think it was perfect." That got a ripple of laughter. "But what you're telling us, Markin, is that, no matter what we do, they're going to kill us and destroy everything. If there's nothing we can do about it, why bother telling us? And what's the point of storing food miles away if there's nobody left to eat it?"

Markin nodded, a grim look on his face. "You're right. There is no point at all. Everything we have achieved here will be gone in an afternoon." He let the words settle on them. "But, we have the time between now and then to organize ourselves to give ourselves a chance against them. We can start by storing part of the harvest, because if we don't and we fight and we win, however unlikely that might seem now, then we'll still starve. And if they don't kill all of us, then whoever is left will still need to eat. And after that, we organize ourselves here to make it as difficult as possible for anyone who wants to take from us."

"How?" It wasn't clear if that was from Flinder or not.

"How? By learning how to fight, how to kill, how to make and use weapons. By making this place harder to get into, so they can't just walk up here like it was some picnic outing. By setting up a warning system so we can either have time to hide or prepare to fight. By doing something that proves we're not ready to roll over and die just because someone in some government building far away doesn't like the idea that we are living and thriving without any respect for them."

"Weapons? We're not soldiers. We're farmers! And where would we hide?" That was Semmik's voice. Even if nobody had been asked to speak, at least the questions were pertinent and everyone was listening carefully, if not sympathetically.

"No. You're not soldiers. Farming is only one thing you do. That doesn't make you only farmers. You can do other things as well. And as for weapons: bows and arrows, slingshots, axes, cudgels, anything that can hurt someone else is a weapon."

"Against guns and chemicals?"

Markin shook his head. "Not chemicals. They won't destroy that way, because it will too easily destroy the food they want."

"What about hiding? How would that work? All of us hide? How? Where?"

"In underground passages we dig, here and in the forests nearby. Maybe up towards the mountains, if we could get enough warning. Hides, going up in the trees." Markin tossed his head angrily. "I don't have all the answers, but I do know that I would rather be able to do something than just wait around to be shot."

"You seem really sure about that."

Markin nodded. "I am. There's stories out there about places which have already been destroyed, wiped out and everyone killed. I trust the people who passed on the stories. One I spoke with heard it from a survivor himself. The reports I've heard before are from a good long distance away. But the latest ones show that the attacks are spreading into other areas. Even if you never heard that, think about it for a minute, will you? We are able to feed ourselves. They are finding it harder and harder. We are surviving, thriving, even, in their eyes. More than that, we are enemies to their way of thinking. And we're succeeding. That must make them mad. Every Revival community will be thought of as harboring the enemy and of having some food stored. If they find us they will come after us because it's easier, they think, to move in, kill us and take the food and go back and eat it. They want to wipe us out. The entire Revivalist movement. It's just a matter of them finding us. And they will. They'll be taking to the skies to scan the land for us. When they find us will depend on which direction they take first, that's all. It's plain common sense."

"And we do all that, this storing and fighting while we have all our other work to do?"

"Yes. It will mean extra work for everyone until we have some means of defending what we have built here."

Although the questions continued for a space, Markin's body language said that he knew they were not going to listen to him. They found too many reasons to ignore the issue. It was too much work, too uncertain, and why bother if they could be killed so easily? Markin answered as carefully and precisely as he could, but he felt they were drifting away from him.

The meeting finished and Markin remained, seated on a milking stool in the corner, looking exhausted. Kris came over to him and Markin gave him a tight smile. "I know you did your best, Kris. But they're not in the mood to listen. I can't say I blame them. Few of them remember those early raids anymore. They believe it won't happen again. They've no reason to trust me or even understand what it could be like when they come. And, Kris, they will come. I know that." He tapped a hand on his chest. "I know it, Kris, like I've known in the past. But I can't convince them, and I doubt I can convince you even." He suddenly felt very old and very lonely and turned his head. The last thing he wanted now was sympathy.

Kris, perhaps realizing that, said, "I will see what I can do to get help. There's value in what you say about making it difficult for people to come here. What was it you had in mind for that anyway?"

Markin rolled his shoulders. "It would be too much work for them to do. We could build a wall around us. We need to take the trees back further so we won't be surprised when they suddenly appear from them. And we could use those trees to make the wall. Or we could dig out a series of tunnels. That would be hard mining work though." He waved his arm to encompass the community. "I can't blame them. I'd hate to have to think about what it would entail, how much it would add to my day if I was them. And then there's moving the harvest and all that would entail. That's not easy either. An early warning system would need to be figured out somehow. Something set up way back down the path. I can't think right now of what that could be. Maybe a few people down there permanently, or rotating them down there? But how would they tell us?" He looked up at Kris and shook his head. "Truth is we've left it too long."

Kris was silent a moment. "Perhaps there's a way we can do something. Not everything you said. That's the best case. The worst case is they turn up tomorrow and kill us all. What we need is something in between. Seriously, Markin, how long do you think we might have?"

"You don't know what's going on out there, what it's like. The government's frightened. And a frightened government is dangerous. That's the reason for the sweeps the security force is doing right now. The people, us, we're not feeding the cities anymore. They can't feed themselves, so they'll take what they can. You know that. This is an old story. And, because we're organized and we're large enough to be found easily, we're going to be easy targets for them, unless we do something to protect ourselves. We're nowhere near as large as some communities, though." Seeing Kris's raised eyebrows, he nodded. "There are some places I've heard of which are maybe ten times the size of us. We're small compared to many. But that only means they'll take their time getting here. It doesn't mean they're going to stop after that. If they can break up the big Revivalist places, they sure as anything will break up the rest. They're not going to want to leave any of us surviving. I'm certain of that."

"But why now? Why not before?"

"My guess? They thought we'd all fail. Then, when we didn't, they didn't think we'd make a big enough difference to anything. But now? With their food and resources threatened, people no longer working the factories, industries closing due to lack of workforce, they'll decide it's worth their while taking us on. They'll be slow and careful about it because we're not going anywhere. We're easy meat.

"I've heard they've already started against the communities that are easiest to get to. They have taken everything they can from them. They get a bigger return for less effort there. They'll be spreading out, though. It depends on the direction they take. If they choose south-east first, then my best guess would be that we could expect them by late-summer next year, maybe later, but not much. By the end of next year for certain if that's where they start." He looked empty. "It's not enough time for what needs to be done." He looked up again at Kris. "I'm sorry. Sorry that I didn't speak earlier and it's too late now. I'm sorry Kris. They're going to come and they're going to kill us." His face threatened to crumple as he waved away the hand Kris reached to him with.

"I trust you in what you say. And you have nothing to feel sorry for. If anything, I should have listened to you more, encouraged you more. I should have trusted you earlier, let you spend longer on the outside, getting more information. Tell me how you know what you know."

Markin gazed off into the distance. He began slowly. "You recall I had been a policeman long enough before Newgrange to have trusted my intuition? I knew which witnesses were lying as they spoke. I *knew* which information I received was useful and which was useless. And I *knew* when something was going to happen. It never let me down. Ever. And now? I'm standing in front of people who will die if they do nothing and I can't tell them how certain I am that I know what I know. Kris, I'm certain there will be bloodshed. I just don't know when." He gestured to his back. "I can feel the tightness there between my shoulders. There's the same catch in my guts and there's like a black cloud somewhere up ahead. That's what happens. I trust all of those signs. There's something bad coming." He grimaced. "But I couldn't tell them that, could I?"

"No, you couldn't. You were right. So, let's do what we can in the time we've got, shall we? At least, we'll go down fighting." He gave a tight grin. "For me, I wouldn't mind having one last fight with them. I'd dearly love to pay them back for Ellenara. I'm sure I can convince enough people that something needs to be done. And you, my friend, you are going to guide us in getting it done."

DESPITE THE PROMISES HE HAD MADE, KRIS COULD GET LITTLE DONE TO fortify Newgrange and neither could he persuade enough people that hoarding what little extra they had away from the community was of any use. Earlier that day, he'd invited Markin to spend some time with him, as the weather was cold and outside work of any kind was a low priority for everyone. Markin wasn't sure what Kris wanted.

"It's not that they're fatalistic, Markin. I think it's more to do with the fact that it doesn't feel personal." The two of them were sitting at the table in Kris's home, the door shut against the winter wind and the slanting, freezing rain it was carrying today. The fire was just warm enough to make wearing extra clothes inside debatable. Kris was sharing some of his precious coffee and they were savoring it, cradling the mugs, taking their time with it. "It's more that they don't believe it could happen. Not here, anyway. Most of them think we're too far away from anywhere to be of interest or be perceived as a threat." He sighed. "I'm sorry. I promised and I can't deliver. You must think poorly of me. Maybe we're all just too comfortable here, or it's been too quiet for too long."

Markin had already realized that nothing substantial was going to happen to protect the village, so it wasn't a surprise. But he did appreciate Kris wanting to tell him to his face. The distance which had existed between them earlier had evaporated with time. "I don't blame you, Kris. I don't blame them, even. I can understand how they think. Why should they act as if it's the end of the world? No, the person I blame is me. I should have said what I thought earlier. People like me, who do what I do; going out to sniff the air elsewhere, they're more cautious, less easy to contact." He made an irritable gesture.

"That was only a part of it. I was also meant to be scavenging for anything we could use and bring it back. I'm sorry, Kris. It just took too much time. Sure, we're isolated here, but we're isolated from other Revivalists. News is hard to come by." He gave a wry grin. "That's why I relied more on my intuition, that gut feeling I told you about, more than on hard facts, because I was running out of them."

Kris took a sip and looked at his friend. "You can blame yourself if you want, but it won't change anything. If you're right, then before the next year is over, it's likely that armed soldiers are going to be marching in here. We fought before, but it's not going to be the same this next time. It's not going to be a pitched battle in streets with both sides using the same weapons.

"If we can't fight them and nobody's interested in storing surplus, then the only hope we might have is if we get enough warning of their arrival to take to the woods and try to hide. Even with ground transport it would take a day to get here, surely? Why couldn't we persuade the people that it would be everyone for themselves? It might suit their mood better if they felt they were responsible only for themselves. Each family to find a spot to hide in then wait it out and see what and who's left when it's all over. Can you think of some sort of warning system for us?"

Markin had often thought about this approach. But persuading anyone to find a bolthole, to prepare a place, even if it was just for themselves, was not going to be easy. Kris was right. They had become comfortable simply dealing with the daily problems of living here. "Early warning will only work if they come by the path and don't come by air and drop in on us." Markin swirled the mug gently, watching the dark liquid. "But, the more I think of it, the more I think they will come by land. That means using the road and the path. They will probably reconnoitre by air, but they will come here with vehicles or by foot. And that's because they will want to wipe us out. Bombing is too uncertain. You can never tell for sure if you got what you were after. Plus, it'd ruin the food they're after and kill the animals they need. But, on foot, they'll come and kill us and make sure this place is finished.

"And coming by land, I can only think of using warning fires, but that would mean they would know we knew straight away and remove any slight time advantage we might have. We can't rely on flashing mirrors if the sun's behind clouds or it's at night. Radio sets would be obvious, but I doubt anything like that can be found or still be in working order; not the way some people reacted against tech. I've not found any, put it that way. There could be something I've not thought of but, at the moment, it doesn't look possible. Not yet, anyway. Plus, of course, anyone we put down there is in immediate danger and also needs feeding and housing. The more you think about it, the worse it gets." He drank the last of the coffee in one long gulp, instantly regretting the impulse. "Maybe it's better to be fatalistic and not mind what happens to us. Maybe they've all got it right and we're the odd ones out."

"We're not alone, Markin, it's just that there's not enough of us to do anything worthwhile. I promise I'll keep thinking of ways of setting up some sort of warning system, if that's the only thing we can do. Will you keep thinking about it as well?"

Markin nodded. "Of course." He shivered slightly. He tried changing the mood a little and wore a lop-sided grin on his face. "But I'm not going back out there just yet, so if you have anything else to drink, I'm your man. I did hear, for example, that someone had been experimenting with a still or some sort of fermentation. And I thought, as you're the head man around these parts, you might have been asked to sample some?"

Kris could not help but laugh at the optimistic look on Markin's face. "Yes. You heard right. Oska made an attempt at alcohol. I think he had the principle of it, but the execution was... ," He gave a dramatic shudder. "I don't know what he put in it, but what came out was disgusting. Disgusting and probably lethal. Even he decided that it wasn't worth his time. So, my friend, in answer to your hopeful inquiry, there's nothing else, except I may be persuaded to find another mug of coffee. A very small mug, though."

"It was worth a try. I accept your offer. But you would think someone here would be able to brew something that didn't kill you when you drank it, wouldn't you? Sometimes I despair of mankind, I really do."

The weather remained cold, but the rain had stopped, leaving a clinging dampness in the air when Markin finally left Kris and set off for his own home which he shared with Bespic. Because Markin spent so much time away for various reasons, it had not made sense to have a home just for him, so he and Bespic shared a place, and he was heading back now to eat with him. The two of them rubbed along well. He and Markin had become friends, not through any positive movement in that direction by either of them, but because they seemed to find themselves in each other's company more often than not. In the end, they had agreed to share living quarters. Perhaps they now were friends, for they knew each other well, easily shared domestic routines and nothing was really new between them. It was, as Markin said, a comfortable arrangement. Bespic's version of it was that it made sense and that was all there was to it.

The usual faint light of the stars were al that shone in the otherwise black sky. The normal darkness of the nights made any outside activity after sundown difficult. Markin took some time to stare up at the heavens, something he used to do a great deal more when he first came to Newgrange. Away from the harsh lights of civilization, he had learned the spread of the points of lights above him with a lengthy fascination that left him sometimes cold and shivering with a stiff neck, but happier for all that. Over time, he had slowly filled his evenings with duty, becoming too tired to do more than cast a swift glance upwards, as if reminding himself that the universe still existed. He stopped now, however, and looked once again upwards, hoping to find momentary relief in the glinting stars, or perhaps some remnants of that old happiness. Although it had been some time since he had studied the night skies, he was fairly sure that there was now a new light, brighter, steadier, and somewhat larger than the surrounding stars. At first, it felt new to him. Then, if not new, then somehow familiar. Could anything be both at once, he wondered? He couldn't be sure, but he seemed to recall that, before the planet Harmony and its accompanying moon had disappeared, it had been of a size and a brightness which would have been a close match for what he was seeing now. He remembered it well: Harmony and the moon vanishing from the skies. Inexplicable and impossible and amazing, but it had happened. He, along with so many others, had scanned the heavens for the missing planet, without success. It had been so many years ago now that maybe his memory of its location and brightness was wrong. He stood silently for a long while, staring, gauging, remembering, but could come to no satisfactory conclusion. Maybe the light was reflecting from an asteroid hurtling toward them, destined to destroy the planet. Somberly, he realized that such an imminent destruction did not match his feelings of the future, and he trusted that feeling still far more than any speculation of a possible asteroid strike. An asteroid was too big to worry about, but this feeling; that was his.

Aware that he was getting cold and stiff, Markin shook himself and set off again, telling himself that he would spend more time another night to look at that spot of light again. He didn't fully believe his eyes. He took care to walk slowly, feeling for bumps and hollows, even though his eyes had adjusted to the dark. The short distance down the gentle slope towards his home still contained dips and bumps sufficient to tip him over if he was to suddenly break into a trot. He took his time.

The difficulty and slowness of such travel brought home to him just how impossible it would be to galvanize the village to take to the woods at night. He could easily imagine the disaster it would be with people heading in the wrong directions and colliding and cursing and getting nowhere. If only there could be a way of providing an early warning system to avoid such a catastrophe. If only he could think of a way. And he caught himself thinking that and grinned. Here he was stumbling in the dark and he was doing just what Kris had wanted him to do; take his mind off what he perceived as his own failure and, instead, start thinking of how he could save everyone again.

He knew he was home because he banged his shin on the old stump that was used as a seat in better weather. Sucking his breath through his teeth as he rubbed his leg vigorously, he limped to the door, just avoiding stumbling into the drainage ditch. He squinted against the sudden brightness of the candles and the fire and blinked rapidly in adjustment as he entered.

Bespic looked up from the table at the side of the room. He was quiet and reserved with a thin face and an untidy band of brown hair around the sides of his bald head. He was working at weaving a basket. "I've left plenty of stew for you and there's some bread as well. A bit chewy, but still good."

Markin hung his coat, gave his leg a last rub and busied himself at the stove, returning to the table to eat.

"What did Kris have to say for himself, then?" asked Bespic, as he examined his handiwork; a large, tightly woven, wide-necked basket, almost completed.

Markin shrugged as he chewed his food. When he could speak he added, "Not a great deal. I think he wanted the company more than anything. But, I did get a mug of coffee out of it."

Bespic placed the unfinished basket on the floor beside him and gave his full attention to his companion, elbows on the table and cupping his chin in both hands. "And now, you can tell me the truth."

Markin took his time, carefully wiping the bowl clean with the bread. "He's as concerned as I am that at some stage the government in

Pannedon is going to see fit to come here and take what we have and probably destroy what they can't take. And, just like me, all the times when I've told you about it, he can't see anything that can be done either. Not enough of the people here see it as a priority. He did get me thinking about an alternative though. It's something I toyed with for a while, but never got anywhere with. What if there was a way we could warn everyone to give them enough time to hide? "

"Is it possible?"

Markin sighed heavily. "That's the problem. There are too many difficulties. We really need phones or some sort of tech to make it work, and *that* is simply not going to run here. Even if there were any to be had."

"So what are you going to do?"

"Do?" Markin snorted. "I don't see what I can do. But I will think about it. That's all."

Bespic nodded; small and swift and precise. "Something will occur. An idea you hadn't thought of maybe. But something. I'm sure." He seemed, to Markin's ears, to sound very certain of his prediction. Indeed, he grudgingly admitted to himself, there was a certain ring of authenticity in what he said, but Markin wished he could share such certainty. Bespic scooped up the basket he had just put down and held it up for his companion's inspection. "What do you think of this?" he asked, lengths of very thin reeds sprouting from the unfinished rim and waving vaguely as he turned it slowly for Markin's inspection. "I think, when it's finished, it might almost be watertight."

Markin nodded approvingly at the tall, wide-lipped basket. Bespic always asked his opinion of his latest experiment and seemed to value them. Therefore, Markin was careful to be honest. "It certainly looks good, very tightly woven." He ran a fingertip over it, making appreciative noises. "Some fine work. It must have taken a lot of time. You've come a long way since your first attempts."

Bespic's face gave way a little, creasing into a thin smile. "I'm aware of my nickname. 'Basket'. It's odd, isn't it, that the name reflects what I was very poor at to begin with, but now I have made this it actually makes sense. A title almost, when it originated as a mark of disrespect and a way of pointing out my failure." He spoke very precisely, the words crisp and definite. He put the basket on the table. "People are very strange."

"Not everyone, surely."

Bespic nodded gravely. "Oh, yes. Everyone is very strange in their own way. Take my apprentice, Pelle, for example."

"Apprentice? Does she know that's what you think she is?"

"She works under my guidance, and I pass along what knowledge I have gained to her. What else could she be?" Markin inclined his head in acceptance and allowed Bespic to continue. "Pelle, as I was saying, looks perfectly normal. A girl growing up here knows about working hard and all that. But I catch her drifting off instead of working."

"And that's strange?"

"Not in and of itself, I grant you. But, when I challenge her about this, I am told that she is listening to the sheep, or some other beast we have."

"I still don't see that as strange."

"But they're not making any noise. There is nothing to hear. That is what is strange. Even a normal, healthy young girl can say the strangest things. Which was, if you recall, my point. People are strange."

Later, as Markin was lying in bed, hugging the covers close against the cold air seeping in under the door, there was something in the back of his head which would not let him alone. Something about what Bespic had said about Pelle. He could not grasp it and look at it so that it would leave him in peace, and he wasn't even sure why it was that he was being kept awake by it. He just knew that there was something there of importance for some reason. If only...

THE WINTER EDGED ITS RELUCTANT WAY INTO SPRING, AND THE ROUTINE AND the work of Newgrange continued as it always had. The usual arguments occurred over the usual things, such as who was responsible for what, and Kris, as he usually did, resolved them as best he could.

Pelle worked with Bespic creating containers for the community, learning from him, making mistakes and having successes, and in the meantime still gazing off into the distance, 'hearing' the animals. Endel had still not said another word but always hummed and bobbed to an unheard song when he was with the cattle. Little Pol wandered throughout the activity, given the small tasks of egg collecting and helping feed the cattle and milk the goats as best she could. She, too, kept her secret songs to herself now that she knew Kris couldn't help her.

Sten was seen sometimes stomping back from the woods beyond the fields often with a stern or disappointed look on his face. Bespic's baskets and containers became better and better. Marianna wove constantly and Sarrah baked and the coffee in Kris's tin finally came to an end. It was a time of work and preparation for the coming year and the harvests later on. Fields plowed, plots dug, seeds sown, dung spread, roofs and fences mended, tools repaired and sharpened, ditches re-dug, cracks caulked and the levees and sluice gates checked and repaired. Everything was business and activity. Everything was as it always was, except that Markin's mood became darker and darker. He also knew that there was nothing he could do about it.

One day, having returned from an unsuccessful scavenging sweep of the nearest villages in the small hope there was something missed earlier, or that he would meet up with someone with definite news, he came back to the village taking the path around the field to end up at the heart of the community, where the largest compost pile was, where communal activities such as weaving hurdles for temporary fencing took place, and the occasional summer cookouts happened around a large fire. He leaned heavily on the large boulder that had been the spot where Kris and he and Ellanara had stood and surveyed the land. He rested there stretching his back against the curve and felt miserable at all the activity around him when he felt so useless, as if he was letting the community down.

As he rested there, gazing inward, not knowing what to do next, Pol came wandering down towards him, her hair in two braids barely reaching her small shoulders and clutching a bunch of grass in her hands, making the sort of wordless sing-song that all children of that age can do. Seemingly focused on her grass and her song she came to an abrupt halt in front of him, becoming silent and lifting her head up to gaze with the quiet and intense concern that only the innocent can have.

"Why do you feel like that?"

The question broke into Markin's reverie and he looked down at the small girl before him. "What do you mean, Pol?"

"Why do you feel like that?" The question came back again as if no further explanation could possibly be needed.

"I'm a little tired, that's all. I've been walking a lot."

She cocked her head. "No. That's not the truth. You feel sad and you feel... I don't know the word, but not sad. Worse than sad. Why do you feel like that?"

Markin looked more closely at her as she gazed up at him, waiting for him to answer. "Can you tell how I feel just by looking at me, Pol?"

She gave an exaggerated sigh. "Of course not, silly! I hear it in you. It's there." And she pointed with the fist holding the grass, the chubby index finger straight out. "That's what I hear. Don't you?"

Markin eased down the boulder until his creaking knees told him to stop. He was closer to Pol now, who still regarded him with an unwavering stare. "I'm not sure I do hear it, Pol. I can't hear you. At least, I don't think I can. I can hear your voice, but that's not what you mean, is it? But can you hear anyone else here?"

"Of course. I can hear everyone. It's just that you sounded different." She studied the clump of grass in her hand, pulling out odd strands from it, her demand for an answer from Markin vanishing as quickly as it had arrived.

"Can you hear everyone, even if they're not right here, like me?" Markin was fascinated by the matter of fact way the little girl was acting.

"Mmmmhmmm." She was still plucking at the bunch in her hand.

"How about anyone working in the woods? Like Flinder. Can you hear him?"

Pol looked up and tilted her head to one side, a faraway look in her eyes. She pointed to the nearest woods, beyond the fields. "He's there."

By now, Markin's knees were hurting enough to make him sit down properly and stretch his legs a little in front of him. "And me? When I'm not here. Can you hear me when I'm traveling away from Newgrange?"

Pol threw the grass away and brushed her hands stiffly in front of her. "You are smaller, quieter then." She held her thumb and finger apart. "Little sounds. I can hear you because I know what you sound like. But I like the sounds the flowers make better. Flowers and mushrooms." She examined her palms carefully before carefully wiping them on her legs to clean them. "I have to go now. Bye." She waved and turned, her braids bobbing, and she stumped off.

Markin remained seated watching her go. Part of him wanted to believe what she said, and another part of him wanted to disregard it as nothing more than the dreamlike statements of a child engrossed in her world. But the part of him he could not ignore was the part which screamed at him that what she had said to him was the truth. It was the part of him that had known when a suspect was lying, when something about a case wasn't right; the part of him he had learned to trust implicitly. And, if that was so, the implications of what she had told him were amazing.

He sat thinking, ignoring the damp ground and the way it was spreading into his clothes. She, Pol, could somehow hear others. He knew he couldn't do that. Not in the way she had meant it, anyway. Therefore, was it only Pol or all the young people who could do that? He was fairly sure that if Sten had been able to do it everyone would have heard about it in great detail a long time ago. Then he recalled what Bespic had said about Pelle hearing things or some such phrase. Perhaps she had the same ability as Pol. Did anyone else have it?

And then it came together. If these children could hear people in some strange fashion and they could do it when they were far away, it would be possible to use them as the early warning system he had given up on. Nobody would have to be sent away. There would be no need for food and shelter far away from Newgrange, they could protect the community from right inside of it.

Optimism surged in him. He needed to do two things. Three, actually. He needed to find out if more than just the two girls were capable of this... thing. He had no idea what to call it even. Second, he had to tell Kris about it so that some sort of arrangements could be made to set up a listening rota or something like it. Pol was still too young to be a reliable listener, but if there were others, then it would be less of a problem. And, third, the children, however many there were, would have to be agreeable to do it. Could they be persuaded to do it and what would happen if they weren't?

A growing awareness of something cold happening to him brought him to the present and he levered himself slowly upright, brushing away the dirt clinging to his rear and giving a little shiver. He looked around him, seeing the land with new, more hopeful, eyes.

Kris was at his table, sorting through a seemingly haphazard pile of notes. The notes were on all sorts and sizes of scavenged paper now kept in a battered tin box which had once housed mechanics' tools. These notes contained records Kris had kept of crops and past harvests, as well as notes he had made on the weather of previous years. In any year he would use them to estimate what the yield and the number of livestock might be. He looked up as Markin knocked on the door-frame, smiled in relief at the interruption, and beckoned him in, gathering the sheets up carefully and weighting them down with the box.

After Markin had told him of his conversation with Pol, Kris scratched at his beard as he thought.

"What Pol said to you reminds me of something she said to me some time ago now. She wanted me to make the mushrooms bigger so she could hear them better, or something like that. But it was definitely about her hearing them in some fashion. I brushed it off as something she had made up. We need to find out how many more there are who can do this. You say you suspect Pelle as well? I know I can't do it, and you say you can't, but maybe some adults can. How do we find out?"

"Can't we just ask them?"

"I suppose we could, but how do we phrase it? 'Can you hear things that others can't?' Sounds like we're looking for the mentally unstable, doesn't it?"

"Perhaps if we ask the children first and then if any adults hear about it, they'd be more likely to own up as well, wouldn't they?"

"But the problem remains; how do we find out?"

Markin thought for a moment. "Why don't we ask Pol if she knows if the others can do what she can? I mean we're only talking about, what, five or six youngsters? After all, she said I sounded different, that's why she spoke to me. What if anyone who can do this also sounds different? It's a good place to start at least, isn't it?"

"Why were you sounding different?"

Markin brushed that aside. "It doesn't matter. How about we speak to Pol? After asking her parents, that is."

. . .

Within a few days of gentle inquiry they had discovered that Pol and Pelle could both 'hear' people and animals. Both of the girls were quite sure that Endel could as well, although they couldn't explain why they were so sure. He still wasn't saying anything, but had fixed Markin with a fierce stare when asked if it was true about his ability. Other than these three, there was Hanna Sippol, a little older than Pelle, who could also 'hear' people, but hadn't realized that it was anything special and was reluctant to admit it to her parents, as she didn't want to be different from them. Once she heard that Pol and Pelle could do what she could do and were agreeable to doing more with it, her heart-shaped face burst into a smile and her blue eyes lit up. The last was Bodren, the youngest of the two sons of Flinder and Sarrah Hander. The elder, Fillip, a stoic boy by nature, slow moving but sturdy, could not do what his brother could, but in keeping with his temperament, seemed not to be upset by it, returning to his work without remark. Bodren, on the other hand, was the opposite of his brother; always usually smiling and whistling. After he had found out that he was someone special in the community, the smile was even wider and his hazel eyes were wide with delight under his mop of black hair.

At that point, Kris and Markin took some time to explain to the parents what they had in mind and to reassure them that there was no danger involved at all. Indeed, it was to prevent danger and to help the community as a whole. Finally, when the parents agreed, Kris and Markin gathered the children together in the barn to talk to them. They were just about to begin their explanation when Sten walked in, all bristle and outrage.

"Why was I not invited to this?"

Markin tried to keep his thoughts from showing as he stepped forward. "Look around, Sten. The only ones we invited here are the children. Not adults. Unless, of course, you have the same ability these children have?" He let the question dangle a moment.

Sten glowered at him and ignored the question. "You know very well that I have spent a great deal of time dealing with the trees and have established what I think is a very good rapport with them. If anyone should have responsibilities for forewarning, it should be me."

"I don't really see how that is?" Markin framed it more as a question than an accusation.

"Because I can hear them. The trees, that is. I can hear them. Therefore you need me."

"That's good," said Markin, struggling to keep a calm tone, "but we're looking for those amongst us who can hear people, not trees. That's not to put down what you are doing, just that it's not the thing we're after right now."

Sten was not to be put off. "I am confident that, given time, I can provide you with what you need. Right now, however, I demand to be included in what you are doing."

Neither Markin nor Kris could think of a polite way of saying what they thought of his suggestion in front of the children. They were saved, however, by Pol, who had been sitting on some hay and throwing wisps of it at Pelle. She stopped what she was doing and looked up at Sten. "The trees don't listen to you. You don't hear them properly or you'd know that they are more afraid of being cut down by us here. They're not that interested in talking to you."

Sten turned to her, but confronted by her innocent gaze and her size, it was his turn to be at a loss as to how to respond and, after huffing a few times, could only muster, "That's what you think."

"No. I know it is true because I listen to them and that's the sounds they make."

Faced with such innocent simplicity, Sten could only glower and stalk out with as much dignity as he could muster after saying, "I shall come back at a later time and resolve this." None of the children laughed, which impressed Markin no end.

"I suppose you want to know why we asked about what you can do and why we asked you to meet us here?" said Markin after a decent interval had passed. "I'll try to explain as best I can and then you are free to ask whatever questions you want." He cast a quick look at them, and their faces all showed a guarded interest, even Endel. "I don't know if you remember, but some time ago at one of the regular meetings there was talk about soldiers with weapons coming here. Do you remember that?" There were a couple of nods and a few small shrugs. "Kris and I would like to find a way that would help us to know when those people were coming, so that instead of fighting them we could have time to hide from them. And that's where you come in. You all can hear things that neither Kris nor I can. What I want to know is this. Can you hear people far away and can you know if they are different people, people who do not live in Newgrange? Because, if you can, then you here today might be the best help possible for everyone. What do you think?"

Pelle was the first to speak up. "I don't know if I can hear other people. I hear people here, but I haven't heard anyone else to know the difference."

"Fair enough," said Markin. "But can you hear people far away?"

Pelle nodded.

"How far away have you heard anyone?"

Pelle screwed up her face in thought. "I heard you once when you had been away for four days and Bespic had mentioned something about being worried about you. So I tried hard and I heard you, but I don't know how far away that was."

Markin showed his surprise. "That's very good, Pelle. Well done. And, thank you. Anyone else?"

"I already told you I could hear you," said Pol.

"You did indeed."

"I haven't tried doing that," said Bodren. "But it shouldn't be too hard, should it?"

"I don't know," said Markin.

"How far away do you want us to hear?" This was from Hanna.

Kris answered this. "Well, there is a road a long way down the mountains from here. That's the most likely place these people will come from. That place would take them about two days, maybe a little less, to get here. That's how far away we need."

"Then why not go there and we can listen for you?" Hanna offered.

"That should be easy enough to do," Kris acknowledged. "Markin here can go, and you can listen to him as he goes. There and back should take about four days?" He looked for confirmation from Markin, who nodded. He had traveled that route more frequently than anyone else in Newgrange.

"And are these people really going to come and take our stuff away?" Pelle asked. There was a fearful look on her face.

"I think so, Pelle. I really do, or we wouldn't be asking any of you to do this."

"Why?" The question came from Pol.

"Because they kill people and rob them and burn homes and destroy things. That's what they do and they will do that to us." Everyone turned to look at Endel. The words had come out almost flat and emotionless and that very lack of emotion, together with the unexpected source, lent them a truth which could not be ignored. These were the first words they had ever heard him speak, and their surprise was evident. He merely sat there, ignoring their reactions, looking at Markin who managed to overcome his own surprise enough to add, "That's very true, Endel. Sad, but very true. That's why we need to know ahead of time when they are coming."

Slowly everyone recovered from the shock of Endel actually speaking. Then Hanna asked, "When will they come here?"

Kris shook his head. "We don't know for sure. But we can make a guess that they will be here probably somewhere around harvest time. So we have a good long time to practice."

Markin looked at the children, at how serious and accepting they were of the news, and wondered if he could ever have been like that as a child. Was it the fact they worked hard, played little and had nothing like the childhood he and so many others had had that had made them this way? Or was it something else, something about the fact they lived with a closer connection to the earth, saw animals being born and raised and then slaughtered which made it easier to accept other people coming to kill them? He had no answers.

"What do you want us to do, apart from listen for strangers?" Pelle asked.

"After we've found out if all of you can hear Markin down at the road," said Kris, "then, I suppose we set some times up and everyone takes turns to listen."

Hanna shook her head. "That won't work at all. Just sitting and listening all day, or even for a long time, is really tiring. I tried it once, following a chicken to see where she went. If I know I have to do that, then I'm not going to be looking forward to it. And that means I will probably make mistakes or miss hearing them."

Bodren agreed. "I don't mind listening, but not all day. Even if it's one day every so often."

"Well, what do you suggest?" asked Markin.

Hanna said, "We all listen everyday. We listen when we get up, when we eat lunch, when we eat dinner and before we go to bed. That way everyone is involved, and if someone is tired or gets sick, it won't matter. That only leaves the night and you said that it took a long time to get from there to here, so even if they start in the night, we'll still have plenty of time to hide."

Kris gave an appreciative nod. "That sounds very sensible, Hanna. Thank you. But what does everyone else think about that idea?" There were nods and sounds of agreement from the children, including Endel.

"Well, in that case," said Kris, "Markin and I would like to thank you for your help and for being able to do whatever it is that you can do. I would have no idea even how to begin this 'hearing' thing, but we are incredibly grateful that you all can do it. The next thing to do, then, is to ask Markin to go down to the road and see if you can all hear him as he goes. If some of you lose him, if you can't hear him after a while, come and let me know so we can work out how far you can hear. That will be good to know as well." He turned to Markin. "When do you think you'll be ready to leave?"

"I can start tomorrow, once I've got some provisions ready."

Kris turned back to the children. "So, starting tomorrow evening, you can all begin to track Markin as he walks down to the road and back again." He scratched at his beard again. " I'll be telling your parents about this meeting and what we've decided. I suppose that's it for today and we should all be getting back to work."

The children got up with thoughtful looks on their faces and set off in their various directions, Pelle taking Pol by the hand, leaving Kris and Markin alone.

"We're asking an awful lot of them, aren't we?" said Kris.

Markin agreed. "But why is it, do you think, that they can do what they can do? Is it something they've been exposed to? Something in the

food we grow here? And why only the children? And yet, here they are."
He picked his next words carefully. "They're different from us."

"Yes. I don't know how it happened and I can't even begin to guess."
Kris gazed off into the distance where a group of villagers were hard at
work in one of the fields, planting seeds by the look of it. "I'll tell you
something, though. The one with his nose put out is Sten. However
much he can irritate me, he is at least trying to do something more than
just survive. He is trying to make a greater connection with the planet,
something which started the whole Revival movement. But, according to
Pol at least, not doing that well. It must be a difficult feeling for him. I
actually feel sorry for him. A little, anyway." He looked at Markin. "Have
we given up on all that? What happened to our ideals? That's probably
why Sten irritates so much. He's the voice of my conscience. He reminds
me of what I should be focusing on, not the harvests and the job
allocations and all the rest of it."

Markin made a noncommittal noise. "The thing that got to me,
though, was Endel. What has that boy been through? I don't even want
to think about it. But the way he spoke -- ," he shuddered, "-- it must
have been something awful. That's the most he's said since he's been
here. What memories is he holding on to and what are we doing to help
him? The answer to that last question, by the way, is absolutely nothing.
And instead we're talking to him about it happening to him again. We
have no idea what he's feeling. Sten's big enough to look after himself.
You can feel sorry for him if you like, but Endel's the one I feel for most."

"Maybe you're right. But, whatever happens, we've just put the safety
of everyone here on the shoulders of the youngest of us. Right or wrong,
it's a heavy thing to have done. Maybe we shouldn't have done it. But it's
too late for that thinking." He took a deep breath. "However you look at
it, we're in their hands now."

6

THE SLEEPER

Neither Meldren nor Javin had seen any of the other people on the island for several days. They had wanted to but had respected what Isselta had said. That didn't stop them tuning in every so often to see if it felt right to visit any of the newcomers.

"Actually, I'm glad of the rest," said Meldren, picking some berries for lunch from their garden. "It's nice to have time for ourselves again without having to worry about whether we're doing the right thing or not." She offered a berry to the sprite who ignored it. She popped it in her mouth, chewed and swallowed. "I don't think I'm that good at working with people."

Javin was sprawled on his back, arms behind his head, squinting into the sky, watching the clouds moving along. "I keep thinking back to when we were first together. We kept thinking then that it was all over but then it started again, with Harmony becoming more and more... different."

"And you think that it's going to be like that all over again?"

Javin levered himself up to a sitting position and patted the ground for Meldren to sit with him. "I think this is just a breathing space. And there's still that cloud, that 'something' up ahead. I think this is the lull before the storm."

Meldren held out the basket of berries to him. "Speaking of that 'something', have you tried to feel if it's any closer yet? Or felt anything about it at all? I can't."

"No. Nothing. And that's -- not worrying, exactly -- but it is strange that we can't get anything else about it."

Meldren ate several more berries. "I wonder when we'll find out what Isselta's been up to." She thought about it a moment, her eyes soft-focusing as she sensed ahead in time. "Actually, I think it's going to be very soon."

THE NEXT DAY, AFTER BREAKFAST, THEY HEARD ISSELTA CALLING TO THEM from outside. Sharing a 'this-is-it' look between them, Javin and Meldren walked out. Expecting to see only Isselta, they were surprised to find all of the others there as well, standing in a fan behind her. But then something else caught their eyes.

Meldren clapped her hands in surprise. "You've all got sprites! All of you. When? When did that happen?" And it was true. Snuggly wrapped around each of them was a sprite identical to her's and Javin's. Some were being stroked gently with a look of wonder and fascination; something which Meldren knew well. Some of the wearers were twisting and squinting in vain attempts to admire their new companions.

Isselta broke into a huge grin, the happiest they had seen her. "*When* it happened was yesterday." She gestured at the others. "Apparently it happened at the same time for everyone. We just found them. They appeared by themselves."

"Mine was on my chair," put in Pep. This started the others all sharing how they were united with theirs at the same time.

Meldren waved her hands at them to quiet them. "That's amazing. Really amazing. And it's wonderful to see you all here... together."

"Well, that's partly why we're here," said Dennet. "We thought that, if we had them as well as you, then it must mean something important. It took us a while to realize that everyone had them. I thought it was just me, until I saw Isselta here with hers. And then we went to see Carmeena, and she had one as well. That's when we guessed it was the same for everyone here. The three of us went to see everyone else and it was true! By the time we'd stopped talking about them, it was late. As nobody could figure out what it could mean, we decided to come here today and see you."

Javin sat down on the ground and indicated that they should do the same. When they were all settled in a semi-circle in front of him, some of them moving gingerly as if fearing that they might dislodge the creatures, he asked, "Have any of you had any strange experiences since you've had these sprites? Something like hearing voices or anything like that?"

There was a general shaking of heads. "We've been trying to find out what they like to eat." This came from Timoss arranging his crutches carefully.

Meldren smiled. "We haven't really got that sorted out yet either. Some days they eat some things that, the next day, they don't want. We don't really know that much about them. Well, we do know that they never seem to make a mess on you." That got some gentle chuckles and more stroking and ineffective squinting. "Like I said, we don't really know that much about them, apart from the fact that they are strange little creatures which I have never felt worried to have around my neck."

Javin took on a more serious tone. "The one thing that we are quite sure about is that these sprites are a way for Harmony to speak more easily with us. Now, I'm not saying that that is the only thing they are for, but that's what Harmony Herself said about them when we first got ours. For all we know, they could be incredibly useful in any number of ways. That's why I asked about anything strange happening."

"How does that happen? How does Harmony speak to you? What's it like?" asked Farran, his lined and drooping face looking the least sad she had seen it, Meldren thought.

She gestured vaguely with her hands, trying to find the right words. "It's really hard to explain. It's more a feeling and a sound together. A beautiful series of sounds, but they make sense somehow, but only while She's there. Afterwards... , well, it's not easy to recall it all. At least, that's what we've found. You know it, but you can't find a way of saying what you know. And it's never the same thinking about it. It's so fresh, so real when She speaks, or sings, rather. And it goes on deep inside your head and a part of you wants to make the same sounds, and another part of you wants to stay in the sounds. And the feelings you get! It can be the most incredible feeling in the world or something so strange that it's scary. But scary in a way that is safe at the same time -- or afterwards. I'm sorry," she said, shaking her head and smiling. "I'm just not good at describing it. It really is something that has to be experienced."

"And, who knows? Maybe that's what you're going to be doing, sooner or later," added Javin. "Maybe She will come to you and maybe She won't. But it's good that you're all here together. It's the first time all of us have been in one place close together."

"Oh," Meldren interrupted. "I should have said that when She comes, if She does, then you can't move. It's like you are awake, can see things going on, but you can't connect with them. And, no, it's not really scary. Like I said before, you feel safe." She smiled. "Which is a good thing, because, you know, when a planet wants to do something to you, there's not a lot you can do to stop it. So it's a very good thing that Harmony takes good care of you, of us, when She comes."

"How do you know when She is coming?" This from Isselta. "Does She arrive gradually or all at once; boom!"

Before either Javin or Meldren could speak, the sprites on each person's neck began to partially unwind and move up to be around the top half of their heads. As they did so, Meldren looked at Isselta and pointed at her sprite, her expression saying, *This is the sign that She's coming*.

Everyone suddenly slumped forward a little, their faces expressionless despite what must have seemed a terrifying loss of control of their bodies. Eyes were open but unable to focus voluntarily. Breathing seemed to be the one thing left to them.

Meldren heard Harmony as She arrived to speak to them. She assumed that everyone was hearing the same thing. It was the musical equivalent of someone gently and carefully introducing themselves to people who could not yet speak the language. It was sonorous and gently chiming, echoing, repeating, continually evolving and gradually asserting itself until it became a strong, sustaining chord, growing louder until it dominated the mind completely. Then, when there was nothing but this weighty chord, it began to dissolve into innumerable rills, arpeggios, lilting phrases and soft, almost hidden tunes, all played simultaneously as if on a hundred different instruments. At that point, it became suddenly clear that all of those intricacies were held within and were part of that one chord and that she, Meldren, was held safely in that self-same chord, contributing to it, making it richer and fuller somehow just by her existence.

Then came the pause, that musical sound of thinking, of breathing, of... being: the sound which Meldren knew from before. And then, the halting, lilting voice of Harmony appeared in her head as though an incredibly skilled orchestra was forming words with only the sounds of the instruments, and there were thunderstorms and tidal waves and tornadoes and earthquakes taking place in the far background, and all of them were Her voice.

"You are... here... now... together.... Now you can... begin. You can begin the... growth?... change?... healing. You are songs.... Songs becoming more real... stronger... bigger." There was another of those infinitely beautiful musical pauses for deliberation; a gentle rhythmic surging of background sound hinting at immense power. "Songs need to be heard... by other... you. More than you here. Songs of ... together? Father sings it is... to make new songs.... I sing with Him the same.... I am not-hide now. All you... now sing realness strong. Be loud songs now. Loud songs."

And, gently, quietly, the music, the harmony that was Harmony, withdrew and faded until the only sounds were of the breeze in the foliage and the small busyness of insects. And, as that happened, so everyone regained control of their bodies. Sprites slid back down to curl around necks and faces showed amazement and confusion in equal proportions. Having experienced this before, Javin and Meldren were the first to recover fully.

They sat, waiting for the inevitable questions. It was Dennet who first addressed them. One hand was at his throat, making sure that the sprite was still with him. "That was Harmony, right? But what did it all mean? And all those sounds! I've never heard anything like that." He looked to the others. "Did we all hear the same thing, or did we each hear something different? I mean, what was it that happened?"

Meldren put her hands up to quiet the nervous, excited chatter. "Yes. That was Harmony. And, I suspect that each one of you heard the same thing. It's quite something, isn't it?" She smiled warmly at the expressions of wonder on their faces. "You've got to remember one very, very strange thing about it. And that is that what you heard in your heads was this planet, the one we're sitting on, speaking to you. Think about that for a moment. This planet," and she patted the ground, "wanted to speak to you, to all of us. And She did it as best She could. Harmony has the same language as we are made of: songs and music. So, when She speaks to us, it's difficult to understand Her. And these sprites we now all have? They help us to understand Her. Without them, it's much harder and more painful."

"So who was the Father She was talking about?" asked Timoss.

Javin pointed up. "The sun. The sun is the Father of Harmony and of all the planets. He sang them into existence, as far as we can tell. And Harmony sings everything into existence here. But the sun is the most important."

Isselta asked, "Do we get to hear the sun?"

Javin shook his head. "You don't want to do that. It's not a song for us here. I think the only time you get to hear the song is when you die. But I'm not sure about that, either."

Pep looked confused. "But what did it all mean, everything She said to us? Not hiding? Realness? What does that mean?"

Meldren answered her. "That's what I meant about there being problems understanding Her. Javin and I were often unsure about what She meant. We still are. But 'realness' is how She speaks about everything on this planet. It's all created with a song or songs. That's real, to Her anyway."

Javin added, "And not-hiding is going back to something that happened quite some time ago. Harmony was being attacked by people from Haven, the other planet. She hid so She could not be attacked. I have no idea how She did it, but, apparently it worked. So, not-hiding I guess would be when She can be seen again. I don't know if any of you noticed a strange thing, a feeling like a rippling, that happened recently? The clouds sort of jumped a bit and it looked like the ground had a wave running through it?" There were a couple of cautious nods. "That is exactly how it felt when She hid. So, I suppose that was when She un-hid." He shrugged. "I can only guess."

117

Isselta, as ever, was first to ask the difficult questions. "Does that mean that we, all of us, have to be able to sing, to create things with songs and that we have to be really good at it? And, if that's the case, why? Why us? Why is that something we have to do? Do we get any say in it at all?"

"We don't know," said Meldren, with a slight shake of her head. "But, if Harmony is changing in some way, changing what She does or how She does it, then I suppose that all of us here have some role to play in that." She raised her hands to show her ignorance. "But what that might be, I have no idea. All I do know is that if Harmony is planning something, She is going to make sure that it gets carried out. So, to answer the last question, it is unlikely that we are going to have any say in it. Sorry."

Both Javin and Meldren had become used to being treated in this way by Harmony, but they could see some were struggling with it. Carmeena, for example, was shaking her head slowly from side to side, but whether in wonder at it all or in fear or rejection was hard to tell. Allegara was sitting stock still, a stunned look on her face, as if nothing in the world made any sense anymore. Enrick and Farran were leaning towards each other as if to find support. The idea that a planet had spoken to them was one thing; hard enough to accept, but the memory of the music in their heads helped them. But to go from that to a realization that the self-same planet wanted, no, required them, to do something was somehow much harder to believe. And yet, that appeared to be the case. Singing songs to create... what? And why? In a child's handspan of an afternoon, everything they thought they knew had been uprooted, overturned and re-made into something barely recognizable. It would take some time, Meldren realized, before any of them would be ready to move on.

AFTER EXPERIENCING HARMONY COMMUNICATING, THE NEXT FEW DAYS SAW various islanders, as Javin now called them, coming to talk with them about what had happened, how to care for their sprite. During the times when they were alone, Javin and Meldren discussed what the next steps should be.

"We have to start teaching them how to sing themselves, before they start experimenting and getting things muddled," said Meldren.

"I don't believe that's the problem." Javin was sitting at the table shelling some pods from a longbean bush in their garden. The sweet, yellow beans inside would make a nice addition to their supper. Meldren was rinsing some leaves in a wooden bowl. "I think, if any of them are anything like us, then they've already been trying things. Remember what it was like for us? Whoo!" He laughed and shook his head at the memories. "I think that what we have to do is what Harmony said; learn to sing together."

"Like when you and I sang ourselves to Littlehaven you mean?"

"I think so. It's one thing to sing something for yourself, to do the simple things. But singing together. That's different. When we sing together, it's because somehow we need to make something which one of us can't do. Or, at least, make it easier or stronger. But if we're saying that all of us islanders have to sing the same song, whatever that is, I have to agree with Isselta. What for? What do we need all of us for when just a few of us, two us, can do so much? It has to be something really big. And that is something I can't even begin to understand." He handed his bowl over and scooped the empty pods together. Before he dumped them in a basket outside to be added to the compost, he turned to Meldren. "What if all of us here are to -- I don't know -- spread the word around Harmony? Get everyone to hear the songs, maybe even get them to sing them?"

"Yes, but why have us sing together? Harmony could simply nudge us to leave and go to various places. Singing together doesn't come into it. I don't think that's it. But nice try."

Later, as they cleared away the remains of their meal and sat sipping at some water, Meldren suddenly twitched upright, spilling her drink. Javin did likewise. She reached to feel the sprite around her neck and shook her head as if to clear it. "Did you feel that?"

"What was that? It felt like I suddenly knew where everyone on the island was. I felt them in my head. It was like a map. But without listening to the songs."

"What's a map?" asked Meldren, brushing the water from her skirts.

"Sorry. I forget sometimes. It's a way of showing where things are with marks, writing and so on. You make the marks on paper or even on the ground. If I drew on the table here with some charcoal and put marks for where Isselta, Dennet, Timoss and the others live, that would be a map."

Meldren considered this a moment. "What's the point of that? I can go and see them."

"But if they were a long, long way away then it might be useful to see how far away they were and you could plan a journey better."

Meldren wasn't convinced. "But you'd have to go there first to see how far it was, wouldn't you? And what's that to do with how you felt in your head just now?"

"Well, it was like I knew where all the islanders were without having to think about it. Is that how it felt to you?"

She closed her eyes as she recalled it. "I suppose so. Something like that." She opened her eyes again. "So I had a map in my head, did I?" She was still fascinated by the strange words which Javin used on occasion and always tried to incorporate them whenever she could. "And my sprite definitely twitched. That's what made me spill the water."

"Mine did too. Just a pulse," said Javin, his hand gripping air in demonstration.

"Which means only one thing," said Meldren heavily.

Javin nodded. "It's Harmony. She must want us all to be connected, I suppose."

"So, can we? Be connected continuously, that is?" asked Meldren. "After all, if She's shown us something, I would guess She wants us to use it. Maybe what just happened was a demonstration, a way of showing us what's possible. It might not have happened to the others."

"The only way to find out is to try, I suppose," said Javin.

"And we do that... how?"

"Same as always, I suppose," he said. "Focus on what it is we want to do, maybe remember how it felt when it happened, and then... I don't know... let it happen, I guess. Ready to give it a try?"

They wriggled into more comfortable positions in their chairs and held hands across the table before shutting their eyes and relaxing. In a short time, they both felt the pulse at their throats as their sprites responded to some invisible contact. And then, as suddenly as before, they were both aware of the others in their heads as distinct points of something which was not music nor a thought, or a picture, but something more like a link or thread. Each person was distinct and the two of them were aware that each person was also linked in that same unfathomable way to every other person. It was a network which they could feel in their minds. Turning their heads made the points of awareness slide in response so that they all kept the same relationships to each other. If they had kept their eyes closed, they could have walked up to any one they wanted to without hearing the songs which were their true selves.

After a moment or two, they opened their eyes and Meldren asked, "Is this something we tell them? After all, it's a little like spying on them, isn't it? I mean, I have heard of people being able to locate lost relatives or objects, but I don't think it's like this. If I shut my eyes, I know where each of them is and I'm quite certain I could tell when they were traveling anywhere."

"But it's not really spying, is it? It's not like we chose to do this. It's something put into us. And besides, I can't tell what they are doing, only where they are. They could be doing anything and I wouldn't know about it, just that they are where they are." He thought a moment more. "I don't think we should be telling them about it. Maybe they will be able to do it as well. And, if that's the case, we'll find out about it soon enough. But if Harmony only showed us, then I suppose it's for a reason She knows about but isn't necessarily going to share with us. So I'm inclined not to say anything about it. For the time being, anyway."

Meldren agreed with a slow, thoughtful nod. "Which leaves us back where we started which is, how do we do this 'loud' singing that Harmony spoke of? What can the songs be about? I confess, I don't know how to think of this. You and I, we sang what was needed. Bigger songs. What does that mean? Songs are songs, aren't they?"

"Maybe," said Javin, trying to understand it all. "But... if we are all singing something together, whatever that is, then it will be louder and that means... ." He gave up, throwing his hands in the air in defeat.

"Louder songs can be heard further away," mused Meldren. "Could it be possible that if all of us islanders sing something together, then we can do something far away from here, like the other side of the world, perhaps?"

"I've just realized something," said Javin. "Before we even get to singing together, they have to learn to listen, to hear each other, like we did. Without that, everyone will be singing different songs. Listening comes first, I think."

His sprite pulsed rapidly for a moment; his immediate surprise changing to humorous resignation. From the look on Meldren's face, hers had pulsed as well. "Looks like we have our answer, doesn't it?" he said.

The next day, they visited each of the other islanders and asked them to gather together as before. When they all had arrived there was a generally nervous shuffling and whispering going on, as neither Javin nor Meldren had given any hint for this gathering. Once again, they were all seated in a semi-circle and there were a variety of expressions; from quiet, curious interest from such as Enrick and Farran, to the more serious, slightly anxious concern exhibited by Carmeena and Allegara. Javin and Meldren had earlier shared some ideas with each other as to what they were going to do.

"You've had the sprites for a little while now," began Javin. "And we've been visited by Harmony. Big changes. And it seems we're all in this, whatever it is, together. We're here now because we all need to learn something today. Which means we all need to be able to learn how to listen to songs, as a group, all together. Now, I'm fairly sure that, if you are in any way like us, you have been experimenting with songs. Am I right?"

A few bowed heads, sideways glances and small attempts to hide behind the next person indicated the truth. Javin was quick to reassure them. "This is good. It's a good thing. You should be interested in what you can do now. This is not about telling you not to do those sorts of things, which wouldn't work anyway, I'm quite certain. This is about something else. When Harmony said about us singing louder songs, Meldren and I realized that can't happen unless everyone can hear the same thing. If we are all hearing something different, the song we sing will not work or it will just be a waste of time."

Isselta piped up. "If we did something that was... I don't know... strange, if we sang something strange, like an animal that wasn't right, or ill or with bits missing, would it live? Would it be... I don't know the words, would it be something that lasted, that could live, even if it was wrong?"

Javin made a '*that's-an-interesting-question*' face. "I'm not certain, but I feel that Harmony wouldn't let it happen. After all, this is Her world. It's Her song which makes everything in it. I don't think we can create new things, new beings, that haven't existed before, because everything has to fit into the one main song. We're not powerful enough, I don't think, to make something that can live outside of Harmony's song. The first settlers here, I'm sure they had to be brought into the existing songs by surviving. They added into Her songs. So, no, I don't think we can create anything at all, only the things which Harmony has already got space for in Her songs." He nodded to Isselta in appreciation of her question.

"Meldren and I have thought about how to do this, and we've come up with an idea. And that's what we're all here for. As it was her idea, I'll let Meldren tell you about it."

Meldren had been picking at her thumb as she shuffled the words around in her head to find the best way of describing what she wanted them all to do. She realized what she was doing, stopped and looked up at them all.

"All songs come from Harmony. So, it made sense to me to see if we can all hear the main song, the underlying song if you like, of where we are right now. Not the ones to do with flowers or the air or each other or anything like that. But the one song which underlies everything here."

"But what is that? What does it sound like?" asked Pep.

"Well, that's what I can't tell you," answered Meldren. "This is a practice. A way to see if you can understand what is going on around you, see if you can sort out the different sounds and see if you can find one common one. It's more about how you listen than anything else."

There were a few puzzled looks. Enrick asked, in his usual soft-spoken way, "How will we know if we are all hearing the same thing? And how would you know if we weren't?"

"Good question, Enrick," said Javin. "We'll know because we'll also be listening to it and we'll be listening in on how you are. You all know by now, I assume, that everyone has their own special sound, their own song? You might also have learned that the song will change a little due to whatever else is going on. So, Meldren and I know what you all sound like. If we can also hear that the same something is going on with each of you, we can be pretty certain that you are all doing the same thing. In this case, all listening to the same thing. Plus, Meldren could probably tell a lot of that by using her talent of watching how your colors change as you are doing this. Does that make sense?" Enrick nodded as slowly and thoughtfully.

Meldren beamed at them all. "Good. Are there any other questions about this?" There was a general shaking of heads. "In that case," she continued, "make yourselves comfortable and just relax. My guess is that, up to now, you've been listening to things around you and trying a few small songs of your own. Food, water, flowers, things like that. But this is different. This is listening deeper for the songs which carry the sounds you've heard so far. The song which carries everything else."

She waited as they all found comfortable positions. Some, like Isselta and Dennet sat upright and cross-legged. Others who were older, like Farran and Carmeena, found it more comfortable to lie flat on their backs with their hands either by their sides or folded on their chests. Timoss, with his painful legs, stretched out on his side, one leg straight, the other drawn up, his head pillowed on his arm.

"Now, when you are ready, close your eyes and let yourself sink into the songs around you, hear them but don't concentrate on them too hard. Listen to one and then another. But, as you do so, listen for what is common to them all. Listen for that common song that's so often hidden underneath. But don't try to do anything other than listen. It won't work. Trust me on this. Listening is enough. Don't try to alter it, add to it or anything else. If you do, your sprite will stop you. Javin and I found that out last night when we were experimenting. Listen and keep listening until no other smaller song can disrupt it. It's about listening and about concentration."

She reached out to Javin and grasped his hand and then the two of them also closed their eyes and relaxed. What Javin hadn't told them was that their new-found ability to know exactly where each one was could also be used to know how far away or close to a song each one was. It was like hearing a tuning-fork. That's how he knew that there had been lots of practicing going on. As long as he or Meldren knew the song they were listening for, they could also hear if the others were in tune with it. That had been their second discovery the previous night.

"And what would have been wrong with allowing us to have this ability before, when they were all new to the island? It would have made helping them so much easier," Meldren had said.

"Ah, but would it have, though? We'd have known something was wrong and that they couldn't hear Harmony, but we knew that already. It would have given us information but nothing to help us use it."

Meldren had huffed but conceded. "But it would have been nice."

It was after this that Meldren had the idea of listening to the 'under-song' as she called it; the song which was Harmony in Her purest form with nothing added. She and Javin had argued in their gentle way about what they should set as a test. Javin had been for something really small; a single flower, a tiny insect, but Meldren had held out for the under-song. They had rarely listened to it themselves, had only heard it on occasion when Harmony had been showing them something She wanted them to understand, but they knew what it was and knew it was always there in the background. Javin had eventually conceded that it was a better target and one which was more of a true test for the islanders.

Now, they sank themselves into the songs around them, dipping beneath the vegetation and the various types of living things, down into the earth and the bedrock until there was the clear, deep, pure thrumming sound of the song which carried all of those things and more as choruses and echoes and harmonics and arpeggios and cadenzas and all manner of variations, creating the world around them.

As the two of them did so, they also kept part of their awareness on the sounds of the others. It was more like hearing with vision in that they could also, with a part of their minds, know if one of the others was getting closer or moving further away, distracted by a particular sound. They could do nothing to change what was happening, only know of it. They let the islanders listen for long enough to know how it was going, who was strongest in this area and who was distracted.

Meldren clapped her hands gently two or three times before asking, "Who thinks they heard it and were able to keep hearing it?"

A few hands went up and she noted that they correlated with what she and Javin had heard. Carmeena had been rock-solid throughout, the best of them all. Enrick and Farran had both been very, very good as well. Isselta had been very unfocused to begin with, but had later managed to home in on the song and hold it. Of the others, Pep had wandered in and out as had Timoss. Dennet had had trouble from the beginning and had never really managed to hold it for any length of time and Allegara had been the same. But all of them had managed to hear the song for at least part of the time. They had had different reactions to it however, which came as a surprise to both Meldren and Javin.

"It felt like I was somewhere dangerous, almost like being up very high and being afraid of falling. But something was there to stop me," said Carmeena.

Farran, on the other hand, said, "That's not how it was for me. It was more like having my parents there either side of me, making me feel so safe. There was nothing like being up high for me, simply a feeling of being safe and... loved." His voice tailed off and he colored in embarrassment.

For Pep, it had been, "...like a really, really loud noise. You know it was very loud, but I was hearing it from a long way off. But loud. Really loud, only in a safe way." Whereas Timoss could only shake his head, his eyes filling with gentle tears, unable to give words to his experience.

The effort had tired them and so they decided to try again the next day. This next time, only Dennet had some trouble tuning in and holding the song, but the day after that, he was as capable as the others. Then they were all finally able to share their experience of it. They all agreed that it began as a simple sound or song, but that the more they listened to it, it became more complex. They didn't really have the words to describe it, just shared feelings. But it made them smile and made them feel as special as when they had found their sprites. After a while the talking and laughing began to die down a little.

As they chatted together, Isselta, as usual, was the one to voice what most of them were thinking. "What do we do next? Do we learn to sing together, or make our own songs?"

Javin answered. "I don't really know. Meldren and I have been talking about it and, well, to be honest, we're not sure what should happen. You should know that before you were all here on the island, we had a feeling of something big happening later on. We mentioned it before. But we could never really understand what it was or get anything more than that. Now you can all hear the song, I've had a feeling that something has changed. It's still the big thing we first felt, but... it's changed somehow." Meldren nodded in agreement as he continued. "If any of you know something about this, get a feeling about it, please do let us know. All we can get is that it's something big and coming soon. But how big and how soon are not obvious."

And, with that, the meeting broke up and everyone drifted away, back to their homes. Javin and Meldren ate a light meal together before walking out to the headland overlooking the ocean. They were wrapped up in several blankets against the cooling breeze but wanted the clear expanse the place offered. "What do you think's next?" asked Meldren. "I get the feeling that, at last, they're all starting to act like a group, instead of a bunch of individuals. They're so much more talkative now, especially amongst themselves."

"Nothing like having a planet in your head to make you want to stick together."

She smiled. "Agreed. So they can all hear the same thing. But what now?"

Javin had obviously been thinking about this already. "The way I see it is that they are much the same as we were when we first started out hearing Harmony. First we listened, then we sang. I suppose that the next thing is for them to sing together."

"Yes, but what? Sing what?" Meldren, tugging her blankets closer, turned to gaze at the distant horizon as if hoping to find answers there. "Singing has to have a purpose. I can't think of a purpose that would fit all of them, unless it's like a learning exercise. But learning what? And more to the point, why are we doing this? What's it all for? For all we know, it's just a waste of time and nothing will happen because of it." She frowned in irritation and uncertainty. "We've helped a few people. We've taught them some very simple things and through it all, the feeling that something else is going on in the background grows and grows. And we're stuck here in the middle of it with no idea about anything, just stumbling along like good little people, doing whatever Harmony wants us to do." She turned away from the horizon to look at Javin beside her. "When we were together at first, there was always something happening.

We couldn't always understand, it but something was definitely happening. It made more sense, I suppose. Not like this." She gave a deep sigh. "I don't like this not knowing. I prefer seeing where things are going."

"But that's not what happened to us at first." Javin spoke gently. "We didn't know what was happening then any more than we do now. I guess that, sooner or later, we'll look back on this time and say that, of course, it was obvious all along just as we do now about when we were first together."

Meldren inclined her head in grudging agreement and sought for his hand in the blankets. They sat in silence for a while, losing themselves in the space before them. After a while, Meldren gave a little shiver. "Let's go back now. It's getting really chilly."

As they were walking slowly along, hand-in-hand, the wind at their backs, she said, "We still haven't decided what to get them to sing." Javin shrugged in reply.

It was during that night that both of them had the answer they sought. They didn't realize that was the case until later in the morning when Meldren spoke of it first.

"I had a dream last night."

"An ordinary dream or...?"

"Not a nightmare, a dream. It was in a strange place. Tall things growing all around. I don't know what they were, but they were tall, straight plants or something. Some of them were bushy. And strange looking homes --"

"And fields which all had very straight edges to them, not like here," finished Javin. "I had that dream as well."

"That's what I saw, for sure!"

"And the tall things are trees. I thought I was having a dream of Haven. I recognize the things in it, the plants, the scenery. But I didn't recognize the place. And you, you had the same dream as me."

"Well, we have had the same dreams before," said Meldren. "But this one was about Haven? Are you sure about that?"

"As sure as I can be. The things I saw in the dream were things I remember from Haven."

"But there weren't any people that I can remember. Did you see anybody?"

Javin shook his head. "No. None. It felt abandoned."

She gave a wry smile. "It was one of Harmony's, wasn't it?" She cocked her head as she recollected something. "Oh! But I forgot. Did yours have a sound to it?"

Javin frowned. "Yes. Now you come to mention it, there was a sound, a song. In the background."

Meldren prodded, "And you can remember it?"

Javin thought a little more before his eyes widened in surprise. "It was the base song of Harmony. Harmony's own song. The one we told everyone to listen to. The exact same one."

Meldren pointed a finger at him, emphasizing her point. "And that's no coincidence. That has to mean something, doesn't it? The song of Harmony but on Haven. Harmony and Haven together somehow. And you *are* sure it was Haven?"

"Positive."

Meldren frowned. "Do you think it's the same song on Haven as here?" She waved that thought aside impatiently. "No. Of course not. If the songs were the same the planets would be the same. So what was that about, then?"

Javin looked just as puzzled. "I agree it can't be an ordinary dream. But..."

"But what?" Meldren prompted.

"Well, I was thinking that last night we were complaining that we had no idea what to get them to sing, or even if that was the right thing to do. And then, in the night, along She comes and gives us this message, this answer. But, like every other time, it's never clear enough to know right away what it is She wants. But," he waggled a finger at Meldren, "what if it's the sound, the song, Her song, which we have to get them all to sing? I mean, She did say about singing loud and strong. Perhaps that dream was a way of saying that we should all try to sing it so loud that it can be heard on Haven."

Meldren gave an involuntary shudder. "That there, what you said.

That gave me the shivers. There's a truth in that. I don't know what it means, but," and she shuddered again, "that idea, that gives me the shivers." There was silence for a while; each feeling that something had happened which was important, but neither able to grasp what it might be.

Finally, Javin said, "I agree with you. There's something going on here which I can't understand. All I know is that it's important to us somehow. But, other than that, I don't know. What I do know, what feels right in all of this, is that we have to teach them to sing that song as best they can. Maybe, just maybe, when we do that, we'll get to know what this is all about and what, if anything, it has to do with Harmony."

With nothing more than that to go on, they arranged to have another meeting with everyone. For the most part, the islanders were comfortable being on their own, but they also enjoyed being together as a group. After the general greetings were over and they were settled, Javin spoke.

"We, that is, Meldren and I, have been thinking about what's the next thing for all of us. I think we have it, but, before we start, has anyone got any questions about the songs or Harmony? Or, have any of you found out more about that thing in the future we mentioned the last time we were all together?"

Farran made a tentative motion with his hand to attract Javin's attention. "I didn't get anything about the future thing, but I did have a strange dream the other night." Javin and Meldren pricked their ears at this. "It was nothing like this place. I don't know where it was. But it felt like it was important. There were no people that I could see and all around there were these tall, pointed plants growing up and the fields looked wrong as well."

"I had the same dream!" said Isselta, turning to Farran. "Tall plants growing and strange houses."

"Me too. The place was abandoned," said Enrick. And all of the others began to nod and add their memories of it until there was a general hubbub of noise and Javin was waving his hands to damp it down.

"We've all had the same dream it seems," he said when he had their attention again. "What you saw, I'm fairly sure, was somewhere on the planet Haven. My home. It's where I came from. Do you recall what the sound was in the dream? What was going on in the background?"

Dennet was the first to answer after a moment's thought. "It was the same sound we were trying to listen to before, wasn't it? What did you call it? Harmony's song?"

Meldren nodded enthusiastically. "That's right. It's the same song, but in the dream it was on a different planet." She looked around. "Does everyone remember that or did some of you hear a different sound?" The nodding indicated they had all hear the same things. "Well, because of that, and we thought that we were the only ones who had had the dream, we thought --"

"We have to learn to sing that song ourselves," finished Isselta for her. In answer to Meldren's quizzical look, she added, "And, because we heard Harmony's song in the dream, the only thing which feels right about it is for us to learn to sing it ourselves." She shrugged. "I can't find anything else which makes me feel so certain, feels so right. So... we have to sing it, I suppose. Then maybe we'll find out what it's all about?" The girl looked around at the others as if to find confirmation in their faces.

"That's very much what we were hoping as well," said Javin.

Timoss asked, "I agree with Isselta that it feels right, but isn't there a danger in us doing this? It's Harmony's song. So couldn't we be danger of making things happen, creating or even destroying things, if we all sing this?"

"Yes," agreed Javin. "I suppose it could happen like that. Or maybe not." He gave a frustrated sigh. "Everything seems to be yes and no at times. But Meldren and I have learned one thing, and that is that if something feels really right, you have that deep-down certainty of what you're doing, then it works out. And, as Isselta here just said, she can't find anything else which feels as right, and neither can Meldren and neither can I. I suspect it's the same for you. Plus, I think that because we're learning to sing Her song, Harmony will be taking a very close interest in what we do. She won't allow us, with our small voices, to do anything which might upset what She is doing. I can't prove that's right, but I think it is true."

And so they began. First they listened together to the song of Harmony which ran underneath everything in the world. Then they started to try to recreate it. The sprites around each of their necks wobbled and swayed and made small crooning sounds but, each time, the song trailed off into silence. After several false starts, Javin clapped his hands to stop them and said, "I don't think it's going to work like this. I think we're doing it wrong. We can't all be singing the same thing because it's not just one simple chord or note. You remember when you first heard it? You all said that it sounded simple but it was more complicated the more you heard it. Well, listen to it again. But carefully. Really carefully." They shut their eyes and bowed their heads again in concentration. "Remember, it's not one plain, clear song. I thought it was at first, when Meldren and I first heard it, but that chord we're hearing is made up of different notes, different tunes almost, all bound together. Some are lower tones and some are lighter and some are quicker and some are slower. Can you hear that?"

Enrick spoke first in his quiet fashion. "I can't hear the quick ones you talk about. Only the lower ones. I can hear the song but if you're right, then it's like I can hear one part of it better. When we tried singing it just now I was trying to sing with all of you and couldn't find the right notes. Some of you were singing things I couldn't hear and that confused me."

"Same here," said Carmeena. "I can't hear what Enrick's talking about and when he was singing I got confused and my song came out wrong."

Allegara, sitting next to her, nodded in agreement. "Same for me. I can't hear those low notes you talk about. But I can hear lots of other lovely sounds. Some of them are lower than others, but not what Enrick was singing.

Timoss said, "Well, I can hear what Enrick is on about, but not what Allegara hears."

"Isn't it obvious?" put in Isselta, impatiently. "If we can only hear parts of it, then those are the parts we have to sing. After all, we're not a planet who can make masses of sounds. We can only make one each. But, together, we can make the whole song, surely?"

"I suppose so," said Javin with a surprised look on his face.

"And," continued Isselta, "I think that there are going to be just enough of us here to sing each part. I do not think that there are any more notes or tunes or whatever you want to call them, only the ones we can hear. Harmony's been planning this all along, hasn't She? Ever since you two first found us, this is what She wants from us, isn't it?"

"That's planning! Long term planning like nothing else," said Farran in tones of admiration.

"Not if you're already dealing with clouds and oceans and seasons. This would be easy for Her." said Javin with a grudging chuckle.

"Amazing," agreed Dennet.

"But obvious," insisted Isselta.

"Just a moment, Javin" said Timoss. "Are you saying you can hear the high notes as well as the low ones? And you, Meldren. Can you hear the low ones as well as the high ones?" When both acknowledged they could, he looked around and said, "But none of us can, is that right?" Nobody contradicted him. This revelation caused puzzlement for a moment.

"Then," said Isselta in a firm voice which really would have suited someone older, "we must be singing this for you two to hear. Because none of us, apparently, are able to hear it all. Only you two." She looked up at them, her head cocked as she appraised them. "I think it's not about us so much, as about both of you. I think this is all for you two. I think," she said, sorting her words carefully, "I think you are going to need to be careful, because this song we're learning, it's got a huge amount of power in it and it's all going to be aimed at you, if I'm right."

Neither Javin nor Meldren could think of any response to make to this, for both of them felt it to be true. They both felt it and they both feared it. It took a moment for them to shake off those feelings and return to the purpose of the meeting. Neither of them, however, wanted to ask why. The answer was not one they felt they wanted to hear.

At first, they splintered into ones and twos as they focused on their individual songs. Then, as they gained confidence in their own parts, so they came together and sang as a choir, quietly at first but gaining both in confidence and volume. As they sang or hummed their parts with more assurance, listening and adjusting to each other, the sprites on everyone's necks unwound a little, enough for the bodies to slide up the backs of their necks, over the tops of their heads and down; the tiny heads coming to rest on their foreheads. The singers continued with barely a blink as that happened. Once in their new position, the sprites began humming in unison with their human companions adding a counterpoint, a depth and an harmonic to each singer's voice, building on it, making it grow and expand. As they all, humans and sprites, gained in volume, so each person felt a power humming, growing, expanding within them; in their chests, in their minds, adding strength to their voices and clarity to the sound. As they sang, so they felt lifted, surrounded and immersed in the song. The space between themselves and Harmony shrank, and they lost themselves inside Her, and the singing of it became easier and purer and louder, and the sprites matched them as they sang.

Javin and Meldren, listening to this fountaining song, found themselves as if trapped by it in a way which was unlike anything they had experienced with Harmony. Later, Meldren was to describe it as standing inside a whirlpool of sound they could not and did not want to break out of. Their own sprites, still around their necks, pulsed and thrummed and sang impossible harmonies which felt and sounded separate from the vortex which held them, but which anchored them and held them tight to the ground, refusing to let them both be swept away by it.

Finally, this amazing chorus began to fade, began to ease, and the two of them felt able at last to move as the music finally released them. The choir lay on the ground, their sprites returned to their usual place round their necks. Although they lay in abandoned postures they were not exhausted, but instead emptied and elated at the same time. The singing had finished but the touch of grace and power was with them still. Before anyone could speak, a warm wind rose up and formed a soft river of air which flowed around them all, caressing them and soothing them further before fading away gently, becoming a breeze and then no more than a breath. And as it faded, each person heard the echo of a word: "Soon."

7

NEWGRANGE

The summer on Haven moved inexorably toward autumn. Tools were sharpened, storage bins were cleaned, and stalls were swept in preparation for the harvest. The sun was still hot, the days were still long, but the smell of autumn was present in the morning when the earth was cool from the night. No matter how hot the days, the water in the river which ran alongside the fields was always teeth-achingly cold, coming as it did from the mountains. You could dip a mug and drink it without worry. Through various channels, it irrigated the fields, and the sound of its bubbling passage was a background to their work. The soil now felt fresh in the hand, not tired and dusty. The rains came in longer, less frantic bursts and everything growing produced seeds and bulbs and roots and leaves in profusion. There was a constant eye on the weather and the talk was of when it would rain and for how long and would it help or hinder the crops or when they were gathered. The natural tension of the culmination of a year's work was everywhere.

But the tension in the air was not just from worrying whether this coming harvest would be enough to take them through the next year with some surplus. It was also because the longer Newgrange was undisturbed, the closer it was to being found and attacked. Everyone now felt that. The fact that the children were acting as an early warning system had given the idea of an attack more credibility than anything anyone could have said. Because the children took it seriously, the adults became more sensitive to the idea that there was a threat and that it was coming. The children's ability to sense people from a distance had been proven conclusively when they had tracked Markin to the road and back. Word had spread quickly and several times one or other of the children had demonstrated their ability. Fears previously ignored had grown to permeate the community. The year which had started out in a tone of optimism and happy disregard for the outside world had taken on a darker sense of unease underlying every activity. Every day now, half-fearful eyes were turned to the children for signs of an approaching force. If the children noticed this interest, this weight of responsibility for the emotional welfare of Newgrange, they showed no signs of it and carried on with their allotted tasks.

But the tension grew. The threat existed. They had nothing to base this on, no news of raids elsewhere, no survivors seeking shelter, nothing. But the very lack of evidence hung heavy on them, dragging at them, so that when they looked each day to the children and saw nothing, it served only to confirm their fears. Each day that passed brought the unthinkable, the inevitable, nearer.

Several times Kris or Markin had to intervene when a routine disagreement over some small and normally resolvable issue erupted into a fight. Punches were thrown and curses were uttered before the quarrelers were separated forcibly, heaving and swearing and glaring at each other before being hauled off in separate directions to calm down. When the usually neat, calm and reserved Bespic had to be dragged off of Sten for some supposed disparaging remark he had made about Bespic's latest basketry, Kris decided enough was enough and called for a full meeting that night.

The weather was warm enough to hold it outside in the middle of the community. Kris scrambled up the boulder. It took more effort than he had thought it would. '*I must be getting old*,' he thought as he caught his breath, surveying them all. The faces he saw looking up at him showed tiredness and tension in equal measure. He knew what he wanted to say but wondered if, now, he could find the words he needed. That thought had never occurred to him in the early days when crisis seemed to follow crisis. He tried out a few phrases in his head before he realized that they were all waiting for him to start. A deep breath and a hope for inspiration and he began.

"This is not the usual meeting. But this is one we need to have now. And I think you all know why." He paused to scan them again, trying to judge their reactions, their feelings. Markin was leaning against the boulder, arms folded, with a scowl on his face, daring any of them to say something out of place. "There is a tension here which is pulling us apart when we need to be together. I don't know about you, but it's almost like I can reach out and touch it." With one hand he grasped the air in front of him as he spoke, and formed a fist. "This fighting and arguing, this is not something we can live with. I mean that. It's the truth, not some figure of speech. If this continues, if this tension and unrest is allowed to go on, then we will fall apart and we will all fail. We will have nothing left."

"When are they coming? That's what we want to know?"

The voice came from near the back and sounded a little like Pelle's father, Tervin. Kris turned in the direction it came from. "We don't know. That's the truth of it. Your guess is as good as mine. But you know that we have done what we can to give ourselves a fighting chance here. Thanks to Pelle, to Hanna, to Bodren, to Endel, and to Pol, these our children, we have a chance. A greater chance than ever before."

"But will they come now or next year?" Was that Semmik?

Markin answered that without altering his stance, the words coming out in a growl. "They will come. That is certain. And more than likely, they will come this year. If not, then early next. But they will come. And you all can feel it, even if you don't want to acknowledge that feeling. Every single one of you knows I'm right because your guts tell you that it's going to happen. There's a clenching there, a darkness like a cloud in our future. It's there because it's real. That's the truth of it. As surely as winter comes, so will they come. Listen to yourselves, to your hearts, and you know it's the truth."

That got a few sidelong glances and some shuffling. Kris was grateful for the words. They touched on the fear beneath the surface better than anything he had said. Before anyone could respond, he spoke up again. "I can see you all agree with what Markin said. And that just makes what we're doing to each other worse. We cannot fight each other. Put this tension to use instead. Each family, each person, everyone here, we must all prepare for it. Only some of you have put some food aside, smoked meats, cheese, the things which will keep and are easy to carry. That's good. But not enough of you have been thinking about this. We need tools for when they have gone, so we need to hide them with us. We need seeds to take and hide. We cannot simply run as soon as we know they are coming. We have to take the heart of this community with us. And the people, you, us, we are only part of that heart. Newgrange exists because of the food we grow, the skills we have, the tools we use. Those we must take with us. The big things like the loom or the bread oven, they will have to stay. But everything else we have that makes us who we are, that has to be accounted for. For they want to break the Revival movement. They will destroy everything that they can reach and find. There will be nothing left for us when we return. And we *will* return and we will succeed again. But if we waste our time fighting each other, then we lose. We lose everything. We lose what we came here to find. We lose our sense of direction. We lose our pride. But worse, we lose ourselves, our souls, our spirits. We cannot fight amongst ourselves. It has to end and it has to end now, today."

"You want us to stop being angry." Semmik was speaking again. "But how? When we're waiting here, waiting to run for our lives? If something goes wrong, it's human nature to take out our frustration, isn't it? Doesn't mean we're going to kill anyone, does it? It just means we're angry and frustrated." He put his hands up as if to dismiss the problem. "It's human nature."

Markin pushed away from the rock to stand upright, looking angrily at Semmik, and spoke before Kris could think of an answer. "It's human nature to do a lot of things. And one of those things is to get angry and resent the person you've had a fight with and lost. One of those human nature things is to think about revenge. One of those things is to stop being a neighbor, stop helping, stop being part of this community because you feel angry. If the fighting continues, then the community dies. You want to be angry and frustrated? Fine. Go right ahead. I can't stop you. Nobody can. But instead of taking it out on other people, you could actually do something useful with it.

"Take that anger and that resentment and that irritation and turn it into something useful. Find places to hide that are far enough apart from anyone else so we don't all get caught. When you're frustrated, go and take provisions there and place them where the animals can't eat them. When you're angry, sharpen a tool, make a new one, dig a hole to hide in, but do something that will keep us together and not push us apart." He was breathing heavily and glaring at them all, Semmik having long since ducked out of his line of sight.

"If all the gods man has created throughout history were to look down on us here, they'd laugh at us for being so useless and helpless. It's as if we're determined to die." Markin flung an arm out to point at Pol who was bored by all the talk, yawning as she leaned against her mother's legs. "The youngest of us here is more capable of helping us all than any one of us so-called adults. I've seen the looks you've been giving them, as if they are our sole hope and help, as if there's nothing we can do for ourselves. It's time that changed! If we can't fight and we stay here, we *will* die. If we can't fight and we run off without real, proper preparation, we *will* die. If we can't be bothered to think of our neighbor and what we can do to help each other, we *will* die." He took a breath to steady himself. Kris crouched down on the rock, not wanting to take away the import of Markin's words, thankful that the right words were being said, even if they weren't his.

Markin continued more quietly. "Remember why you came here. Remember how angry and scared you were then. You wanted this place to be your paradise, your haven. I was frightened. Kris was frightened and angry, and with a good deal more reason than most of you. But that anger then didn't break us apart, it brought us closer together. We had a common idea. And that's the same today. We've proved this can work, that we can live as we want. But our common idea now is to avoid being killed for doing just that. Yes, we will probably see everything we've worked for broken, burned, and destroyed, but that doesn't mean we were wrong. It simply means that we will rise again afterwards, stronger, better, happier.

"We've all given up everything once. Now we get to do it again. And for the same reason as before: because we know it is the right thing to do. Getting angry with each other, thinking we can't do anything to save ourselves; these are the wrong reactions. I can't tell you what to do, but I can ask that in two days' time, each and every one of us has located a place to hide away safely, that we each have earmarked what we will take and what we will leave and that we are ready to move. It should be at least a day's travel away to lessen the possibility of being found. Don't tell anyone else where you are going, don't show anyone else, because if we know only our safe place, then we cannot lead them to anyone else's. Between here and the mountains is a big enough area to hide all of us in without stumbling over anyone else. But be sure you look to your neighbor first. Do they need food? Would they benefit from one of your tools? What about clothing? Water? We share and then we scatter. And we scatter to survive. Remember that." He ended, looking tired and drained.

Kris had been watching them all as Markin spoke. The tension he had noticed as the most obvious emotion had now been replaced by a look of determination. There was now a palpable feeling of resolve and a willingness to look each other in the eye. He stood up now and added, "And when they have come and gone and taken what they have taken, we will meet here at this rock once more. This is the center, the place we will start from again. Once we are certain they have gone, we meet back here and we re-build for two reasons. First, because we can, and second, because they cannot beat us. But we have to be able to re-build. That's what we take with us."

There were more nods and determined looks, a metaphorical squaring of shoulders. The meeting ended not because Kris ended it but because there was nothing which could be added. They dispersed quietly and soon only he and Markin remained. He scrambled down from the rock and squatted down to look at his friend, now slumped against the boulder as if his legs could no longer support him.

"What you said, Markin? That was wonderful. I never knew you could speak so well. It was everything I wish I could have said, but you did say it and you said it better. Thank you."

Markin shook his head tiredly. "I wouldn't have had to say anything if only they could have felt what was coming a long time since." He sighed. "Maybe, if we can't even feel something that big coming at us, maybe we don't deserve to live here. There's got to be more to living than only going by what you think and by justifying what you do with logic. There's nothing logical about what I feel, but it's more important than any argument I can give." He reached for a hand-up from Kris. When he was upright, he said, "I'm going to go home and I'm going to sleep. I'm too tired trying to get them to listen to and acknowledge what they ignore most of the time."

Kris watched him walk slowly away and wondered if Markin thought he was as useless and ignorant as the rest of them. And, because he couldn't feel the future rushing at him as strongly as Markin obviously did, he realized that he probably was counted amongst the useless and ignorant.

FOR THE NEXT SEVERAL DAYS, THE ENTIRE COMMUNITY OF NEWGRANGE WAS galvanized into taking action. Something had changed in them after hearing Markin. The minimum work necessary in the fields ensured that the harvest would be as good as it could be. Everyone was spending time in the woods, mostly going uphill toward the mountains, into the denser areas of forest, finding places where they could hide. They took with them digging implements and clay pots and leather bags of food to store. Some, like Carra and Tervin Sippol, didn't come back for three days, causing Kris to wonder whether they had decided to leave the settlement for good, despite, or maybe because of, being parents to Hanna. Although he wouldn't admit it, he gave a sigh of relief when he saw them trudging slowly back to their home. Tervin nodded and gave a weary smile and wave when he saw Kris, which presumably meant that they had found a place to make their own.

There was a tangible sense of community and togetherness. The tension was still there, of course. It was evident mainly in the way that everyone kept checking on their supplies, re-packing or simply bringing baskets with them as they worked. Bespic could not make containers quickly enough. The children were watched, but without the same fear. Now, they were looking for the signal to move, to act and not simply to despair. People also scanned the skies. If there were any surveillance craft up there, they weren't seen or heard. Too high or too quiet.

Whatever the reason, the sky was not going them any warnings. Despite this, gradually, a new sense of peace and a new normality was established.

One day, as the sun was setting, Kris was enjoying the peace, sitting on the ground outside his home watching the shadows slide as he chewed on a piece of bread. His thoughts were far away, his eyes seeing the past, when he became aware that someone was standing near him, patiently waiting to be noticed.

Angling up, he saw it was Endel, the normal, blank look as always on his face. Since the original meeting, the boy had said nothing. It was as if the words he had spoken were a false memory, not actual speech. Beckoning the boy down beside him, Kris asked, "Is there something I can do, Endel?" Kris felt fairly sure that if this was the time for a warning from the children, Endel would not have been the one chosen to deliver it. Endel knelt on the ground. He watched Kris silently.

Kris repeated his question, wondering what it was that could have made Endel seek him out rather than Semmik or Marianna.

Endel's gaze was unnerving in its steadiness. The only sign that anything was going on was the movement of the lips as the boy chewed on them. He broke the silence abruptly, just as Kris was wondering what next to do. "They're not going to let us live. They're coming to kill us all. They'll find us and they'll kill as many as they can."

An icy feeling ran down Kris's spine. "What do you mean, Endel and how do you know this? What makes you say it?"

There was still no flicker of emotion on the boy's face. "I saw it. In the night."

"What do you mean, you saw it? Was it a dream you had? Last night? Is that what you mean?" Kris felt an urgent need to understand what this was about.

"I saw it. It is real. They will find us and kill us."

Kris tried to think for a moment and push away the fear that clutched at him. It had to have been a dream. After all, this boy had obviously suffered so much before he came here. And yet... and yet his words, so quiet, so unemotional, had hooks on them which had snagged something deep down in him, tugging it reluctantly into his awareness. Markin would have known what to do with this news. But he didn't. Or he didn't want to know. Surely, if the soldiers were on their way, the other children, some of them at least, would have said something. Wouldn't they? What if they had lost the ability? What if Endel was the only one who could sense them and because he didn't speak he had left it too late? What if it was really only a dream? How could he be sure? "Does anyone else think this? Are you the only one who had the dream?"

"Maybe."

"Does that mean you haven't told anyone else about this?"

Endel shook his head.

"Are they coming now? Are they on their way now?" Kris knew he was treating this as real as the bread he had eaten despite his wish for it to be nothing more than a boy telling him of a bad dream. "Is there something we can do?"

Again, Endel shook his head.

"Do you know when this will happen?" Kris did not want this to be real. But some part of him was sure that it was; a part of him which he could normally dismiss logically. Not this time.

Endel inclined his head and gazed at the ground, his eyes half-lidded as he sought something inside of himself. It looked, thought Kris, as if the boy was listening to, or looking at, something private, something hidden away from everyone else. Kris wanted to hurry him, yet he also wanted Endel to take his time and be sure. A part of him inquired why he would want to know the time of his own death.

Finally, Endel looked across at Kris, who found himself holding his breath. The boy shrugged.

"You don't know!" Kris felt an anger rising. Here he was, listening to a boy telling him that they would all die but not telling him when. The unfairness of it stung. He wanted to reach out and cuff the boy to the ground, roar at him and beat him. But, instead, he clenched his fist in his lap and ground his teeth.

Endel's expression did not change. If he saw the anger in Kris, it did not reach him. Instead, he half-closed his eyes once more, but kept his head up, as if daring Kris to see what he was seeing. As Kris was about to shout at him to stop, Endel spoke. "They will be here in three days, I think. Three days. Possibly later."

That rocked Kris back and he flung his arms behind him to catch himself. The anger was gone, replaced by urgency. "Are you sure? What about the others? Have they seen this as well? Do they know what you know?" The questions spilled from him. But Endel, untouched, unmoved, without emotion, only added, "They're not seeing as far as me. They'll tell you tomorrow. The killing will happen later."

"We should start leaving now then. I'll spread the word" -- he paused -- "but, if only you can see this far, will they believe it?" Doubt suddenly assailed Kris. Should he wait for the other children to confirm what Endel said? And what if they didn't? Then what? What if Endel was right about the attack but wrong about the time? If he went round to everyone tonight and then nothing happened, they would never be able to trust any future message of an attack. He needed more than this to act on.

He scrambled to his feet, leaving Endel behind, and made for Pol's house. She had been the first to let slip about what the children could do. If anyone could help, it would be her. If she could, that was. He banged on the door just as the last rays of the sun faded and the world began to slip into the nightly gloom. When Pol's father, Berd, opened it with a puzzled expression on his face, Kris wanted to push past him and confront Pol. Instead, being invited in, he masked the eagerness in his face and asked if all was well, exchanging the polite formalities.

Finally he was able to ask, "May I speak with Pol for a moment? It's nothing to worry about. It's something that I think she might be able to help me with and I really would like to be able to sleep well tonight, but this will keep bothering me if I don't ask her." It sounded to him as if his words were spilling from him without control. He felt stupid and silly, like a young boy trying to hide something that anyone could see.

He forced a smile. "Some time ago, she asked me to make the mushrooms bigger so she could hear them better. I thought nothing of it then, but... well, with all that's been happening, I would be hugely grateful if you could spare her for no more than a few moments while I ask her about some mushrooms I've found growing out back of my home. It's silly, I know, but with all the extra work that's been happening, I plain forgot, and with the night so warm and everything, I won't be more than a moment or two... ?" He brought his babbling to a stop. He left the question dangling as he watched Berd and Jenni exchange parental looks of question and answer, until with a curt nod and a smile, Berd turned to Kris and said, "Surely! No problem. I doubt she's asleep yet anyway. She usually sings quietly to herself a long time after we tuck her in. Not too long, mind."

Kris breathed out heavily, releasing the breath he had unconsciously held in. "Of course, of course. I know it's silly, but thanks anyway."

Soon, he was piggybacking Pol to his home, the remaining day glow being sufficient to walk quickly and safely. On the way, he tried to think of what to say to the child snuggled against his back. Finally, inside, he shut the door and carefully lowered the almost-sleepy girl to a chair. He hunkered down in front of her, but before he could say anything, Pol sneezed once, her hair flailing around her face, and then, wiping her nose with the heel of her hand, she said, "You're very afraid, aren't you?" She didn't say as if she were concerned for him, more like she was dispassionately reporting something of no personal concern. First she wiped her hand down her leg and then carefully brushed her hair back with her fingers. "You have heard they are coming, haven't you? Was that Endel?" She narrowed her eyes at Kris. "Yes, it was." Then she, like Endel, half-closed her eyes for a moment before nodding. "Yes. They are coming. Coming quick."

"So we should leave now, Pol?"

The little girl, with her feet swinging in the air, shrugged.

"But if they come, they'll find us, won't they? So we should leave, yes?" Some part of Kris was annoyed at himself for leaving the decision to the youngest person in Newgrange. Another part of him was frantically searching for an alternative course of action.

"They'll kill everyone they find, you know," said Pol in a serious voice. Again, the chill down Kris's back at the certainty in the words.

"Everyone, Pol? Really? Is there nothing we can do?"

Pol's bottom lip jutted out; her signal that she was thinking. "Only the ones who are here. They'll only kill the ones who are here when they see them. That's all. Just those."

"But that means all of us, Pol."

She gave a heavy sigh of impatience at his ignorance. "No. It means only the ones they see will be killed. The others who aren't hiding won't be."

"What others? Who are you talking about, Pol? What do you mean?" Kris had been genuinely frightened, which was bad enough by itself, but now he had confusion to add to it.

"I can't tell you because I don't know who they are. But they won't be killed." She screwed up her face as she tried to find words for something only she could see. "I can see things like Endel and Hanna and Pelle and Bodren can. We can all see things. But we can't see everything! There's something I can't see and I don't know what it is. All I know is some people will come."

Kris tried to make sense of it but gave up. "I'm going to tell everyone to start leaving right now, Pol. We can't take chances. We have to leave."

"Uh-huh." She yawned. "Can I go home now? I'm sleepy."

That night was frantic. Kris rounded up Markin to help him rouse the community after briefly telling him about Pol and Endel. They both took lanterns and began the process. Some people were reluctant, wanting Hanna and Bodren and Pelle to confirm the message, but the look on Markin's face and the fear in Kris's were enough to persuade most of them to get moving.

By the first light of morning, Kris looked back from the edges of the forest, feeling much older than his years. He could see a few people moving around him making quiet, determined progress, Markin's rolling walk making him obvious off to the right. He and Markin had been the last to leave, making sure that everyone was accounted for. Some had waited until dawn to set off to make sure they didn't get lost, whilst others had decided to make for the trees right away and then find their way. It had been chaotic for a while in the darkness. Now he saw the smoke rising from the chimneys from fires that had been lit to make it look like there were people living there, and, with an ache in his heart, admired the neat, rectangular fields with the harvest almost ready. So much work. So much love. And they were abandoning it on the word of their children. He shook his head in disbelief at the difference in the past day and night. Yesterday was a world he could never go back to. And what lay ahead was uncertain at best, disastrous at worst. Here he was, a leader without anyone to lead. An idealist whose idea was being dismantled before his eyes. What did he think he could ever have done to change things? He should have given up when Ellenara died. They should have been together always. Going on alone had been too painful, except he never wanted to admit the pain. He shouldn't have used anger as a motive for himself. And here he was now. This, he thought bitterly, is what failure tastes of and looks like. He called to Markin and raised his hand, though whether it was in greeting or farewell he no longer knew.

8

THE SLEEPER

Javin was not asleep. He was sitting at the table in the moonlight, gazing out of the window at the sea and watching the light flicker and ripple on the waves in the silver pathway, listening to the ever-changing underlying song out there. Meldren's breathing was a gentle background sound, softly mimicking the surf he could hear hitting the distant cliffs. There was nothing he could blame for being awake. He just was. There was no restlessness, no irritation, no indigestion, no premonition, just this wakefulness. He sighed, quietly, ran his fingers along the sprite's body as it lay still around his neck; it having joined him after he had left the bed, and wondered how to spend this time. There was no pre-dawn glow on the horizon, so he supposed that sunrise was still a long way off.

With nothing better to occupy him, he decided to try to sense more about the islanders, how they fitted into his and Meldren's life and what was going to happen. What *had* happened to them both when the islanders had sung at them? That was the only way of describing how it had felt; being sung at. It was yet another strange experience in what was becoming a life full of strangeness. Strangeness was normal now. How others lived, how he had once lived; that was strange to him. So what should he call this now? A normal life? Ordinary living? He smiled to himself at the futility of these thoughts. There was a 'before' and an 'after', and through it all, he was himself. Different abilities, different beliefs, different awarenesses, but he remained himself. That was all that mattered. That and Meldren.

Coming to that comforting conclusion, he felt his way into the surrounding land and the songs it rested on, tried to touch the strands of the future, and there was nothing. However he tried it was the same; an absence of anything he could latch on to.

He leaned his arms on the table and tried to think again of what to do with this unusual alertness. And then he realized something. Being this awake was unusual, but, even more unusual was the fact that he could feel nothing at all around or before him. He could hear the small songs making up the world, but there really was a silence beyond that. It wasn't that he had lost his ability, he realized. It was that there was nothing for him to listen to. If he had to put a human name to it, then it was the equivalent of a breath being held, of waiting in silence or silent preparation. But how could that apply to a planet? How could Harmony be doing those things? And for what possible reason?

Now that he had recognized a pattern, he felt the immediate confirmation of the truth of it in his mind. Now, also, he thought to share this with Meldren. He knew she would be -- not angry -- disappointed, if he didn't. But he was loath to disturb her. Nevertheless.... .

He was about to wake her when her sudden intake of breath and movement of her head indicated she had woken up by herself. Seeing Javin beside the bed her first sleep-slurred words were, "Are you well? Is anything wrong?" But then she waved away any answer he might have made and said, "No. Your colors are fine. Something's about to happen though, isn't it? It's Harmony again." This last was said with a note of tired resignation.

Javin helped her sit up, smiling and prodding a blanket behind her. "I was about to tell you. How did you know? Is that why you woke up?"

She scrubbed her face free of sleep and yawned once. "How do you or I know anything? I woke up and that's the first, no, the second thing to come into my head."

He kissed her on the forehead. "Thank you for putting me ahead of a planet. It makes me feel special."

She reached up, soft and warm from sleep, wrapped her arms around him and gave him a long, considered kiss on the lips. Her sprite, having wrapped itself around her, crooned gently as she did so. "That's because you are special, my love. But it doesn't change the fact that Harmony is up to something. And, if we're aware of it, then it probably is going to involve us in one way or another."

"You're right. I was trying to find out more about whatever it was, but got nowhere fast. I'm wide awake and it's a long time until dawn by the looks of it."

She gave a deep chuckle. "And you were all alone and wondering what to do, weren't you? I have the answer right here," she patted the bed. "If anything's going to happen, I'm certain Harmony will let us know in good time. Now, stop wasting time." She lay down again and opened her arms to him.

Later, when the sun was well above the horizon and the air was still, Javin stirred and rubbed his eyes and yawned. The first thing he saw was Meldren sitting at the table, putting a new braid in the front of her hair, sweeping it to one side of her head. She heard him and gave him a fleeting smile as she focused on securing the braid with a tie behind her right ear. "Don't worry, you haven't missed anything. I've been trying to hear anything but it's useless."

"I know," said Javin as he levered himself reluctantly from the bed."It's what I was doing in the night. Perhaps that was what woke me up; the absence of things, like when a clock stops ticking."

"A clock?"

Javin gave a wry smile as he scratched his head. "I'm sorry. That's one of my words again, isn't it? It's a machine for telling time. And before you ask, I know very well that nobody here on Harmony needs one of those because everyone knows what the time is. Now, I'm going to get dressed and have some breakfast. Have you eaten yet?"

"Mmmhmm. And I think you'd better hurry," she said, pointing. "I think we're about to have company." Javin looked where she was indicating and saw Isselta walking along the path, distinctive because of her small, slim body. Beside her was someone else, Dennet perhaps by the look of it. Behind those two was another person, indistinguishable from this distance. "They'll be here soon."

Javin was just about presentable by the time Isselta and Dennet arrived and had finished a hasty breakfast by the time the last of the islanders, Carmeena, had sat down outside.

"Why don't they come inside?" whispered Javin.

"Politeness?" ventured Meldren, breathing into his ear as she brushed away some invisible dirt on his shoulder.

Together they stepped outside to greet everyone. As usual, Isselta was first to speak, her young, serious face tilted up. "There's something not quite right and we thought we should come to see you." She looked around at her companions. "It's like everything's stopped, except it hasn't, but it feels like it has. What's happening?"

Meldren, sitting cross-legged by now, said, "You all have as much talent as we do. We don't know any more than you. We both felt it last night. It's almost like something's waiting to happen. Is that how you feel it?" Everyone nodded.

Javin smiled. "I don't suppose you thought just one of you could come and ask? You do realize that we're all together again, don't you? And I'm guessing that it's not an accident." He watched them looking around at each other as what he said sank in.

"Oh!" exclaimed Isselta. "Does that mean that whatever it is is about to happen?"

Javin arched his eyebrows in answer. There were the beginnings of conversations as Meldren looked at him and gave him a slow, sweet smile. Then a breeze arrived, seeming to come from all directions at once into the space where they were all sitting. It built quickly into something approaching a wind which swirled around them all, circling so that each person there felt wrapped in it for a moment. As it did so, they each heard the air carry the word "Now" before everyone's sprites rose up and arced over their heads as before.

The islanders looked in surprise at each other. Without prompting they began to sing Harmony's song again, only this time it was quicker to reach that state of purity. No-one was hesitant or off-key. It was a perfect blend of sound and each sprite contributed to the song its wearer was making, giving the whole a depth and a resonance which would have been impossible if only human throats were making it. Neither

Javin nor Meldren felt any compulsion or invitation to sing. They were the audience.

Without thinking, Meldren shuffled closer to Javin and they held hands as the song became both louder and also somehow more pure. As it swelled around them and filled them so that they could feel its vibrations deep inside, so they seemed to see a swirling of the air around them. This motion, at first like the shimmer of a heat haze, became thicker and more substantial until they could see the islanders hazily as if through a fog. At this point the song began to carry them with it. That was the only way to say it. It felt, as Meldren was to recall later, as if the sounds were solid enough to hold and lift them up and carry them with it wherever it wanted them to go. There was a roaring in their bodies, a vibration around them which energized them and made the wall around them all but opaque. Or, maybe the islanders had faded, leaving only the faint impressions of their bodies to be seen. Without seeing it happen, both Javin and Meldren felt that everything was moving quicker and quicker, or else they were moving quicker and quicker and everything else was staying where it was. The only constant of which they were aware and which could not be ignored or shut down was the song.

As the speed of either themselves or everything else increased, so there was another, more powerful song which arrived. It filled the gaps left by the islanders' singing; gaps which only became apparent when they had been filled and completed and it made them into something better, more encompassing. It meshed seamlessly with the first song and laid a road of sound for the two listeners and they, unknowing, slid along it, hurtling toward a target they did not know existed. As they slid, so they felt pinpricks in their minds. It was the same 'knowing' they had experienced when they first realized they could locate any of the islanders. Only, this time, it was not the islanders they were locating. This time, there was a greater distance involved. But they knew they were moving towards those pinpoints at speed, because of the way they grew larger, more certain in their heads. And the speed increased and the pinpoints grew larger.

9

NEWGRANGE

K ris was hunkered down in his hideout listening to the staccato bursts of small arms fire and soldiers shouting. It sounded far enough away to be coming from Newgrange. The entrance to his shelter was covered by bushes. The space he was curled up in was provided by two rocks leaning together forming a small space with a low ceiling. He had scraped a small depression in the earth to give himself a little more room, and had piled the dirt into a small bank closer to the entrance which, he hoped, would make it harder for any casual observer to see inside. He supposed that they were firing into the homes down in Newgrange to see if anyone came running out. He doubted they would be killing the animals.

Finally, the shooting stopped and he could make out more voices shouting and animals complaining. From what little he could see outside and from what his stomach was telling him, he had been hiding for about a full day. He wriggled around to make it possible to take a sip of water from a leather bottle and broke off a small piece of dried meat to chew on. He thought he could probably make the food and drink last for another day if he was really careful. That had to be long enough! They wouldn't spend more time than they had to looking for any people. And, if they were all as well hidden as he was, then the soldiers down there in what was left of Newgrange would give up and go. The tension of waiting and not being able to move had eased after hearing their arrival. Knowing that what they had all feared had finally arrived was, in a strange way, a relief. He stayed awake as long as he could, but exhaustion finally made him sleepy.

Some time later he awoke feeling guilty at not bearing witness to every noise which pointed to the destruction of his community. He realized that he had woken because a current of air had carried the smell of distant smoke with it. He closed his eyes, knowing that all that hard work, all those hours and hours of dedication were being destroyed.

The smell of smoke finally began to fade. Kris began to doze again but a shout nearby caused him to try to sit up suddenly so that he cracked his head hard on the rock above him. Gritting his teeth against the pain he tried to focus on what was happening outside. From the sounds, he gathered that some troops were combing the area, calling to each other. It was difficult to know how close they were. Then there was what sounded like a challenge. Voices were raised; shouting and demanding. Kris wasn't sure, but it sounded like Flinder's bass voice responding, the tone of it seemed as though he was pleading. He couldn't hear what was said, but the several shots and the ensuing silence told him enough. He wanted to do something other than nothing, but he lay still, holding his head and trembled in fear and shame.

A little later, the same thing happened again; the shouts, the heartfelt pleas followed by gunfire and silence. And then again. Kris didn't want to identify the voices, didn't want to know who was being murdered. It was enough to know that it was happening. They were taking their time in finding and killing people. He had no idea how anyone else who was listening to this was coping, he knew only that he could not stay inside his shelter and hear these murders taking place. Better to be outside, in the air, seeing the sky and the trees and the mountains than being alone inside this shelter masquerading as a tomb.

Suddenly claustrophobic, sobbing wordless sounds of misery and anguish, he clawed the earth away, ignoring broken nails and torn flesh to grab the bushes and heave at them until their roots broke free of the soil and he could hurl them from him and stand upright.

As he did so, he heard a sound unlike anything he had ever heard before: stranger than anything he had heard, but not frightening. It sounded like a chorus of voices or some strange instruments being played. But it was unlike any song he had ever heard. The sounds it made held him fast and filled him, somehow, with hope.

He was standing in the open on a rock-strewn slope, surrounded by trees, looking down toward the small and now smoldering ruins of Newgrange. Away to his right and downslope from his position he could just make out some troops moving slowly through the trees. A short way to his left there was a wide, empty space created by a forest fire which had been started by a lightning strike some years before. The sound seemed to be coming from there. He made a tremendous effort to turn, feeling a prickling in his back, expecting to be shot. He turned his head enough to see that there appeared to be a shimmering glow forming in the center of the clearing which grew in solidity at the same time as the strange sounds grew louder.

He was unable to tear his eyes away from what was happening. Slowly, the sound grew louder and clearer until it rang like a bell within him. The shimmer became more solid; the glowing transparency giving way to something more like glass. Inside Kris could see the outlines of two figures becoming more defined until, with an abruptness that was almost painful, the sound stopped, leaving an emptiness in the world. The silence was the reverse of the sound; just as intense and just as all-encompassing. With the silence, the not-quite-glass vanished and the two figures inside it became real human beings; breathing, moving, looking around. A man and a woman, dressed strangely in some sort of dull-colored cloth, barefoot, and with what looked like matching large necklaces. The man had cloth around his head to keep his hair out of his eyes. They were half-facing away from him but he could see that they looked puzzled, frightened almost and clutching each other's hands as if unwilling to be alone.

He felt that the silence around them lasted longer than he would have thought possible as the two newcomers exchanged glances, pointed at something, looked up, then had a short conversation which appeared to consist of the man reassuring the woman about something after which they seemed to come to a decision. With a curt nod to each other, an exchange of tight, nervous smiles, they began to peer around them as if trying to locate something. They didn't notice Kris at first but they eventually turned toward him and appeared uncertain what to do next. Then the woman, who, Kris noticed (surprising himself with the level of detail he could perceive as if that one sense was overcompensating), had long red hair, some of which was gathered back from her face by a fancy braid which ran from above her left temple to end behind her right ear. She gripped her partner's hand tightly with hers which had short, neat nails and some green stains on the knuckles, and she moved toward him. They both seemed oblivious to any discomfort from having bare feet, as the man was a step behind at first but then they were both striding easily across the space until they stopped a short distance in front of him.

When she spoke, it sounded like a dialect, in that he almost understood every word she said, but had to concentrate very hard to make any sense of it. The shock and suddenness of it all had apparently taken away some of his thought processes. He knew only that he didn't know what the woman had said. He shook his head dully to indicate his lack of comprehension. The man spoke instead, and his words were more intelligible but still with a strange accent to them.

"We're here to find the ones who can hear the songs. I'm sorry if we frightened you."

Kris had no idea what they were talking about. It was all he could do to breathe.

The man's brow wrinkled as he peered over Kris's shoulder. "What are those people doing?"

Finally, as if some elastic restraint inside him had snapped, Kris found himself able to move. He turned in the direction the man was looking and saw the troops. They were still moving uphill with their weapons held in threatening postures.

Seeing them, Kris pushed at the man. "You have to get away! They will kill you both. They're killing all of us." He pushed again but the man seemed not to notice. "You have to go. Now!"

Finally, the man seemed to become aware of Kris pushing at him and shouting. He took one long look at the approaching troops before taking a step back and gazing fiercely into the woman's eyes and whispering something. She held his gaze and nodded curtly when he stepped back and said, "I think we can hold them up for a while. Yes?"

If Kris thought their arrival had been strange, it was nothing compared to what happened next. The two newcomers closed their eyes and began to... he wasn't quite sure what to call it, but he supposed that the word 'sing' was the closest. But that wasn't the strangest thing. As they began, what he had originally thought were necklaces unwound and arched up until they formed a straight line from the back of the necks pointing at the sky. But then those necklaces (which were really creatures with small heads and tiny eyes, he noticed) also began making a strange noise, utterly unlike anything he had ever heard of. It raised the hairs on the back of his neck and he felt something invisible move past him, rushing away toward the troops.

Kris didn't know if it was safe to move or not, and didn't dare to look behind him until the noise, the sounds or whatever it was faded away. The necklace creatures collapsed and wound themselves back around the necks of the two strangers and the man, looking over Kris's shoulder again, appeared satisfied. Kris took that as a sign that it was safe now and he turned to see what had happened. The troops were still there, but were not moving. It was as if they were statues, held in place somehow.

It was Kris's turn to be jostled. The man, when Kris could get his bearings again, was saying, "It won't last for ever. We are not killers. But they are slowed. If you are still here when it stops, they will still kill you. Do you understand? You have to leave while you can!" The man's dark features saddened as he looked at Kris. "I'm sorry we can't do more, but we have to find them." And, with that, the two of them turned and hurried away.

Kris only realized he was shaking when he tried to move after them. His legs didn't work that well and he stumbled and fell on all fours. The logical part of his mind was yelling at him that he was in shock and needed to rest and drink some water. The survival part was urging him to get up and get moving. But the shocked part was having trouble taking in everything which had happened and wanted nothing more than to sit and not think. With these conflicting demands pulling at him, Kris struggled to get to his feet again. Unable to decide rationally what to do next, the most basic, primal aspect of him kicked in and forced his limbs into motion, away from the present danger. So he stumbled and ran like a drunken fool, bouncing off trees, ignoring the whip of branches on his face and the pain from stubbed toes and bruised knees until he could run no more. Sobbing from the effort and the shock, his legs buckled beneath him and he sank to the ground, numb to everything around him.

As the road of sound enfolding Javin and Meldren came to an end, both of them were aware that the scenery had changed. They were no longer where they had started from. That, in itself, was not a cause for concern so much as everything felt... not wrong, but... different. They were in a clearing. Meldren looked around, disoriented, but was caught by the sight of what was growing around the edges of the space they were in. She pointed questioningly at them. Javin nodded and said, "I see them. The trees. The trees we all saw in our dreams. I recognize them. That means we must be on Haven! Haven? But how? Why?"

"Haven?" echoed Meldren. "Not Harmony? Really?" her eyes wide.

"Yes. It feels different here. *I* feel different here. But it's how I remember it. The air's different. Look at the sun. It's bigger, like I remember it." Meldren's eyes widened still further as she looked up. "We must be here for a reason. There must be people here for us to find," Javin guessed. "I assume you've got the same feeling of the direction they are in as me?" She nodded, still staring around, trying to take it all in. The ground at her feet had worn, pink-grey boulders peeking through the earth, not the familiar dark grey ones of the island. "Then I suppose we'd better get going and find them."

Before he could do anything, however, Meldren grabbed his hand, squeezed it and indicated a direction with her head. Javin turned and saw the man standing just at the edge of the clearing, staring at them. The trees were spaced haphazardly but close enough together to make it hard to see into the depths of the forest. Javin didn't know what to do, but Meldren held on to his hand tightly and walked towards the man. At that moment, Javin fell in love with her all over again. In a strange place after the strangest of journeys, here she was determined, direct, unfazed by it all, apparently. He was amazed at her fearlessness and her beauty. He jogged a little to match her stride and they stopped in front

of the man, who seemed too shocked to do much more than gape at
them.

"We have to find some people. The ones who can hear the songs. I
don't know who they are, but is there a quick way to get to them? Yes?"
Meldren spoke urgently.

The man seemed incapable of understanding at first, so Javin
repeated it for him and added an apology for frightening him. That was
when he saw the movement further away, deeper within the trees
slightly downhill from their position. He saw people in uniforms,
carrying weapons. He had no idea how many there might be, but there
were enough of them to make him concerned. His staring at them made
the man turn. At first, the other man didn't see anything, but then it was
obvious that he had spotted them as well, for he became very agitated,
pushing and shoving at them both and telling them to run away. "They
will kill you both," he kept saying.

Javin could recognize soldiers when he saw them, but Meldren was
still dealing with the new surroundings. He recognized the danger. He
was also aware that he didn't feel frightened. It was more an
exhilaration, a sense of being fully alive which left no room for fear.
Seeing them, still feeling the beacons in his head, Javin suddenly found
that he knew exactly what to do. Maybe it was because of his state of
exhilaration or maybe it was from some other source beyond him, but he
knew. He leaned in close, to get her full attention and whispered, "There
are people coming to kill us. I don't believe we would have been sent
here to be killed, so let's slow them down, like Harmony did to hide from
those ships."

Perhaps it was the matter-of-fact way in which he spoke or the
implicit trust Meldren had in him which caused her to look at him as if
he was talking about what to eat. But he knew she had understood,
maybe because she had been made aware of the solution in the same
way he had. As he stood back, he said, "I think we can hold them up for
a while. Yes?" And that was it. The agreement, the awareness of what to
do, the joining together, the act of singing -- it all came together in an
instant. Somewhere inside them, or in Haven or the sprites, there was the
knowledge of what to do, how to sing, what to sing. And so they began,
and they felt their sprites rise up and sing with them, guiding the sounds

to the soldiers to wrap them inside the song and hold them there. It was effortless and beautiful and liberating all at the same time.

When they had finished, and they knew when that was because it felt perfect to end at that point, Javin grabbed the man and tried to shake him into hearing what he had to say. He kept telling him that they had slowed the soldiers down, not killed them and that the man should leave right now if he wanted to survive after the song had died away.

Without waiting to see if the man acted on his words or not, Javin took Meldren's hand again, grinned at the excited glint in her eyes, said, "He's not going to help us find them," and they took off in the direction of the nearest pinpoint in their heads. They half ran, half walked through the woods, homing in on the nearest beacon that was calling to them inside their minds.

As they jogged along, Meldren said, "I don't know how we got here, but we did. Do you think the islanders are still singing? I can't hear the song anymore. Does that mean that we are we going to have to stay here?"

Ducking under a branch, Javin said, "I don't think so. But I have to believe that if Harmony sent us here, then She will look after us and get us back somehow. At least, that's what I want to believe."

"Then what do we say to these people, the ones we're heading towards? If we don't know if we're going back, what's the point of us being here?"

Javin came skidding to a halt. "That's it! You're right! What *is* the point of us being here if not to help these people? And that means we *have* to be going back to Harmony."

He began to jog again, catching up to Meldren. "How long do you think we have to find them, assuming we know what it is we are meant to do?"

"Well, we did know what to do with those soldiers back there, didn't we? That came from somewhere that wasn't me. So perhaps it's safe to assume that it'll be the same for helping these people."

"Let's hope so." She continued a pace or two. "What are soldiers, anyway?"

"People who are trained to obey orders and to fight other people, basically. There's more to it, but that's all you need to know right now."

Meldren jogged on again a little way in silence. "That's just silly, isn't it? And they agree to that?"

From Meldren's point of view, it did look very silly indeed, Javin realized. He also realized that, after being away from Haven for so long, the idea seemed less than sensible to him as well. "Yes. But that's what they are. And there may be more of them near here." Javin slowed down to get his internal bearings. He pointed to a large jumble of boulders that could be seen in amongst the trees ahead. "I get that's the nearest one. How about you?"

She closed her eyes to check on what she sensed and then nodded. They approached the boulders but could see no sign of anyone. They stopped and looked around. "But they have to be here!" said Meldren.

Javin circled the boulders. "Hello! Anyone here?"

"This has to be the place. Unless something has gone very wrong. Where is everyone?"

As Meldren spoke, there was a rustle of greenery to one side of the pile and a small head poked out and smiled at her. It was a young girl, much younger than Isselta, thought Javin. The child scrambled out, stopping half way to turn back and speak to someone else. "It's the people who have come for me. I have to go with them. They need me." Then she was standing up and smiling at Javin. "My name is Pol. What's yours?"

"Javin," he said, surprised at the sudden appearance. "And, and, and that's Meldren," he added, pointing toward her as she came from behind the rocks. Meldren paused, a startled look on her face, as she saw how young Pol was.

Pol didn't seem to notice. Instead she tugged at Javin's hand saying, "We have to hurry up now. I know where the others are. But I can't run as fast as you, so you'll have to carry me." And she reached up her arms to him who, still coming to terms with Pol's appearance, scooped her up and balanced her on his hip. "That way," said Pol, pointing across the slope. "That's where Endel is. He's quiet, not like the others, but he's closest." She bounced up and down to urge Javin into motion. "Come on! Hurry up!"

"But what about these people?" Meldren pointed at the man and woman who had, by now, also come out of hiding and were standing there looking just as confused as Meldren. "Are they your parents?"

"We have to go!" said Pol urgently.

The man, probably Pol's father, thought Javin, had a look he could not decipher. "She's Pol, our daughter. And you are?"

"I'm Javin and this is Meldren. We had no idea we were looking for your daughter. We are not going to harm her."

The man's eyes were filling with tears and he reached out blindly to find his wife's hand. "She's been talking all the time about two people coming for her. We didn't know what she meant. And then, well, here you both are." He drew his wife closer to hug her, trying to control his breathing, fighting back his tears. "Pol is... I don't know the word. She's a special girl and can do things and see things we don't understand, but she's always been right when she said something is going to happen. You'll take very good care of her, won't you?"

"But what about you?" said Meldren. "Can't you come?" But the answer was already in Javin's head.

The man shook his head. "No. We will stay. I believe that Pol will come back. We have to wait here. We have to hide and wait." He reached out to the girl: a delicate, tender gesture of love and farewell. "You be good now, won't you? Look after yourself. We'll be here, waiting for you, when you get back." The mother could no longer restrain herself and rushed to give Pol a tearful kiss and a hug. Whispering, 'we'll miss you,' she returned to her husband and strained to hold back more tears as she sought comfort in his embrace.

Pol watched them, her head cocked to one side, as if she was assessing them for some value, some hidden meaning. Then she waved a hand at them and a smile flicked on and off. "You need to hide now. They're coming again." Then she urged Javin to move by swinging her legs as if riding.

Javin was reluctant to leave, but with Pol urging him and her parents apparently knowing about this before, he looked for reassurance from Meldren, who, tears streaking her cheeks, gestured her helplessness.

"We promise we will do everything we can to look after Pol and bring her back safely," said Javin as he turned away.

"Why does she need to go with you? Why do you need her?" her mother cried out. They were the questions Javin had hoped would not be asked.

He turned back, despite Pol's urgings. The woman deserved an explanation. It was the least he could do for her. He tried to keep his voice calm and reassuring. "We know that your little girl is very special and that, because of it, she needs some special training that she can't get from anyone here. We're going to be teaching her how to use the gifts she already has and then she can come back here again and help a lot of people." It sounded almost plausible as he spoke, and he wasn't sure where the words came from, but he hoped that she would not want more details. The stress he felt erased them from his mind as soon as they were uttered. True or not, what he said seemed to give some ease. The woman's face creased into a watery smile and she bobbed her head in thanks and turned to bury her head in her husband's chest. He looked out over her head and mouthed, 'keep her safe' at Javin, who nodded grimly.

Without waiting to see whether they went back into hiding, Javin, Meldren and Pol left in the direction Pol had indicated.

"This is definitely not turning out how I thought it would," said Meldren, wiping at her tears.

"Do you think all the others will be as young as this one?"

"My name is Pol, and all the others are older than me," the child said as she bounced along. "You'll see. Endel will be waiting for us and then you'll see."

They continued through the forest, having to make occasional detours to avoid denser stands of trees, until Pol pointed. "There's Endel."

If Javin and Meldren were expecting an adult from what Pol had said, they were surprised when they saw that Endel turned out to be a young boy. He was standing in a stray patch of sunlight. Coming up to him, they looked round for his parents. "They are hiding. They are not my parents. They know I have to go with you," the boy said. That was all he said.

Pol pointed in a new direction. "That way. Next is Bodren. He's a boy, like Endel."

"Another boy?" said Meldren, holding on to Endel's hand. "Are they all children and you're the youngest?"

"Yes," said Pol. "And we have to hurry up, because the others are coming to find us."

"Do you mean the soldiers", asked Javin. "We slowed those down before we found you."

"More soldiers. The ones coming from the village, after they gathered up the animals. They're coming. We have to hurry."

Javin and Meldren exchanged harried looks and set off again to find this Bodren. Again, when they arrived, he was waiting for them. His parents and, presumably, his brother were with him. The same anxious, scared faces as before and the same hasty and insufficient explanations and reassurances were said, and off they went again. This time it was to find Pelle and, after her, Hanna where it was all repeated.

It was slower to get to the last two, because Meldren had to keep shepherding the boys and hurrying them along, helping them over fallen trees, and holding branches aside for them. As they neared where Hanna was, they could make out shouts and explosions coming from somewhere behind them, a little downhill from their position but closing quickly it seemed. Javin hoped fervently that it was simply scare tactics and that nobody was actually getting hurt, but he had a bad feeling. None of the children seemed to be that concerned about it.

"That's the last one. Now what?" Meldren asked Javin after collecting Hanna and hearing the heart-wrenching farewells of her parents. They had kept moving away from the sounds of the soldiers behind them. They were standing on a slope leading down to a small, lively stream. Obviously this was a fold in the hillside cutting across their line of progress and going down would be easier on everyone. Looking back the way they had come, they had been, he now realized, moving steadily uphill throughout the time they had collected the children. But going down was to go nearer to the soldiers. He wanted to get back into the deeper part of the forest from where they had just come and be out of sight. Seeing the sky above him did not make him feel homesick. It made him feel vulnerable.

"We have to get back to Harmony."

"I know! But how? We can't go back to the clearing we arrived in.

There are too many soldiers now. We'd never make it. Not with the children. Plus, I don't know where it is anyway. What do we do?" Meldren's voice rose sharply.

He looked around for inspiration. "All I feel is we have to be together, be able to hold hands. We can't do that here." He saw Meldren nodding in agreement. He wondered whether they should follow the stream uphill, or cross it somehow to the trees on the other bank which would take time and make them too visible for too long. He could not decide. The weight of responsibility for the children pinned him down.

In desperation, Javin asked Pol because the little girl had seemed to know what to do before. "Where do we go now, Pol? Where's the next place we go? We have to get somewhere safe. Do you know where?"

Pol shook her head, her lower lip jutting out to make her lack of knowledge clear. But Endel reached out and tugged down on Meldren's hand. She looked down at the serious young face as he pointed to follow the bank uphill and pulled at her to follow him. Meldren looked to Javin and raised her brows, and shrugged as if to say, *what do we have to lose?*. So, the little group of children and adults followed along behind Endel. It was hard scrabbling up the slope, avoiding the loose rocks and slippery tussocks of grass, but the ground to their left finally flattened and the trees offered a welcoming gloom once more. They kept winding their way between trees, scrambling over rocks and trying hard to ignore the sounds of weaponry which seemed to be getting nearer as Endel led them ever onwards.

Just when Javin thought that they were never going to find a place that would serve them, they stepped out from the sun-speckled ground into bright, unblocked sunlight. The reason for this space was clear. There was a single, very large boulder, looking like it had in the far past rolled down from the mountain and sunk in the ground, pushing up a thin wall of earth on the downslope. It had obviously displaced much more, as there was scant vegetation growing around it and the trees uphill from it were thinned by its passage through them. The lack of space around it and the shape of it was such that it forced them to scramble up and occupy various small ledges and flat surfaces and still be able to be within arms' reach of each other. Meldren screwed her face in pain briefly as she missed her footing and slid for a space, grazing her shin, before she was able to stop herself.

Javin did a swift headcount to reassure himself that nobody had been lost. The crackling ripple of gunfire and something more destructive appeared to be getting nearer. Perhaps, he thought, they were being tracked in some fashion. That didn't explain the shooting necessarily, and it wasn't something he wanted to dwell on. Breathing heavily from the exertion and the stress, he made a *'what-now'* face at Meldren. She had regained her composure by now, thought for a moment and appeared to have an idea.

"We have to listen to the same song that brought us here. That must to be the way we go back, mustn't it?"

"But what about the children? Can they do that or do we simply hold on to them, or what?"

Having come to a decision, Meldren seemed more determined. "I don't know, Javin. All I am sure of is that if Harmony sent us here and she wants these children, then She'll find a way to do exactly that. We can only do what we feel is right. And that is hearing the song." She had to raise her voice slightly as the firing came closer. "We don't have any choice. There's no time for anything else, is there?"

Javin heard the truth of her words and tried to calm his breathing enough to focus on the sound he was searching for. He found it hard to do. He thought briefly of what would happen when the soldiers found them, but that thought was disrupted by a soft hand on his shoulder. Turning, he saw that it was one of the other girls -- Hanna? Pelle? -- looking at him with a gentle smile on her face as if there was nothing to be concerned about.

"We can all hear you both very clearly. If you hear what you need to, we will all hear it as well. Don't worry. We'll be safe for long enough. You can do it."

Hearing this maturity, this careful reassurance, given in such a young voice calmed him down. He made a thin, brisk smile of thanks at the girl, gripped her hand in appreciation and took a deep breath to begin the focus he required. Nearby, Meldren was doing the same and, together, they listened for the complex note or chord or sound they knew only as Harmony. As they did so, both felt their hands being taken by the children so that they all formed a ragged circle. Something flowed into the adults, something that felt like peace and strength combined. As they felt it first in their hands, and then as it flowed to their hearts, so they heard the song and felt the whirlpool begin to form around them. Now the song was stronger and the whirlpool clearer, stretching out, encompassing them all. Again, they felt movement, speed and distance as the sounds of gunfire faded. The road they had traveled before, laid before them by that richer, more glorious voice, unrolled before them again. Soon they began to hear the islanders' voices again, becoming clearer and clearer until, with a gentleness which hid a vast strength, the other, richer voice, faded away, and only the islanders' voices remained and the whirlpool began to disintegrate around them once more.

Javin opened his eyes to see Isselta standing there, a look of amazement on her face. "That's not possible!"

"Actually," he said, "it is. And it's not much fun at all." Then he slumped to his knees; the fast receding adrenaline surge leaving him empty and weak, and he emptied his stomach. Meldren urged the children toward the islanders wordlessly before she too sank to the ground, breathing heavily before she, too, vomited.

10

THE SLEEPER

Meldren woke the next day, feeling tired and muzzy-headed and with no recollection of when she had fallen into bed. She tried to decide whether or not the previous day had actually happened. Javin lay snoring lustily beside her, sprawled out on top of the blanket, fully dressed. She realized she was also still wearing her clothes. They felt uncomfortable now. She swung her legs out, sat on the edge of the bed, and looked down at her shin to see the scab and the bruising from the rock. Patting around it tenderly to find the extent of the damage, she had to admit to herself that it had all happened. But then a thought struck her and she whipped her head round and shook Javin awake. Grunting and rubbing his eyes, he tried to focus, squinting his eyes at Meldren. "The children? Where are they? Who's looking after them? Do you know? I can't remember anything from when we got back."

Javin struggled to sit up and scrubbed his face with his hands, his voice still husky from sleep. "They must be with the islanders, mustn't they? I think I remember Carmeena and Allegara talking to them. We'd better go and find them, I suppose. We're responsible for them."

They gulped some water down after splashing their faces and waited for their sprites to settle themselves. They were heading out when Javin put his hand on Meldren's arm then he tapped his head. "Slow down! We were able to find them before by what was in our head. We should try that now, shouldn't we?"

Meldren shook her head in disbelief at not thinking of this herself. She closed her eyes and felt for the pinpoints that were the children. First, she found the islanders mapped out in her head, but then she went past those, deeper inside her head, and located the children; brighter, sharper but smaller somehow than the islanders. She realized that these bright spots were spread out. Calling up the islanders again, she realized that the two sets were together. Obviously, some time after she and Javin had arrived, the two groups had got together and left them both alone. She made sure that she checked on them all, counting the pinpoints twice to be certain, before waiting for Javin to finish his own search.

"They all seem to be here, and they all seem to be with the islanders, from what I can tell. How about you?"

"Yes, that's what I saw as well."

Meldren gave a huge sigh of relief and slumped down thankfully on the doorstep, suddenly weak from relief. "Well, at least we don't have to worry about them for a moment. But we should go and see them very soon."

Javin joined her on the ground. "I agree. But, I think we could do with something to eat first. I am starving. It feels like I haven't eaten for days and days. My stomach's empty."

"Hmmm. That's not that surprising, is it?"

Javin looked puzzled for a moment before his memory kicked in and a scowl spread across his face. "Oh! Yes. The vomiting. What fun that was!"

Later, after a quiet breakfast of freshly harvested fruits and some dried meats -- quiet because they still felt tired and slow -- they were walking towards where Carmeena lived, as that was the closest of the pinpoints. As they walked, they tried to come to terms with what exactly had happened the day before.

"We really went to another planet, didn't we? And we went there because of the songs being sung?" Meldren made a sweeping gesture with her hand as if to dismiss this impossibility. "How can that even happen? And what happened here when we were there? Did all the islanders keep singing for the whole time we were there? There are so many questions about this. You do realize that we've kidnapped children and brought them here and I don't know why. I can't explain it. But it needs explaining because it's a very wrong thing to do by itself." She felt herself beginning to panic.

"I know I'm going to have to live with the looks on their parents' faces for the rest of my life," Javin said quietly, making her relive those moments as well, taking her attention away from her panic. "So I think we had better find out what we were sent to do and do it well so that we can take these children back to their families as soon as we can. I made promises to them that I have no way of knowing how to keep. I don't feel good about myself, either. There has to be more to this than kidnapping. Harmony must have a larger plan. If only we could see what it was."

"Are we bad people?" Meldren asked, trying to shake off her feelings of guilt.

Javin gave a slow shake of his head. "I don't think so. It's not like we planned any of it. But to those parents, the people we left? Maybe we are bad."

"We've always trusted that what Harmony wanted was good, haven't we?" she persisted. "What if we're wrong about that? What if this is nothing more than a game to Her? What if we've been tricked all along and She only wanted to see if we would obey Her?"

"I can't believe that. It would mean that everything we've felt, all the things we've sensed, everything was wrong. And it didn't and it doesn't feel that way." He made slashing motions of denial as he spoke.

Meldren found herself wanting to agree with him. But these children? The islanders were welcome to come or go. But the children now here meant responsibilities of a whole different order.

They walked on a little way in silence. "Javin, do you think those -- what was the word? -- those soldiers killed their families? There was a lot of shouting and loud noises. It didn't sound good."

"I don't know. I really don't know. We know that they were good at hiding, but maybe the soldiers had equipment to help find them somehow. I wish I knew for certain. It must have been awful -- no, unspeakable -- to have to say goodbye to your child and watch him or her leave with strangers." He looked at Meldren with haunted eyes. "That love and hope and trust has to be repaid. It has to."

Meldren reached for his hand to squeeze it. "We'll do all we can, you know that. And Harmony has to help. You're right about Her, I know. It's the scale of what we're involved in that made me think like that." Javin hugged her to his hip as they walked. "I'm sure She will make it clear what we have to do," she continued. "After all, this is happening because She started it by telling us to find the islanders. She's got to have a say in what's going on."

"I agree."

"Then there's the children themselves."

"What do you mean?"

"I haven't been around that many children, but I was one once. And I know that how they reacted was not anything like I would have if I had been in their shoes. They're all so serious! I would have been screaming and crying. But not them. It was as though they all knew what was going to happen before we did and they weren't bothered by it at all. I'm fairly sure that they are not going to be small, scared little things. I mean, even the youngest, the first little girl we found, even she was so certain about everything. I'm willing to bet a whole year's weeding on the fact that whatever this is all about, they already know about it."

Javin gave a rueful smile. "Then I can only wish that we knew as much as they did."

"I have enough problems accepting the fact that we were on another planet, there and back, in one day." said Meldren.

"'Same here, and I'm not completely sure that I like the after effects."

"If it *was* yesterday. For all we know, we could have been asleep for two or three days."

"True enough. But sleeping is certainly better than feeling like the inside of my head has been hammered flat, or hammered flat *and* then throwing up," he said.

Carmeena and Hanna sat outside, eyes shut against the sun, leaning back against the wall, enjoying the warmth, as if they had not a care in the world. As Javin and Meldren approached, Carmeena, without opening her eyes, said, "We've been waiting for you and enjoying the sun. Hanna here also enjoyed seeing the moon last night. She enjoyed it a lot, for a very long time indeed." Then she gave a jaw-cracking yawn. Hanna opened her eyes and leaned in to whisper something to

Carmeena, but the woman flapped a hand at her and said, "You ask them."

The girl peered shyly up at Meldren and asked, "Can I have one of those little animals around your necks? Like Carmeena has?"

Meldren squatted down by her, grateful to see how calm she was. "I'm sorry, I've forgotten your name."

"Hanna," said the girl.

"The answer to your question, Hanna, is that I really don't know. Nobody here is sure where they come from or how they got theirs." She stroked hers gently, remembering. "I woke up one day and it was around my neck. Javin here, he found his in a tree. One of Harmony's trees. Carmeena, I think you found yours on your bed, didn't you?" The woman, eyes still closed, nodded. "What it means is that they seem to turn up and get found, one way or another. So, the answer to your question is definitely maybe."

The girl seemed to consider that a moment. "So why *are* we here, then? I know something is meant to happen, but I don't know what."

Meldren and Javin exchanged relieved smiles. "That's exactly what we want to find out as well. We were talking about it on the way over here. All we know is that we were sent to you to find the ones who could hear the songs. That's what we were told, anyway. But... you're not scared or want to talk about anything which happened yesterday? I mean, here you are on a different planet, far, far away from your home. Is there anything we can do to help you? It must be a shock, surely? You do know you're not on Haven anymore?"

Hanna thought for a moment before giving a firm shake of her head. "I know. No, I like this place. It has really nice sounds. They're different from the ones I was used to. But I like them just as much. The moon sounds really, really nice. And the night is so much longer here. And the days."

Meldren's eyes widened at these words. "You can hear the sounds easily?"

"Oh, yes," came the swift reply. "I've always been able to hear them. The animals were always the clearest to me, but, if tried hard, I could hear other things. But here, it's all much easier to listen to them."

Carmeena finally gave up on dozing and gave a short bark of a laugh.

"You should have heard what she was telling me she could hear last night. And I thought I was beginning to be better at it. And then she... ." Her words tailed off and she shook her head in disbelief.

"I think," said Meldren carefully, "that one of the reasons you're here is to learn what to do with the songs. That's what everyone here is learning as well. It's one thing to hear the songs, it's another thing to understand them. Maybe there will be other things as well, but that's probably a good place to start. But are you sure that you are not worried about being here, on a different planet? Away from your parents?"

"I think it will be fine," said Hanna, in a very considered way, much as an adult would respond politely to being asked if there was enough to eat on a table overflowing with food.

"Is there anything we can do to help?" Meldren was looking at Hanna but it was Carmeena who answered.

"Yes! Tell her that the moon will be there again tonight and the night after that, and the night after that, and that I, at least, need to sleep more than a half span at a time."

Hanna and Meldren exchanged guilty grins. "But it is pretty. And it has a beautiful song. But I will try to let Carmeena sleep tonight."

"I'm sure you will, Hanna. And Carmeena will be very grateful, won't you?" Meldren couldn't stop grinning.

Carmeena's face twisted into a 'I'll believe that when it happens' look, but then nodded slowly to negate it and ended up reaching around to give Hanna a reassuring pat on her leg.

"Is there anything we can do for you both? Have you enough food, for instance?"

"We'll be fine, thank you," said Carmeena, stifling a yawn. "With enough sleep I can cope with anything."

Making their way to the next home, that of Enrick, Meldren said, "See what I mean about her? Not a bit worried about what's happened. All she's interested in is the moon."

"That and what she's here for," said Javin. "For all we know, she's keeping all her emotions bottled up and can't or won't let them out yet." He jerked a thumb back over his shoulder. "Right now, she could be having a screaming fit." He looked back over his shoulder at the home. "Well, a quiet screaming fit, but you know what I mean."

"You don't believe that any more than I do, Javin. Besides, if anyone's going to have the screaming fit, it's going to be Carmeena."

The two of them walked past where Farran lived, knowing from their internal map that there was no child with him. "I'm not sure whether to be sorry for him or not," said Meldren. "He was always lonely, had that very lonely feel to him. It's in his song all the time. But I can't help wondering whether having one of these children might not have helped him somehow."

"Perhaps it was that very song that is a part of him which made it so that he would not have one. Maybe it would have made him feel even more lonely."

They continued on their way to where Isselta lived. Meldren had already half-guessed who would be there, and when the small, blonde-haired child waved at them from the doorway, she knew she was right. "What's her name, again?" asked Meldren quietly.

Javin had to think a moment. "Pol, I think?"

They approached the home where Isselta was pouring out some water for them all. Meldren saw that she was smiling, a wide, genuine, happy smile, the like of which had rarely settled on the girl's face. '*At least, that's an improvement*,' she thought. The bruised look was fading more and more.

"Hello! How are you Pol? And Isselta? Is everything fine? Can we help in any way?"

Pol also had a wide smile which filled her eyes and bunched her cheeks and lit her whole face up such that her happiness radiated out from her, engulfing anyone close by. You could not fail to be affected by it. "The moon is beautiful! And the flowers have lovely songs as well, don't they? Do you like the songs they make? I do. Even the tables have songs here! Much more than at home." The words tumbled from her.

Javin squatted down to be at Pol's level. "When I first saw the moon, I really liked it a lot, just like you. I was born on Haven, same as you, so it was a big surprise for me as well. It is beautiful, isn't it?" They began chatting and exchanging flowers and stones and talking about the sounds they each made.

Meldren took the water Isselta offered and drank it gratefully, for the day was becoming warmer. She was feeling better now that she had seen how the first two children were reacting to their new places. She still felt both responsible and guilty but her panic had lessened. She asked, "How are you two coping?" already sure of the answer.

Isselta looked just as happy as Pol, eyes twinkling over the rim of her mug. She put it aside. "She's amazing! We've been getting each other to listen to our favorite songs. She's right about the table! I never even thought that it would have much of a song, but she knew it straight away. And she really has fallen in love with the moon. Again, I never thought to actually listen to it. I knew it was there in the sky, but seeing it and hearing it are two totally different things."

Meldren smiled at her enthusiasm. "It sounds like you are doing just fine together. Is there anything Javin or I can do for you? We're going round to visit all of the children. We should have done more when we got back, but... well, we were exhausted."

"You looked it! We split the children up between us because you looked so awful. Sorry, but you did, what with the throwing up as well. We did it without much thinking and you two sort of trailed off on your own, looking as though you were already asleep. Well, we did make sure you got back safely. But," she grinned excitedly at Meldren, "did it really happen? The two of you going to another planet? What was it like? You'll have to tell us all about it, you know. You can't keep that sort of thing to yourselves. Especially as we all had a part in it."

"I meant to ask you about that," said Meldren checking to see that Javin and Pol were still entertaining each other. "Did all of you keep singing for the whole time we were gone? I mean, what happened here?"

"The sprites did a great deal of it, to be honest. At first, it felt like there was something else taking us over. I'm not sure how it was for others, but for me, it felt like I had the most amazing energy. Powerful: that's how it felt, but it wasn't my power. And the sprites kept up the song all the time. After you two disappeared, which was most definitely an interesting thing to see, by the way, we all kept up singing for a while but it was too hard to keep doing it that loud for long. Not for the sprites though. They kept up the song, even when we were trying to eat! We took it in turns to have breaks for food and drink and so on. And then, later on, the sprites started making more noise and we began to join in again. Then we got louder, like at the beginning and -- whoosh! -- you two came back again." Isselta became more serious for a moment. "I just realized something. None of us thought any of it was strange until you both came back. The whole time you weren't here, with the sprites singing, and us doing nothing, we never thought any of that was strange. Until you came back, that is." She suddenly giggled. "And that is strange, isn't it? The fact that we didn't think it was strange."

Meldren laughed. "I do know exactly what you mean."

"When are you going to tell us about what happened? I've asked Pol, but all she says is that she knew you were coming to get her and the others."

"Has she said anything else?"

Isselta shook her head. "Why?"

"Two things. One, there were people hiding where we ended up. Others were looking for them. Javin said those others were trained to fight, and that they would kill us if they could. I've no idea why, but I believe him. It's his home after all. We were worried that Pol's parents might be found and maybe killed." Isselta shook her head in disbelief, her eyes wide, jaw slack. "Yes. That bad, really. And the second thing is, neither Javin nor I really know what happens next. It's not like any of us have had much of a chance yet to understand, or have a say in what's going on. Obviously, they must be here for a reason, but what that reason is we don't know. Yet."

Isselta was still shocked. "They were killing the parents? I can't believe it."

"Maybe, yes, and I'd like Pol not to think too much about it. Each of the children seems as if they know lots of things which are going to happen. Maybe they do. Maybe not. But, we don't know anything about Pol's parents and I'd like to keep it that way... ?"

"Oh, absolutely! But so far, Pol hasn't mentioned anything about her parents. It's almost as if she has blanked them out of her head. Not like me. I didn't want to think about my father after what he did. But it was hard work keeping him out of my head. He wanted to keep being in my mind a lot. I've got used to it and it's easier for me now, but I still don't spend any time thinking about him. And I don't spend much energy on it either. But, for Pol? It's like they've been shut off so she *can't* think about them. That's the only way I can explain it."

"Hmmm. If I'm honest, I don't know what's best, Isselta. I truly don't. We've brought them here, we have a responsibility to them. But, beyond that... ?" Meldren let the words hang there as she watched Javin giving rides to Pol on his back, running to and fro and making strange noises. She smiled and called out, "What is that strange noise you're making, Javin?"

He lowered Pol to the ground and held her hand. "It's a horse. An animal on Haven. They use them for riding and hauling loads. I was being a horse, wasn't I, Pol?"

"Yes," she piped. "And not a very good one, either. He wasn't doing what he was told." Her smile was clear and she was still radiating happiness. But then, in an abrupt change of mood, she let go of Javin's hand and walked to Meldren and looked up at her with a serious, searching look on her face. "You're meant to teach us things here so we can go back and teach others. But I don't want to go back just yet. I like it here. I like those things round your necks and I like the moon in the sky at night and I like all the new songs I can hear. Can I stay longer?"

Meldren bent down, hands on knees, to look at the little girl. "You can certainly stay here longer. But how do you know that you are here to learn from us? Who told you that?"

Pol gave one of her exaggerated sighs. "Nobody told me. I just know it. Don't you? Don't you know it as well?"

Meldren cocked her head. "I know that we have to do something for you all. Javin and I need to talk about it some more yet to make sure we teach you the right things." She stroked her sprite with one finger of her other hand. "And maybe you'll have one of these for your very own."

Pol jumped up and down excitedly clapping her hands, her mood now switched back to happiness. "Oh, yes! That would be wonderful! Thank you! Thank you!"

"Wait a minute. Don't get too excited," said Meldren, trying to rein the girl in. "I can't say for certain that you will, only that it is possible." But Pol still kept jumping around, grinning and laughing, wrapped in the thought of having her very own sprite.

Meldren turned to Isselta. "So much for helping her. I think she's just helped us out. Now all we need to do is work out what to do. Are you sure there's nothing we can get you for her, or... ?"

Isselta waved away the offer. "We'll be fine. We have enough food and plenty to do. Later on, we'll go and see the others and have a party or something. Go to the beach maybe. We'll be fine."

"Sounds like a good idea. But I don't think Carmeena's going to be too much help. She is missing her sleep. A lot! We'll leave you two to it, then."

"We'll be fine," said Isselta. "Don't worry about us."

So Javin and Meldren set off again to visit all the other children, where the same sort of thing was repeated with minor variations: enjoyment of the new surroundings coupled with a lack of concern or interest about what might have happened back on Haven. Even Endel, who was living with Enrick, looked positively happy, if careful with his words.

By the time they returned to their home, Meldren was a little off balance emotionally. She tried to explain it to Javin when she said, "I don't know how to respond to them. It's like they are in their own worlds and we have no way of understanding them. And they're so young!" She looked worried again.

"Were you able to see anything in their colors when you were with them?"

Meldren tried to think back but shook her head. "I wasn't looking that carefully. I should have been, but everything is crazy. But when I did look I saw nothing out of the ordinary. Their colors seemed very bright, lots of flares around their heads and stomachs when they were speaking about the moon and the songs, but, other than that, nothing that I think might help us." She gave another sigh. "Pol said something about teaching them before going back. But what if they have to go back to be hunted again? And are we both really going to leave them alone back on Haven? If not, does that mean we have to live there as well?" She rubbed her forehead with the heels of her hands. "I don't want to live there, Javin. I know it's your home, but..."

"I don't want to live there, either," he said. "Maybe the children are dealing with everything in a way we can't understand." He put his arm round Meldren's shoulders and she rested her head on his shoulder as they sat watching the sky from their doorstep. "Maybe we're trying to do too much at once. Perhaps what we should be thinking about is what we have to teach them. Why else bring them here if not to help them in some way? And you and I both know that being able to listen to songs, to understand them, is a huge help in so many ways." She nodded. "I say that we should focus on that first and let everything else wait. What do you say?" He kissed the top of her head. "By the way, I like your braid," he whispered.

That caused her to turn and smile gently and kiss him in return. "You're sweet. I also think you're right. But can we figure out the 'what' part of it in the morning? I'm very tired still."

"Of course."

THE TRAINING OF THE CHILDREN STARTED OUT IN A HAPHAZARD FASHION. This was because, despite what Pol had said and what both Javin and Meldren had thought, it wasn't necessarily easy to do.

First it was necessary to understand exactly what the children could already do. That they were precocious was obvious from the beginning. It seemed that they were all naturals, as far as hearing the sounds around them. What became clearer after a time was that they had no idea at all that those self-same songs (as they were learning to call them) were responsible for the world as it was, and that all of those songs came from the same place; from the planet.

Growing up as they had with this skill had left them with a perception of the world which had become normal but which, in turn, had made it difficult for them to see the truth of those same songs in a new way. Isselta described it one day when she was relaxing, watching the ocean and listening to the song of a shoal of fish below the surface song of the ocean, taking a break from looking after Pol. Meldren was beside her, having tried to understand what exactly was going through Pol's head and also taking a breather from the disconcerting directness of the child.

"It's like she's only seen running water in her life and then, one day, she wakes up and there's only ice all around. There's absolutely nothing in the experience of water to get her ready for ice. The two are totally different, but the same thing."

"Ice? What's ice?"

Isselta made a vague gesture, trying to explain something that, to her, was obvious. "Ice is water when it's frozen. Really, really cold. Much colder than it ever gets here. Remember, I came from way away from here where there was snow and ice and not much green. And before you ask, snow is also water but very cold and falls like rain, but in soft, cold flakes that are white and cover everything. Have you ever seen really tall mountains and they have some white at the top?" Meldren made a *maybe* face. "Well, that white stuff is snow because it's cold at the top of mountains. Ice is cold as well but it's hard, solid."

"I've heard the word, but never knew what it was. To me water is the stuff I drink and makes up the ocean. I've been in cold weather, but I've not seen snow falling. So what you're saying is that Pol -- and the others -- can't link the sounds they hear to the idea that they are really songs which can change things."

Isselta nodded. "Exactly. If all they've ever heard is the songs, why would they then think that those songs can be made by something or someone else?"

"But," argued Meldren, trying to make sense of it, "what about when we came back, when you sang us back here? They said they could hear us and that if we heard the sound, they would hear it as well... Oh! I see what you mean! No matter what it did, it was still just a sound. We heard it, so they heard it and it must have come from somewhere they had never listened before; exactly like they talk about how the moon sounds wonderful. It's only another sound. They haven't connected the idea that the moon's song is what is making the moon. They have it the other way round: the moon makes the song."

"I'm sure that's what it is," said Isselta. "So, all you have to do is find a way of making them see things differently. Hear them differently, that is." The two sat in silence for a while, letting the idea percolate. "If you want my suggestion," the girl said, "I'd try what you did with us when we first arrived. Let them hear Harmony as She really is and then sing them something; a flower maybe, or a rock. Anything at all would do. Once they get the idea, there'll be no stopping them, I guarantee it."

"Now *that* is a good idea, Isselta. Why didn't I think of it before?" She grinned at the girl. "The only thing left after that is to work out what

happens next. A minor detail, I'm sure. At least, I hope it will be minor."
Isselta was silent, gazing off again, half-focused, withdrawn, her lively
mind elsewhere. "Are you getting anything about what this is all about?"
Meldren asked. Isselta's face didn't look that much older than Pol's, she
thought. Bigger in body, taller, but still a child herself. But when she
spoke, it was like listening to an adult. Isselta was as precocious in her
own way as Pol, Meldren realized.

It took a moment more before Isselta replied, dragging her gaze and
her focus back to Meldren beside her. "Not a feeling. More like an
understanding of something. Think about it. We have these children
here. They're incredibly talented to begin with but they've been brought
here to learn something else. And then, at some point, they're going to go
back again."

"And... ?" prodded Meldren.

"And everything about them is like they are seeds."

"Seeds?"

"Yes. Seeds. They're small. We take them and give them something;
feed them, if you like. And that knowledge that they gain here has to be
used back there. We put them back and they grow. Meldren, hasn't it
occurred to you that Harmony might be more interested in seeing if what
you and Javin can do, and the rest of us here have learned, can happen
on another planet? Those children, they're the seeds; the ones who are
taking what happens here and growing it somewhere else. They will be
spreading the idea, the songs, the understanding of the planet. What else
would you call it, except seeds?"

Meldren's eyebrows arched in surprise at the idea. "That's certainly
thinking in a bigger way than I was! I was only concerned with getting
them back and what they would do. But your idea, the way you see it... ,"
she sucked in her breath as she thought about it, "that's possible.
Actually, what you've just said reminds me of something that Harmony
spoke of, way, way back before it all became so confusing. I can't
remember the exact things She said -- you know how that is -- but it was
something to do with the Sun's song. But the Sun isn't responsible for
what happens here on Harmony. He's more about *all* the planets, not one.
But Harmony talked as if some song the Sun was singing was going to
be spread, or shared." Her brow furrowed as she tried to recall what she

could of Harmony's visit. "Also I am almost positive She used the word 'seed' or 'seeds'. And here you are using the same word about these children. I don't believe in coincidences like that. There is always a reason." She hugged her knees to her as she, in turn, gazed out. "Ice and seeds. I shall have to tell Javin."

ONCE ISSELTA'S IDEA WAS ADOPTED, THE TRAINING OF THE CHILDREN WENT very quickly. Rather than go from place to place and work individually, Javin thought it would be easier and quicker to gather them all in one place and take them through what Isselta had said.

That's why they were all seated in the open ground near Javin and Meldren's home where the previous group meetings had taken place. The children were quiet and almost fidget-free. They had chosen to sit in a close little group with Pol in the middle of them all, snuggled up against Hanna. None of them had, as far as anyone knew, referred to their parents back on Haven, or had seemed upset in any way. If he had not known, Javin would have assumed that the children facing him were with their parents. But the adults were only there because they wanted to share in what was happening.

Javin remembered how different and strange it had felt when he had first arrived on Harmony. He had felt so alone. Then, of course, he had been told he could never go back. Now, finding out that there was a way, he didn't want to. But, for these children, he was concerned that some of the same feelings he had had might be present. Besides, he reminded himself, he had been responsible for bringing them here. He was, he knew, trying to feel better about himself and his actions.

Pelle spoke up first in answer to his questions. Javin by now knew all their names. "I like it here. But I also like it back home. I like the animals back home. You don't have any here."

"Well, actually we do, but no big ones on this island." He tried to listen into them and hear anything which seemed out of balance, not harmonic, or suppressed or distorted. Yet again, there was nothing which caught his ear. "Have any of you thought about what will happen when you go back? I suppose I should ask if anyone wants to go back, first?"

Endel, the boy with the serious, pinched face put his hand up. "None of us *want* to go back, but we know we will have to. And when we go back, we will have to teach the others. I would like to stay here, but I know that I can't." There was some solemn nodding of agreement from the other children and Javin felt a slight shiver down his spine at the way in which the boy spoke like an adult facing and accepting his responsibility. Their lack of resentment could not stop him from feeling compassion for them for having had their childhood taken from them and given tasks which any adult would have found daunting. He wondered briefly how long each of them had known what was ahead of them, and whether any of them had wanted to run away from the future. Here and now he saw only serious faces as if they were preparing for some sort of test. Perhaps they were.

"Is this something you've always known? Did you grow up knowing it?"

The other boy, Bodren, spoke. "We've known since we came here. We only know a bit at a time, though."

Hanna took it up. "To begin with, we all were only able to do certain things like hear the sounds around us. And not all of them. I liked animals, Pol here liked plants and mushrooms so on. But after a while, we were able to hear more things and then we got to knowing other things."

"Like knowing when you were coming," added Pelle. "We knew someone was coming, but we didn't know who and, at first, we didn't know when."

"And we didn't know where we would be going until after you came for us." This from Bodren again. "It was just a bit at a time."

"And as for going back... ?" asked Javin.

"We knew that not long after we arrived." Endel picked up the thread. "Not that we knew what we were going to be doing back there, only that we were going back. And then, this morning, when I woke up, I knew the rest of it. Same as for everyone else here." He gave a shrug as if to diminish what he was saying; as if it was normal.

"But you don't mind this happening to you?"

Bodren spoke again. "Why? What would change? We know that we have to go back and help others. If we said we won't do it, it would still happen, wouldn't it? I've known something like that ever since I was really little. It's been in some place inside me all the time. I know it is there. I'm used to it."

"Yes, like something has been growing inside me," added Hanna, as she held Pol's hand. "I'm used to it, like you are used to the moon here. I have always felt that there was something I had to do. I just didn't know what it was. But now I do, it all feels right inside."

Then little Pol spoke up. "Have you always had two hands?"

Taken aback, Javin nodded, wondering where this was going.

"So it's always been normal for you, hasn't it?"

Another nod.

"And you can do things, make things with your hands, that you couldn't do at first." She gave an eloquent, slow shrug. "That's how it is for us. We've always been able to do things, and we've got better at doing them." She looked up at him in a very serious manner. "I think you should stop feeling like you do right now and help us to learn what we have to do."

It was the seriousness and calm acceptance of the children, especially Pol, which disturbed Javin. He thought of Isselta telling him and Meldren that she pitied them for not having a choice. And here he was pitying these children. He tried one last question.

"What about your parents back on Haven? Don't you miss them?"

Bodren answered first. "Some of them are probably dead. Not all of them. Some will have survived. Some will probably have gone away after the soldiers left." Again, the chills.

Endel added, "It's like you being here on this island. You like being alone. We like being alone. Having people who look after us and feed us, people who care for us; it is hard to see them go, but it is also easy in a way. We're not like them. We're like ourselves. We like being together. Maybe, someday, we'll find others who are like us. I can't see that yet. If there are some adults who are like us, that will be good as well. But, here, together, that's more important."

What else did they see or understand that he didn't? He felt as if he was standing in front of a new and strange race of beings that only looked like children. He wondered if, at some point in the future, when things were settled for them, any or all of them would break down and admit that they missed other people and being loved. Somehow he didn't think so. He didn't know what to say or do for a moment, until Pol said in her quietly decisive fashion, "I think you need to teach us now."

That brought him back to the present and he beckoned Meldren over to start them listening to the deep song, the song underneath everything; the song that was Harmony.

It went well. The children learning incredibly quickly that, not only could they hear songs, but that they could sing them as well for themselves. All the adults' sprites unwound a little to where the heads with the bright, beady black eyes were resting on the shoulders, from where they stared at the children, making small, staccato noises.

Then came the chaos and excitement as they began to experiment with the new knowledge and sing new songs. The only problem was keeping an eye on what was happening. If it hadn't been for the other adults there, he seriously doubted whether he and Meldren could have managed. Endel was quietly singing a large metal knife, and the look on his face gave Meldren nightmares before she stepped in and said that it wouldn't last on Harmony as there was no metal for that there. He stared at her and shrugged and began to sing a cow into being just off to one side.

Bodren was singing a log and some bread onto the ground in front of him. Pelle was singing some baskets while Hanna was singing a brightly colored scarf. Pol had found some space for herself and was giggling happily underneath the biggest mushrooms anyone had ever seen.

It took a little while before the children were able to focus on anything other than the new ability they had suddenly discovered. Javin called out in a loud voice, "We need to stop now." The sprites immediately stopped their strange punctuated noises and the song-creations faded away. "This is getting confusing," he said, "and people could hurt themselves or find themselves too close to something being sung. It's too crowded here. If you want to practice, then you should do it back at your homes where someone else will be able to help and guide you. From what we've seen here, nothing you sing will last because of our sprites stopping it. But, before we all separate, are there any questions?"

There was a brief silence, before Endel asked in that now-familiar flat one, "When do we go back to Haven and start what we have to do?"

"I think," said Javin, "it will be sooner than we want. But, in the meantime, go back to your homes and practice, and Meldren and I will come round tomorrow for any help or to answer any questions you might have."

After everyone had left, Meldren asked him, "Do you think they are going to be safe? All sorts of things could go wrong, couldn't they?"

"I don't think so," said Javin. "They've all got this mission they have to fulfill, whether they want to or not. That's plain from what they said. I don't think they'll hurt themselves or anyone else. All the islanders, the *adult* islanders that is, are good enough to prevent things happening. At least, they should be. And if they're not, then they have the sprites and *they* are closer to Harmony than anything else. They'll make certain that the children are safe. Because Harmony wants them safe."

She thought a moment. "The sprites did seem to be keeping things under control. When you called a halt, the sprites stopped as well. And then the things the children had sung faded straight afterwards. There has to be a connection, doesn't there? I wonder if that's got anything to do with why none of the children have got a sprite yet; to hold them back a while?"

"Probably. Maybe. I don't know, to tell the truth." He felt tired. Or was it irritability? "Perhaps that 'det-det-det' noise they made was not a song at all but a way of breaking up any other song, to stop things getting out of hand. I get the feeling that they won't be able to sing anything without a sprite nearby." He ran his hands through his hair in a gesture of frustration. "What have we got ourselves into, Meldren? Children acting like adults. Amazing talents and hopping between planets like it's nothing at all? I thought I knew what 'strange' was. But this... ?"

"Your language, the things you say on Haven; that has lots of different words," said Meldren. "Isn't there a word in it for something as peculiar as what we're doing, for what's happening here?"

He snorted and shook his head. "I can think of some really good ways of swearing that you don't have here, but not a way to describe this. 'Bizarre' is about the only word that comes close, and it's way beyond bizarre, if you ask me."

Meldren played with the new word, trying the emphasis in different places, drawing out the vowels. "Biiiizaaaaarre, bizzzzzaaaaaaaare, bizzzzzzzzzar, Yes," she smiled at him. "That sounds a sufficiently strange word for what is happening. I like it. This is a bizarre."

He couldn't help smiling in return. "Not 'a' bizarre, just 'bizarre'."

"No. This is not just bizarre, this is *very* bizarre."

———

MELDREN'S GUESS ABOUT THE ROLE THE SPRITES PLAYED IN CONTROLLING THE children's exuberant exploration of the skill of singing things into being proved correct. Over the next several days, it became clear that the children, by themselves, had to focus a great deal more in order for them to bring anything into being at all. Even then, there were occasions when both her and Javin's sprites, as well as the sprite of whichever adult's home they were visiting, began making the staccato sounds. It was an effective way of preventing childish enthusiasm from getting out of control. Plus, it had the effect of forcing each child to focus very clearly on the precise details of the song and, beyond that, to listen to Harmony's song more clearly in order that whatever was sung would fit within Her world. The effort was tiring and each child ended the day very sleepy. Of which Carmeena greatly approved.

Each child wanted be fast and to make things as quickly as they could. But the leash of sound created by the sprites held them back.

"Why do you think they are not being allowed to sing some things, or sing them quickly?" asked Javin as they were walking away from Dennet's home after getting Bodren to realize he needn't try everything at once and that he needed to listen as well as sing. The boy had been spending time with Dennet on the cliffs watching the ocean. Dennet had been teaching him about the various colors and what that meant about the life in the ocean. Bodren, like the others, had never seen an ocean and had been fascinated, but had struggled to see what Dennet saw.

"I suppose it's a way of training them to go more slowly."

"Yes, but why? All of the islanders could do this sort of thing quickly. It was easier for them and they weren't able to listen as accurately as the children."

Meldren stopped, Javin walking on half a pace further before she caught his hand. "That's it, I'm sure. It's to do with the listening. Everyone here on the island was born on Harmony. Well, except you, but you don't count because of what's happened. They grew up knowing what Harmony sounded like, even if they didn't want to hear Her later on. She's always been there in their heads. But these children, they come from another planet, another song. I think they have to learn to listen to the underlying song of the planet. We don't even think about it now, but Harmony's always there, way deep down beneath any song. I think that's the reason why the children are being taught to slow down, so that, when they get home, they'll automatically tune in to Haven's song first."

They began walking again. Javin said, "You might be right. But I think things aren't going as fast for another reason as well."

"And that would be... ?"

He smiled. "Ah, now, that's the problem. I have this sort of feeling," -- vaguely waving his hands in the air -- "that there's another reason for them being here apart from learning songs. Why don't you see if you get the same thing."

They walked on in silence as Meldren let her mind roam around the children being here and what they were learning. Javin was right, there was a hint of something, a small obstacle of some sort blocking her view of the children as a whole. It was as if, by trying to look at it, it got smaller or slid from view in some way. That alone was enough to tell her that he was right.

"Same for me," she said. "Whatever it is, I am at the point of not desperately wanting to have an answer straight away. I've learned enough by now to know that, if it's something Harmony wants us to know, we get to find out sooner or later."

"Usually sooner," agreed Javin.

"And not always what we want to know, either," she added.

The following day, they were at Allegara's. During the times when Pelle wasn't practicing songs, Allegara was showing the girl what she could do. Her talents, which she hadn't used in a while now, since living on the island, were finding things and creating heat with her hands. Javin and Meldren arrived just as the two of them were discussing talents in general, and Allegara's in particular.

"I can see why finding something you've lost would be useful," said Pelle, "but what's the point of making things warm?"

Allegara answered, acknowledging their arrival with a lift of her chin. "We, all of us, we all have five things we can do. Touch, taste, smell, see, and hear. That's what everyone can do. But you already know that you can do something else that isn't on that list, right? Why do you want to hear the songs and sing them?"

"I don't *want* to do that," said Pelle. "I just can. I've always been able to do it."

"Exactly. And I've always been able to find things and use my hands to heat things up. Up until now, you didn't realize that there was any point to hearing songs. But, now, there is. Everyone here can listen to Harmony and can sing songs of one sort or another. But, before that, everyone also had a talent; something that they can do which isn't on that list of five things. And I do mean everyone. Everyone on Harmony has a talent." She looked to Meldren. "Isn't that right?"

"Absolutely! Well, apart from Javin here. But he wasn't born on Harmony, so he's different." And then she had a sudden realization. "And none of you were born here, either, were you?" She paused, thinking.

"And... ?" prompted Javin, as the other two were staring at her.

"Well, that's the answer, isn't it? That's what we couldn't see. What we were asking about yesterday. It's that none of the children have any talents."

Pelle looked confused. "I thought listening to the songs and being able to sing them were talents?"

"Oh, I'm sorry," said Meldren. "I mean what we on Harmony call talents. The things that Allegara said aren't on the list of five."

"Like what?"

"Well, Pelle, Allegara's already said what she can do. I, for example, can see colors of things. Colors that help me understand what people are saying or feeling. Others can see far, far away. Amleek, the sailor who comes here, he can see what the weather will be like a few days ahead. Dennet can tell what fish are swimming near the surface. I know he's been trying to share that with Bodren. There's lots of different things, things we call talents. Apart from the songs around us, is there anything else you can do that others back home couldn't do?"

Pelle thought for a moment, a frown on her face. "I don't think so."

"And what about any of the others? Hanna, for instance, or Bodren? Do you know if they can do something like that?"

"No."

Meldren smiled in triumph. "Then that's the other thing you're all here for."

Pelle considered this. "Is that why we haven't got our sprites yet?"

"Like I said, I'm not sure how they get here or who gets them. But, if I'm right about this, then I think that the sprites might appear -- might, mind you -- when you all have found your talents."

"But how do I know what my talent is?"

"Trial and error, I suppose," said Javin. "Why not let Allegara teach you hers and then you can see if you can do the same?"

"And if I can't?"

"I guess that we'll have to get together as a group again and see what any of us can teach any of you." He smiled at the girl. "You'll end up being able to do something, I'm certain of it. Otherwise, why would you all be here?"

"To be prepared for going back home," came the flat reply.

After a few abortive attempts to teach the children on their own, Meldren followed up on Javin's idea and arrangements were made to bring them all to the meeting place. Recognizing that this now was where everyone tended to end up anyway, Javin and Meldren had spent a little time singing it into a place where it was more comfortable to sit. There were soft, green ledges which had small, earthen banks behind to rest on. The whole area had been made into more of a bowl shape, a small amphitheater; the floor having been lowered so that it was easy for all to see and hear. They also sang a small pond to one side, for anyone who wanted a drink. It attracted some admiring and thankful glances, especially from Timoss who was always looking for a comfortable place to ease his legs and who now had a special place of his own, shaped just for him, where he could rest his legs in relative comfort.

The weather was warm but the breeze coming off the sea had a coolness which meant staying in the sun was the way to remain comfortable. Meldren thanked them all for coming. She had a bowl covered with a cloth at her feet. She asked which of the children had learned a new talent. There was a shaking of heads. Carmeena said, "Actually, it's not that Hanna can't do anything, it's more like my talents aren't the ones she's going to have. There were a couple of times when it seemed like she was going to get it, but, in the end, it didn't happen."

"Thanks, Carmeena. I agree with you," said Meldren, turning to the children. "You've all heard about talents by now. At least, what we on Harmony mean when we use the word. I think every one of you children has a talent inside you waiting to come out. It might be, however, that the talents which the adults here have are not the ones inside you, in which case, we'll have to sort that out later. But, first, I want to make sure that all of you are able to let your talent out. And, for that, I've been thinking that there is something similar for all of them. So I want to take a moment to get you all in the right state of mind for it. Who knows, but it might let you find your talent anyway. Ready to try?"

She looked around at the young faces, all of them focused intently on her. As she was about to start, Pol spoke. "I think that the sounds you have are the right ones for us."

"What do you mean, Pol?"

The child tried hard to find words to explain herself more clearly. "I hear things in people. Songs, I suppose. And what I hear now sounds a good song. I can't explain it. But it has a good sound."

"Well, thank you, Pol. I appreciate you telling me. Now, to begin. Whenever you hear songs, you use one part of your head or your mind, whatever you want to call it. It's the part which knows music and song and all the sounds. You don't have to do anything to use it, except decide to use it. Does that sound right to you?" She took the small nods as a sign to move on. "But, a talent is something else. It happens in another part of your head. It's not the same part as the sounds. What I want you all to do now is to close your eyes. Relax. Be comfortable. Wiggle around if you need to. And then, when you're comfortable, let your mind feel the weather. Not the songs of the wind or the clouds, but feel what the weather is doing now and what it will be doing tomorrow. Remember, no songs here, just feelings. You're not going to be hearing sounds, but you are trying to let feelings in. And those feelings might be a warmth in

191

your back, or a tingle in your hand, or seem like a blank space in your mind." She waited as the children attempted to follow her instructions. She watched their faces. "Don't try hard. Simply feel the weather for tomorrow and let it come to you." Another pause as she took the cover from the bowl. "Now, let's try something else. Forget about the weather. We'll come back to it later. Get relaxed again but this time see if you can make the water in this bowl here at my feet get hot. No songs, remember! This is something different. Get used to knowing there are other things than songs to help you feel your way around the world. Can you feel the water getting warmer as you focus on it? Let it happen. Don't force it. Let your mind do the work by itself."

Again, a silence and Meldren, along with all the adults, watched the bowl. After a moment, there was perhaps a wisp or two of steam coming for it. Meldren clapped her hands. "Well done. Let's all open our eyes."

When they were looking at her, she dipped her finger carefully in the water and nodded appreciatively. "It's very warm! Well done, whoever did that. Who did do that, by the way? It could be more than one of you."

"How would we know?" asked Endel.

"It would have felt like an easier thing to do, a feeling like a part of you reached out to the water," said Allegara, whose talent this was.

A tentative hand went up. "That sounds a bit like what I felt," said Hanna.

"Good. Well done. It will be easy for you to be certain if you practice on your own. What about the weather? Did anyone feel an answer to that one?"

Pelle said, "I felt warm and then something like water on my head. What does that mean?"

"Sounds to me like a nice day but rain later on," said Javin. "The easy answer is to wait and see. You'll know if you're right. And, another thing, if it does happen like you said, and it's not a lucky guess, then you'll have a feeling, a certainty, like something sliding into place. It's a way of knowing that something you were thinking of, something you felt, was correct." He looked at the others. "That's true for all of you, by the way."

"Did anyone get anything else?" asked Meldren. When nobody volunteered anything she said, "In that case, if each of the adults can explain about their talent or talents and maybe think of something for the children to try? Oh, before that though, you can have more than one talent. Normally one stronger one, stronger than the other and usually only two. Although there's no reason why you couldn't have three of four, I suppose. Now, who would like to be first?"

And so began an afternoon of experiments.

Enrick began by explaining his talent of being able to 'see' what was hot or cold. He told them which of the children was warmer than the others (Endel) and who was cooler (Pelle) and asked them to see which of two stones he put out was the warm one. He added, "It might not look like very much, but it is useful. You can see if a fire really is out, for example, or if an animal is hiding somewhere. Things like that. And the other thing I can do I'm not sure is a talent. I can somehow get animals to trust me. It seems to work every time, at least with the animals I've met. But, like I said, I'm not sure it's a real talent, but I'd be happy to teach any of you what I can."

Farran stepped up and didn't say anything at first. With his slumped shoulders and lined face on which a smile would have seemed lost, he looked a distant, lonely figure. He simply gazed intently at one of the rocks Enrick had left and there were gasps from the children when it rolled along and came to a stop at his feet. He picked it up and held it in the palm of his hand and then took his hand away, leaving the rock suspended in mid-air before taking hold of it again. "There's a size limit to what you can move. If this is your talent, then your limit might be more or less. But it can be very helpful when cooking or gardening." Looking at their faces, he explained, "Sometimes something needs stirring and you're busy doing something else, or, your back aches and yet you've got weeds to pull out. That sort of thing."

Perray, with her gentle smile, asked for something from any of the children. Bodren gave her a round wooden bead from his pocket. Perray took it and held it as she shut her eyes. Then she began to describe what she saw; the forest where it had come from, Bodren's father (she called him an older man, but Bodren knew who she meant) carving it carefully, where it had rolled into a corner of the room the time Bodren thought he had lost it. "Banith could do that," Javin whispered, leaning in to Meldren, referring to one of the traders he had first traveled with on Harmony.

"Shhhh", said Meldren, putting a finger to his lips.

After that, Perray said that she could also find water underground.

"How?" asked Hanna.

"I can feel it sometimes. Other times, I get a shivering in my arms and legs. It depends. But you can do it in all sorts of ways. The person who showed me used a stick. It's useful for finding where to dig a well."

Timoss said he would happily talk to any of the children if they came to him, but that he would rather sit out if they didn't mind. "I can make plants grow strong and quick, and if that is something that you think might be your talent, then I'd be happy to share what I can. One other thing that I can do, but I'm not sure if it's a talent, is I hear people as a noise. They're not songs, but noise. The more people, the more noise." With a wave of his hand he encompassed all the people present. "Normally, it would have been hard to be here with this number of people, but since I've learned more about the songs, it's become easier."

"Is it loud, then?" asked Endel.

"Sometimes," admitted Timoss. "Plus, I learned that the noise I heard from a person was telling me something about them; whether they were angry or sad or happy. But often it was simply too much at once." He considered for a moment. "I really don't know if it's a talent or not, or nothing more than annoying."

"Is that why you hurt your legs?" It was Pol's distinct treble voice.

Timoss looked down and away for a moment, his long, black hair falling over his face. When he spoke, his voice sounded a little rough. "You could say that. It had something to do with it."

"Why don't you mend them if they hurt?" the girl persisted.

"Sometimes I wonder that myself," said Timoss quietly.

Meldren stepped in to the silence and asked for the next person.

Dennet got up and said, "I really don't have much to tell that you don't already know. If you want to know how to see which fish are swimming beneath the surface of the water, I'll help you." Then he gave a big beaming smile at them all and sat straight back down but then bolted up again and added, "You can see other things as well. Not just fish." And down he sat again.

Allegara showed them, again, how to heat water or to help ease pain by applying that heat to a person's aches and pains.

Carmeena told them that she could bring something to them, if they were all quiet. She shut her eyes for a while. At first, nothing happened, but then everyone started to notice that there were more of the small insects called zips, named after the noise they made. They were brightly colored, about the size of a fingernail, red and gold and blue, and always on the move. Yet, here they were flying closer and closer to Carmeena, more and more of them, until they almost hid her from view. At which point they began to settle on her and cover her like a living cloth. She opened her eyes and smiled at them all before thanking the zips and, with a slight puff of breath, scattered them in all directions. She added that she could also know what the weather would be like; mainly fair weather or storms in her case.

Isselta was the last to stand up. She came over to Meldren and asked if she should talk about her talent, given what she had shared about her perception of Pol.

"Well, if you don't say anything to them," said Meldren quietly , "it would make them come and pester you more and more. At some point, either Pol and the rest of them will choose to deal with what happened, or they won't. Here, with everyone else... ?" She shrugged. "So, yes. Go ahead and tell them."

Isselta started by telling them a little about herself, but only that she had come from a long way away where it was very cold and there was a lot of ice and snow. The children didn't need any explanation of those words. She left out why she come to the island. And then she began to tell them what her talent was. "You know that, sometimes, you can look at a person and know that they aren't feeling well, or they're sad? My talent is something like that. I can look at a person -- more accurately, I can look inside a person -- and see what is going on in their heads that is making them ill or unhappy or sad or whatever. In most cases, people keep things like that to themselves. Pol, here, for example, can see how people are from the songs inside them, can't you?" Pol nodded gravely, her frown showing how hard hard she was concentrating on what was going on. "The big difference is that, when I see the private thing, the thing they are keeping to themselves, especially if they don't even want to know about it, and then I tell them about it and why it's hurting them, they often get a lot, lot better." She looked around at them all, including the adults. "This is not something that is fun to do, like rolling pebbles or having insects and animals come to you. In fact, it can be hard work at times and it's difficult to know when to use the talent or not. Sometimes, you can make people very angry because they don't want anyone else to know what they have hidden inside themselves." She gave an apologetic smile as she looked over to Meldren. "Most of the adults here know what it's like for me to look inside them, so I suggest that you ask any of them how they felt about it. I suppose you'd call this talent of mine a type of healing."

Instead of the usual muted chatter which followed each of the other presentations, there was silence until Endel asked, "What about Meldren and Javin? What are your talents?"

Javin stepped forward, smiling. "I can honestly say that I don't have one. I was born on Haven and, before I could learn what talent I might have, Harmony came hurtling into my life and that was pretty much the end of it. Oh," he added, "I did find that I was able to see out of other animals' eyes a couple of times. But I have no idea whether that was daydreaming or a talent." There was a ripple of laughter at this.

Meldren said, "Some of you already know that my talent is to see colors around people and things and that those colors help me to understand more about what I'm looking at. It's a bit like what Timoss was saying about the noise he hears. It was a talent that grew gradually for me. I didn't start out seeing colors. So you might only begin to see them occasionally at first, but it's something that you can learn to do. I'm happy to help with that," she concluded. Then she clapped her hands and said, more briskly, "Who now has an idea of a talent they think they might have? Remember, a talent is not something you wish for or want, it's something already inside you which is waiting to find a way out. So, if you heard something that made a part of you inside sit up and take notice, that might be your talent. Did that happen for anyone?"

Each child's hand went up. But Endel also had a question. "What's the point of having a talent if you can sing a song to make something happen instead? I mean, we could sing water to any place we wanted, for example. Why go looking for it?"

"If you can sing a song, that's good," answered Javin. "But, no matter how good you are at singing, you can only sing one song at a time.

Sometimes, it's much, much easier to use your talent to make your life easier, or better, or be of more help to people while you sing the songs that really count. If you did nothing but sing songs to get you over obstacles, then you're wasting your ability. Songs are used when they are the best way of dealing with an issue. They're not the answer to everything."

"Which," interrupted Meldren, "is exactly what I tell Javin whenever he complains about getting on Amleek's boat to go to Littlehaven." Javin smiled a little sheepishly. "He gets sea sick. He could use a song, but, if it's only an upset stomach, that can be overcome with time on dry land. Can't it?" she said, addressing this last to Javin.

"I have yet to convince her that it's 'only' a little upset stomach," he smiled at her. "But what she says is true. Songs are not the answer to everything. Take Farran's talent, for example. Weeding a field while checking on something else is incredibly useful. Talents are what everyone can do. Songs are what only some can do. At least, that's what I think. Don't make the mistake that talents are useless compared to songs. They're not. They're incredibly important, because whatever talent you end up with is going to go a long way toward defining you as a person and how you are going to live your life. Even more so than singing songs."

"How do you know when a song is the best way of dealing with an issue?" persisted Endel.

Meldren knew how she recognized such times, but wondered how to explain that to a young boy. "Perhaps the best way of thinking about it is like this. If the thing you're thinking of doing with a song takes only a little effort, or maybe the use of a talent, then you shouldn't sing it. There's a lot you can learn by actually doing things for yourself instead of taking the easy way out and singing. You will never understand what fun and frustration there is in cooking your own meal if you only ever sing food. You will never understand the difference between eating what you have watched and tended and spent time on, and eating something that took no time at all. There is a difference and it's called life. You have to experience life, know what it is like to be alive, because that's what these bodies we have are designed for. Besides, the longer you live and the more experience you have of living, the easier it becomes to know when a song is called for and when it isn't."

Endel nodded thoughtfully, as if not completely persuaded, but willing to give her words due consideration.

That brought them all to the point where they were going to make a choice about talents. It was decided that the children should go back with whichever adult they thought could help them with a talent. If it didn't work out, then, the following day, they could find a different one. If there was a child without a talent beginning to show, then they would need to rethink things. And so, after some to-ing and fro-ing, everyone ended up with someone else. Meldren noticed that each child had picked a separate adult from the one they usually stayed with, except for Pol who stayed with Isselta. They said their farewells to them all and promised to check in with them all the following day.

THE NEXT DAY, AFTER TAKING SOME TIME FOR THEMSELVES TO RELAX; TO NOT listen to anything, to not watch colors, to enjoy the weather, Javin and Meldren finally sat and tuned in to the songs of the adults and children to see if there were any large problems or obvious dissonances which would require their help or attention. Happily, everything sounded harmonious. It seemed as though everything was moving along nicely, even if they didn't know where it was all going.

It was a warm morning, with some clouds way off to one side and another gentle breeze. Congratulating themselves on what appeared to be a peaceful day ahead, they decided to put off visiting until the afternoon and enjoy the time alone. With this in mind they headed out the back, down the slight slope to the garden. It had been ignored long enough to make the weeds the dominant feature. They contemplated it without much enthusiasm for a moment, debating where to start, when they heard a noise. It sounded like someone shouting. Going back up to the house in order to get a better view, Meldren heard it again. Definitely a shout, but beyond that... ?

Looking out of the doorway, she saw a figure running toward her. At first, she couldn't place who it was, until she noted the long, black hair.

And then she couldn't believe it. But it was, without a doubt, Timoss. Running! No crutches, no limping, but running free and easy and yelling something.

She called to Javin. Both of them were at the door when Timoss arrived, covered in sweat, gasping for breath and trying to say something. Meldren brought him inside, poured some water and encouraged him to speak as soon as he could. He was still gasping and shaking his head, but whether he was angry or wonderfully happy was difficult for her to tell, even when looking at the colors around him. They waited for him to regain his breath and speak. Finally, Timoss, after gulping the water, wiped his mouth with his sleeve and waved a hand at his legs.

"Look what she did!"

"I saw you running here," said Meldren. "I couldn't believe it at first. But who is 'she'? Who did this?"

"That girl. The smallest one. Her. She did it."

"Pol?" said Javin. "Really? But are you glad or angry about this? I can't tell." he asked.

Timoss screwed his face up, shook his head and made claws of his hands as if trying to grasp something. "I don't know myself. That's the annoying thing. Part of me is incredibly happy to walk again without pain. That part is fantastic. Wonderful! I never thought I would be able to."

"And the other part?" asked Meldren.

He shook his head. "There's the another annoying thing. I don't know. Angry, maybe? Insulted? I don't know how to describe it. It wasn't my choice!"

"Maybe you should simply tell us what happened. That might help," she said.

He put the drink down and paused a moment to gather his thoughts. "I was sitting in my home, at the table. You know that Hanna is working with me on making plants grow quick and strong? I think she will be very good at it indeed. But that's not the point. We were sitting at the table, practicing with some seeds and seedlings, when the little one, Pol, came in and... ."

"And... ?" Meldren nudged.

"And she *did* something and I felt my legs straighten out." There was disbelief on his face as he stared down now at his legs. "I actually, literally, felt them straighten out. I saw it happen! The bones moved, other things slid around inside and then the pain... the pain was really, really bad for a split second. Not more than that, but I think I screamed. That made Pol jump and then the pain stopped and my legs felt... well, they felt like legs again. Not two useless lumps I drag around. I had no idea what happened. I didn't hear a song or anything like that. I didn't know what to do, what to say or anything. It's a shock. Still is. The next thing I knew I was running. Me! Running! Can you believe it? I don't remember starting, but here I am." He looked around as if he couldn't quite believe where he was, still breathing heavily, shaking his head at it all.

"And there was no warning about this? Pol didn't say anything? Or Isselta?" Javin asked.

"Nothing. Like I said, it wasn't my choice. It had nothing to do with me. I was sitting at my table one minute, talking about seedlings and the next, I'm off running on legs that were new."

"Why did you run? And why run here?" asked Javin.

"I don't know. Scared, I suppose? Maybe? Wanted to see if they worked? I've no idea. I just got up and ran. I suppose I'm here because I started out heading this way. I wasn't thinking about that. I wasn't thinking about anything really. I ran and here I am. Otherwise I'd be at the other end of the island by now."

"Overall, you're probably more happy than angry, then?" asked Meldren.

"Oh, I'm happy all right. At least I think so. It's a shock. Having that done to me out of the blue? No warnings at all. That, well, that doesn't feel right to me. But I think I'm more happy than anything. Probably."

Javin had a serious look on his face. He said to Meldren, "I think we need to see Pol and Isselta, don't you?"

"The sooner the better," she agreed. "We need to find out more about this." She turned to Timoss. "Are you going to need anything? Can we do anything?"

Timoss waved them away. "No. Not at all. I feel a bit foolish, to tell you the truth, now I'm here. I'll start back in a moment or two. You don't need to wait for me anymore. If you have to do something, go and do it."

They arrived at Isselta's to find Pol, red-faced and runny-nosed from crying, and shouting at Isselta who looked just as upset from trying not to shout back. When they saw Javin and Meldren they both rushed to them saying in tandem, "You have to tell her!"

It took a few moments to calm them down enough to begin to understand what they were saying. Isselta, apparently, had been telling Pol off for making Timoss's legs whole and straight without his permission, and Pol was arguing that she did it because it was the right thing to do once she had heard what was wrong with him, "like you told me to."

"I didn't tell you to go and do anything, only to listen," said Isselta.

"But what I heard was hurting him," argued Pol. "I was trying to help him and have the pain stop."

"Yes, but you can't go around doing that to everyone."

"I wasn't! I was only doing it to him!"

"Enough!" said Meldren, stepping between them. "Nothing is going to get solved here by shouting and arguing like this. We need to find out what happened and then, maybe, we can find a solution. But, this arguing has to stop. Agreed?"

Pol snuffled a quiet 'Yes', and Isselta looked upset at being accused of arguing like Pol, but managed a curt nod of agreement.

"Good," said Meldren, taking a deep, calming breath. "Let's go inside and sit down, shall we? Then you, Isselta, you can start by telling us what it was that you have been teaching Pol, here."

Still a little upset as being seen in the same light as Pol, Isselta seated herself at her table, waiting for the others to sit where they chose. Pol sat on the floor half-turned from Isselta, who chose her words carefully and spoke slowly. "I was teaching her how to listen to the hidden sounds inside people: the things they don't want to hear themselves. I didn't realize she can hear other people from far away, so I didn't know she was listening in on Timoss. I can't do that. I have to be with the person. I was telling her about how, when you know the hidden thing, it's not always a good thing to tell the person about it. Not until they're ready to hear it. I thought she'd understood that, because she walked out and I thought that the lesson was over. Until I heard the scream."

"But I didn't mean to make him scream," said Pol through her pout. "I keep telling you that."

"Pol!" said Meldren with a warning finger and a voice which brooked no argument. She looked at Javin who, from the way he was leaning against the wall with half-closed eyes, she knew was listening to the songs of them all to see if that would give him some more information about what had happened. He nodded at her to carry on.

"Now, please tell me, Pol, what you did. Nothing else. Just tell me the things you did in the order you did them, please."

Pol's pout had grown deeper by now and she was glaring up at Isselta. Meldren leaned down from her chair and gently tapped the child on her knee, repeating her request.

"I did what she told me to do," began Pol, every word a poke at Isselta, whom Meldren just managed to hold back from retorting.

"Pol! This time, tell me what *you* did, not what Isselta said."

Pol considered this request a moment, the pout sliding into a deep frown. "I listened, really, really hard to Timoss. I didn't know I wasn't meant to listen to someone. Anyway, I listened, and I heard about his legs."

"Can you explain what you mean by hearing about his legs?"

"I mean that I heard the secret thing, like she told me to do. He had bad legs because he didn't like being near lots of people. It hurt him. So he went somewhere but fell down. A long way down. And his legs hurt. That's his secret, that he doesn't want to have people hurt him anymore." Pol gave a big, quivering sigh as she finished, as if the memory was sad. Her voice gentled a little. "I don't like hearing him like that. And then I went to see him and the secret, the sound of his secret, it got louder. So I got as close I could, and then I... , I... ,"

"What did you do?" coaxed Meldren, watching Pol's colors flash in a series of swift changes which she interpreted as emotions of pain and sorrow and regret.

"I stopped the pain of being amongst people and made his legs better." Pol's face suddenly crumpled up and she began to cry again, but this time not in anger but in the way all young children do when faced with emotions they don't fully understand or want. "I didn't mean to hurt him. I was trying to help him. That's all."

Meldren lifted her up into her lap and held her close, crooning and rocking as the girl cried her confusion, head buried against her chest. She looked to Javin to see what he could offer.

"From what I can hear," he said quietly, "she did something quite remarkable for someone so young. The song I can trace back from her... it was impressive. Not something that she should be doing on a regular basis, but impressive enough for all that."

When Pol had gone from crying to snuffling, Meldren asked her, "Do you know why Isselta got angry with you? Do you?" There was a tiny nod. "Can you tell me why?"

"'Cos I didn't ask," came the muffled reply.

"That's correct. You didn't ask. What you did was very, very clever. Lots of people couldn't do what you did. But that doesn't make it right if you do that without asking the person involved." A shadow fell across her and she saw Timoss had arrived. She made a silent 'shhh' at him. "Just think," she continued talking quietly to the little girl, "if someone did something like that to you without asking you or warning you that it was going to happen? Something like... oh, I don't know, like taking away all your hair." Pol's pudgy hand appeared and touched her head in reassurance. "You wouldn't like that, would you?" Again a tiny movement of the head. "Tell me, Pol. Do you think you will do something like this again? Before you answer, you need to know that what you can do is very, very good. But, if you do it the wrong way, like this, it's not a good thing and people will not like you for it. Do you understand that?" Another tiny nod. "S0, do you think you are going to do this again?"

Pol wiped at her nose with her hand. Her voice was shaky. "I promise. I promise I won't."

Meldren pried her away from her body to be able to look at her, although the girl didn't want to meet her gaze. "I believe you, Pol. I do. And now, there's a way you can make it right." Pol's head lifted. "Timoss is here and you can apologize to him. Will you do that, please?"

There followed another tearful interlude which ended with Timoss crying and Isselta looking as if she might. By the time everyone had settled down and were sharing some fruit Isselta had sung for them and everyone was beginning to smile again, Javin looked outside and noticed that the rain had started falling. He gave a soft laugh. "Raining. Just like Pelle felt it would yesterday. I'd say that's another person with a talent. We should go and congratulate her."

Once the two of them were back home again, after having congratulated Pelle, they put off visiting the other children. They felt unsettled, still dealing with the issues that Pol's healing had brought up.

Meldren, toweling herself dry, asked, "Have we done the right thing? These talents are more like fun to the children. Growing up on Harmony, we learn about them gradually. We grow into them more. It took me years to learn to see colors everywhere and understand what they meant. And that's how it's always been. But we've thrown these children into it without any guidance, without any background. We're trying to make them adults in one go." She draped the town over the back of a chair, pushed at her hair distractedly and sighed. "They're going to go back and they're going to have to cope with everything that gets thrown at them on Haven and without anyone to turn to. It's asking so much. It may be asking too much."

Javin chewed at his lip a moment before he spoke. "I wish I knew for certain that everything would turn out well for them. But, like Isselta said, they're the seeds. One way of looking at them as seeds or seedlings is that we're able to give them the nourishment, the help they need before they go back. Just imagine what it would have been like for them if they hadn't come here. Back on Haven, what would have happened if they had found out the things they could do without any help at all? Sure, we'd like to give them more, but it's better than nothing, isn't it? Better than they would have had. They're learning a lot, and like you said, it's all happening at once. And that's the thing, Meldren. It's not the same as if they had been born here. They're not like any children we've ever met. They can do more with greater ease than you or I would have thought possible. We were made ill learning what we've learned. They just bounce off of things and carry on and adjust and get better. We have to trust that Harmony knows what's best for them, and that She or Haven will look after them. We have to," he repeated. The way he said it sounded like he was trying to convince himself.

"I hope you're right. I really do. But it seems so unfair putting this much on them. And for what? They go back and teach others? Really? But would any adults listen to them? Who'd listen to Pol, for example? She's so tiny. And Endel worries me. There's some dark stuff hidden in him. He needs supervision. But then they all do! You saw the place where they were living. It's dangerous. Yes, they have some skills, but they don't have the experience to go with them. How are these few children ever going to be seeds for anything there?"

Javin shrugged helplessly. "I don't have the answers, Mel. I wish I did. Let's go and see everyone when the rain stops. Tomorrow maybe? Perhaps that will give us some ideas, something we can do for them."

Meldren nodded distractedly, staring out at the rain, still worried about what was facing the children and what would happen to them when they returned home. She could not shake off the guilty feelings about bringing them here which had returned more strongly than before.

THE WEATHER MATCHED MELDREN'S MOOD; DARK AND DREARY. THE RAIN which had begun on the previous afternoon, had carried on throughout the night, and it was still drizzling the following morning. Everything felt clammy to the touch, there was an unaccustomed chill to the air and, coupled with a restless night's sleep, neither Javin nor she felt in the mood to go and be cheerful and encouraging.

Nevertheless, they set off after breakfast, each with a blanket thrown around their shoulders, shivering momentarily as their feet brushed through the droplets on the ground.

"This does not feel like summer any more," said Javin.

"It isn't. It's more near winter than anything else. We've just had a really late, warm autumn, that's all."

"I don't care what it is, I prefer the warmth. And there's no reason why we can't have nice, warm winters, as far as I'm concerned," he said.

A wan smile from Meldren. "You don't recall last winter very well, do you? It was like this at times then."

"I probably only remember the warm days, not the cold ones," he muttered. "They're nicer memories."

As if in response to his complaints, the drizzle gradually became mist and the mist eased into nothing more than a dampness and the dampness was drifted away on a breeze which also shepherded away the clouds to let the sun warm the air. The whole process was completed by the time they had finished talking with Farran who, today, was working with both Endel and Pelle on moving things without touching them.

"Most of it is not trying very hard to do it," Farran explained in his deep, slow voice. "The talent is in allowing your head to get on with it and not interfere, but keep a guiding hand, so to speak."

Javin laughed, the better weather having improved his mood. "I can still remember very clearly how difficult it was for me when I was trying to do this once. I must have looked a fool; almost bursting out of myself I was trying so hard. I could have used you then, Farran. I really could have used you."

Farran shook his head. "It wouldn't matter whether I was there or not. If you don't have it in you, you can't do it, no matter how hard you try."

"And these two can?" asked Meldren.

Farran nodded. "Certainly. They only need some help here and there, but they've got the basics of it just fine."

"One thing I've always wanted to know about this talent," said Javin. "What's the size limit you can move? Or do I mean the weight? Do you know?"

Farran scratched the top of his bald head as he considered his reply. "Biggest thing I moved was a dead mandria once. Not far, mind you. But I moved it. But is that the biggest I could move? I don't know. Maybe. Maybe not."

Javin gave a low whistle of appreciation. He knew how big the gentle beasts were. They were used for hauling, mainly, and he had loved being around them. He couldn't conceive what it would be like to move one simply by wishing it to happen.

Before they left, Endel came up to them. "We know what Pol did. All of us know now. We wanted to tell you that we understand better. We are learning a lot here. But how to use it when we get back; that's going to be more difficult. But we will try."

Meldren, seeing his serious face and hearing the firmness in his voice, could have burst into tears at the distance she felt between the child standing before her and his childhood. She managed to smile, but his demeanor stopped her from hugging him. She made do with gripping his shoulder firmly and saying, "We are sure you will do wonderfully well, Endel. And thank you for telling us. Both of us really appreciate it."

Walking away in the sunshine, blankets now bundled under their arms, Javin turned to Meldren. "How are you feeling now?"

Meldren wiped her nose and sniffed a little. "They obviously are trying to learn to do the right things. That's good. And the fact that they seem to be able to know what the others are learning is good as well. I hope it's going to be enough, that's all."

The children generally seemed to be coping well with everything they were learning. Bodren was out with Perray learning about finding water. He had located what he thought was some water in one area and even got how far down it was. Perray wasn't going to let him get away with that and had him dig down to see if there really was water there. The look of satisfaction on his dirt-smeared face at the bottom of a damp hole was wonderful. "That'll teach him more than anything I can tell," said Perray. "Having to prove it, to work for it; that's the most important thing. It's not just talent that works; you often have to put muscle into it as well." She leaned down and ruffled his hair affectionately. "He'll be fine now, won't you?" Bodren smiled and nodded enthusiastically before returning to his digging.

Timoss appeared to be over the previous day's drama and he and Hanna were busily engaged in learning how to encourage plants to grow strongly and quickly. The two of them were seated on the ground. It was strange to see Timoss looking at ease there, thought Meldren. Between the two there were some small plants, and Hanna was concentrating fiercely on trying to make them grow. The little plant swayed to and fro, even though by now the breeze had faded, and it shivered as if straining toward something. She stopped and smiled happily at the two visitors. "This will be so useful! Imagine getting seedlings ready ahead of planting. The harvest will come quicker and there will be bigger harvests. It will help everyone so much!"

"You're obviously enjoying yourself," said Javin, cocking a questioning eyebrow at Timoss who gave a small, quick nod in return.

"Oh, yes!" said Hanna.

"It will take time to work with larger numbers," said Timoss, "and you would probably become very tired. You should start with only a handful of seedlings before working on a field. Work up to it. But, having said that, there's no reason why you can't work on a bag of seeds to get them stronger and ready to germinate. That should be much easier on you. Remember, you're not trying to make them grow quicker with a song, but you're finding what's inside them and making it bigger and easier for the seedlings to find it so that they can do all the growing themselves. Plus, some plants might be more difficult than others. The best thing, of course, is to try and note the results, so you know what works and what doesn't."

Hanna's grin got wider and wider.

They called on Allegara to find Pol there. The girl beamed at them when she saw them, the problems of the day before apparently banished from her mind. "Look at this," she said proudly, pointing at a steaming bowl of water. "I made it hot myself."

"She did indeed," said Allegara. "And, what's more, she's a quick learner."

"It will be very useful if somebody's hurt," said Pol, more seriously, sounding suspiciously as though she was repeating what Allegara had told her. "Making them warm will make them feel better. And then I can make them all better myself. *After* I've asked them, of course," she added with a mock-serious face.

After a final check on Carmeena and Enrick to make sure they were having no problems with Hanna, who was dividing her time between them, they ambled back homeward again. But instead of heading home, Meldren took Javin's hand and walked to where there was a clear view of the ocean. They sat on the blankets wrapped in their thoughts for a while.

"I think things are sorting themselves out," said Meldren. "I nearly burst into tears, though, when Endel came up and spoke. Such an old way of speaking, and he's so young still. I felt so helpless, so useless."

"Do you still feel he needs supervision?"

"Maybe I do, but maybe that's only because I want to help as much as I can." She considered for a moment. "No. He'll be fine. I have to trust that it will all be fine. Perhaps doing what he's doing is the best cure for whatever pain he had inside."

"They've come a long way in a short time," he said. "The next thing to consider is when do we go back? And then what? Do we leave them there straight away or do all of the islanders come with us? How long do we stay? How would we know? I can't believe they're going back on their own -- ,"

"I wouldn't allow it," said Meldren sharply, ignoring the fact that she knew she would have no say in the outcome. "That's not happening. But you are right. We know what the next step is, but not when it is." She wound a lock of her hair round her fingers, twirling and untwirling it. "With the speed of things, I get the feeling that it's going to be sooner than we like."

"When have I heard that before? When has anything ever happened when we wanted it to happen?" He puffed out his cheeks in exasperation. "When Harmony wants it is when it happens, but She never tells us in advance."

She flicked her hair out of her face, folded her arms across the tops of her knees and put her head to one side on them, looking at Javin. "Do you get a feel for it, for when it is?"

"No. Not really. I know it's soon. But, beyond that, seeing a specific day... ?" He shook his head.

"Same here. Perhaps they'll all wake up with sprites and that will be when it happens."

"And if they don't?"

A gentle snort of laughter. "Then someone's going to be very annoyed."

OVER THE NEXT SEVERAL DAYS, BOTH OF THEM FELT A TIGHTENING INSIDE them, a nearing of the day of departure. They moved around constantly, encouraging and helping, teaching when they could. Always, they were answering questions and telling stories to help with the children's understanding. They sang food when it was needed, carried tools or whatever else was required, applauded and enthused, listened to adventures and experiments, and spread calm when frustration boiled over or excitement threatened to overwhelm the teaching. There was no sign of a sprite however, so the internal ratcheting continued, still looking for something to show that the end had arrived. It was as though everyone was preparing for a test without knowing what the test was about or when it would be held.

On the fourth day, as they were heading out once more, they met the children on the path. They were walking in a group, with the adults a little way behind. They stopped and there was an almost tangible shell around them, filled with silence, as if something benevolent but invisible held them all, preventing them from doing anything more than look at and appreciate each other.

It was Pol, the smallest, the most precocious, and seemingly the least afraid who spoke. "We have to go back now. It's time."

"How do you know?" asked Meldren, after she had found her voice.

Hanna answered. "We feel it. Haven is pulling at us. You won't feel it like we do because you are part of Harmony." She looked directly at Javin. "Even you now are part of Harmony." She looked away again, at her fellow travelers. "But we are part of Haven, so we can feel Her and we know it's time to go."

Meldren felt the truth of the words and saw in the repeating flickering colors around them that the children all knew the same thing and were comfortable with that knowledge. "Do you know anything more than that? Like, who goes from here and who stays? Or how long anyone from here will stay there? Or where you will arrive on Haven? When we went, to find you, it was very rushed and we knew nothing about it. We didn't even know where we were going." She indicated Javin. "We would like to know a little more this time, if that's possible. We'll take you there, but I'd like to be better prepared, that's all."

"Why don't we go to the meeting place to sort this out a bit better?" said Javin.

When they were all gathered and seated, Javin said, "Does anyone here know more than the fact that this is the time for the children to go back? I mean, I feel it is right, but beyond that, not very much. Anyone?"

There were some shrugs and silence for a moment as people used their various abilities to discover what they could. Timoss said, "I'm not sure, but I think it feels like a change coming here, to this place. I know it's a change when the children go back, but I feel a change for me as well. And it's not that it's the children. At least, I don't think it's just that."

Carmeena nodded in agreement. "That would explain the feeling I got as well." She made a chopping movement with her hands. "It's as though there's a finish, a completion somehow. But I'm not sure what it is. And it feels, like Timoss said, it feels more personal than just the children leaving."

Farran added, "It feels scary for me. Not in a big, bad way. But unsettling. Yes, that's a better word. Unsettling."

Gradually the rest added their feelings and interpretations to form a picture which Meldren summed up for them all. "Thank you for this. Obviously, the children here are the central concern. And we all feel and know it is time for them to return. But, from what you've said, it sounds like there is a bigger change for you all than simply saying goodbye to them. Personally, I didn't get that same sort of feeling. It was much weaker; almost non-existent. And Javin? Did you get anything like they have been talking about?" Seeing him shake his head, she continued. "So, if I was to make a guess, I'd say that all of you and the children are going to be facing a new challenge somehow. And that would mean, I think, that all of us are going to go to Haven. That's the only thing which makes sense of these feelings, as far as I can see. The thing is, for how long and what do we do there?"

Isselta, who, Meldren noted, had finally lost the tension she normally carried in her shoulders, spoke up, "Well, we can't expect the children to do everything by themselves when they arrive, can we? I mean, would adults believe them or even understand them? I think we are going so that we can help them there. But, I don't know how long that would be. But it would make sense, wouldn't it?"

"I have to say you're right," said Javin, after a moment. "I'd never really thought about what would happen beyond simply returning to Haven." He smiled at the children, Pol in particular. "I know you are all very clever and capable, but I have to believe what Isselta said. And, delightful and wonderful as Pol is, for example, some people back there might not want to spend any time listening to someone as young as you are." The look on Pol's face made him think that anyone who did ignore her would very soon come to regret it.

Meldren also wondered what anyone would make of Isselta. She still looked very young, but the granite core of her had made her someone who was much older. Was she a child because of her size, or an adult because of her abilities? But, if first impressions were what counted, Isselta would not be listened to as an adult. She was on that borderline of youth and maturity. She was sure, however, that anyone who patronized Isselta would be very swiftly corrected.

"We are all going it seems," Meldren said. "I have no idea how that is going to happen, who is going to sing us there and back, but, " she shrugged, "I suppose that's going to be taken care of somehow." She gave a wry smile. "That attitude comes from being 'helped' by Harmony in the past. She's always up to something, even if we only get to understand it later. The one thing we've learned to trust is that She will look after us, even if we have doubts about it at the time." Then she became more businesslike. "Now, what about food? We don't know what will be there when we arrive. We should at least eat here or take some with us. Once we're there, we'll sort things out properly. I'm not leaving in a rush, that's all I'm saying. Plus, I'd like to know there's something to eat that doesn't require much preparation. We might arrive anywhere. Somewhere far away from food, for instance."

So began the preparations. There was a buzz of excitement in the air. People were chattering slightly louder than usual and laughing nervously. There was a sense of something new, exciting, scary, yet alluring. Everyone agreed they were too excited to eat now, so they focused on thinking about what food to take with them. This took some discussion. The obvious choices were things like cheese and dried meat and fish, together with berries and other fruits. But then came the problem of how to transport them. Pelle resolved that by singing up some baskets which she recalled from working with Bespic. These were filled and passed around. Then Javin sang some leather strips which were also shared so that everyone had something with which to tie their basket to them.

Finally, after checking and re-checking everyone, Javin and Meldren felt that they were ready. Before they all began to sing, however, Javin stepped forward to speak, but Hanna beat him to it.

"We haven't got sprites! I thought we would have sprites before we went back." The other children nodded in agreement.

"I'm sorry, Hanna," said Meldren, "but I did say I had no idea if they would appear or not. It looks like they haven't. But, perhaps there'll be something else for you. Maybe it's waiting for you on Haven, whatever it is."

Her words did not appear to cheer the children up, but it was too late to do anything about it.

Now Javin was able to say what he had wanted to. "I think it's only fair to say that we have no idea what is going to happen in the next few minutes. It seems to be that we are all going to Haven. It's also true that we have no idea how long any of us will be there. Perhaps we should all be prepared for anything at all. But I wanted to warn you that I have no idea what is going on, how it will work or anything else."

"Sounds about normal, then, doesn't it?" said Isselta with a huge grin on her face, although Meldren was sure she saw some fear in the back of her eyes.

Meldren looked around at the others to see how they were reacting to the news. "Why don't we just all sing the best we can and find out for ourselves? The one thing we do know is that Haven is going to be looking out for the children and Harmony will be doing the same for us. Speaking for myself, I'd like to have an adventure" -- short pause -- "which turns out to be safe and enjoyable."

Javin said, "I'm not sure that's what an adventure is, but I like what you said." Turning to the rest, he said, "Let's start singing!"

11

NEWGRANGE

The song which wrapped them around, held them and guided them came from themselves, their sprites and from something or someone bigger and stronger than all of them put together. Again, as before, they slid along it, held within it, spun from the sounds around and within them. They did not see Harmony recede or Haven approach. The song was their reality, until it began to fade. As it lessened, the wall it had built became translucent and they began to feel textures with their feet, and feel the movement of air around them bringing new smells. As it left them entirely, they felt their bodies responding to this new environment, adjusting and reacting in various subtle ways to the different light, different weight, different air, different everything. They found themselves in a wide space, much wider than their previous arrival point. It was sloping gently. In the uphill direction a long way behind them there were snow-topped mountains, to which Isselta drew Meldren's attention briefly. Further down the slope there appeared to be some sort of tumbledown buildings, but generally the place seemed to be uninhabited. Nearby, there were one or two tall, branching growths -- "That's the trees we saw in our dreams," said Javin -- and open sky. Overhead, the sun, much bigger here, caused much interest amongst the islanders.

The sprites began to coil back down to their accustomed positions around the necks of their hosts. The children looked around as everyone tried to take in their new surroundings.

"Do you know where we are?" asked Meldren.

Bodren pointed at the buildings. "That's Newgrange. That's where I live." Javin noted the use of the present tense.

"Are you sure? It doesn't look like anyone's there now." Javin found it difficult to listen for songs in the scenery. He hadn't yet adjusted to Haven.

"There are some people here," said Endel. "They're hiding, I think. Or maybe they just don't want to be outside. We should go down there."

"Is it safe?" asked Farran. "I'm new to all this, but how can you tell?"

Endel shrugged as if it was self-evident. "Because it is."

"So," said Meldren pointing uphill toward the mountains and trying to get her bearings, "is up there the place where we first landed and found you?"

The children nodded.

"The soldiers have all been gone a long, long time ago," Pol said. "It's safe now."

"Safe it may be," muttered Javin, "but it doesn't exactly look welcoming."

"Excuse me!" said Isselta. "But has no-one here appreciated the fact that all of us, and everything we carried, all the food and everything, has arrived here in one piece, safe and sound? Not to mention the fact that it happened sooooo fast! Is nobody amazed by that? I am." The look of mingled pleasure and amazement on her face as she spread her hands, palms up, inviting others to join her in appreciation of this event, brought smiles to everyone's faces. "It's amazing. It's the most amazing thing that's ever happened to me, and to just about everyone here as well. So, no, I'm not going to march down to a collection of broken-down huts straight away and whatever else is waiting for us down there. I want to take the time to thank the whoever or whatever it was that made this happen and take in the new sights and sounds, even if it's only for a moment or two, thank you very much." Then her face broke into the biggest grin ever and she giggled.

To see Isselta reveling in the moment made Meldren realize how much she had changed since she had first known her, and also how much she and Javin had been taking for granted in their lives after Harmony had shouldered Her way into them. She looked to Javin and smiled and laughed; Isselta's enthusiasm was proving to be infectious.

"You know something, Isselta?" said Javin. "You may well be right."

"Of course I am," she rejoined, eyes twinkling.

"Maybe we should all take a moment or two for ourselves. Let ourselves become used to this place, get a feel for it, maybe even begin to learn the songs here once we can adjust to it. Why don't we have something to eat before we do anything? If there's something we need to do something about, the children here will let us know, wouldn't you? I'm sure it won't hurt if we don't get to those huts down there for a while, will it?"

The suggestion seemed to fit the mood of the group, glances and smiles and words of wonder and appreciation being exchanged before they sat down and began to swap basket contents with each other. At first, the children were unsure how to react. Pelle seemed anxious at first, keeping looking down to the remains of the village, as did Bodren. Endel's normally dour face didn't register much of anything. Pol and Hanna exchanged questioning looks but nothing more than that. Gradually, however, they all relaxed and even seemed to be enjoying themselves and they soon tucked into the food with genuine appetites.

Meldren found herself sitting next to Endel. "How many people do you think are down there?"

He half-closed his eyes a moment. "I'm not sure, but I think there are more than thirty. But it's hard to get a feel for them all."

"Thirty? And how many were there when you left?"

The boy thought a moment. "I didn't count. But there were more than that. A lot more."

"What do you think happened to the others, then?"

"Some were killed. Some would have left to find somewhere else to live."

The unemotional nature of the boy when he spoke was something Meldren still could not get used to.

"What are you going to tell them when we get down there?"

He shrugged, as if he hadn't given it any thought. "I suppose we could tell them we're back," he said.

When the food had been eaten and they were becoming more used to being on Haven, they tidied themselves up; running hands through hair, brushing dust and dirt from each other's clothes and generally attempting to make ready for the coming meeting.

Conversation lessened and there was a palpable sense of anticipation emanating from them as they began to walk toward the village. Getting closer, they could see that most of the huts were badly damaged by fire. Most had roofs missing or with large holes in them as if they had been deliberately torn down. One or two looked like there had been attempts to patch up the larger holes in the roofs and walls. As they left the last of the trees behind them, they crossed ground which had stunted or sickly-looking plants in them. Off to one side, the river splashed and dashed against its banks, its liveliness a stark contrast to the evidence of destruction all around. Ahead of them, they could see a large boulder which seemed to be sitting in the middle of where the houses were. They came to a halt beside it. There was silence, but Javin and Meldren could feel themselves being watched.

"Hello! Anyone here?" called Javin. Still nothing stirred.

"The children are here," called Meldren. "We've brought them back, just as we promised we would."

That news was what changed everything in a heartbeat. Making wordless sounds, some tired looking, emaciated people came out from their hiding places. Children and parents or step-parents reunited with such painful emotions on the part of adults as to make those from Harmony feel like intruders. Some people were standing and watching listlessly, faces thin with hunger and exhaustion. Seeing them so lost and hopeless, the newcomers all wished they had come back much, much sooner and they also all felt guilty at how they had just eaten so much.

When the reunions had finished, Pelle introduced the new arrivals. "These are the people who have helped us to learn new things so we can help you here. They've come to help as well."

"But where are you from?" asked the man holding on to Pelle's hand, her father by the shared shape of the nose. "You look... different somehow."

Javin put his hand on the man's arm as he spoke. "You might have difficulty believing this, but we are from Harmony. The other planet? We've come here to help you. We met very briefly when Pelle came with us."

"From Harmony? Where's your ship? We didn't hear you land. I don't understand." Confusion and something like fear showed on his face.

"This is not going to be easy to explain and I have a feeling that it will take more than a day or two to accept. It's hard enough for me to accept what I'm telling you, but we didn't come in a ship. I don't even know how to begin to tell you what did happen, how we got here. Maybe some of the others might tell what they think, but it's true, we have come from Harmony to help you and the children."

"Are you saying our children *went* to Harmony as well?" He hugged Pelle closer as he spoke as if frightened that she would disappear again. "They've been there all the time?"

"Yes." Javin decided to keep his answers short from now on, in the hope that it would simplify matters.

"How? How did they get there? What happened?"

"They got there the same way we arrived here." It was obvious from the look on the man's face that this was all too much to take in. "That's not important," he said. "The important thing to realize is that we're here to help you, and your children are back with you safe and sound and they will answer all your questions as best they can. My suggestion is to go back to your homes, enjoy your children, talk with them. We would only be intruding. You should be catching up on what's happened. We'll talk some more soon. We're not going away. And I promise we'll try to answer every question you have. But, for now, enjoy being together again." As he was speaking, he was guiding the man by his elbow to get him moving. As he let go, he said to Pelle, "Tell them what you can. We'll stay back there in one of the first huts we passed. If you need us, that's where we'll be."

The girl nodded and encouraged the others to walk away with her, although she could not stop the adults staring. Soon enough, Javin, Meldren and the islanders were alone by the boulder.

"I don't know about you," said Meldren to no one in particular, "but this is not anything like I thought it would be." She shivered, not just from the dampness in the air, but also as she looked around at the shattered remnants of the community. "These people... they deserve better than this. They looked as though they are starving to death. Does anyone know what the time of year is?"

"My best guess is winter," said Javin. "Late winter perhaps, by the look of the plants. But I could be wrong about that."

"Winter, and they have nothing to eat? Unless we do something, they are all going to starve."

Isselta's earlier happiness and excitement had evaporated. She looked like a frightened and lonely young girl again. "This," she said, gesturing around her, "this is not what I thought of when I used the terms seedlings for those children. How can anything be expected to grow and spread here? Why have we come?"

Farran agreed. "This matches my feeling of being scared and unsettled." He made a vague gesture of dismissal with his hand. "This is not good."

"Everything's been destroyed," added Carmeena. "How can this be the right place? Perhaps we were sent to the wrong area. Maybe there was something wrong in the song we were singing?" There was a note in her voice; a note of hope that she was right and that this mistake would be corrected soon.

They stood gazing around, feeling dismal and lost.

"I'm not going anywhere," said Javin with more determination than he felt. "We were sent here for a reason. We might not like it, but we're here and we have to make the best of it. It's my planet, if you like, but that's not the reason for me saying this." He scanned the faces around him, noting the shock as they tried to adjust to the situation they had found themselves in. "I'm saying this because we have spent time with those children. We have helped them grow and learn. They are a remarkable little group." He gave a tight smile. "It's not like we're totally useless, either. We are also capable of doing things ourselves. Yes, this is not what I was expecting. But we're not helpless. We had better start planning right away, because sooner or later, those children and those adults are going to be wondering why we really did come here. And if we do nothing but sit around saying how awful things are, then maybe they'd be right to ask that question. So... ," He took a deep breath. "A couple of things you need to know. This planet has shorter days. It's going to get dark soon." When some glanced up to gauge the height of the sun, he said, "You're going to have to learn that the sun here is different. It's bigger, for a start. Plus, there's no moon. Get used to the idea. Second, we need to hear this planet's song. We need to know what this planet is singing. If we are going to use songs to help, they have to be songs which fit here. We can't assume that the songs we used on Harmony will work here. Maybe even the sprites won't be of any help. But we won't know unless we start listening. Let's find a bit of shelter and do that right now. The quicker and the clearer we hear it, the quicker we will be able to help. First thing after hearing is to sing food. After that, we'll work out priorities. But food comes first for them all. Agreed?"

A few nods.

"Good. Now, let's get to work. We'll go to that hut over there," he said, pointing at a building back along the way they had come. It had a partial roof, but three of the walls looked in reasonable repair. "That's going to be our base for the time being. When we get there, go through your baskets for anything edible. Keep it safe for later. Then, start listening, and listening carefully. As soon as you think you can hear it, understand it, then try a small song. Something like a, like a... ," he looked around. "Like the wood the walls are made of. Try singing a small stick. We'll start small and slow and build on it. Well... ?" And he took hold of Meldren's hand and set off, expecting the others to follow. Which they did, but slowly at first.

"That was impressive, my love," whispered Meldren.

"Thanks. I felt it was more desperate than impressive. But I'll take the compliment."

THE MORNING OF THE FOLLOWING DAY FOUND THE ISLANDERS IN A BETTER frame of mind. Several early song experiments had failed, but, over time, the failures were fewer. Those failures had been small; the wood being sung had faded or never appeared or, in Dennet's case, had looked like wood but was able to be bent and twisted like a piece of thick leather.

Javin was quietly cursing the fact that they had not brought extra clothing or blankets. It was colder and more damp than they were used to, making focusing on songs harder. Everyone had started the night sitting as close together as they could and the loudest sounds had been the shivering breaths in the dark. They knew the night was going to be shorter than back on Harmony, but that knowledge hadn't turned into understanding yet, so that the first night had seemed to drag on endlessly until Isselta had said, "Fire is fire, no matter where you are, surely? So what worked on Harmony ought to work here, shouldn't it?" As nobody could think of an argument against it, she had tried and a small blaze had taken hold of a piece of wood they had been using for experiments. Others had quickly torn some more from the walls, or had found some on the floor and added to the blaze to the point where their bodies had been sweating in front but still cold in back. As a result, there had been a constant shuffling and rearranging of places around the fire.

As the morning arrived more quickly than they were used to, they began turning their attention to food. "What food do they have here, Javin?" asked Perray. "Shouldn't we know that before we try to sing some more?"

He shook his head. "I'm not sure. I can remember food when I was here, but I was living in a big city. I never grew it. I only bought it, traded for it, I mean. I think we shall have to ask them about what they eat. And don't forget the children will know more about that than we do. They should be able to be more helpful about that."

Some were feeling tired after such a restless night, and wanted to sleep. Javin agreed that those who really needed to sleep should go ahead. "The rest of us, however, need to be seen, need to be doing things. We're here to help, remember, even if we're not sure what we're doing. Then they will, hopefully, begin to accept us and begin to accept what we can do. And remember, the days are shorter, just like the nights. It'll take some getting used to, but we'll have plenty to occupy ourselves." He stood up. "Those who need sleep, stay here. I can't guarantee it will be quiet, but make the most of it. The others come with me and Meldren and let's see what we can do to help these people."

"How did you know I didn't want to go to sleep," said Meldren, grabbing at his hand as he left.

"That's easy," he grinned. "You'd never not want to know what's happening."

She narrowed her eyes at him and bared her teeth in a silent snarl, turning it into a smile. "I'll remember that, Javin. You might live to regret it."

He ducked in quickly and planted a kiss on her cheek. "But it will be worth it, my love."

"Hmmmm."

Carmeena, Farran, Enrick and Timoss decided to try to sleep. That left Javin, Meldren, Allegara, Isselta and Dennet to set off to the large, central boulder, where they could see a few of the people waiting for them.

It soon became obvious that the children had made some progress toward explaining everyone's arrival yesterday. It had been greatly helped by some demonstrations which had taken place. Apparently, Pelle had moved some smaller stones around, Endel had done much the same sort of thing, and Hanna had taken some failing plants and had encouraged them to look more sturdy and healthy. The adults of Newgrange had witnessed these events and more and had asked many questions. But the progress had been at the expense of sleep and Pol looked very tired and Bodren also yawned lustily.

"I think it would help if we introduced ourselves," said Javin, who then did just that, explaining that some of the group were sleeping. In return, one of the men called the names of those present.

"I'm Kris," he said, "and here are Pelle's parents, Oska and Venna. Pol, over there you know, she is with Berd and Jenni. Then we have Bodren with Sarrah and Fillip. Sadly, Flinder died." He paused briefly, the memory clearly causing him pain. "That's Semmik and Marianna with Endel." He put his hands up in resignation. "I'm sorry. It's too much to take in all at once, I know. Perhaps it will be easier to learn names more slowly." He stopped again, taking slow, deep breaths as if recovering from exertion. "I would love to be able to offer you some food, but, sadly, as you can see, it is in rather short supply here. I apologize." He attempted a warm smile, but the empty, flat eyes had no room for humor.

His shoulders sagged. "What I really want to know is, if you have come here to help us, what can you do for us? The children have shown us some tricks, but we need more than that."

"First, they are not tricks. They are talents which will prove useful to you. As for us?" Javin beckoned the islanders to come closer. "We can do a lot, but you need food first. To help with that, we need to know what sort of things you eat. What sorts of food do you usually have here?" He beckoned Endel to him as well. "Endel, we need to know the foods you eat. You lived here, so perhaps you can remember what they were well enough to make them?" Endel nodded at Javin and then drew Bodren to him with another motion of his head where they began to talk quietly.

Leaving them to it, Javin saw Kris's eyes fill with tears. "That's the problem," the man said. "We don't have any food. Not normal food. We used to eat bread and meat and vegetables, but they left us nothing." He wiped his cheeks and his eyes signaled an apology for the display of emotion.

"Bread we can do," said Javin, indicating to Isselta and Dennet to begin, and ignoring the confusion on Kris's face. "The other thing is you need to live in something which is weatherproof, not these huts. Meldren? Can you and Allegara work together on these? Warm, packed earth floor to begin with, no drafts and a waterproof roof. I'm going to go with -- Kris, was it? -- and find out how else we can help here."

He pointed to the river. "Is that your only source of water?"

Kris nodded as he looked around, still confused by the sudden organization. "Yes. We used to have it running in channels, but... ," he stopped, pointing at the torn up ground where the channels used to be. Everything seemed to be too much effort for him. When the singing began, Kris was taken by surprise. It wasn't just the strange sounds and rhythms, but also the way the sprites rose up from the necks of the Isselta, Dennet, Meldren and Allegara. He turned to Javin and gestured at his own throat, his whole face a question. "I've seen those before, haven't I?"

Javin looked harder at Kris. "I recognize you now. You were there when Meldren and I arrived to take the children. There were soldiers coming. I remember you."

"I was too frightened to remember much. But I do remember those things round your necks."

"I'm glad you survived. These creatures," said Javin stroking his own sprite, still coiled around his throat, "they can help us in many ways. We'll do our best to help everyone here."

Despite the words, Kris was obviously confounded and overwhelmed by what he was seeing happening. In front of where Isselta and Dennet and Pelle were standing, fresh bread appeared on the ground. Enough for a loaf for everyone present, with plenty left over. He had hardly made a step toward the inviting loaves, when he saw what Meldren and Allegara were involved in. As he watched, walls appeared to mend themselves, a door seemed to drift into focus along with a window, and then, after a pause to consult with one of the onlookers, a roof with thick, new thatch. It all seemed to be spun out of the air; as if invisible strands were being collected and woven and made into something tangible. Off to one side, Endel and Bodren were singing a different song, and an enticing smell of fresh cooked meat wafted across the area. The two boys stopped and stood back a little and both were grinning hugely, the sight of such happiness on Endel's face was a great relief to Javin. Then Bodren put his hand to his mouth in realization and sang a large dish to put the meat on, instead of leaving it on the ground.

Every one of the villagers was making toward the food, making noises of wonder and amazement, as well as appreciation.

"-- Where did it come from?"

"-- Who are they?"

"-- Is it real?"

"-- Can we eat it?"

"-- I don't believe it, but I can smell it!"

Soon everyone was eating, including all the visitors from Harmony: Carmeena, Farran, Enrick, Perray and Timoss having joined them when the smells of the fresh food dragged them awake. They yawned as much as they ate at first, but the food soon revived them, just as it did for everyone else. There was chattering and even some laughter to be heard from the villagers, who kept glancing at the newcomers from the corners of their eyes, as if everything would vanish if they stared directly them. It must, thought Javin, seem very much like a dream to them, having fresh, hot food where there had been none. He motioned Pelle to him and asked, "What's the weather going to be like tonight and tomorrow?"

She half-closed her eyes, fingers and thumbs rubbing gently against each other as she sensed ahead. "Cold tonight, like last night. But no rain. Not for another... two days, I think. It will be cool in the daytime, but nothing really bad is coming."

"Thanks. Pelle. I think it might be a good idea if we had a big bonfire here in the middle so that everyone can keep warm while we finish off the huts and it'll be easier to feed everyone if they're in one place. Can you ask Bodren to sing some wood for it? We'll need a lot to keep it going, so that's going to be his job for the rest of the day. Tell him to rest when he feels he needs to. I don't want anyone doing too much. We've only just arrived here, and we've got a lot to do yet. Oh, and can you ask Endel to sing some raw meat so we can cook it later on?" The girl bobbed her head and left to pass the message on to Bodren first, who was sitting with his mother and brother, and then on to Endel, sitting near to what Javin guessed were his parents.

After eating and resting a little, the reconstruction of the village progressed more quickly, now that the others had joined in. Huts were sung and even some furniture appeared. However, none of islanders were used to songs which had metal in them, so things like knives and shovels were given over to the children to sing, rather than have such items be damaged or mis-shaped in the process.

Everyone was busy. The villagers, beginning in a daze of disbelief which was slowly replaced by a sense of wonder, began to help out where they could; guiding the design of a hut, showing where a window should be, or how wide a hearth or tall an oven needed to be. Javin asked Meldren to work at singing them all some clothing. "Anything at all will be useful; for us and for them. Something thick, some blankets, anything which will keep us warm. Pelle has said the weather will hold but be cool for a while. So you've got plenty of time."

"I can do that," said Meldren. "But what about you? You're looking tired. Shouldn't you be taking a rest? You're keeping everyone organized and busy, which is great. But you need to look after yourself as well."

Javin rubbed around his eyes and yawned. "I promise that tonight I'll rest more and then tomorrow should be a little easier. At least I hope so.

But we need to get these people out of the weather, well-fed and clothed warmly before we do much else. Until then, I don't really think I could rest that much anyway." He gave a tired smile. "But, I promise to sleep a long time when it's done."

She leaned in and kissed him. "Just make sure you do, that's all."

THE EVENING ARRIVED; THE SUN SETTING SPEEDILY, ACCORDING TO THE islanders. By that time, everyone looked tired, no matter who they were or where they were from. Those from Harmony had been focusing hard all day, singing new songs, listening to how they fitted in to Haven's basic song. They felt drained, their heads aching from concentrating, their bodies still trying to come to terms with being on a new planet. The villagers were tired because although they still lacked strength, they had been working as hard as they could to repair their homes. And the children were tired from working for far longer than they had ever done.

Bodren had done a magnificent job of creating a large pile of wood for the fire, just as Endel had sung much meat, and had also experimented with singing some of the vegetables he remembered. Both were slumped on the ground, exhausted but proud. As before, Isselta sang the fire up and they all gathered around and began roasting meat on long skewers, chewing on some bread provided by Hanna who had worked on it quietly with a little help from Pol who had dozed off several times during the day.

Hardly anyone spoke at first, grateful for the food and the rest. Gradually, as bellies filled and bodies warmed, conversations began and a low buzz of voices spread.

Javin found himself sitting next to Kris, with Meldren the other side of him. Kris was looking a great deal better than previously. Gone was the morose, tearful expression to be replaced by one of cautious optimism. He even let loose a few small smiles as he was speaking.

"I can't thank you all enough," he said. He waved his hand to include everyone and everything there. "We would have died without you. And it wouldn't have taken that long, either."

Javin dismissed the praise with a brief toss of his head. "We are happy to help you all. But, tell me something. What season of the year is it? Because the fields will need planting for crops, won't they?"

"It should be mid-spring, but the winter was long and hard." A sad look crossed his face. "Very, very hard. Some people died when the soldiers came. They were shot. That's what happened to Bodren's father. He heard them coming and tried to divert them away. He did, but he got shot doing it. Several others were found and killed. Most of us were, I think, plain lucky. After they had run off all our animals, they burned the homes and they sprayed something on the land. I don't know what that was. Poison probably."

"I thought the crops looked strange when we arrived. That would explain it."

"I caught a glimpse of what happened to the land," put in Perray who was wandering past on her way to get more food. She wrinkled her nose. "I got it from one of the plants. It wasn't a pleasant sight."

In answer to the question Kris obviously had, Javin said, "Another one of the talents; being able to see what has happened in the past to something." He gave an apologetic shrug and motioned Kris to continue.

"We had taken food with us, plus a lot of us had stored food in our hideouts. When we got out and saw what they'd done" -- he caught his breath and gestured an apology for the emotion -- "some of the survivors decided to leave and find somewhere else. That left the ones you see now. Apart from those who died during the winter." He sighed. "Older and weaker. Some, I'm sure, died of broken hearts." He pointed downhill beyond the village. "We buried them as best we could. The rest of us decided to stay and see if we could wait out the winter, maybe trap some food, eat some fresh shoots and so on. But the winter, it just kept on being winter. We had so few tools left. I didn't tell you that, did I? No. They destroyed everything they could find, including tools. We only had the ones we hid with us. Not enough. The soldiers won't be coming back, however, because they destroyed so much. To them, this is now wasteland. It looks like one to us as well."

"I can see how everything looks, Kris. But, tell me, why did it happen? All I know is that we arrived to find these children. We didn't know that's who we were looking for, but anyway... We met you, of course. We got here and there were soldiers. Are you saying that those same soldiers did all this back then?"

Kris nodded. "Yes. It was the same time as you arrived. Seeing you both was the strangest sight, and there was me feeling scared and confused. I think you saved my life that day."

"It was a strange time," agreed Meldren.

"But why did the soldiers do all this?"

Kris let out a slow breath. "That's going to take a bit of telling. First, though, I think you owe me some answers. The children and everything?"

"That sounds fair," agreed Javin. "What do you want to know. Or shall I guess?"

Kris gave a wry grin. "I get a feeling I might not understand some of the answers, but I'll take that chance. First thing is, how did you get here?"

Javin turned several possible explanations over in his mind. "You must have heard lots of things today. Lots of ideas and explanations?" Kris nodded. "The reason for that is that none of us really know how we got here. That's the first thing. The second thing is that even if I told you what we think we know, it wouldn't make a great deal of sense. But," he held up his hand as if to excuse himself for any mistakes he might make, "since you asked, I'll give it a try. I've never tried explaining this to anyone before, so it might come out wrong. You can ask others if you like and see if what they say makes more sense.

"We came here, we think, because of a very strong song, or music, if you like. Sounds. That's what brought us here. Very powerful sounds. That, or something like it, was able to carry us quickly and safely from Harmony to here. That's about as far as I can go in explanations. Which, I know, isn't very far at all. Next question?"

"You're right, it doesn't make any sense, but I think you're being honest. Either you do know how you got here but don't know how to explain it, or you don't know and you're making it up. Doesn't matter which in the end, does it? I accept that I'm not going to know the 'how' part of it. But there must be a 'why' part you can answer. So... why are you here and what about the children? Well, two questions in one, I suppose."

"The children: they're first. We knew we had to come here to find and bring back something. And, I know that sounds crazy as well, but you must have had a strong feeling to do something that you couldn't explain? It was like that for us and so we followed that feeling, and we arrived here and that's the time when we found out it was the children we had been sent for." Javin breathed out a sigh. "That must have been so hard, letting the children go with us. I don't know how they did it, their parents. We were strangers and we took them. They must have had nightmares after that."

"I'm not so sure about that," said Kris. "From what I can tell, the parents had been listening to those children for days, being told that some people were coming for them and that they would be safe and that they'd come back. It helped, at least as far as I can tell."

"That's a relief," said Meldren, leaning around Javin to speak. "I know that Javin was worried about it all, worried about what the families were going through. We all were, actually." She smiled at Kris. "Thanks for putting our minds at rest about that. We didn't want to cause anyone any pain."

Kris nodded thoughtfully to himself. "But that still leaves the other question. Why are you here?"

"This is going to be one of those strange answers again," said Javin. "We're here because the children said it was time to come back. We had no idea why, but we all felt that we should come, in a group this time."

"You do that sort of thing often, do something just because you have a feeling?" interrupted Kris.

"There'd be no point in having them otherwise, would there?" smiled Meldren. "We trust what we get and we do what is necessary because of it."

Kris smiled. "I'm getting used to your accent, even if I have trouble remembering your name. You'll have to forgive me if I ask you to say something twice. But you remind me of my friend when you say that. He trusted his feelings." He shook his head. "I wish he were able to hear what you're saying. Actually, I wish I could do what he did; listen to those feelings better." He shook off the sadness with a visible effort. "But that doesn't really answer anything, does it?"

"Perhaps the best answer to the question of why we're here is something one of the people who came with us said." Javin peered around and pointed out Isselta who was talking and laughing with Pol's parents, the firelight flickering on their dirt-streaked, happy faces. "That girl there, Isselta, she said that we should think of the children as something like seeds. We've taught them things, helped them learn new things, and now, we've brought them back and they can grow into adults here and pass on what they know to others, until... well, until enough people have got the message."

"But what is that message? What did you teach them?"

Meldren helped Javin out, trying to speak more slowly and clearly for Kris' sake. "You said you wished you could listen like your friend. Well, the children and the rest of us can listen to things you might not be aware of. We can hear sounds you didn't know existed. And, if you can hear those sounds and you can make some of them yourself, with the help of these little creatures round our necks, you can do a lot of things. That's how we're making the huts, how the bread and meat appears. All the things we're doing, they're done with songs." She screwed her face and bit her lip to show she was aware of how it sounded to Kris. "That might sound too strange at first, but it's true."

"But it's not just that," added Javin. "Things like knowing something without being told, like finding water underground, like moving things without touching them. All of those things don't use songs. Those are what anyone can do. I'm convinced of it. I've seen enough to know it's real and true. And your children can do those things. Maybe some of the adults will find they can do them, too. It might only take seeing someone else do it to make it possible for them to do it as well."

Kris expression showed he was having trouble coming to terms with what he had heard. "Seeds? That's how you think of the children?"

"It's not such a bad idea really, is it?" said Meldren. "After all, every child is a seed of the parents. It's just that, here and now, they are carrying more than what they were born with. They're going to be spreading ideas and talents around."

"And if their parents don't go along with this?"

"Look at them," said Javin. "Look at what they can already do. Do you honestly think they will listen to their parents' fears? All the people who came with us, we've all seen enough of what they can do to make it obvious that, no matter what you or I might think, they are going to do things their way. After all, they were the ones who told their parents not to worry about going off with strangers. After that, everything else will be easy in comparison."

"Maybe you're right." Kris sounded doubtful.

"Only one way to find out." Javin slapped his hands on his thighs, determined to change the subject. "Now, you promised me some answers. Like, what happened here and why did it happen?"

Kris thought for a moment. "This is going to be easier to understand than what you just told me. At least, I hope it will be. The best way I can think of explaining it is by saying that this place, Newgrange, is, or was, one of many others like it around the planet. There were lots of people who didn't like the military coup which happened many years ago. But we'd had those before in our history, so we figured it would sort itself out. Only it didn't. This one wanted to go to the stars and find other people. It wanted to know we aren't alone in the universe." He shrugged. "It sounds fine by itself, but what it actually meant was that everything here was geared to that. Industry, science, education, the media, you name it. And the people were monitored, snooped on more like, more than ever before. All for the glory of a couple of spaceships. And then we were told that Harmony, your planet was threatening us." He looked at the shock and disbelief on their faces and nodded. "That's really what we were told. So we sent those ships to Harmony to neutralize that threat. Not my words, by the way. Again, it's what we were told. Well, it didn't happen for whatever reason and the ships came back and everyone on board was dead. It made the whole military organization and everything they had been doing look foolish. And Harmony disappeared! That was something they couldn't account for, and it made them mad. That's when everyone began to question more and more why they were still being obeyed." Kris gave another shrug. "If you can't beat them and you don't want to join them, the only other option it seemed was to move away from them. So that's what this place and others like it are about. We didn't have the power to take on the military. Especially not in the mood they were in after the failure with Harmony. We thought if we went away they'd ignore us. Let us live how we wanted. And, if we failed, it was down to us. We wanted to control our own lives again. Live with a little more self-respect and respect for the planet, instead of ripping it apart for some stupid dream that was going nowhere. The trouble for them was that more and more people thought like that." He gazed into the bonfire. "I was the one who found this place and got it started. Actually, it was me, my wife and a friend who started it. I'm the only one left. My wife was killed early on in one of the fights that were always breaking out then. My friend, the one I said trusted his feelings, he was also killed by soldiers the same time as you arrived to take the children." He shook his head at the memories. "That's the reason I never left. If I did, I'd be leaving them behind, as well as the idea we shared. Everything I wanted to create was here." He rubbed at his eyes. "Besides, it's too late for me to start anything else."

Javin shifted around to see Kris more clearly. "Are you telling me that government soldiers came here because you wanted to live how you wanted to live? Really? That sounds... ." He threw his hands up at his failure to find the words for that he felt.

"Bizarre?" said Meldren.

"Yes," Kris nodded. "That's a good word for it."

"But why?" Javin asked again. "Why would they do that to you?"

"You have to realize, it's not just us that got attacked. We heard that it had happened to other places like ours. And, before you ask why again, it's because the government, if you want to call it that, wants to keep everything like it always has been. We were rejecting everything; all of our history since we first arrived here. That's a big thing to do. We called ourselves Revivalists, although I'm not sure why. It had a good sound to it I suppose." He shook his head and smiled wistfully. "I don't think any of really understood how big it was going to be or how much it would annoy the government." He picked at a callous on his hand, his voice lower. "A government faced with more and more people rejecting its ideals can do one of two things. One, you agree with the majority and get in line with how the people are thinking and change how you act and what you do. That is noble but unlikely. Or, two, you decide that because you have the power and the ability, you must destroy the opposition and reinstate the status quo. Kill enough of them and destroy what they have built, prove their ideas are weak or wrong and, sooner or later, they'll give in and move back to the towns and be good little citizens again." He chewed at the callous and then spat. "That's the reason for all this, and why it's happening over and over again in different places. We're just one little community. But we represent a lot of problems for the government."

Javin felt all sorts of emotions running through him."When Harmony disappeared, we knew that there was an attack coming, but we didn't know how to deal with it." He looked at the expression on Kris' face and tried to think how to describe that time when he and Meldren had given guidance to a planet and gave up. Instead, he said, "I can never explain it to you in a way which would make any sense. But one thing you should know is that I was born on Haven." After hearing what Kris had to say, he didn't know what he wanted to say. Apologize? Sympathize? Share his disappointment, his lack of knowledge of events here? He realized he did not understand Haven at all. He felt Meldren move closer to him, as if aware that what was about to be said was important for the both of them. He felt her hand at his waist and he reached to squeeze it, still looking at Kris. "Hard to believe, I know, by looking at me. But you probably heard of my parents."

That made Kris look up. "Who were they?"

"My last name is Sarnum. I'm Javin Sarnum."

Kris frowned in thought for a moment. "Sarnum? But that was the name of the last elected head of government. Marak? Marak Sarnum? But he and his wife were killed, weren't they? By the soldiers in the coup. What's-his-name took over. Mikkan, that's the name. General Mikkan. I seem to remember something about a son, but he wasn't found or was found dead. I can't remember the details now." He peered more closely at Javin, as if trying to find something in his face he could identify. "And you're saying that you're the son that wasn't found? But you came here from Harmony. Or that's what you say, anyway. How can that be?" There was skepticism in his voice.

"I was found after my parents were killed. I was hiding. I think Mikkan wanted to keep me so that, later on, when I was older, I could be used in some way in the government. You know, give it an air of legitimacy. Something like that. Or, maybe, he just felt sorry for me. I was kept out of sight, educated and everything. I was moved around a lot. But, in the end something must have changed, because they left me to fend for myself in the city after doing something to my head so I had a false identity and only partial memories of my past. They messed up my mind for certain. Anyway, I survived in Pannedon for a while. Then one day I was living there, and the next, I'd been drugged, had *all* my memories wiped and shipped off to Harmony. I don't know why any of it happened. It took a while for me to get my memories back. You can ask Meldren. She was there when it happened. Or, at least, she was the first to know. Weren't you?" he asked, turning to her.

"I don't know everything that happened to him here," she said. "But I do know he was completely useless on Harmony at first. Didn't know the first thing about anything. Didn't know anything about his past until a healer helped him." She hugged him from behind, rested her chin his shoulder and smiled at Kris. "He told me about his parents, and I know when people are lying. He never did lie about his life before Harmony."

Javin smiled. "She really can see when people are lying. That's a fact. It's one of those talent things I mentioned earlier. Some time later, you can test her if you like and she doesn't mind?" He half-turned to check with her.

She laughed. "I don't mind."

"Why are you telling me this anyway?" asked Kris. "If it's as true as you say it is," he dipped his head at Meldren, "then don't you have some sort of right to be -- I don't know -- the opposition or something? The constitution never allowed for hereditary power, but your presence could at the least make life difficult for the ones in power."

Javin laughed easily for the first time since his arrival. "There is absolutely no chance that I have any interest in being part of governing a whole planet. I have enough trouble trying to live my own life, let alone telling others what to do with theirs. No, that's not something I have any interest in doing. Besides, I like it better on Harmony." His choice was obvious as he tilted his head to rest it against Meldren's and smiled.

"So why did you tell me, then?" asked Kris.

Javin became serious again. "Because I wanted you to know that I'm someone who cares about this place, this planet. It used to be my home. It's where I came from, and it's somewhere that a part of me still cares about. You said that you couldn't leave here because too much of your past is here. Well, my past is here as well, and I'd like to at least do something that might help make things right. There's that child in me who still needs to see Haven as a good place."

Kris looked long at him; not quite skeptical, not quite accepting. Finally, he gave a curt nod, making up his mind. "I think I can understand that. But what you've overlooked is that this place, Haven, is not a good place right now." He swept his arms wide. "Otherwise this wouldn't have happened here or other places as well. Maybe, one day, it will be a good place again, the sort of place you have in your mind, but it's not today. That's for sure."

EVERYONE SLEPT WELL THAT NIGHT: FULL BELLIES, HARD WORK AND A LARGE bonfire saw to that. The next day everyone was bleary-eyed, yawning, lethargic and slow to get started. Some more wood was dragged from some of the outlying ruined homes, the bonfire was coaxed back into life and everyone began to feel more alive again. Plans for the day were discussed and tasks agreed on and allocated. Some more fresh bread was sung, and someone found an intact pot to boil some water in. Someone else found some herbs to add. A few mugs were brought out and the hot tea was shared around. The difference in everyone was evident. There was a lightness, a feeling of assured hope, a strengthening of will. Above all, there was happiness, laughter and joking, shared smiles between the islanders and the villagers. There was a sense of coherence which had been missing before.

Javin watched it all but couldn't join in as easily as the others. He stood to one side, hugging his mug, chewing on his lip, a distance in his eyes. Meldren noticed and, excusing herself from a group of women who wanted to know how she coped without anything on her feet, went to him.

"Why the look? I can see your colors and they are not how I'd like to see them. What can I do to help?"

He gave her an abstracted smile. "I'm sorry. I was just thinking about our conversation last night with Kris."

"What about it?"

"This isn't how things should be."

She looked around at the buzz of activity in puzzlement. "What's wrong with it?"

"It's what happened here and those other places, and why it happened." He shook his head. "That's what's wrong." He turned to look directly at her. "And who's to say that it won't happen again? Everyone could still be murdered for being here. Just for being here. That's simply not right."

"Of course it's not right, Javin. I agree. But what can we do about it? And, even if we knew what to do, how do we do it? We're not on Harmony any more. It's not like we have a right to do anything beyond what we're doing here. We're helping these people in a way that works for them. But as for changing how other people act? Is that what we're going to get involved in next?" She reached for his hand. "The truth is, my love, that we're very much on our own here."

He sighed heavily. "I know. But... Harmony sent us here to help her sister. She pushed us to come and take some of Haven's children to teach them and bring them back again. I can't believe that we've been sent here to rebuild one village and go again. Think about it." He became more animated as he followed his thoughts. "Any time we've had closeness and communication with Harmony, something big, something grand was involved. This here, this village, it's small. A small thing. Sure, getting here was an adventure, something new. But this can't be all there is. It goes against every experience we've had. There has to be something bigger than this. It's not necessarily about whether we have the right or not. We're here because of a planet, not because of our desire to make things happen." He grinned lopsidedly, "Of course, the trick is, as you said, my love, what happens next and how do we fit into it? "

"We do what we always do, of course," she replied quietly, drawing him close by putting her arms round his neck and leaning in to rest her forehead against his. "We ask. We ask Haven. The answer will come somehow. But She needs to know what it is we're asking. It's no good us just standing here and complaining. We have to let Her know what we want from Her." She stood back, a briskness in her voice. "So, my love, are you really sure about what it is we want to know?"

"I think so. I think what we want to know is what it is we are really here to do. What is the big thing Haven wants from us? What did She bring us here for? That's the question."

Meldren smiled and gave a brief nod of approval. "Good. So now we can get on with helping out, can't we? I mean, you don't think you're just going to be allowed to be left standing there waiting for an answer, do you?" She took his hand and started walking. "Come along with me and I'll find you something to do."

He laughed at the mock seriousness in her voice. "Certainly. Whatever happens, I suppose we'll deal with it."

"You're right about the 'we' in that sentence," she said over her shoulder, a smile in her voice. "You're not going off alone. If you're wanting to do something adventurous, then I have to be with you. That's a simple fact. Anything else would be an injustice."

He stopped suddenly, causing her stop and look back questioningly. "You know something I've just realized? You used the word injustice? Well, I'm angry at the injustice of it all. I've never allowed myself to be before now. I didn't get angry when I got my memories back. But now? Now, now I can feel it." He felt something he couldn't quite name. Was it anger or was it a realization of loss: loss in his life, of his memories, loss of innocence in children? "I'm angry because this... these murders shouldn't have happened. I'm angry at you and me and everyone being dragged here without ever being told why. I'm angry at being kidnapped, and that happened so long ago that it seems stupid to be angry at it now. I'm angry at not being able to live how we want to live; always being dragged off to something we don't understand until much later. When do we get to say what happens to us? When do we get to choose? Ever? Or is always going to be like this?" He swept his arms in a wide arc encompassing Newgrange and all the people, past and present in it, and beyond it, the whole world and his own history on it. "I'm angry at everything. Every little thing! The children who haven't had a childhood over there. People starving to death here because the fields were poisoned. It's *wrong*!"

Meldren wrapped him tight. "What you said made your colors be the brightest I have *ever* seen. Big, strong flares around your head in particular. Which means," she said, pushing him off to cup his chin and look into his eyes, "that what you said had a force to it unlike anything you've said. A truth. And, yes, I can feel angry about those exact same things as you do. But it's not as true for me, not as personal." Tenderly, she stroked his face, her eyes soft and warm. "I'm glad you found the anger inside of you. If you hadn't, it would have festered and grown and become something ugly. So, I'm proud of you for acknowledging it. Hold on to it though because, sooner or later, you're going to want that anger. If we really are going to do something big for this planet I'll guarantee that whatever we need will be more than us being nice and polite and normal. We'll need your anger. Our anger. Because I can feel some of it inside me as well." She looked into his eyes. "Now, let's get back to the others. We've still got work to do." She gave an encouraging smile. "Well there's one good thing come out of it."

"What?"

"If Haven didn't get that message of yours, then She's absolutely deaf and we can go back home to Harmony sooner than we thought."

He gave a wry grin. "I don't deserve you, you know."

"I agree. You don't. I will let you kiss me, though, because it's something you should do more often." She sighed theatrically. "One more thing I have to teach you." But her eyes were smiling and laughing.

By the time they were among the others, Javin had regained a calm outward face, although Meldren could see in the way the colors were dancing around him, pulsing out and closing in tightly, just how unsettled he still was. The day passed quickly in work; the homes being completed inside and out, clothing being sung.

The most dramatic moment of the day was when Pol got to show off her talent. Kris had gashed the edge of his hand on a sharp sliver of timber he was moving from out of one of the ruined huts they had decided to use for firewood. He gasped in pain, holding his hand from which blood was flowing freely. He paled and there was a look of panic in his eyes as he realized the extent of the injury. Pol stopped piling the brushwood and kindling that had been collected and marched, not ran, to him where he was leaning against the boulder, grimacing and surrounded by several anxious villagers trying to help. Without a word, she pushed through them and reached for his damaged hand. She held his thumb, turning his hand palm up, and the steady, focused attitude of the child held him back from pulling away or remonstrating. He was still shaking with the pain and shock of it, but she ignored him and half-closed her eyes, her high-pitched voice singing a song that was barely audible. The other tiny hand hovering over the cut didn't seem to be do anything. There was a sudden gasp of surprise, not pain, from Kris, and he finally did jerk his hand back from her to hold it in front of his face as if it no longer belonged to him. There was no evidence of a cut, only the quickly drying sticky residue of blood. His jaw gaped, his eyes wide as he looked at Pol as if she were a stranger.

Meldren was close by, having seen Pol's determined walk. She put a reassuring hand on his shoulder. "Don't ask how it was done."

"B-But... ," he spluttered.

"That was one of the things she learned from us. She might be the youngest and the smallest but, from what we've seen, she's also amongst the most talented. It would mean a lot if you thanked her," she said.

"Th-Thank you, Pol. Thank you." He was still in a daze. The villagers who had witnessed it were in a similar state of shock, taking turns to examine the hand disbelievingly.

Meldren took him by the arm. "I think you need to sit and rest for a while and get over the shock. It will also give you some time to get used to the idea of Pol and the others being here and doing things like this."

He nodded absently.

Pol was standing nearby looking unsure of herself. "That was very good, Pol," said Meldren. "Well done."

"But I didn't ask permission," the girl piped back, inspecting the blood on her hand.

Meldren grabbed a handful of grass and gave it to Pol to wipe the blood away. She squatted down to be at the child's level. "With something like that, he was in need of help, wasn't he?" A nod as she scrubbed her hand. "Without help, he would have lost much blood, yes?" Another nod. "Sometimes, when people have been badly hurt like that, they need help but are too shocked to ask for it or to listen to what someone is saying to them."

"Does that mean you aren't going to tell me off?"

"That's exactly what I mean, Pol. You did a good thing here."

"But I should still remember to ask?"

"If you're ever in doubt, Pol, always, always ask. And be prepared to be told no. Just because you ask doesn't mean you can get on with healing. You have to listen to the answer."

"I know," she said in a sing-song fashion. "I promise."

"But right now, Pol, you deserve a big hug." Pol's face broke into a wide, happy smile as she threw the grass away and put out her arms to Meldren, and the two of them held on to each other tightly.

Kris took a while to recover from the twin shocks of injury and sudden healing. When Meldren went over to him later, still sitting in the doorway of his home, he looked up at her. "Now I know that you really are from another planet and that these children, the ones I thought I knew, they're not the same as us." He held up his healed hand. "This? This is so different, so strange, so... ," his voice tailed off.

"Don't say that," said Meldren, "These children are not strange. Just because they can do something you can't doesn't make them strange. They're still children. And if you go around thinking they are strange, different, separate or however you want to call them, then that's how they will end up."

Kris looked confused.

Meldren sat down beside him. "Look at it this way. If you keep thinking of what they can do that you can't, then eventually they will feel unwelcome and unloved and they will end up as outcasts. And that's not what any of us are here for. We're here to help. But if you can't look at Pol, for example, without seeing something strange and something to be scared of, then you're hurting them and yourself by pushing them away. Do you have any idea just how brave all of them were when they were with us on Harmony? A different planet, strangers all around them teaching them strange things? And do you know what they were thinking all that time? It was about what they had to do when they came back here. They were thinking about how they would be helping you here. So, please, don't start making them out as something to be scared of. All they want to do is live here and help. Don't push them away because one child did something wonderful for you."

Kris gazed off into the distance, absently rubbing at his hand. "I had a friend. I told you about him. He helped start this community. He did something I couldn't do. He could feel when bad things were going to happen." His eyes became sad and a thin, tight smile appeared. "He was the one who warned us that we would be attacked. None of us really believed him. I thought I did. I told him I did. But I didn't. Yet he was my friend, my helper, the one I could talk to, explore ideas with. So I went along with what he said and together we helped plan things." He looked at Meldren sitting next to him, a grim expression on his face. "I should have been a better friend. I should have believed in what he said. I never could feel the things he talked about. I always felt -- I don't know -- less than him. Lacking something in myself, if you like." He shook his head sadly and gazed off into the past again. "But he saved us. Because of what he felt, because he made me act, we're alive today. It's down to him and to what he felt and to his courage in telling me about that feeling. He probably knew I didn't believe him. Not deep down."

He swept some hair from his face and then brushed gently at his eyes with his fingertips. "And now, there are others here, doing things he could probably understand or at least appreciate, even if he couldn't do them himself. And I'm doing what I did before: not believing it, wanting it to be something else, thinking that I'm missing a part of me. I'm thinking about why I can't do what Pol did and not liking myself because of my inability when, instead, I should be thanking her and finding out how I can make things easier for her. If I couldn't support and believe my friend, then I can at least begin to make it up to him, to his memory, by looking after these children and not being scared of them, not seeing myself as useless or worthless. So," he said, forcing a smile, "maybe your idea of them being seeds was right in more ways than one. It's planted a seed in me, to get me thinking in new ways."

Meldren nodded and they sat together in silence for a while, watching the work going on around them.

THE THIRD DAY WAS SPENT IN THE FIELDS. NEARLY EVERYONE WAS OUT, pulling weeds and dead and dying plants. That was the day that Hanna's earlier wish was granted, but not in the way she had thought.

Hanna had asked about whether any seeds were available, and whatever could be found was brought out and given to her. When Hanna had all the pots spread out around her as she was seated on the ground, a lot of the villagers stopped to watch her, pretending they were taking a break from the work in the fields. Timoss stood to one side, watching his protege. Hanna held her hands over each pot in turn and cocked her head, eyes closed, as if she were listening to something. After she had done this over each pot, she took three of them and placed them to one side, telling her audience, "These won't grow. They are spoiled in some way. The rest of them I think I can make grow strong and quick. But we need to make sure the soil is ready for them."

She set off for the fields where the islanders were standing in a group, the onlookers trailing behind. Hanna arrived to hear Isselta say, "I don't know for sure what the song should be for here. But, I do know that this soil has got something in it that stops plants growing. If you listen, it sounds as if there is some sort of chaotic noise. It's not a song, it's noise. And that is making the plants weak and die."

"A poison, you mean?" asked Farran.

"Well, Kris did say that the soldiers did something to the soil and Pep also mentioned having seen the soil being sprayed," said Javin, "so that sounds as if it's right. The point is can we change the song here, make it so the soil is good enough to grow plants in again?"

"What we need is a sample of good soil," said Carmeena. "But where from?"

There was a brief silence which was ended by a grunt of laughter from Timoss who had accompanied Hanna. "The field is poisoned, but everywhere else is fine, isn't it? All we have to do is grab a handful of soil from somewhere which is not a field!" He spread his hands and made a face which plainly said, 'Obvious!'

They separated, sharing embarrassed smiles, to get their samples. Javin saw Hanna standing nearby. "Is everything all right, Hanna?"

"Yes. I wanted to see if I could start the seeds growing yet."

"Soon," he reassured her. "We're just going to make the soil ready for you." He stopped and peered more closely at her face and pointed. "What's that you've got on you?" he asked.

Hanna brushed at her face. "What do you mean?"

Javin pointed to his own cheek. "You've got something here."

"What? What is it?"

"I'm sure it's nothing. Probably just some dirt. Let me see."

He held her face gently in his hands and examined her carefully. It looked like there were a series of dotted lines on her cheek. They were thin and formed an intricate swirl which covered most of her cheek. He moistened a finger and rubbed gently but nothing changed. He rubbed again, a little harder. Again, nothing.

"Just a moment," he said as he closed his eyes and listened to her. She watched him carefully, wondering whether to be afraid or not, wondering what he was hearing. She held her breath without realizing. After a moment, he opened his eyes and looked at her, smiling to reassure her. "No. There's nothing to worry about, Hanna. Your song is still sounding as it should. It's not changed. But there is something else added. A small note, a background chorus; something like that. And, as far as I can tell, it's coming from your cheek." He listened again for a moment. "It's not just you. I can hear the same chorus; delicate and lovely in both Pol and in Endel." He jerked his thumb at the two others working some way off. He beckoned to Hanna as he set off. "Come with me and we'll see if what I think is happening actually is what's happening."

He called Endel over and motioned to Pol and as soon as he saw them, he nodded to Hanna. "Hanna, what do you see on Pol and Endel's faces?" Hanna looked and was surprised.

"They've got markings on them, on their faces!"

"And, Endel, what do you see on Hanna's face?"

The boy nodded. "Markings. A pattern." He looked at Pol. "Same as Pol."

"What are they? What's happening?" asked Hanna.

"First, there's nothing I can hear that says you should be worried. They don't hurt, do they? You don't even know they're there, do you? Second, I think you've got what you wished for, Hanna." She was puzzled, not able to recall anything like that.

"Remember when you first arrived on Harmony and you saw our sprites? And you said you wanted one and asked when would you get one? Well, I think your wish has been granted. I think that these patterns on your faces are what Haven uses instead of sprites."

"Ooooh! We've got our very own sprites!" squeaked Pol, giving a little jump of excitement and pointing at Endel's face.

"What do they do?" asked Endel. "What are they for?"

"Hmmmm. Perhaps they're like our sprites. They help us sing difficult songs, as you know. But they made it easier for Harmony to talk with us. I suppose that means the same sort of things for you. Haven will find it easier to speak with you, perhaps. Or, maybe, they're going to help you sing songs better, make them stronger or louder somehow." He shook his head. "Really? I think you're going to have to find out for yourselves what they do."

"What shall we call them?" demanded Pol. "We need to give them names."

"What's wrong with calling them sprites?" asked Endel.

"We can't call them that, silly," came the swift put-down. "Sprites are sprites. These are something else. So we need to give them new names," and she poked at the pattern on Hanna's cheek. Hanna batted her hand away.

"Why don't we call them something like worms? They look like worms," offered Endel.

"Yuk! Not worms," said Pol making a face to go with the words. "Definitely not worms."

"You think of something, if you're so clever," he demanded.

Pol considered a moment, bottom lip jutting out, staring hard at Hanna's face, which Hanna found very disconcerting. "I think we should call them wrigglies, because they wriggle."

"What do you mean, 'they wriggle'?" asked Hanna.

"Yours is changing. It's wriggling," explained Pol.

Endel leaned in to take a closer look, then examined Pol's face. "She's right, they're moving."

Hanna with a horrified look, clapped a hand to her face. "I can't feel anything happening."

"Why would you, if they're meant to help us?" said Endel in a very reasonable tone, which only served to annoy Hanna.

"Because I've got something under my skin! That's what's the matter. And it's alive!" Hanna could feel tears burning in her eyes. This wasn't how she had imagined it would be. She didn't want something on her face she couldn't get rid of. The thought of it made her shiver in disgust.

Nobody would look at her without seeing this thing on her. She was going to be ugly her whole life. It was too awful to imagine.

Javin stepped in and knelt down to reassure her, his hands on her shoulders. "Let's not jump to any conclusions about these things, whatever they are. I know they are meant to be a way of helping you. It's a scary thing, having something like this happen to you and you not knowing what it is." Hanna bit her lip and nodded in agreement even though she didn't really want to.

"But it's nothing to worry about. I know that. Believe me, when I first had this sprite around my neck, I didn't dare go to sleep in case it choked me or did something else. It's the same for you. You need to get used to it. We know nothing about what it can do or anything. But, being scared of it won't help much."

"But it's going to make me look ugly!," she wailed, her bottom lip trembling.

"No, it's not. It's going to make you look different, that's all. Ever since I've arrived, I've noticed people staring at our sprites and wondering what they are. I feel different because of that. Ask any of the islanders and they'll tell you the same. But I'd feel even worse if my sprite wasn't with me. It's going to be the same for all of you. Don't think that it's going to ruin your life. It's not. It's going to make your life so wonderful that everyone you meet is going to envy you. And, trust me on this one, but you're going to find someone who sees only you and nothing else. Just like I see Meldren. I don't see her sprite. I see only her. It's going to be the same for you." He gave her an encouraging smile. "It's not like you're on your own. You have these others here with their own ones. That's going to be a great help." He planted a kiss on her forehead. "Now, do you think you're going to be all right?"

Hanna gave a tentative nod, her bottom lip under control again. "I think so."

"Good. We ought to show the others and let them know this is a good thing. Especially the villagers."

"Why don't we call them ribbons?" said Endel suddenly. "My mother had ribbons in her hair. Long and thin and pretty. I remember them. Ribbons." A spasm of grief appeared and vanished in a moment. And then he was his normal stoic self.

"I like that," said Pol decisively. "I'm going to call mine a ribbon, because it sounds nice."

"I never knew that about your mother," said Hanna, but Endel had closed down again, offering nothing more. "I like it as well," she said, putting a hand out to him, but he was seeing his past.

"Ribbons! Ribbons! We've got ribbons!," said Pol, dancing away to spread the word.

Javin watched her, shaking his head and smiling. "I think it's going to be too late to change it now. Ribbons it is." Pol ran up to each person she could find and pointed at her cheek before running off again. "It'd be nice to watch her, but we do have some work to do. We have to make sure these fields are going to be able to grow crops again." He dusted his hands on his knees and got up. "I should have collected a sample of good soil, but I'm sure the others will have enough."

Hanna pulled at Javin's hand, inclining her head toward Endel. "I think we should be able to do this together; make the soil good again. What do you think, Endel?" She had a new feeling, a new certainty that hadn't been there before. Maybe, she thought, it was because Endel had shared something with her, making her feel special. Or, maybe it was something to do with these things in her cheek, these ribbons. She didn't know which it was, only that the feeling was there and she had to follow it.

Javin had that faraway look in his eyes which, she knew, meant he was listening to her song. He smiled at her and urged her on, but she waited to see what Endel would say. Endel looked at her a moment, as if seeing something new in her, before nodding solemnly.

They were soon at the group of islanders who were all holding clods of earth from beyond the field boundaries. Javin caught their attention. "Hanna here thinks she will be able to help us with making these fields ready. And, good news. You've probably heard the word 'ribbons' from Pol, who's still racing around here somewhere. But this is a chance to see them properly. We have our sprites, but Hanna and the others now have their own special somethings: ribbons. Would you and Endel like to show them?"

Hanna felt very self-conscious to begin with as she tilted her head to allow these friends of hers to see what had happened to her face. She was worried that they would think it ugly and she would see it in their faces. But her fears were swept away by the looks of admiration and interest and the words and, even better, the hugs of congratulation. There were questions about the ribbons, but Javin gestured to them to let Hanna and Endel speak for themselves.

"I don't know where it came from," she said, seeing a few knowing glances shared amongst her listeners. "I don't know what they can do yet. But... ," she looked for help from Javin who urged her on with a smile. "I don't know how to say it, but I think we, Endel and me, we can make these fields well again quickly." She felt unsure of her words, but trusted her feelings. She worried whether these people, who knew so much more than she did about working with songs, would think she was trying to show off. She held her breath.

"From what I can see," said Meldren, "the way your colors are glowing and reaching out wide around you, I believe you." She looked around at the islanders. "We all had to start somewhere, so why shouldn't you do this? After all, this is your planet. You're the ones who should be doing it. We're here to help and support. But, beyond that, it's going to be up to you." She beamed at Hanna. "Yes, it can be a little scary when you start, but, trust yourself and trust your feelings. Now, would you like us to leave you or... ?"

"Oh no," said Hanna quickly, happy to feel the support. "I think I'd like you all to be close, wouldn't you, Endel?" He shrugged.

"It's all yours then," said Meldren, with a sweep of her hand.

Hanna stood still and let herself hear Haven's familiar song. The song behind everything came through clearly; more clearly than ever. Without looking, she reached for Endel's hand. He didn't pull away, which at some level surprised and pleased her. When she felt that she could hear what she wanted, how to change the song of the soil beneath her feet, she gave a quick squeeze of Endel's hand to alert him and began to sing. After a moment, Endel joined in with his clear treble, singing a slightly different version, a counterpoint to her song, giving it nuances and intricacies she alone could not provide. Her eyes were shut and she felt the song flow through her in a way she had never experienced before. There was a strength in her which she had not known. The song became richer and the tones deepened; impossible tones for either of them.

Suddenly, it expanded, lifting off and becoming something she would never have believed possible. A part of her mind realized that what she was hearing was not her voice alone, nor was it Endel's. There was something else, something which felt like it was her, but it was a new part of her; more complex, more intricate, more powerful than just her. It carried her and Endel and the song they sang, and it was as if they were the center of sound as it rippled away and out from them, changing, pulsing, pushing, yet leaving them still and strong, in the middle of it all.

Something inside her knew that it was done, even if she could not name what had happened. There was a completeness inside her that she did not want to disturb. She stood in silence in a kind of rapture at what she felt; eyes shut, breathing strong and deep, feeling a part of everything -- the world, the ground beneath her feet, the people around her -- which was indescribable and full of joy. She was dimly aware that Endel's hand was still in hers and that he was gripping hers tightly. And that was wonderful as well and made everything richer and better.

Finally, as if an echo was fading within her, she became more aware of herself as an individual, as Hanna. And with that feeling came the reluctant admittance that she had to open her eyes and be that girl again. When she did, she was surrounded by smiling, happy faces. The islanders, seeing her awareness return, moved to congratulate them both on what they had achieved.

"It was wonderful to watch you and hear what you were singing," said Allegara. "I have never seen or heard anything like it. You were both superb." Hanna caught sight of Endel from the corner of her eye and saw that he was grinning as well. Allegara hugged Hanna and Dennet hugged Endel, being closest to him. The others stood around congratulating them, reaching out to pat them on their shoulders or head; whatever could be reached.

"How do you feel about those ribbons on your face now, Hanna?" asked Javin with a smile.

Hanna blushed and bobbed her head. "I feel fine, now. Thank you."

"Did they feel any different, when you were singing?" asked Meldren. Both children shook their heads. "You won't have noticed that they changed when you sang, then?" In answer to their looks, she added, "When you were singing, the patterns changed." She pointed at her own face to illustrate her words. "When you started, they were in a sort of swirl. But, as you sang, they moved. Just like our sprites move for certain things, yours moved as well. They started out on the cheek, but then they moved up to form a patten on your forehead. Sort of like a circle, but with spokes. And it kept whirling." She moved her fingers to show as them best she could. "Then, when you stopped, it went back to the cheek again, didn't it?" she said, looking for confirmation from the others, who all agreed in nods and words.

"That's... that's strange, isn't it?" asked Hanna.

"No stranger than what happens with our sprites," replied Meldren, still smiling at her.

Suddenly, Hanna realized that this new thing under her skin, this ribbon, was not something to be ashamed of. It was a badge. A badge which showed all the world that she was different, but in a good way. Javin's next words confirmed it for her.

"Welcome to how it feels to be special," he said.

Those words were quite the nicest things Hanna had heard in a long time. Better yet, Endel was still holding her hand.

THE NEXT MORNING, JAVIN AND MELDREN WERE SITTING ON THE DOORSTEP of one of the newly sung homes. Side by side with a new blanket wrapped around both of their shoulders, they were watching the villagers go about their daily tasks. The weather was still cool with a fresh breeze carrying a hint of dampness. The clouds were ragged and looked like they were in the process of breaking up, the sun filtering through here and there.

"What are you thinking?" asked Meldren.

"That this place is going to survive after all. Hanna's got crops looking like they're growing quickly, especially with Timoss helping her. Everyone's got a weatherproof and warm home. There's clothing now for them all. Bodren's doing a wonderful job with firewood, Endel's doing the same with meat. Pelle's making storage containers and metal blades, and Pol, well, Pol's being Pol."

"And...?" prompted Meldren.

"And it feels like we've done all we can here. It's up to them to finish it however they want. But, at least, now they are going to be able to survive until food becomes a little more available." He found Meldren's hand with his. "Maybe it's time for us to go."

"How do you feel about everything? Still angry?"

He considered this a moment. "Maybe. Yes. Actually yes, I am. But it's down deep. The other day, when it happened, it was raw and fresh. Now? Now it's more like it's matured into something... harder." He made a face. "No. That's not quite right. It's there, but changed in some way but it's there still. I can think about what happened here, what happened to me, and I can still feel angry but it's under control." He lifted her hand to kiss it. "Not that losing my temper then seemed to do any good. I think if someone got in my way, argued with me about these things, I probably would lose my temper. And I don't recall Haven answering in any way. Have you had any strange dreams? Any unusual feelings? No. Neither have I. So, perhaps we're not meant to do anything about it. Maybe it was important for me to see how angry I really was. Maybe it's going to be the children here who do things. We've only been called in to help rebuild this village and help these few people, and that's the extent of it." There was a pause. "Unless you have a feeling otherwise? I confess, I've been too wrapped up in what we've been doing here to have spent any time on trying to feel out the future."

"What I have noticed," said Meldren, "is that I'm not noticing being among these people. They're not bothering me like I would have thought."

"Well, we were noticing something like that on the island," said Javin.

"Timoss had the same sort of problem, but we suggested he could learn to control it. We should have taken our own advice." Meldren raised her eyebrows and gave a small shake of her head. "Why didn't we even think of doing that earlier?"

"I never thought of it," admitted Javin.

"Neither did I. Which makes it all the more interesting that we seemed to have had it happen to us anyway. I wonder who was responsible?"

"Could be anyone or anything," said Javin. "It could be Harmony or Haven or even Pol, for all we know." They both smiled at the memory of the excited little girl running around showing everyone her 'ribbons'. "Do you think we have anything else to do here? Anything that Haven wants us to do, that is?"

Meldren tilted her face up to catch a fleeting patch of sunlight and closed her eyes. After a moment, she opened them and had a puzzled expression on her face. "Something. Yes, definitely something. But it's nothing like that black cloud we had much earlier. There's something else. It's even less easy to put into words, though."

Javin went back to gazing outside. "Well, whatever it is, it's going to be interesting. Maybe not in the way we would think of it at the time. Later: that's when we'll call it interesting." He waved at Kris who was walking across towards the fields, but who changed direction when he saw Javin and Meldren.

"Mind some company?" he asked, squeezing into the narrow space beside Javin. He nodded greetings at Meldren and said, "I felt like I should try one more time to convince you to do something about the government." He put a hand up to stall Javin's reaction. "Hear me out first. You say you've no interest in organizing people, when what's happened here over the past few days shows how wrong that is. As the son of a legitimate leader who was overthrown in a coup, you would definitely have a right to challenge the legitimacy of the government, given what I can recall of the constitution. But what really made me want to ask you again was because of the amazing things you can do." His gesture took in the whole community. "Look at what you've done here. You might not want to admit it, but you all have tremendous power. Power to do things, change things and make them right. Surely that's something you should consider? You can really make changes to this world. All you have to do is go to Pannedon and show them what you can do. Who's going to stop you? I mean, really? If you want it, it's yours. Not that I have a vote or anything like that, but if I did, you'd get mine. What do say? Are you willing to try?"

Javin and Meldren exchanged looks. "I don't know where to start, Kris," began Javin. "I told you before, I've no interest in staying here. I love Harmony now. And I love this woman here next to me. She was born and brought up on Harmony and, if I'm right, she'd stay with me here if I asked her to, but she'd miss her home just as much." Meldren smiled and gave a gentle nod.

"Yes, I am the son of the overthrown leader, but, honestly who would give me a second look? I can't prove any of that. That's not going to work. And then there's the power you speak about. Do you know where that power comes from? It comes from the planet, not from us. Everything comes from the planet. And that means if the planet doesn't like it, it won't happen. It's not up to me or Meldren or any of us to decide what to do. We are only helping the planet."

"But that's what we need," exhorted Kris. "We need someone who will take care of it. Help the planet and it helps everyone."

"And everyone will see it that way, will they? No, Kris. I appreciate your faith in us, I really do. But it's not going to work. And the main reason for that is because I'm not interested in making it work."

Kris sighed, looking glum.

Meldren looked thoughtful and asked, "Why did you come over here, Kris? I'm not being rude, I just wanted to know if anything had happened that made you think of asking Javin again."

He scratched his beard as he thought. "I can't think of anything. I was walking along and saw you two, and Javin waved, and so I came over." He frowned. "Tell you the truth, it wasn't until I sat down that I thought about asking you again. In fact, now I think about it, I was half-surprised at myself when I began speaking. Sounds stupid, doesn't it? Makes me sound stupid anyway."

"Actually, no. No it doesn't, Kris," said Meldren with a thoughtful look at Javin. "In fact I'd say it's making some sense."

"In what way?"

Meldren gave a little smile of satisfaction. "I think you're the answer to a question we had been asking. A question about what do we do next. All we have to do now is work out what the answer means."

Kris looked even more confused. "I have no idea what you're talking about." To Javin, "Do you understand what she's saying?"

"I think I do, actually. When something is out of the ordinary happens, we have learned to listen to it. You just said that you were surprised at what you did, and despite my saying earlier that I had no interest in ruling anything, you came back and said it again; no lead up, no small talk, just leapt right in. There's a message in it, I'm sure. Now we need to understand what Haven wants us to do."

"Haven?"

"I told you that everything we do comes from the planet. We're on Haven, we asked earlier what to do, so the answer has come from Haven." He shrugged. "It's obvious."

"To you, maybe," said Kris. "I'm having some trouble with that." He paused. "But, can I ask one thing?"

"Of course."

"I know it sounds silly and everything, but could you tell me what it is you're going to do when you find out what it is? If I'm going to change how I think, I've got to start following through on things and not ignore them. If I had a feeling, I'd like to know what it led to."

"Of course," said Meldren. "We'll let you know, just as soon as we do."

After Kris had left, Meldren said, "It does make sense, you know. After all, we don't have the same connection with Haven as we do with Harmony. It makes sense that there would be a different way for Her to speak to us."

"I remember Harmony trying to speak with me at first. It was unpleasant."

"Yes, but She was using me to talk to you. Maybe She's passed on some ideas to Her sister? The point is, Haven's got through to us. Now we have to work out what it is She wants."

"What was it that Kris said that got your attention the most?" asked Javin.

"Power," said Meldren, after a moment's thought. "I've never heard what we do spoken of like that. He wanted us to use that power to change things."

"That's what got my attention, too."

Meldren hugged her knees closer to her chest. "What if that's the answer?"

"What? Using power?"

"Think about it. What if we did change things because of what we can do? But that would only make sense if we changed things at this place he mentioned."

"Pannedon?"

Yes, Pannedon. What if we go there and change things, but not because we want to be in charge? By the way, what is a 'vote'?"

"It's a way of showing you support someone, that's all. But the point you were making... ?"

Well, if we don't go and be in charge, then the only thing which makes sense is if we change the ones who are in charge already, doesn't it?"

"What? Like throw them out?"

"No! Change their minds, I mean. Kris said that what we do looks amazing. What if Haven, through us, did something amazing there and that made them change?"

"Like what?"

"I don't have all the answers. We can work that one out. But, first, do you agree with me?"

He leaned back, resting on his hands behind him with his head tilted up to the sky, and shut his eyes. "Yes. I do. It feels right. I have no idea how it would work or what we'll do, but it feels right." He opened them again. "Do we set off right away or wait?"

"I have no idea where we're going, or how long we'll be gone, but I want to have something to eat first and then we'll tell Kris, like we promised. And then... then we set off, I suppose." She rested her chin on her knees, a wistful look on her face. "Is it always the right thing, going places because it feels right?"

"I remember you saying what's the point of having feelings if you don't do anything about them. Maybe we don't get to say no in that case. But I also remember you saying you wanted an adventure."

"You don't have to be so good at remembering things, you know."

"No, I don't. But it is fun."

"I won't vote you."

"It's 'I won't vote for you'."

"I won't do that, either."

"It's still fun."

"BUT HOW WILL YOU GET THERE?" ASKED KRIS, BEFORE ROLLING HIS EYES AND adding, "I'm asking someone who came from another planet." He grinned at the two of them seated on the floor in his home, as furniture was in short supply still. "I wouldn't understand it even if you could explain it. But what are you going to do when you get there?"

"We need to talk to the people there about how you think about things and about how you feel about the government," said Meldren. "You are certain that yours isn't the only place to have been attacked?"

"I can't know for certain, but Markin, my friend who was killed, was absolutely positive that it was so. And he gave very convincing reasons. Plus there's the lad, Endel."

"What about him?" asked Meldren.

"I'm fairly sure that he was a survivor of one of the raids." He told them of the boy's arrival and what he had said the first time he and Markin had brought the children together. "I think he's seen too much for one of his age."

"How do you think things going here in general?" Javin said, changing the subject to avoid answering direct questions whose answers would show they had no idea what they would be doing.

Kris nodded thoughtfully. "I think everyone here likes what has happened. No. I *know* they all like what has happened. After all, we're warm and dry and can eat again, and there are crops growing in the fields. Who wouldn't like that? But, if you're asking how everyone thinks about what you all can do, that's not quite so easy. For example, Pelle has been making baskets for us as you know. She was apprenticed to someone who was also killed. But what's strange is that, when she works, it's as if she's weaving them out of nothing, or half making them with her hands and reeds and the other half sort of appears. It's... well, it's unsettling to watch. And then she makes knives and other blades in the same way. It's strange seeing beautifully crafted objects being made like that. Like I said, it's unsettling."

"It's hard to accept that children can do these things?" suggested Meldren.

Yes, it's partly that. But it's also because they make it look easy! I think it makes some of us, some adults that is, it makes us feel useless. Like we have to wait for a child to help us grow crops or get firewood, or make food or heal us when we have accidents." He held up the hand which Pol had healed as an example.

"Seeing the children doing those things is strange, isn't it?" said Javin. "I felt the same sort of things you're talking about when I was first on Harmony. Everyone seemed to be doing incredible things, and I was... , the polite way of saying it was that I was absolutely useless at everything. I felt stupid and slow and without any possible talent." Kris was nodding vigorously in agreement. "But it's not true here. Maybe you never will be able to do even half of what they can do. But you and all the rest of the adults here, you have ideas and plans and dreams for bigger and better things. The children are only working inside your dreams. They're not making new ones for themselves. Someday, perhaps, some of them will. But, until then, they're only fleshing out what you saw and worked so hard to produce. You can feel slow, if you want. You can feel stupid if you like. But without the adults, this place wouldn't exist. You might remember that, next time you see a knife appearing out of nowhere. You made this place out of nowhere as well." Javin softened the words with a smile.

Kris smiled and with a lift of his chin acknowledged Javin's words. "Thank you. I hadn't looked at it that way. You know something? You'd have given me a run for my money in persuading people way back when. But," -- taking a deep breath -- "do you think we adults can learn to do what they do?"

"Maybe not all of you," said Meldren. "But I would be very surprised if no-one can do some of the things they do. It takes time and practice. And you might find it hard having someone like Pol as your teacher."

Kris laughed. "That would be interesting!" Javin and Meldren exchanged glances and began to get up, dusting their hands on their clothes. "What happens now?" Kris looked as if he wanted to act as chaperone or guide or do something that would involve him in some way.

"I think we'll go back to our place so nobody need know what we're doing and we won't cause a scene that way," said Javin.

"I don't know what to say." Kris gave a wry smile. "Mainly that's because I don't know what you're going to be doing there, so I have no advice to give. I'll just wish you luck in whatever happens and hope to see you back, safe and sound, as soon as possible."

Javin half-turned to go but stopped and said, "Actually, there is something you can do. What's the name of the leader of the government now? Do you know?"

"Why didn't I think of that?" said Kris, rolling his eyes. "His name, at least, the last name I heard, was Pekillin."

"Pekillin?"

"Yes. Mikkan was in charge after your father, but he resigned or left or something and appointed another soldier in his place. Pekillin succeeded him. He was once a general but now, supposedly, the architect for world peace, brought about mainly by killing off anyone who opposes him." A look of concern crossed his face. "You should be careful, you know. Whatever it is you're going there for, whatever you are going to do, this man is powerful. He's held power there for a good long time. He knows how to use it. Pannedon is not a safe place for you."

"I promise we'll be careful. And I promise we'll come back," said Meldren, giving him a quick kiss on his cheek, which caused him to blush unexpectedly.

"See that you do."

Back in the privacy of their hut, which now had a hearth for a fire, some rushes on the floor but not much else, Meldren asked, "Two things, Javin. One, how do we know where to go and secondly, what do we do when we get there?"

He tugged at his ear. "Find a road to follow. Follow that to bigger roads and from there to Pannedon. To find Littlehaven we followed the rivers to the sea. I thought it would be much the same here, but maybe Haven will have other ideas about it. As for what we do there, I'm still not sure. But Kris was right. We should be careful."

"I don't think we've ever been careful. We've gone in to whatever or wherever we had to and did our best. We might have been frightened afterwards, but not before."

"I didn't say I was frightened."

"Then why all the talk about being careful? The first time we came here to collect the children, we barely got out."

"We didn't have time to be frightened," argued Javin.

"And we don't have time now, either. Remember what has happened here. Not just the deaths and destruction, but also what happened to you. That's all part of it. That's why we're doing this."

Javin saw the look on Meldren's face and felt the anger begin to burn in him again. "You're right. They need to be shown."

Meldren tapped his chest. "Don't you lose that anger when we're there. This is where we are going to make things right." He nodded. "Now, Haven," she said looking around, "we know You're ready for us, so take us there now." She cocked her head as if listening for something. "Help us find the roads that lead to Pannedon." Swiftly, their sprites unfurled to swiftly reposition themselves around the top of their heads, straining upwards. They simultaneously unleashed a shrill squeal which rose higher and higher until it was beyond hearing.

At the same time a deep, rich sound erupted from the ground beneath their feet, washed upwards over them, wrapping them within it, shutting the hut and Newgrange away from them, lifting and spinning them up and up until they could see the mountains beneath them. Haven then hurtled them away, carrying them inside Her song, dipping them down to swoop over burnt out villages and hastily dug burial mounds, over ragged men, women and children looking broken and despairing, following the signs of murder and destruction, always carried out in beautiful countryside, far from any town.

Seven, eight, nine times more this happened. Then they saw, as if projected on the wall of sound around them, many more such places, many more such graves, many more starving, injured, disconsolate people. Each sight filled their heads with whispered songs of lost hope and longing, of fond memories and despair: all the small songs lost in destruction. Those, too, faded, and still they traveled. Then, ahead of them, there were more buildings, closer together, taller. There were areas which looked run down, dirty, jumbled: places that looked unsafe. The outskirts of a large city passed beneath them. And then they were there. The sprawl of buildings, the grand design of them; all these pointed to it being the center, the place where all roads led. This was Pannedon, and they were drifted and lowered gently in the song until they felt the ground beneath them again and the song seeped away, back into the earth, and they were standing there, beside a vast building. Their sprites relaxed and resumed their normal positions around their throats.

"That I wasn't expecting to see," said Meldren.

"Nor me."

They both stood for a moment, unable to shake free of what they had been shown. Finally Meldren asked, "Where do we go?"

"Here," said Javin indicating the entrance with a tilt of his head. "This building is where the government meets. I think I recall it. There should be a lot of people inside."

"Good," came the clipped reply. "After what we've seen, I'd love to meet them."

They half-ran up the wide stone steps and pushed open the huge doors. Ahead of them was a wide corridor, but empty of people. Their bare feet made no sound as they walked along, peering in at the various doors they passed.

"There's nobody here," said Javin, looking around. "There were always people here." He paused to get his bearings or to hear something. There was only silence. "It's been a long time now, but I'm sure that if we keep going down this main corridor, we'll come across some information, a sign or something."

At a crossing of corridors there were several signs. He pointed them out. "You'll have to tell me what they say," said Meldren.

"Here," said Javin, scanning them before pointing down another corridor, this one carpeted and with intricate decorative lighting running along the walls. "Down here. There's the parliament rooms, and he's got be somewhere close to them. I think I remember this corridor. I used to play along here when no-one was watching. If it wasn't this one, then it was one very like it."

Still no-one was to be seen or heard as they hurried along. It felt as though something large but insubstantial was holding its breath.

"There has to be someone here, surely? Why would we be sent otherwise?" Javin looked around. "There," he pointed. "This is the place." Ahead, the lighting became more subdued, the carpet thicker, the stone giving way to wood. "I remember it. Those doors. They're what I remember: the big brass handles and that carving on them. Inside, that's where he'll be if he's here." Javin's eyes burned as the memories of his boyhood came back.

They pushed through and into an empty outer office, and then through more doors and more eerily vacant rooms before they finally found what they were looking for. Behind two large doors with some sort of emblem carved on them was Pekillin's office. He was reading some papers in a folder on his large desk and muttering quietly to himself as he did so. He was a tall, thickset man, going bald, with a sour, downturned mouth. The room was large and comfortably furnished with another smaller desk and chair to one side and four soft armchairs and a low table on the other. Wood paneling and high windows made for a heavy atmosphere. Along the walls were various portraits in frames. His sharp, blue eyes skewered them both as they entered.

"Who are you and what are you doing here?" His voice cut at them; dismissive and angry at the same time. A voice used to being obeyed. "And what have you done with my assistant?"

Javin and Meldren stood, trembling slightly from the adrenaline rush of their journey. "You're Pekillin?" asked Javin.

"Of course I am. Why would you ask?" He stood up behind his desk, closing the folder and for the first time seemed to notice how they were dressed. "Who are you anyway, coming in here looking like homeless people, dressed in rags? Who let you in? And what are those things round your necks?" He pressed one of several buttons on a panel on his desk and called out, "Security! In here. Now!"

All three waited. Javin and Meldren waited quietly, controlling their breathing, not taking their eyes off him. Javin listened to the song of the room and the man, trying to hear anything that sounded like a threat. There was something in the desk, he felt. Meldren, he was sure, was studying Pekillin's colors. The tension between them grew the longer nothing happened, and Pekillin's expression changed from arrogance to the beginnings of concern. Finally he pressed the button again. "Security? In here, now!" The demand this time was a little more shrill.

"I don't think they're coming, do you?" said Meldren quietly after another short pause. "All the rooms we came through were empty. I think it's just the three of us here."

"Sit down," said Javin, his voice harsh.

Pekillin looked amazed that anyone would be speaking to him in this way. Javin repeated his words. Pekillin, glowering at them, opened a drawer in his desk, took out a gun. "You don't come in here and give me orders. Now, you will either explain yourselves or I will shoot you myself."

Seeing the gun seemed to bring everything into sharp focus for Javin. He realized that was what he had heard earlier. Knowing the song, he knew what he needed to change about it. It was easy. He hummed what he heard. Pekillin raised the gun and aimed it at Javin. As he did so, it came apart in his hands, pieces of metal falling to his desk, where some of them appeared to melt. Pekillin flinched back as if bitten, shaking his hand free of what remained of his weapon.

"Sit down!" shouted Javin. "How dare you threaten us like that! You don't even know why we're here!" Pekillin looked in shock at the remains of his weapon and then back to Javin. Javin leant forward on the desk. His sprite partially unwound itself and struck out, hissing. This was enough for Pekillin, who stumbled back into his chair.

"Who are you and what do you want?" There was still some bluster left.

"I can tell you, but you won't believe me anyway," said Javin, still leaning over the desk, his voice a tight whisper. His sprite stayed swaying from his neck, its tiny eyes fixed on Pekillin. Javin reached up to touch the sprite whereupon it withdrew and coiled back around his neck. Meldren dragged two chairs in front of the desk and both of them sat. "We have some questions for you. And we'd like some explanations as well. But first, I want to know whether or not you killed Marak Sarnum" he asked.

The question obviously confused Pekillin. "Who? Kill who?"

"Marak and his wife, Sallinam. Did you kill them?"

"Marak?" Pekillin looked bewildered. "Marak Sarnum? Do you mean the civilian who used to be in this office?"

"I mean the rightful head of the government who was assassinated. Did you kill him and his wife?"

"Why are you asking this? This happened a long time ago." Seeing the look on Javin's face, he added, "No. No I didn't. I didn't kill them. Either of them. Is that what this is all about?"

"Did you order them to be killed?"

"No! I was just a junior officer then. It was Mikkan who ordered them killed. I had nothing to do with it." And he pointed to one of the images on the wall behind him. "Him. He did that. But he's dead now. He died a few years ago. Why are you asking these questions?"

Javin looked to Meldren for confirmation. She nodded saying, "We've only just met, but the colors now are clearer then earlier. I'd say he's telling the truth."

"So who have you killed?" Javin asked.

"I'm the head of the government. I don't go around killing people."

"We'll ignore the gun in your desk, shall we? But what about the Revivalist communities? Are you responsible for those deaths?"

Pekillin said, "So that's what this is about, that you're Revivalists? I should have guessed from the way you are dressed. Why should I tell you anything? You're the ones who are trying to bring this government down."

Javin ignored him. "Why go after them, the Revivalists?"

Pekillin looked from Meldren to Javin in astonishment. "Is this really what this is about? You want to discuss politics?" He shook his head in disbelief. "I don't believe this is happening." He took a moment. "Look, even you must realize that governments make rules for the good of the people. You cannot have people deciding to make their own rules and ignore the legitimate government. That's anarchy!"

"I might argue about this being a legitimate government, but it's not as important as what's happening to these people. They are your people," said Javin.

Pekillin dismissed him with a flick of his hands. "Government is not about the few, it's about everyone. We have a duty to make sure everyone is fed and clothed and housed and everything else."

"So those who didn't like your government and what it was doing, you had them killed and took everything they had?" Javin's contempt was obvious.

"You can't have anarchy...," began Pekillin.

"How many places? How many dead? Do you even know?"

Pekillin shook his head. "This conversation is pointless. You have no authority here. Just because security seems to have a problem does not mean I have to explain myself or my government to you. Take this up with your representative. I refuse to answer any more of your questions." He sat back in his chair and looked off to one side.

Javin nodded and appeared to relax, sitting back in his seat, crossing his legs and smiling, but his voice when he spoke was like ice: sharp and cold and relentless. "We came here from a place called Newgrange. You've probably not heard of it because it's a long way away and most of the people there are dead now, thanks to you. And, before that, we came from Harmony. You remember that place? It's the other main planet. Does that help?"

That made Pekillin sit up and look at Javin. "Harmony? The planet? It disappeared. That's ridiculous. You can't have come from there. Where's your ship? You're obviously lying."

"And yet, here we are," said Javin in his quiet, reasonable, utterly cold voice, indicating their simple clothing with a small sweep of his hand. "And do you want to know the other thing? The 'who am I' thing?" He smiled, but it never touched his eyes while he let the silence expand a moment. "I'm Marak's son, Javin. The one who 'disappeared'. I don't expect you to remember me, what with you being such a junior officer back then. But, trust me, I'm the son of the murdered ruler." He leaned forward in his chair, still smiling. "That gives me a personal interest here, wouldn't you think?"

A thin smile crossed Pekillin's features. "You can't prove that. And the constitution would not allow you any power anyway. What you say means nothing. You have no authority here even if you are who you say you are."

"I know that," Javin said as if chiding a wayward infant. "I'm not here to take over from you."

Pekillin said, "Then what is it you do want? Why are you here? If you don't want revenge, why are you here?"

"Because I want to make things right here. Actually, it's not me who wants to make things right. We're here as spokesmen for someone else." Before Pekillin could ask who that was, he added, "What makes you right and those people you killed in their little communities wrong? I want to know why you think that way."

Pekillin exploded in anger. "Government is about progress, not stagnation! If everyone did what they do this whole planet will be no better than when the first settlers arrived. We'll have nothing. No technology, nothing." He counted off on his fingers. "Education dies, research dies, science dies. It all dies. Hospitals close, schools close, factories close, people will starve. We're trying to keep ourselves alive here!"

Javin nodded thoughtfully, as if in appreciation of the argument. "But why does this government have to run the whole planet? Why not just the cities and towns that want you? You want everything for yourself but won't allow anyone else even a small part. Worse, you're killing those who disagree. But education can still continue, healing can still take place, perhaps there's not such a need for so many factories, and science could take off in new directions even with a smaller government." He spread his hands. "It only needs some adjustments. But you're unwilling to adjust. You want it all your way."

"Don't make it sound so simple when it isn't." Pekillin rubbed at his face in frustration. "We tried negotiating with them. We tried offering payments. We tried everything we could think of. But they weren't interested in sharing what they grew. They just wanted to live in tiny communities by themselves with no thought for others. What they're doing is anarchy. They even hid from us at first and they are still hiding and are willing to let the rest of us starve. They left the factories and the offices empty and they stopped working. They are the ones who are irresponsible! More and more responsible citizens have come here and to other large cities, looking to us to help them. We have a duty to them. Don't you understand?"

Javin ignored him and turned to Meldren. "What do you think of all this?"

She addressed her answer to Pekillin who was still looking both angry and frustrated at the same time. "We have no say at all here. But there is someone who would like to be heard. I think it's time for you and everyone else to hear what She has to say." She stood up. "They're getting impatient. We should go." She gestured at Pekillin to get up and follow them.

"Who is this woman you are representing? And why isn't she here instead of you?"

Javin shook his head. "You wouldn't believe me if I told you. Come along."

Outside, in the corridor, Meldren tilted her head and closed her eyes. "This way," she said, and set off.

Javin nudged Pekillin. "It would be wise to follow her. Remember the gun?"

Pekillin said, "But this leads to the Chamber. There is no session today. No one is here."

"Listen," said Meldren. There was the sound of many voices ahead, but muted somewhat. Walking down the corridor to the end, they faced two huge doors. These were the doors to the chamber where the members of the government normally convened. The noise was coming from behind them. When the doors were pulled open by Meldren, a wall of noise rolled out to meet them.

Inside there was copious seating with desks arranged in almost circular tiers with a large area at the bottom of the arena where there were three larger desks and chairs. Everything about it was comfortable. The roof arched high overhead. At its apex was a large circle of glass to help illuminate the interior. Angry shouts rose from all sides as they entered. The place was packed with people, some of them tugging at similar doors on the opposite side of the chamber unsuccessfully.

-- "What is going on?"

-- "Is this you wiping out the opposition again, Pekillin?"

-- "Why have you locked the doors against us?"

-- "I demand an explanation."

The irate voices rose as he was walked between Javin and Meldren to the focal point at the bottom of the arena. Seeing the two strangers, more voices were raised with questions, accusations and insults. Javin winced at the noise as did Meldren. They waited for the noise to die down a little. Their silence, their icy demeanor as well as their strange clothes and bare feet, acted to dampen the emotional outbursts. So did the suddenly oppressive atmosphere. It felt like there was a thunderstorm about to happen, but inside the building.

Javin and Meldren watched them all. Pekillin stood between them in front of the desk before Javin indicated to him with his head that he should sit down. He gave Pekillin a warning glance that he should not move. Javin then took one step forward. Meldren came to his side and held his hand. Keeping her gaze fixed straight ahead, Meldren whispered. "This is where we find out what we're here for."

"There's something and somebody you need to hear," said Javin over the few remaining voices. He gripped Meldren's hand tightly as he felt the tendrils of the song which had carried them here. From Meldren's stiffening, she felt the same presence. He let it build within him, feeling it rise up, letting him be, but using the two of them to sense this room and these people. There was a song driving this power; an implacable song rising and filling him. The song of Haven. He swallowed hard as he realized that he had no idea what he was about to say, but that it wouldn't be him saying it anyway. He heard the gasps as both their sprites slid from their necks up to new positions around the tops of their heads, the sprites' own heads standing upright from their brows.

He pointed to the doors they had entered from and felt a presence within him using his voice to speak. It was his voice but with something extra, something more potent in it. "You have ignored me for many of your years. You have hurt me and abused me for too long. And now, when some of you are able to listen, to hear me, to appreciate me, you kill them." The voice which was using Javin's throat was lighter than his. Slightly higher-pitched, but with a far greater resonance and richness. It was a woman's voice. There was a background to it made up of a complex music. It was not an angry voice. Neither was it condescending. If anything, it was merely a voice delivering facts or conveying a decision not open to discussion or reversal. It was firm and powerful, commanding attention. Javin wondered what it was doing to his throat to speak like this. He could do nothing to stop it. As the reverberations of the words died away, the silence was total for a moment.

"I have brought these two here to make you listen at last. I can use them to communicate what I cannot." Javin felt his arm being moved up into the air. Meldren's moved with it, their hands still clasped together. Their hands were taken down again. It felt embarrassing to be manipulated in public like a puppet.

"Is this some sort of trick or a recording?" called a voice at last from somewhere near the rear of the auditorium. "Who's meant to be speaking to us? Who are you?"

Suddenly the tension within the chamber ratcheted up. The oppressive, electric atmosphere increased and fearful anticipation gripped everyone's mind. All voices were stilled by it. Javin felt a little of it himself, but was more aware of the slow surging power building within and around himself and Meldren. As the silence stretched -- or time stretched -- the power within Javin slid partially into the ground seeming to spread outwards. As it did so, he heard the song behind it all begin to change in intensity and in its focus. It was no longer directed at him. It was under the entire building. He could feel it gather itself, ready for something he could not foresee.

"Think back first," are the answer, "and explain to yourselves how you all came to be here. You cannot, because you do not know how it happened. And yet, here you all are. I brought you here. I am your home. I am the one who first gave you shelter. I am the one you do not wish to see or hear. I am the ground upon which you live." A pause again. "Watch as I give a small piece of my true self to remain here always to remind you of this."

The voice had grown huge and commanding, straining the limits of Javin's throat. Now it died away as the ground began to shake, imperceptibly at first. Some tried to leave, but the doors remained stuck. The ground continued to shake and, in front of where Javin and Meldren were standing, there began to be a perceptible bulge beneath the carpet. There were cries of fear and anger from the nearest rows, but the very air seemed to suck them up into silence.

Javin, along with everyone else, watched with fascination as the bulge quickly began to grow larger. He heard the song behind it gain depth, and there were added harmonics which had not been present before. Bigger and taller it grew until, with a sharp sound which made everyone start, the carpet gave way with a loud rip. Beneath it the concrete and stone were shattered. And still the mound grew. At some point, someone gasped and there, in front of all of them was a tall green shoot; the beginning of a plant. From that point on, everything changed more rapidly. The plant, or whatever it was, sprang upwards rapidly, thickening and throwing off more and more shoots. What was becoming a central trunk widened and took on textures and appeared to harden at the same time as it thrust higher. The growth was accompanied by groans and cracks as the trunk widened and branches reached out. Desks and chairs were tossed aside as it grew and spread. Some people were knocked off their feet and crawled away in fear.

It was a tree of huge dimensions. And still it rose, the canopy spreading over the whole of the interior, leaves rustling in an unseen, unfelt wind. The trunk kept expanding and the top kept moving upwards until, finally, the crown of this goliath brushed the roof and tapped gently against the glass there, as if threatening to breach the building above as well as below. But it did not. Broken pieces of furniture littered the base of the massive trunk.

Again there was a silence, but this was a silence of awe and amazement.

The voice coming through Javin, gentler, but no less commanding, spoke again. "This remains here always: a part of me you cannot ignore. Always you will be reminded of who you are sheltering under. Always, you will consider me and my needs. Those of you who can hear me, those will be my children, my special seedlings. The songs they sing will grow. I will not permit them to be harmed any more."

The power driving the voice began to fade and Javin felt the song slip down and away, leaving him his body to himself. He swallowed to reassure himself that he could and turned a glazed, tired, surprised face to Meldren who looked shaky and pale. She made a silent 'o', then whispered, "That wasn't what I was expecting." Their sprites shifted back to their usual positions around their necks.

Javin coughed gently, his throat feeling raw. "We might have to explain things here," he said, feeling his mind become clear again. He spoke as quietly as he could to Meldren. "And I think after that would be a really good time to leave, don't you?"

Meldren nodded in agreement, staring around the Chamber and the confused and awe-struck people. "I would love to go home now. But we need to finish this."

Some of the people were beginning to inspect the tree more closely; touching the trunk or reaching up over their heads to feel the leaves and twigs. Slowly, the quiet whispers of surprise and shock grew into a more general hum of noise and conversation. A buzzing of speculation and wonder built. Javin turned to check on Pekillin. He was now slumped back in his chair, a dazed look in his eyes. What he had experienced in his office and here had left him helpless to do anything more than watch.

Turning back to the people, Javin raised his voice, wincing at the sharp pain he felt. "Sit down and listen. Sit down. Sit down now and listen." Meldren took up the call and kept repeating it, and slowly people began to obey, finding places to sit from where they could still see these two ragged-looking strangers. Eventually, everyone was quiet again.

Meldren spoke to them this time. "This tree, which is not really *just* a tree by the way, will watch you. Please, don't any of you even think about cutting it down. It really would be a bad idea. Someone is going to ask what's the point of what you have just seen. And the answer is that a change has to happen on Haven." That caused a buzz of reaction. "The reason this tree is here, the reason we are all here today, is to mark a change in the way you and the world interact. Enough people now have decided that they do not want your government and what it stands for. They are the Revivalists." The mention of the name caused a low buzz of noise to break out, which Meldren was happy to wait for it to cease. She continued, "If you refuse to change your attitude to them and what they represent, you will be punished."

"Ah! Now I understand," someone called out. "You're threatening us. We do what you want or you will do something to us. Why didn't you say so at the beginning? Why all this fuss with a tree? For all we know it will fade away as soon as you leave."

Javin could not see who the speaker was, but turned in that general direction. His voice sounded ragged. "You misunderstand. The two of us? We're not threatening you at all. Something far more powerful *is* threatening you, however. You think this tree is some sort of joke? A special effect, perhaps? You could not be more wrong. Let me see if can explain it more clearly. You may have immensely powerful technology, but you can't stop a hurricane, or an earthquake, or a volcano, or a tidal wave, or a drought, or a plague of insects, or any of those things which are not yours to control." He let them think about that for a moment. "This planet is the one who is threatening you. And if it can grow such a tree here in so short a time, consider what else it is capable of. It is a power you cannot match. This tree is a reminder of that power." He looked around at them all, noting with satisfaction that there were more thoughtful faces than angry ones. "This isn't a game. How you change is up to you. The people who respect this planet, the ones who truly listen to it; those are the ones who are now protected"

He put his arm around Meldren's waist. In a whisper he said, "I hope Haven heard all that and it was said right, because if I'm wrong we're going to look very, very stupid indeed in a moment." Addressing the people again he said, "We are not the people to supply you with the details. That is for you to work out for yourselves. It is time we left you alone to do just that. We wish you well." He grasped her waist a little more tightly and, with his eyes closed, whispered, "Come on, Haven. Don't let us down! Please?"

As he spoke, so he felt the now-familiar surge under his feet and the song filled them both and they became wrapped in it as their sprites lifted once more and keened their piercing notes. The scene before them faded away, but not before they saw the looks of shock and surprise on the faces of the people, some of them rising from their seats as if to rush toward them and prevent them from going. And then, they were away and moving fast.

The return journey was much quicker and more direct. The song unfolded from them and sank back down into the ground as they realized they were back at Newgrange, in the hut they had started from. It was early evening from the look of the light, although they weren't sure which day it was.

They looked at each other in amazement and their legs buckled. "My throat feels awful," moaned Javin, coughing as he lay curled on his side."

Meldren was holding her forehead tenderly. "That was incredible... it was... ."

"I know exactly what you mean. But I don't ever want to do that again."

They managed to sit up, leaning against each other.

"Maybe I'll understand it all one day, but right now... ?" Javin coughed again at the effort to speak.

"Oh, definitely. That thing that fell apart in his hands? All those people? The noise! And the tree! It was huge and beautiful. Right to the roof! And all I could do was stand and stare at it! And what about when it put our hands up in the air?"

"That just felt embarrassing," said Javin in a whisper as he massaged his throat. The two of them were silent, lost in their thoughts for a while before Javin nudged Meldren gently and breathed, "It's all your fault, you know."

"I'd like to hear this."

"You did say you wanted an adventure, remember."

"Not that again."

"Who else am I going to blame?" He smiled at her.

She considered this for a moment as she rubbed at her temples. "Good point. I shouldn't have said it. It's all my fault obviously. But if I own up to it, you have to feed me. I think I can manage to eat something. That's a good change at least." Javin pointed at his throat. "Oh no. No excuses. I feel bad as well, but it's your job to get food."

He reached a hand to her and together they managed to stand up. "I can't sing anything right now," he whispered. "We'll have to go and find out if anyone has some food to spare."

She patted him on the shoulder. "My head is bursting. But it's from the journey, not all the people. It could have been a lot worse, I think. You and I will have to sit down and talk about what happened." She squeezed her eyes against the pain. "But not now. Let's find some food. We'll have to tell them what happened. But not now." She tried to ignore the throbbing in her head as she thought. "I know, let's go and find Pol. She can make us well. And, if she can't, then one of the others will do it. Until then, I'm not telling anyone anything."

Walking slowly, holding on to each other, the two of them left the hut and went out into the gloom of the evening, following the smells of cooking and the sounds of people enjoying themselves.

BY THE NEXT MORNING, EVERYONE HAD HEARD THE STORY OF WHAT HAD happened at Pannedon at least twice. Kris slapped his thigh as he laughed at the description of Pekillin's face as his gun dismantled itself. That was after he had asked for the gun's dismantling to be repeated several times with descriptions of the metallic mess it had turned into. Timoss wanted to hear more about the tree and Allegara wanted to know what it felt like to have your body taken over by a planet. Javin and Meldren had been helped back to feeling strong in their bodies again by both Pol and Isselta. Pol's 'ribbon' writhed into different and fascinating patterns as the child had focused on them. By the time they had finished, Javin was able to speak easily again.

"You don't have to find anything in my head, Isselta," said Meldren when the girl had approached her to help.

"I know that," she said, smiling. "But I've been helping Pol and she's been helping me. Together, I think we're pretty good at what we do. Now, if you'd let me help... ?" Meldren found out that Isselta was as good as her word. Meldren was quickly able to stand, walk and eat without feeing sick.

Both she and Javin still felt somewhat lethargic, however, and were happy to sit and watch the activity around them in the weak sunlight which tempered only a little the cool breeze coming off the mountains.

"We should be going home soon," said Meldren, tugging her blanket more closely around her as she nibbled on some bread. "We've done what we came here to do, haven't we? We've done everything that's been asked of us. Whether or not those people change isn't going to be up to us, is it?"

"What if they don't change?" asked Javin. "Do we have to come back and do it all over again?"

"It's not our world, Javin."

"Then why were we dragged here in the first place? And why now? Why not sometime later?"

"Probably because we were the only ones who could do what we did. Look around. They're all doing wonderful things. They've all learned so much so quickly. But we're the ones who have been taken over by a planet. None of these have. And I wouldn't wish it on any of them."

"But that still doesn't answer why now? Just because Harmony wants to help Her sister? Is that it? Or am I missing something?"

"Maybe." said Meldren, giving it some thought, "Maybe it's because there are enough people here on Haven who want a change. Before there weren't. Now there are. And if Haven felt their songs disappearing, then perhaps She thought it was time to help them out. Think about what She said through us about hearing them."

"She called them seedlings and that She would protect them."

Meldren gave a little shrug as if to say *'That could be proof, couldn't it?'*.

"That's a lot of maybes and perhapses," said Javin.

"If enough people want a change and Haven thinks its a good change, but they're stopped... ," Meldren trailed off. "Oh, I don't know. I'm just guessing. But the point is we were here because we were the ones who could do what Haven needed doing. And that's less of a guess, but I'm still not certain."

He sighed. "I hate to think you're right, but I think you're right. There's always something we have to do."

"It only seems like that now. When we're back, it will seem different." She licked her fingers clean of any remaining crumbs. "Speaking of going back, what is really keeping us here?"

Javin pointed to where Farran and Bodren were working together in the field. "Waiting for them, I suppose. They're still helping the children, after all."

"Why not ask them, then?"

Javin leaned his head on her shoulder and gave a gentle snort of laughter. "I love it when you're logical."

She planted a kiss on the top of his head. "And when I'm not?"

"Love you anyway."

"Good answer." She sniffed at his head and then at her arms. "And we are both filthy and need a good wash. Your hair definitely needs washing. I suspect mine does as well."

They waited until the evening and everyone had come back to eat and rest. The weather had warmed up during the day. A long and spectacularly brilliant sunset had closed the day as a large fire was built again and everyone sat around it, chatting and laughing as they had done that first time. To Javin's eye, the central boulder looked different somehow. Tilted perhaps? But not quite in the same position as it was . At least, that's what he thought. Javin beckoned Carmeena over and invited her to sit with him and Meldren.

"How long do you think you need to be here helping the children?"

Carmeena looked around at the other islanders. "I don't know. It's not only that we're helping them, they're also helping us."

"Isselta said that yesterday," said Meldren. "What do you mean by that?"

Carmeena puffed out her cheeks as she thought about how to say what she wanted. "Speaking for me, I can work with animals; make them trust me, come to me. That's a talent of mine. I began working with Pelle and she was a quick learner. And, the other day, she asked, why don't I attract other things to me? I didn't really understand what she meant, so she said, 'How about asking for the air to trust me?' I still didn't understand. She explained that, if the air could trust me, could come to me when I called it, surely that would mean that it would look after me, keep me dry when it rained, or be still around me when it was blowing hard." She gave a lop-sided smile and shook her head. "We tried it when we saw some rain coming. And, would you believe it? It worked. We stayed dry. I'd never thought of that before. But she was the one who brought it up."

She pointed across the fire to Farran. "He was working with Endel, moving things. And, apparently, Endel came up to him and said, 'If we can move things along the ground, why not move them above or below it?' And he pushed all the rocks in the field way down below the surface, making the soil much easier to work. Not all at once, mind you. A few at a time. But it was the idea which was new. That was after he gave it a try on that big boulder in the middle of this place."

"Ah. That would explain why it looked different," said Javin.

Carmeena looked at him. "They're seeing things we didn't see, thinking of things we didn't or couldn't or wouldn't think of. Maybe it's because they're so young and it's fresh for them, but I'm finding it really interesting being with them. I'm learning. The truth is, they're like my family now. I lost my child, and here I've been given a second chance. Not just one child, though. I have all of them." She stared into the fire a moment watching her memories in the flames. "I would find it hard to leave them, if you want to know."

"What about the others?" asked Javin.

"You'd have to ask them, but I'm fairly sure it would be the same for them as well. Perray, for example," she said, pointing her out, "Pep lost everyone who meant anything to her. Didn't want to be with people for fear of losing them again. But now? Look at her. Laughing, happy. And her braid has gone. She got rid of it, got rid of her past, and doesn't need to keep touching it anymore. She's now got something to do that makes sense to her. What would she do, what would any of us do, if we went back? Back on Harmony is where we left our pain. But, like I said, you'd have to ask all of them and not rely on what I say."

Later that night, Javin and Meldren wandered away from the fire.

Meldren looked up at the stars. "I can't get used to having no moon here. Now I understand why the children were so excited." She looked back down to Javin beside her, a darker shadow surrounded, to her eyes at least, by shifting, glowing bands and streaks of colors. "It looks like it's just you and me are going back, then."

"I've been thinking about that. It makes perfect sense to have the children and islanders working together, teaching each other. But I have a feeling that there's more behind it. For example, as Kris just about admitted, it would be hard to take lessons from young children. But if the islanders can do it? That makes them the teachers of other adults. Plus, they will help protect the children, because at some point, those children will want to leave. Like Isselta said, they're the seedlings, and they will have to travel and spread the word about what they can do, about what happened here. And they will need adults for a while yet."

"There's something else you're not saying," prodded Meldren. "I can see it around you."

"The other reason I think it makes sense is that there needs to be people here, people with talents, who are able to keep an eye and an ear on things in Pannedon. And, more than that, be able to do what's necessary, what Haven needs them to do, if that's what's required. It makes sense them staying here. I never really thought it through until just now." He paused a moment. "I hope they don't have to have Haven speak through them. Just let them be able to hear Her would be good enough, I'm sure."

They walked a little further, hand in hand, letting the cool night air slide past them.

Meldren brought them to a halt. "We should make sure we say goodbye properly. In the morning, we'll let Kris and the children and the islanders know." She chuckled. "Can't call them islanders any more, can

we? How about calling them the moon people? Or we could call them --
."

"-- The gardeners," said Javin. "Because they're looking after the seedlings."

"Hmmmm," said Meldren appreciatively. "I like that. Except I'm not going to tell them that's what we're calling them." She nuzzled up to him. "My clever boy." She sniffed. "And you really must do something about your hair."

12

THE SLEEPER

The next morning, they said their farewells, offering to each islander a chance to go back to Harmony. Each of them rejected it saying much the same thing as Isselta. "We have a place here. People need us here. We can help and there's so much more to do and to learn, not just about this planet, but about what the children can do. And, yes, we will also keep an ear open for what Haven wants from us. We're not entirely stupid." And she grinned, the happiest of girls, finally looking and acting as if nothing bad had ever happened to her.

When everyone had said their goodbyes and uttered their thanks, Javin and Meldren, feeling a little lost, a little lonely almost, stood by the central boulder holding hands. They bowed their heads, both in farewell but also to focus their hearing on the song that would take them back. Their sprites unwound a little and began humming. The sound acted as a lure to attract the richer, fuller song of Harmony which reached out to them, enveloped them and held them safe. They gave one final look at the people before everything faded and they felt the ground dissolve beneath their feet.

Some time later, they had no idea how long, their feet felt earth beneath them again as the music and the sounds slid away and their sprites took up their resting positions around their necks. They looked around and found that they had been taken to the little amphitheater near their home. Memories of the faces of the ones who remained on Haven flitted before them briefly before they shook themselves free of them and smiled at each other.

"Let's go home," said Meldren, "and see how our garden is doing."

"That sounds good," said Javin. "But let's take the long way and walk along the cliffs. I'd like to see the sea again. I've missed it."

"Me, too."

As they walked, they began to enjoy the feeling of being alone together. The small hiss of wind through leaves and branches, the smells of the ocean; these felt right. No longer responsible for others, they began to let themselves become unentangled from the ones on Haven, finding happiness and lightness in the freedom they now had.

Meldren was resting her head on Javin's shoulder, looking out to sea and letting the wind refresh her. "Javin!"

"I said I'd take care of my hair, and I will."

No. Not that. Look." And she pointed. "There's Amleek with perfect timing. He's on his way here. We'll be able to get some fresh food in Littlehaven."

Javin groaned. "Can't we please stay on the ground for a little longer?"

She ruffled his hair. "Oh, you make such a fuss. We can even wash your hair there."

"You're still not making it attractive!"

She kissed him on the cheek. "Think of it as a small adventure then."

———————

THAT NIGHT AT ORLAND'S THEY SLEPT PEACEFULLY; HAIR CLEAN AND stomachs full. Far, far away, the Sun sang the songs carrying news of the seedlings, those fresh, new notes in its unending symphony of creation. The tiny, stuttering series of small notes entering and adding to it were caught and examined by His distant relatives. A song with questions and answers passed back and forth until an agreement was reached and the next stage of this strange experiment was set in motion. Harmony's Father sang a note of thanks to His distant relatives and waited for it to unfold.

PREVIEW: AMBASSADORS OF HARMONY

Chapter 1

The unusual sound of raised voices nearby caught Myrella's attention. She put down the tedious report on projected harvests and tried to catch what was happening. There seemed to be some sort of argument going on in the outer office and then, suddenly, the doors to her office were flung open and there stood Mannert, her secretary, with a stunned look on his face. Pushing past him was an excited looking young man, who had obviously been running, as he was still panting hard.

"What is going on here?" she demanded. "Why all the excitement?"

Before she could speak further, the young man burst out, "We've been found!"

His obvious excitement along with Mannert's amazement meant that those words had a deeper meaning than was at first obvious to Myrella.

"What do you mean? Who has found us? Explain yourself."

The man was now standing directly in front of her desk. He had a look almost of ecstasy as he drew himself up, gave a small bow and in a more formal voice marred slightly by his attempts to control his breathing, said, "Madam President, it is my honor to report to you that we have been contacted from a deep-space ship which has recently arrived at the edge of our solar system, and that the occupants of that ship are human." Then his excitement broke through again and he exclaimed, "We're no longer alone! We've been found. There are others like us out there!"

Myrella felt a numbness, which another part of her mind translated as shock. "When did this happen? How do you know about it? Where are they?" The questions tumbled from her without her seeming to have anything to do with them. This moment was everything everyone had ever hoped for since the very first settlers had landed and looked at a sky they did not recognize on a planet they did not know.

"The message was received a few hours ago now," the man explained, still beaming in an almost inane fashion, his eyes wide and bright.

"I'm sorry," asked Myrella. "I don't know your name." She wanted a moment more to allow this news to become real.

"Brokka, Madam President," he said, bobbing his head as he did so but not losing the smile. "Assistant chief of the observatory. I was attending a conference here in Pannedon when I received the message -- "

"Where's the chief?" she interrupted.

Brokka reined himself in a little, assuming something approaching a serious expression. "Essarin. His name's Essarin, ma'am. He was on vacation. But he has been notified and asked me to relay the news for him. He is hurrying back here but thought you should know first." Again the formality broke and he gave that huge, face-splitting grin again. "Isn't it the most wonderful thing ever to have happened? We can finally be with our own kind again!"

Mannert, normally the personification of self-restraint and gravitas, had by now given up any pretense of formality as well, sinking down into an armchair and shaking his head in disbelief.

Myrella was going to indicate a seat for Brokka, but realized she was shaking and clasped her hands together instead as she tried to control herself and inclined her head instead. "Please, Brokka, sit down and tell us what you know."

He perched on the very edge of the seat, leaning forward in his excitement. "It was early this morning. Very early." He paused a moment as he tried to gather his thoughts. "Are you aware of the sort of work we do, Madam President?"

"Looking at stars or something like that, I presume?"

"Actually that's only a very small part of what we do. Mostly we look at computer images and compare them. That's when we're not actively researching or... ." He caught the look on Myrella's face and hurried on. "The point is, what we found was that there was a swift moving point of light that hadn't been there several days before. We did some maths and realized it was small and close, relatively speaking. So we turned some other telescopes toward it and found it was transmitting signals. At first, we didn't hear very much, but then... well, what it boils down to is we heard them! They must have been hearing us from the first moment they entered our system and they have probably been broadcasting ever since. They were saying who they were and that they wanted to hear from anyone who could hear them."

"What did you do?"

"Nothing, Madam President. I called Essarin as soon as we knew. He said to tell you first and that we shouldn't do anything without your say so. That's why I came here so quickly."

Myrella sat back in her chair for a moment, her mind racing as she stared blankly at the ceiling. The shaking had stopped when she finally said, "Who else knows of this?"

"Only the two other astronomers who were there."

"And where are they now?"

Brokka shook his head. "I don't know. Gone home I assume."

Myrella snorted in exasperation. "Brilliant! So everyone's going to know far sooner than we'd like. That means we have to get organized here and quickly. We have to be in control of this." This was what she was used to; making decisions. And what she was used to made her feel less out of control. She snapped fingers at Mannert. "Wake up, man, and take some notes. We have so much to do. This is going to be a day to remember for certain."

Myrella had been blessed with clear, smooth skin which seemed wrinkle-free, meaning it was easier for her to appear younger than she looked. Not that she had spent much time worrying about appearing youthful. Her jaw-length hair had some grey strands at the temples but was straight and easy to maintain. She had a very direct gaze, with clear, brown eyes and her straight nose above thin lips meant that the first impression she made was invariably one of determination and focus with little time for irrelevance. She didn't mind people thinking that of her, as long as she could relax in private, laugh and generally let the weight of the day fall from her. But this news, she knew, was not going to give her much time to relax in the days ahead.

The next few hours were a frantic blur. There was an emergency session ordered where every representative was informed of the news. Along with that there were the press releases to prepare at the same time as various roles and tasks were assigned. That was the start of much discussion which occasionally became heated, especially when the content of the message which was to be sent in answer was discussed. Then there were all the arrangements to be made to welcome the newcomers. There was some confusion at first about this until Brokka informed them that it would take a long while to arrive from the edge of the system.

"They have to decelerate, lose a lot of speed as well as maneuver. Best guess would be about 30 to 40 days before they are here. That's assuming that they have technology we can understand. It could be very different, but we will be tracking them during that time, so there's no need to worry. The delay between our sending and their receiving will, of course, decrease as they approach."

"Looks like you'll have all the time you need," said Myrella to the small group assembled in her office. "Let's not panic over this, but go at it steadily. We want everything to be right when they arrive."

Corrivan was, despite Myrella's misgivings, actually helpful and contributed several intelligent suggestions. She wondered what he was up to and what advantage he thought he would gain from cooperating with her. Later, when all the tasks had been decided upon and allocated, everyone else had left and all that remained was to try to assimilate it everything, Myrella found herself and Corrivan alone together in her office. It felt good to have it almost to herself again. The wood-lined walls gave it a sense of formality and hinted at purpose and power enhanced by the carefully tended parkland visible through the windows. Inside there were, apart from her large desk and chair, two smaller desks, one of which could double as a table for informal meals, three sofas and several armchairs. Additionally there were two cabinets facing each other on opposite walls. With the soft carpet on the floor, it was, above all, a comfortable and accommodating space where she could work and think as well as relax when necessary. With the windows opaqued as they were now, it could feel secluded and very private. Right now, Corrivan was seated in one of the large and comfortable chairs near the wall furthest from her desk.

"A truly wonderful day," he said, with apparent sincerity.

"A busy one, certainly." She decided, just this once, to give him the benefit of the doubt. She went to one of the cabinets and poured two large drinks. "Momentous, for us all. To mark it, have a drink with me," she said, offering him one as she sat in the chair opposite.

He accepted with a slight inclination of his head. Normally, his sour expression seemed condescending to Myrella, but now, he looked merely tired. He cradled the drink in his long, thin fingers and there was a silence which, if not companionable, was lacking in the usual hostility.

"What do you think will happen because of this?" Corrivan asked finally. "I know others have asked the same thing, but, between the two of us, what do you really think will happen?"

Myrella squeezed her eyes shut and pinched the bridge of her nose, trying to lose the headache she could feel building. She felt tired and didn't want to have to think of what was going on outside. She was also reappraising her attitude toward Corrivan, who had been a long-time political thorn in her side. Why was he taking this cozy 'you and I' attitude now? It made her think more carefully before answering. "I don't know." She opened her eyes. "I suppose that everyone will go mad with excitement for a while, but I doubt that anyone is going to stay as excited right up until they land here. But beyond that? Who knows? We're assuming they're human like us, but what if they aren't?"

"Then how would they know our language?"

She shrugged. "It's just a thought, that's all." She picked up her drink and took a sip. "What do you think is going to happen?"

He looked directly at her. "I think this will see the end of the Revivalists. That's what I think."

She held his gaze for a moment, looking into his disturbingly pale blue eyes, trying to decide whether this was the time to get into a fight. It was the same agenda he was always bringing up. Was it worth countering him now? She decided against it, despite a deep desire. "Not that again, Corrivan. I don't see why you are so opposed to those people. And don't give me your usual speech about duty and progress and the like. Frankly, I'm too tired to listen to it. There's that rather large tree in the debating chamber to remind us that we cannot ignore the planet. I think the Revivalists are one of the reasons that tree is there. So, despite what you or I might think or want, that particular notion of yours is not up for discussion right now."

He merely gave the slightest shrug as if to say 'If that's the way you want it'.

"That aside for the moment, what else do you think will happen?" Myrella took another sip.

He finished his drink in one long gulp, put the glass down and laced his fingers over his stomach. Myrella wanted to slap the smug look off his face. Instead she waited.

"Quite obviously there will be significant technology available. That was pointed out earlier. Trading will take place, there will be some sort of diplomatic presence: those are to be expected. But having the universe opened to us will create entirely new tensions and factions within the people as a whole. What will happen because of that is hard to say, but there will be those opposed to the intervention of an outside power. Whether you want to label them Revivalists or not, it's going to happen. And, those in favor of these new explorers... well, they are going to be pushing for more and more of whatever they have to offer." He spread his hands. "That's just human nature, I'm afraid."

"And what if we are considered so -- what's a good word? -- backward," said Myrella, "that we are treated not as equals but as inferiors, not as trading partners but as a resource to be used up? Then what? I'll tell you," she said before he could intervene. "It will be a most difficult time indeed, more difficult than your assessment suggests. Dreams and hopes will be slowly whittled away to nothing. Everything will be hugely unsettling. In fact that's what's going to be happening whatever the end result is."

Corrivan nodded. "And that, of course, my dear woman," -- Myrella's jaw tightened -- "is why there must be a very strong leader at the head of a united group who will be ready to enforce law and order as necessary." He smiled, although Myrella thought it looked more like a sneer.

"And you, my dear Corrivan, are so in touch with what the workers want." Oh, yes, she could sink a dagger as well. He came from a factory worker's family. That, of itself, was nothing to be ashamed of. But he always preened as if he was some sort of nobility and never admitted his lowly beginnings. She hated those who were not true to themselves. And disregarding his roots, pretending they were not as they were, made him reprehensible in her eyes. She took pleasure in the barb, even as she reprimanded herself for doing it. "You would be President, I assume?"

He made a self-effacing gesture. "That's not for me to say, of course. But I do wonder why you and I are sitting here. Talking. It's not like you at all."

"Because, as a leader, as President," she let the word linger between them, "I have a duty to speak with everyone. Even those I disagree with. And, as you are one of the leading opponents of this government, I felt it right to see what your thoughts on the day's news would be. I had hoped to be surprised, but am not overly dismayed to find I wasn't."

"I thought, perhaps, we could be speaking of some sort of alliance, you and I," he said. "In light of the civil disorder which we both acknowledge will occur, it would make much sense."

Myrella allowed herself a genuine smile. "I think the word 'alliance' would be incorrect for what you had in mind. Until or unless there is a wish for a change, or a new government is put in place with a mandate to change this executive role I now occupy, I believe I will choose to stay on as President. After all, I am the first woman President in the history of our world. It would be such a shame if I were to step aside before my work was finished, wouldn't it?"

Corrivan's face was expressionless. "I wish you well, in that case Madam President. I have duties of my own to see to. If you'll excuse me?" He rose, gave a curt nod in her direction and left, the rigidity of his back reflecting the anger he was suppressing.

Myrella watched him leave, grateful for the heavy door which made slamming it an impossibility. She gulped the rest of her drink, swallowing her anger with it. "You can come in now, Mannert."

Her secretary opened the door, obviously having stationed himself nearby when he saw Corrivan leaving . "I did not think you would mind my overhearing. It seemed... prudent. I did hear most of it, and from what I heard I don't think there's anything new there, Madam President. He's going to make trouble out of this in some fashion. But that was always going to happen, wasn't it?"

In answer, Myrella poured another drink for herself and one for Mannert, indicating he should sit down in the chair lately occupied by Corrivan. "The only disappointing thing about it was that he couldn't be bothered to hide his intentions." She took a sip. "This day will go down in history, Mannert. It will probably be a holiday of some kind in the future. How many hundreds of years have we been on this planet? And we always wished that we weren't alone. But being alone, being apart from our own kind for that amount of time, that has to have changed us in some way. Maybe it's changed us so that it's not going to be such a celebration as we thought. Maybe we've changed enough so that we don't really want to have that connection any more. Perhaps we are so used to being alone that anything else just wouldn't feel right. Perhaps we'll resist it as an intrusion." She made a gesture of frustration. "I don't know what's going to happen. Not in the details anyway. But one thing's for certain, there's great change going to happen because of it. We're never going back to how were were, even yesterday. And all Corrivan can think of is stirring up trouble." She shook her head, more in sorrow than anything else. "Some people are beyond belief." She tapped a finger against her glass as she thought about the day's events. "Well, Mannert, that's what this tired woman thinks about it. What do you think? The people on this ship: what are they like? What will they do? What do you think's going to happen?"

Mannert looked at her with sympathetic eyes. He had been her secretary for many years, suffering the ups and downs of political life with her. Despite that, he was sitting upright in the chair, as if he could not really relax with her. His hands were clasped around the glass as if protecting it. "Whoever they are, they have the same basis as us, coming from the same stock, so to speak. We share, at some level, a common heritage. They are people just as we are. So, at their most basic I believe they are like us. Better technology of course, but essentially like us."

Myrella gazed blankly at the ceiling, wishing irrationally that it was all over and everything settled. "I'm afraid you're right. Very afraid."

ABOUT THE AUTHOR

Andrew Elgin grew up in England where he studied history and enjoyed philosophy and played with computers. The things about being human which couldn't be as easily explained, such as intuition, began to fascinate him more and more until, in the end, he decided to stop teaching and explored the ideas which attracted him more.

Whether in short stories, novels or nonfiction, Andrew seeks to make this 'other' aspect of being human the foundation of what he writes. He firmly believes that to become fully human is to discover and develop this hidden natural talent for 'knowing.' He seeks to entertain with his writing, but also to present an opportunity for you, the reader, to explore the undiscovered territory within you. Andrew writes nonfiction under his real name, Nigel Percy.

www.ingramcontent.com/pod-product-compliance
Lightning Source LLC
Chambersburg PA
CBHW07055826026
47161CB00002B/647